THE RED REDMAYNES

Eden Phillpotts

Dover Publications, Inc.
NEW YORK

This Dover edition, first published in 1982, is an unabridged and unaltered republication of the work that was originally published by The Macmillan Company of New York in 1922. (This was the first publication anywhere, preceding the British edition by a year.)

Manufactured in the United States of America
Dover Publications, Inc.
180 Varick Street
New York, N.Y. 10014

Library of Congress Cataloging in Publication Data

Phillpotts, Eden, 1862-1960.
  The red Redmaynes.

  Reprint. Originally published: New York : Macmillan, 1922.
  I. Title.
PR5177.R4 1982   823'.8   81-19499
ISBN 0-486-24255-2   AACR2

CONTENTS

THE RED
REDMAYNES

THE RED REDMAYNES

CHAPTER I

THE RUMOUR

EVERY man has a right to be conceited until he is famous—so it is said; and perhaps unconsciously, Mark Brendon shared that opinion.

His self-esteem was not, however, conspicuous, although he held that only a second-rate man is diffident. At thirty-five years of age he already stood high in the criminal investigation department of the police. He was indeed about to receive an inspectorship, well earned by those qualities of imagination and intuition which, added to the necessary endowment of courage, resource, and industry, had created his present solid success.

A substantial record already stood behind him, and during the war certain international achievements were added to his credit. He felt complete assurance that in ten years he would retire from government employ and open that private and personal practice which it was his ambition to establish.

And now Mark was taking holiday on Dart-

3

moor, devoting himself to his hobby of trout fishing and accepting the opportunity to survey
his own life from a bird's-eye point of view, measure his achievement, and consider impartially
his future, not only as a detective but as a
man.

Mark had reached a turning point, or rather
a point from which new interests and new personal plans were likely to present themselves
upon the theatre of a life hitherto devoted to one
drama alone. Until now he had existed for his
work only. Since the war he had been again
occupied with routine labour on cases of darkness, doubt, and crime, once more living only
that he might resolve these mysteries, with no
personal interest at all outside his grim occupation. He had been a machine as innocent of any
inner life, any spiritual ambition or selfish aim,
as a pair of handcuffs.

This assiduity and single-hearted devotion had
brought their temporal reward. He was now at
last in position to enlarge his outlook, consider
higher aspects of life, and determine to be a man
as well as a machine.

He found himself with five thousand pounds
saved as a result of some special grants during
the war and a large honorarium from the French
Government. He was also in possession of a
handsome salary and the prospect of promotion,
when a senior man retired at no distant date.
Too intelligent to find all that life had to offer in
his work alone, he now began to think of culture,
of human pleasures, and those added interests

and responsibilities that a wife and family would
offer.

He knew very few women—none who awakened any emotion of affection. Indeed at five-and-
twenty he had told himself that marriage must
be ruled out of his calculations, since his business
made life precarious and was also of a nature to
be unduly complicated if a woman shared it
with him. Love, he had reasoned, might lessen
his powers of concentration, blunt his extraordinary special faculties, perhaps even introduce an
element of calculation and actual cowardice before great alternatives, and so shadow his powers
and modify his future success. But now, ten years
later, he thought otherwise, found himself willing
to receive impressions, ready even to woo and
wed if the right girl should present herself. He
dreamed of some well-educated woman who would
lighten his own ignorance of many branches of
knowledge.

A man in this receptive mood is not asked as
a rule to wait long for the needful response; but
Brendon was old-fashioned and the women born of
the war attracted him not at all. He recognized
their fine qualities and often their distinction of
mind; yet his ideal struck backward to another
and earlier type—the type of his own mother
who, as a widow, had kept house for him until her
death. She was his feminine ideal—restful,
sympathetic, trustworthy—one who always made
his interests hers, one who concentrated upon his
life rather than her own and found in his progress
and triumphs the salt of her own existence.

Mark wanted, in truth, somebody who would be content to merge herself in him and seek neither to impress her own personality upon his, nor develop an independent environment. He had wit to know a mother's standpoint must be vastly different from that of any wife, no matter how perfect her devotion; he had experience enough of married men to doubt whether the woman he sought was to be found in a post-war world; yet he preserved and permitted himself a hope that the old-fashioned women still existed, and he began to consider where he might find such a helpmate.

He was somewhat overweary after a strenuous year; but to Dartmoor he always came for health and rest when opportunity offered, and now he had returned for the third time to the Duchy Hotel at Princetown—there to renew old friendships and amuse himself on the surrounding trout streams through the long days of June and July.

Brendon enjoyed the interest he awakened among other fishermen and, though he always went upon his expeditions alone, usually joined the throng in the smoking-room after dinner. Being a good talker he never failed of an audience there. But better still he liked an hour sometimes with the prison warders. For the convict prison that dominated that grey smudge in the heart of the moors known as Princetown held many interesting and famous criminals, more than one of whom had been "put through" by him, and had to thank Brendon's personal industry and daring for penal servitude. Upon the prison staff were not a few men of intelligence and wide experience who could tell the detective much germane to his work. The psychology of crime never paled in its intense attraction for Brendon and many a strange incident, or obcure convict speech, related without comment to him by those who had witnessed, or heard them, was capable of explanation in the visitor's mind.

He had found an unknown spot where some good trout dwelt and on an evening in mid-June he set forth to tempt them. He had discovered certain deep pools in a disused quarry fed by a streamlet, that harboured a fish or two heavier than most of those surrendered daily by the Dart and Meavy, the Blackabrook and the Walkham.

Foggintor Quarry, wherein lay these preserves, might be approached in two ways. Originally broken into the granite bosom of the moor for stone to build the bygone war prison of Princetown, a road still extended to the deserted spot and joined the main throughfare half a mile distant. A house or two—dwellings used by old-time quarrymen—stood upon this grass-grown track; but the huge pit was long ago deserted. Nature had made it beautiful, although the wonderful place was seldom appreciated now and only wild creatures dwelt therein.

Brendon, however, came hither by a direct path over the moors. Leaving Princetown railway station upon his left hand he set his face west where the waste heaved out before him dark against a blaze of light from the sky. The sun was setting and a great glory of gold, fretted with lilac and

crimson, burned over the distant earth, while here
and there the light caught crystals of quartz in the
granite boulders and flashed up from the evening
sobriety of the heath.

Against the western flame appeared a figure
carrying a basket. Mark Brendon, with thoughts
on the evening rise of the trout, lifted his face at
a light footfall. Whereupon there passed by him
the fairest woman he had ever known, and such
sudden beauty startled the man and sent his own
thoughts flying. It was as though from the
desolate waste there had sprung a magical and
exotic flower; or that the sunset lights, now deepening on fern and stone, had burned together and
became incarnate in this lovely girl. She was
slim and not very tall. She wore no hat and the
auburn of her hair, piled high above her forehead,
tangled the warm sunset beams and burned like a
halo round her head. The colour was glorious,
that rare but perfect reflection of the richest hues
that autumn brings to the beech and the bracken.
And she had blue eyes—blue as the gentian.
Their size impressed Brendon.

He had only known one woman with really
large eyes, and she was a criminal. But this
stranger's bright orbs seemed almost to dwarf her
face. Her mouth was not small, but the lips were
full and delicately turned. She walked quickly
with a good stride and her slight, silvery skirts
and rosy, silken jumper showed her figure clearly
enough—her round hips and firm, girlish bosom.
She swung along—a flash of joy on little twinkling
feet that seemed hardly to touch the ground.

Her eyes met his for a moment with a frank, trustful expression, then she had passed. Waiting half a minute, Brendon turned to look again. He heard her singing with all the light-heartedness of youth and he caught a few notes as clear and cheerful as a grey bird's. Then, still walking quickly, she dwindled into one bright spot upon the moor, dipped into an undulation, and was gone—a creature of the heath and wild lands whom it seemed impossible to imagine pent within any dwelling.

The vision made Mark pensive, as sudden beauty will, and he wondered about the girl. He guessed her to be a visitor—one of a party, perhaps, possibly here for the day alone. He went no farther than to guess that she must certainly be betrothed. Such an exquisite creature seemed little likely to have escaped love. Indeed love and a spirit of happiness were reflected from her eyes and in her song. He speculated on her age and guessed she must be eighteen. He then, by some twist of thought, considered his personal appearance. We are all prone to put the best face possible upon such a matter, but Brendon lived too much with hard facts to hoodwink himself on that or any other subject. He was a well-modelled man of great physical strength, and still agile and lithe for his age; but his hair was an ugly straw colour and his clean-shorn, pale face lacked any sort of distinction save an indication of moral purpose, character, and pugnacity. It was a face well suited to his own requirements, for he could disguise it easily; but it was not a face calculated

to charm or challenge any woman—a fact he knew
well enough.

Tramping forward now, the detective came to
a great crater that gaped on the hillside and stood
above the dead quarry workings of Foggintor.
Underneath him opened a cavity with sides
two hundred feet high. Its peaks and precipices fell, here by rough, giant steps, here stark
and sheer over broad faces of granite, where only
weeds and saplings of mountain ash and thorn
could find a foothold. The bottom was one vast
litter of stone and fern, where foxgloves nodded
above the masses of debris and wild things made
their homes. Water fell over many a granite
shelf and in the desolation lay great and small
pools.

Brendon began to descend, where a sheep track
wound into the pit. A Dartmoor pony and her
foal galloped away through an entrance westerly.
At one point a wide moraine spread fanwise from
above into the cup, and here upon this slope of
disintegrated granite more water dripped and
tinkled from overhanging ledges of stone. Rills
ran in every direction and, from the spot now
reached by the sportsman, the deserted quarry
presented a bewildering confusion of huge
boulders, deep pits, and mighty cliff faces heaving
up to scarps and counter-scarps. Brendon had
found the guardian spirit of the place on a former
visit and now he lifted his voice and cried out.

"Here I am!" he said.

"Here I am!" cleanly answered Echo hid in
the granite.

"Mark Brendon!"
"Mark Brendon!"
"Welcome!"
"Welcome!"
Every syllable echoed back crisp and clear, just tinged with that something not human that gave fascination to the reverberated words.

A great purple stain seemed to fill the crater and night's wine rose up within it, while still along the eastern crest of the pit there ran red sunset light to lip the cup with gold. Mark, picking his way through the huddled confusion, proceeded to the extreme breadth of the quarry, fifty yards northerly, and stood above two wide, still pools in the midst. They covered the lowest depth of the old workings, shelved to a rough beach on one side and, upon the other, ran thirty feet deep, where the granite sprang sheer in a precipice from the face of the little lake. Here crystal-clear water sank into a dim, blue darkness. The whole surface of the pools was, however, within reach of any fly fisherman who had a rod of necessary stiffness and the skill to throw a long line. Trout moved and here and there circles of light widened out on the water and rippled to the cliff beyond. Then came a heavier rise and from beneath a great rock, that heaved up from the midst of the smaller pool, a good fish took a little white moth which had fluttered within reach.

Mark set about his sport, yet felt that a sort of unfamiliar division had come into his mind and, while he brought two tiny-eyed flies from a box and fastened them to the hairlike leader he always used, there persisted the thought of the auburn girl—her eyes blue as April—her voice so bird-like and untouched with human emotion—her swift, delicate tread.

He began to fish as the light thickened; but he only cast once or twice and then decided to wait half an hour. He grounded his rod and brought a brier pipe and a pouch of tobacco from his pocket. The things of day were turning to slumber; but still there persisted a clinking sound, uttered monotonously from time to time, which the sportsman supposed to be a bird. It came from behind the great acclivities that ran opposite his place by the pools. Brendon suddenly perceived that it was no natural noise but arose from some human activity. It was, in fact, the musical note of a mason's trowel, and when presently it ceased, he was annoyed to hear heavy footsteps in the quarry—a labourer he guessed.

No labourer appeared, however. A big, broad man approached him, clad in a Norfolk jacket and knickerbockers and a red waistcoat with gaudy brass buttons. He had entered at the lower mouth of the quarries and was proceeding to the northern exit, whence the little streamlet that fed the pools came through a narrow pass.

The stranger stopped as he saw Brendon, straddled his great legs, took a cigar from his mouth and spoke.

"Ah! You've found 'em, then?"

"Found what?" asked the detective.

"Found these trout. I come here for a swim sometimes. I've wondered why I never saw a rod in this hole. There are a dozen half pounders there and possibly some bigger ones.''

It was Mark's instinctive way to study all fellow creatures with whom he came in contact. He had an iron memory for faces. He looked up now and observed the rather remarkable features of the man before him. His scrutiny was swift and sure; yet had he guessed the tremendous significance of his glance, or with proleptic vision seen what this being was to mean during the years of his immediate future, it is certain that he would have intensified his inspection and extended the brief limits of their interview.

He saw a pair of broad shoulders and a thick neck over which hung a square, hard jaw and a determined chin. Then came a big mouth and the largest pair of mustaches Brendon remembered to have observed on any countenance. They were almost grotesque; but the stranger was evidently proud of them, for he twirled them from time to time and brought the points up to his ears. They were of a foxy red, and beneath them flashed large, white teeth when the big man talked in rather grating tones. He suggested one on very good terms with himself—a being of passionate temperament and material mind. His eyes were grey, small, set rather wide apart, with a heavy nose between. His hair was a fiery red, cut close, and of a hue yet more violent than his mustaches. Even the fading light could not kill his rufous face.

The big man appeared friendly, though Brendon heartily wished him away.

"Sea fishing's my sport," he said. "Conger and cod, pollack and mackerel—half a boat load —that's sport. That means tight lines and a thirst afterward."

"I expect it does."

"But this bally place seems to bewitch people," continued the big man. "What is it about Dartmoor? Only a desert of hills and stones and two-penny half-penny streams a child can walk across; and yet—why you'll hear folk blether about it as though heaven would only be a bad substitute."

The other laughed. "There is a magic here. It gets into your blood."

"So it does. Even a God-forgotten hole like Princetown with nothing to see but the poor devils of convicts. A man I know is building himself a bungalow out here. He and his wife will be just as happy as a pair of wood pigeons—at least they think so."

"I heard a trowel clinking."

"Yes, I lend a hand sometimes when the workmen are gone. But think of it—to turn your back on civilization and make yourself a home in a desert!"

"Might do worse—if you've got no ambitions."

"Yes—ambition is not their strong point. They think love's enough—poor souls. Why don't you fish?"

"Waiting for it to get a bit darker."

"Well, so long. Take care you don't catch anything that'll pull you in."

Laughing at his joke and making another echo ring sharply over the still face of the water, the red man strode off through the gap fifty yards distant. Then in the stillness Mark heard the purr of a machine. He had evidently departed upon a motor bicycle to the main road half a mile distant.

When he was gone Brendon rose and strolled down to the other entrance of the quarry that he might see the bungalow of which the stranger had spoken. Leaving the great pit he turned right-handed and there, in a little hollow facing southwest, he found the building. It was as yet far from complete. The granite walls now stood six feet high and they were of remarkable thickness. The plan indicated a dwelling of six rooms and Brendon perceived that the house would have no second story. An acre round about had been walled, but as yet the boundaries were incomplete. Magnificent views swept to the west and south. Brendon's rare sight could still distinguish Saltash Bridge spanning the waters above Plymouth, where Cornwall heaved up against the dying afterglow of the west. It was a wonderful place in which to dwell, and the detective speculated as to the sort of people who would be likely to lift their home in this silent wilderness.

He guessed that they must have wearied of cities, or of their fellow creatures. Perhaps they were disappointed and disillusioned with life and so desired to turn their backs upon its gregarious features, evade its problems, as far as possible, escape its shame and follies, and live here amid these stern realities which promised nothing, yet

were full of riches for a certain order of mankind. He judged that the couple, who designed
to dwell beside the silent hollow of Foggintor,
must have outlived much and reached an attitude
of mind that desired no greater boon than soli-
tude in the lap of nature. Such people could only
be middle-aged, he told himself. Yet he remembered the big man had said that the pair felt
"love was enough." That meant romance still
active and alive, whatever their ages might
be.

The day grew very dim and the fret of light
and shadow died off the earth, leaving all vague
and vast and featureless. Brendon returned to
his sport and found a small "coachman" fly sufficiently destructive. The two pools yielded a
dozen trout, of which he kept six and returned
the rest to the water. His best three fish all
weighed half a pound.

Resolved to pay the pools another visit, Mark
made an end of his sport and chose to return by
road rather than venture the walk over the rough
moor in darkness. He left the quarry at the gap,
passed the half dozen cottages that stood a hundred yards beyond it, and so, presently, regained
the main road between Princetown and Tavis-
tock. Tramping back under the stars, his
thoughts drifted to the auburn girl of the moor.
He was seeking to recollect how she had been
dressed. He remembered everything about her
with extraordinary vividness, from the crown of
her glowing hair to her twinkling feet, in brown
shoes with steel or silver buckles; but he could

not instantly see her garments. Then they came back to him—the rose-coloured jumper and the short, silvery skirts.

Twice afterward, during the evening hour, Brendon again tramped to Foggintor, but he was not rewarded by any glimpse of the girl; but as the picture of her dimmed a little, there happened a strange and apparently terrible thing, and in common with everybody else his thoughts were distracted. To the detective's hearty annoyance and much against his will, there confronted him a professional problem. Though the sudden whisper of murder that winged with amazing speed through that little, uplifted church-town was no affair of his, there fell out an incident which quickly promised to draw him into it and end his holiday before the time.

Four evenings after his first fishing expedition to the quarries, he devoted a morning to the lower waters of the Meavy River; at the end of that day, not far short of midnight, when glasses were empty and pipes knocked out, half a dozen men, just about to retire, heard a sudden and evil report.

Will Blake, "Boots" at the Duchy Hotel, was waiting to extinguish the lights, and seeing Brendon he said:

"There's something in your line happened, master, by the look of it. A pretty bobbery to-morrow."

"A convict escaped, Will?" asked the detective, yawning and longing for bed. "That's about the only fun you get up here, isn't it?"

"Convict escaped? No—a man done in seemingly. Mr. Pendean's uncle-in-law have slaughtered Mr. Pendean by the looks of it."

"What did he want to do that for?" asked Brendon without emotion.

"That's for clever men like you to find out," answered Will.

"And who is Mr. Pendean?"

"The gentleman what's building the bungalow down to Foggintor."

Mark started. The big red man flashed to his mind complete in every physical feature. He described him and Will Blake replied:

"That's the chap that's done it. That's the gentleman's uncle-in-law!"

Brendon went to bed and slept no worse for the tragedy. Nor, when morning came and every maid and man desired to tell him all they knew, did he show the least interest. When Milly knocked with his hot water and drew up his blind, she judged that nobody could appreciate the event better than a famous detective.

"Oh, sir—such a fearful thing——" she began. But he cut her short.

"Now, Milly, don't talk shop. I haven't come to Dartmoor to catch murderers, but to catch trout. What's the weather like?"

" 'Tis foggy and soft; and Mr. Pendean—poor dear soul——"

"Go away, Milly. I don't want to hear anything about Mr. Pendean."

"That big red devil of a man——"

"Nor anything about the big red devil, either. If it's soft, I shall try the leat this morning."

Milly stared at him with much disappointment. "God's goodness!" she said. "You can go off fishing—a professed murder catcher like you— and a man killed under your nose you may say!"

"It isn't my job. Now, clear out. I want to get up."

"Well, I never!" murmured Milly and departed in great astonishment.

But Brendon was not to enjoy the freedom that he desired in this matter. He ordered sandwiches, intending to beat a hasty retreat and get beyond reach; then at half past nine, he emerged into a dull and lowering morn. Fine mist was in the air and a heavy fog hid the hills. There seemed every probability of a wet day and from a fisherman's point of view the conditions promised sport. He was just slipping on a raincoat and about to leave the hotel when Will Blake appeared and handed him a letter. He glanced at it, half inclined to stick the missive in the hall letter rack and leave perusal until his return, but the handwriting was a woman's and did not lack for distinction and character. He felt curious and, not associating the incident with the rumoured crime, set down his rod and creel, opened the note, and read what was written:

"3 Station Cottages, Princetown.

"DEAR SIR: The police have told me that you are in Princetown, and it seems as though Providence had sent you. I fear that I have no right to seek your services directly, but if you can answer the prayer of a heart-broken woman and give her the benefit of your genius in this dark moment, she would be unspeakably thankful.

"Faithfully yours,
"JENNY PENDEAN."

Mark Brendon murmured "damn" gently under his breath. Then he turned to Will.

"Where is Mrs. Pendean's house?" he asked.

"In Station Cottages, just before you come to the prison woods, sir."

"Run over, then, and say I'll call in half an hour."

"There!" Will grinned. "I told 'em you'd never keep out of it!"

He was gone and Brendon read the letter again, studied its neat caligraphy, and observed that a tear had blotted the middle of the sheet. Once more he said "damn" to himself, dropped his fishing basket and rod, turned up the collar of his mackintosh, and walked to the police station, where he heard a little of the matter in hand from a constable and then asked for permission to use the telephone. In five minutes he was speaking to his own chief at Scotland Yard, and the familiar cockney voice of Inspector Harrison came over the two hundred odd miles that separated the metropolis of convicts from the metropolis of the world.

"Man apparently murdered here, inspector. Chap who is thought to have done it disappeared. Widow wants me to take up case. I'm unwilling

to do so; but it looks like duty." So spoke
Brendon.

"Right. If it looks like duty, do it. Let me
hear again to-night. Halfyard, chief at Princetown, is an old friend of mine. Very good man.
Good-bye."

Mark then learned that Inspector Halfyard was
already at Foggintor.

"I'm on this," said Mark to the constable.
"I'll come in again. Tell the inspector to expect
me at noon for all details. I'm going to see Mrs.
Pendean now."

The policeman saluted. He knew Brendon very
well by sight.

"I hope it won't knock a hole in your holiday,
sir. But I reckon it won't. It's all pretty plain
sailing by the look of it."

"Where's the body?"

"That's what we don't know yet, Mr. Brendon;
and that's what only Robert Redmayne can tell
us by the look of it."

The detective nodded. Then he sought No. 3,
Station Cottages.

The little row of attached houses ran off at right
angles to the high street of Princetown. They
faced northwest, and immediately in front of them
rose the great, tree-clad shoulder of North Hes-
sory Tor. The woods ascended steeply and a
stone wall ran between them and the dwellings
beneath.

Brendon knocked at No. 3 and was admitted by
a thin, grey-haired woman who had evidently been
shedding tears. He found himself in a little hall

decorated with many trophies of fox hunting. There were masks and brushes and several specimens of large Dartmoor foxes, who had run their last and now stood stuffed in cases hung upon the walls.

"Do I speak to Mrs. Pendean?" asked Brendon; but the old woman shook her head.

"No, sir. I'm Mrs. Edward Gerry, widow of the famous Ned Gerry, for twenty years Huntsman of the Dartmoor Foxhounds. Mr. and Mrs. Pendean were—are—I mean she is my lodger."

"Is she ready to see me?"

"She's cruel hard hit, poor lady. What name, sir?"

"Mr. Mark Brendon."

"She hoped you'd come. But go gentle with her. 'Tis a fearful ordeal for any innocent person to have to talk to you, sir."

Mrs. Gerry opened a door upon the right hand of the entrance.

"The great Mr. Brendon be here, Mrs. Pendean," she said; then Brendon walked in and the widow shut the door behind him.

Jenny Pendean rose from her chair by the table where she was writing letters and Brendon saw the auburn girl of the sunset.

CHAPTER II

THE girl had evidently dressed that morning without thought or care—perhaps unconsciously. Her wonderful hair was lifted and wound carelessly upon her head; her beauty had been dimmed by tears. She was, however, quite controlled and showed little emotion at their meeting; but she looked very weary and every inflection of her pleasant, clear voice revealed it. She spoke as one who had suffered much and laboured under great loss of vitality. He found this to be indeed the case, for it seemed that she had lost half herself.

As he entered she rose and saw in his face an astonishment which seemed not much to surprise her, for she was used to admiration and knew that her beauty startled men.

Brendon, though he felt his heart beat quicklier at his discovery, soon had himself in hand. He spoke with tact and sympathy, feeling himself already committed to serve her with all his wits and strength. Only a fleeting regret shot through his mind that the case in all probability would not prove such as to reveal his own strange powers. He combined the regulation methods of criminal research with the more modern deductive system,

23

and his success, as he always pointed out, was reached by the double method. Already he longed to distinguish himself before this woman.

"Mrs. Pendean," he said, "I am very glad that you learned I was in Princetown and it will be a privilege to serve you if I can. The worst may not have happened, though from what I have heard, there is every reason to fear it; but, believe me, I will do my best on your account. I have communicated with headquarters and, being free at this moment, can devote myself wholly to the problem."

"Perhaps it was selfish to ask you in your holidays," she said. "But, somehow, I felt——"

"Think nothing whatever of that. I hope that what lies before us may not take very long. And now I will listen to you. There is no need to tell me anything about what has happened at Foggintor. I shall hear all about that later in the day. You will do well now to let me know everything bearing upon it that went before this sad affair; and if you can throw the least light of a nature to guide me and help my inquiry, so much the better."

"I can throw no light at all," she said. "It has come like a thunderbolt and I still find my mind refusing to accept the story that they have brought to me. I cannot think about it—I cannot bear to think about it; and if I believed it, I should go mad. My husband is my life."

"Sit down and give me some account of yourself and Mr. Pendean. You cannot have been married very long."

"Four years."

He showed astonishment.

"I am twenty-five," she explained, "though I'm told I do not look so much as that."

"Indeed not; I should have guessed eighteen. Collect your thoughts now and just give me what of your history and your husband's you think most likely to be of use."

She did not speak for a moment and Brendon, taking a chair, drew it up and sat with his arms upon the back of it facing her in a casual and easy position. He wanted her to feel quite unconstrained.

"Just chat, as though you were talking of the past to a friend," he said. "Indeed you must believe that you are talking to a friend, who has no desire but to serve you."

"I'll begin at the beginning," she answered. "My own history is brief enough and has surely little bearing on this dreadful thing; but my relations may be more interesting to you than I am. The family is now a very small one and seems likely to remain so, for of my three uncles all are bachelors. I have no other blood relations in Europe and know nothing of some distant cousins who live in Australia.

"The story of my family is this: John Redmayne lived his life on the Murray River in Victoria, South Australia, and there he made a considerable fortune out of sheep. He married and had a large family. Out of seven sons and five daughters born to them during a period of twenty years, Jenny and John Redmayne only saw five of their children grow into adult health and strength. Four boys lived, the rest died young; though two were drowned in a boating accident and my Aunt Mary, their eldest daughter, lived a year after her marriage.

"There remained four sons: Henry, the eldest, Albert, Bendigo, and Robert, the youngest of the family, now a man of thirty-five. It is he you are seeking in this awful thing that is thought to have happened.

"Henry Redmayne was his father's representative in England and a wool broker on his own account. He married and had one daughter: myself. I remember my parents very well, for I was fifteen and at school when they died. They were on their way to Australia, so that my father might see his father and mother again after the lapse of many years. But their ship, *The Wattle Blossom,* was lost with all hands and I became an orphan.

"John Redmayne, my grandfather, though a rich man was a great believer in work, and all his sons had to find occupation and justify their lives in his eyes. Uncle Albert, who was only a year younger than my father, cared for studious subjects and literature. He was apprenticed in youth to a bookseller at Sydney and after a time came to England, joined a large and important firm of booksellers, and became an expert. They took him into partnership and he travelled for them and spent some years in New York. But his special subject was Italian Renaissance literature and his joy was Italy, where he now lives.

He found himself in a position to retire about ten years ago, being a bachelor with modest requirements. He knew, moreover, that his father must soon pass away and, as his mother was already dead, he stood in a position to count upon a share of the large fortune to be divided presently between himself and his two remaining brothers.

"Of these my Uncle Bendigo Redmayne was a sailor in the merchant marine. After reaching the position of a captain in the Royal Mail Steamship Company he retired on my grandfather's death, four years ago. He is a bluff, gruff old salt without any charm, and he never reached promotion into the passenger service, but remained in command of cargo boats—a circumstance he regarded as a great grievance. But the sea is his devotion, and when he was able to do so, he built himself a little house on the Devon cliffs, where now he resides within sound of the waves.

"My third uncle, Robert Redmayne, is at this moment apparently suspected of having killed my husband; but the more I think of such a hideous situation, the less possible does it appear. For not the wildest nightmare dream would seem more mad and motiveless than such a horror as this.

"Robert Redmayne in youth was his father's favourite and if he spoiled any of his sons he spoiled the youngest. Uncle Robert came to England, and being fond of cattle breeding and agriculture, joined a farmer, the brother of an Australian friend of John Redmayne's. He was supposed to be getting on well, but he came and went, for my grandfather did not like a year to pass without a sight of him.

"Uncle Bob was a pleasure-loving man especially fond of horse racing and sea fishing. On the strength of his prospects he borrowed money and got into debt. After the death of my own father I saw a little of Uncle Robert from time to time, for he was kind to me and liked me to be with him in my holidays. He did very little work. Most of his time he was at the races, or down in Cornwall at Penzance, where he was supposed to be courting a young woman—a hotel keeper's daughter. I had just left school and was about to leave England and go to live with my grandfather in Australia, when events happened swiftly, one on top of the other, and life was changed for all us Redmaynes."

"Rest a little if you are tired," said Mark. He saw by her occasional breaks and the sighs that lifted her bosom, how great an effort Mrs. Pendean was making to tell her story well.

"I will go straight on," she answered. "It was summertime and I was stopping with my Uncle Robert at Penzance when two great things—indeed three great things—happened. The war broke out, my grandfather died in Australia and, lastly, I became engaged to Michael Pendean.

"I had loved Michael devotedly for a year before he asked me to marry him. But when I told my Uncle Robert what had happened he chose to disapprove and considered that I had made a serious mistake. My future husband's parents were dead. His father had been the head of a firm called Pendean and Trecarrow, whose business was the importation of pilchards to Italy. But Michael, though he had now succeeded his father in the business, took no interest in it. It gave him an income, but his own interests were in a mechanical direction. And, incidentally, he was always a good deal of a dreamer and liked better to plan than to carry out.

"We loved one another passionately and I have very little doubt that my uncles would have raised no objection to our marrying in the long run, had not unfortunate events happened to set them against our betrothal.

"On the death of my grandfather it was found that he had written a peculiar will; and we also learned that his fortune would prove considerably smaller than his sons expected. However, he left rather more than one hundred and fifty thousand. It appeared that during the last ten years of his life, he had lost his judgment and made a number of hopeless investments.

"The terms of the will put all his fortune into the power of my Uncle Albert, my grandfather's eldest living son. He told Uncle Albert to divide the total proceeds of the estate between himself and his two brothers as his judgment should dictate, for he knew that Albert was a man of scrupulous honour and would do justly by all. With regard to me, he directed my uncle to set aside twenty thousand pounds, to be given me on my marriage, or failing that, on my twenty-fifth birthday. In the meantime I was to be taken care of by my uncles; and he added that my future

husband, if he appeared, must be approved of by
Uncle Albert.

"Though jarred to find he would receive far
less than he had hoped, Uncle Robert was soon in
a good temper, for their elder brother informed
Uncle Bob and Uncle Bendigo that he should
divide the fortune into three equal parts. Thus
it came about that each received about forty thousand pounds, while my inheritance was set aside.
All would have been well, no doubt, and I was
coaxing my uncle round, for Michael Pendean
knew nothing about our affairs and remained
wholly ignorant that I should ever be worth a
penny. It was a marriage of purest love and he
had four hundred a year of his own from the business of the pilchard fishery, which we both deemed
ample for our needs.

"Then broke the war, on those awful days in
August, and the face of the world changed—I
suppose forever."

She stopped again, rose, went to the sideboard,
and poured herself out a little water. Mark
jumped up and took the glass jug from her hand.

"Rest now," he begged, but she sipped the
water and shook her head.

"I will rest when you have gone," she answered; "but please come back again presently
if you can give me a gleam of hope."

"Be very sure of that, Mrs. Pendean."

She went back to her seat while he also sat
down again. Then she resumed.

"The war altered everything and created a
painful breach between my future husband and my

Uncle Robert. The latter instantly volunteered
and rejoiced in the opportunity to seek adventure.
He joined a cavalry regiment and invited Michael
to do the same; but my husband, though no more
patriotic man lives—I must speak still as though
he lives, Mr. Brendon——''

"Of course you must, Mrs. Pendean—we must
all think of him as living until the contrary is
proved."

"Thank you for saying that! My husband had
no mind for active warfare. He was delicately
built and of a gentle temperament. The thought
of engaging in hand-to-hand conflict was more
than he could endure, and there were, of course, a
thousand other ways open to him in which he
could serve his country—a man so skilful as he."

"Of course there were."

"Uncle Robert, however, made a personal thing
of it. Volunteers for active service were urgently demanded and he declared that in the ranks
was the only place for any man of fighting age,
who desired longer to call himself a man. He
represented the situation to his brothers, and
Uncle Bendigo—who had just retired, but who,
belonging to the Naval Reserve, now joined up
and soon took charge of some mine sweepers—
wrote very strongly as to what he thought was
Michael's duty. From Italy Uncle Albert also
declared his mind to the same purpose, and
though I resented their attitude, the decision, of
course, rested with Michael, not with me. He was
only five-and-twenty then and he had no desire but
to do his duty. There was nobody to advise him

and, perceiving the danger of opposing my uncles' wishes, he yielded and volunteered.

"But he was refused. A doctor declared that a heart murmur made the necessary training quite impossible and I thanked God when I heard it. The tribulations began then and Uncle Bob saw red about it, accusing Michael of evading his duty and of having bribed the doctor to get him off. We had some very distressing scenes and I was thankful when my uncle went to France.

"At my own wish Michael married me and I informed my uncles that he had done so. Relations were strained all round after that; but I did not care; and my husband only lived to please me. Then, halfway through the war, came the universal call for workers; and seeing that men above combatant age, or incapacitated from fighting, were wanted up here at Princetown, Michael offered himself and we arrived together.

"The Prince of Wales had been instrumental in starting a big moss depôt for the preparation of surgical dressings; and both my husband and I joined this station, where the sphagnum moss was collected from the bogs of Dartmoor, dried, cleaned, treated chemically, and dispatched to all the war hospitals of the kingdom. A busy little company carried on this good work and, while I joined the women who picked and cleaned the moss, my husband, though not strong enough to tramp the moors and do the heavy work of collecting it and bringing it up to Princetown, was instrumental in drying it and spreading it on the asphalt lawn-tennis courts of the prison warders' cricket ground, where this preliminary process was carried out. Michael also kept records and accounts and indeed organized the whole depôt to perfection.

"For nearly two years we stuck to this task, lodging here with Mrs. Gerry. During that time I fell in love with Dartmoor and begged my husband to build me a bungalow up here when the war was ended, if he could afford to do so. His pilchard trade with Italy practically came to an end after the summer of 1914. But the company of Pendean and Trecarrow owned some good little steamers and these were soon very valuable. So Michael, who had got to care for Dartmoor as much as I did, presently took steps and succeeded in obtaining a long lease of a beautiful and sheltered spot near Foggintor quarries, a few miles from here.

"Meanwhile I had heard nothing from my uncles, though I had seen Uncle Robert's name in the paper among those who had won the D. S. O. Michael advised me to leave the question of my money until after the war, and so I did. We began our bungalow last year and came back to live with Mrs. Gerry until it should be completed.

"Six months ago I wrote to Uncle Albert in Italy and he told me that he should deliberate the proposition; but he still much resented my marriage. I wrote to Uncle Bendigo at Dartmouth also, who was now in his new home; but while not particularly angry with me, his reply spoke slightingly of my dear husband.

"These facts bring me to the situation that

suddenly developed a week ago, Mr. Brendon."
She stopped and sighed again.

"I much fear that I am tiring you out," he said.
"Would you like to leave the rest?"

"No. For the sake of clearness it is better you
hear everything now. A week ago I was walking
out of the post-office, when who should suddenly
stop in front of me on a motor bicycle but Uncle
Robert? I waited only to see him dismount and
set his machine on a rest before the post-office.
Then I approached him. My arms were round
his neck and I was kissing him before he had time
to know what had happened, for I need not tell
you that I had long since forgiven him. He
frowned at first but at last relented. He was
lodging at Paignton, down on Torbay, for the
summer months, and he hinted that he was engaged to be married. I behaved as nicely as I
knew how, and when he told me that he was going
on to Plymouth for a few days before returning
to his present quarters, I implored him to let the
past go and be friends and come and talk to my
husband.

"He had been to see an old war comrade at Two
Bridges, two miles from here, and meant to lunch
at the Duchy Hotel and then proceed to Plymouth; but I prevailed upon him at last to come
and share our midday meal, and I was able to tell
him things about Michael which promised to
change his unfriendly attitude. To my delight he
at last consented to stop for a few hours, and I
arranged the most attractive little dinner that I
could. When my husband returned from the bun-

galow I brought them together again. Michael
was on his defence instantly; but he never harboured a grievance very long and when he saw
that Uncle Bob was not unfriendly and very interested to hear he had won the O. B. E. for his
valuable services at the depot, Michael showed a
ready inclination to forget and forgive the past.

"I think that was almost the happiest day of
my life and, with my anxiety much modified, I was
able to study Uncle Robert a little. He seemed
unchanged, save that he talked louder and was
more excitable than ever. The war had given him
wide, new interests; he was a captain and intended, if he could, to stop in the army. He had
escaped marvellously on many fields and seen
much service. During the last few weeks before
the armistice, he succumbed to gassing and was
invalided; though, before that, he had also been
out of action from shell shock for two months.
He made light of this; but I felt there was really
something different about him and suspected that
the shell shock accounted for the change. He was
always excitable and in extremes—now up in the
clouds and now down in the depths—but his terrible experiences had accentuated this peculiarity
and, despite his amiable manners and apparent
good spirits, both Michael and I felt that his
nerves were highly strung and that his judgment
could hardly be relied upon. Indeed his judgment was never a strong point.

"But he proved very jolly, though very egotis-
tical. He talked for hours about the war and
what he had done to win his honours; and we no-

ticed particularly a feature of his conversation. His memory failed him sometimes. By which I do not mean that he told us anything contrary to fact; but he often repeated himself, and having mentioned some adventure, would, after the lapse of an hour or less, tell us the same story over again as something new.

"Michael explained to me afterwards that this defect was a serious thing and probably indicated some brain trouble which might get worse. I was too happy at our reconciliation, however, to feel any concern for the moment and presently, after tea, I begged Uncle Robert to stop with us for a few days instead of going to Plymouth. We walked out over the moor in the evening to see the bungalow and my uncle was very interested. Finally he decided that he would remain for the night, at any rate, and we made him put up with us and occupy Mrs. Gerry's spare bedroom, instead of going to the Duchy Hotel as he intended.

"He stopped on and liked to lend a hand with the building sometimes after the builders had gone. He and Michael often spent hours of these long evenings there together; and I would take out tea to them.

"Uncle Robert had told us about his engagement to a young woman, the sister of a comrade in the war. She was stopping at Paignton with her parents and he was now going to return to her. He made us promise to come to Paignton next August for the Torbay Regatta; and in secret I begged him to write to both my other uncles and explain that he was now satisfied Michael had done his bit in the war. He consented to do so and thus it looked as though our anxieties would soon be at an end.

"Last night Uncle Robert and Michael went, after an early tea, to the bungalow, but I did not accompany them on this occasion. They ran round by road on Uncle Robert's motor bicycle, my husband sitting behind him, as he always did.

"Supper time came and neither of them appeared. I am speaking of last night now. I did not bother till midnight, but then I grew frightened. I went to the police station, saw Inspector Halfyard, and told him that my husband and uncle had not come back from Foggintor and that I was anxious about them. He knew them both by sight and my husband personally, for he had been of great use to Michael when the moss depôt was at work. That is all I can tell you."

Mrs. Pendean stopped and Brendon rose.

"What remains to be told I will get from Inspector Halfyard himself," he said. "And you must let me congratulate you on your statement. It would have been impossible to put the past situation more clearly before me. The great point you made is that your husband and Captain Redmayne were entirely reconciled and left you in complete friendship when you last saw them. You can assure me of that?"

"Most emphatically."

"Have you looked into your uncle's room since he disappeared?"

"No, it has not been touched."

"Again thank you, Mrs. Pendean. I shall see you some time to-day."

"Can you give me any sort of hope?"

"As yet I know nothing of the actual event, and must not therefore offer you hope, or tell you not to hope."

She shook his hand and a fleeting ghost of a smile, infinitely pathetic but unconscious, touched her face. Even in grief the beauty of the woman was remarkable; and to Brendon, whose private emotions already struck into the present demands upon his intellect, she appeared exquisite. As he left her he hoped that a great problem lay before him. He desired to impress her—he looked forward with a passing exaltation quite foreign from his usual staid and cautious habit of mind; he even repeated to himself a pregnant saying that he had come across in a book of quotations, though he knew not the author of it.

"There is an hour in which a man may be happy all his life, can he but find it."

Then he grew ashamed of himself and felt something like a blush suffuse his plain features.

At the police station a car was waiting for him and in twenty minutes he had reached Foggintor. Picking his way past the fishing pools and regarding the frowning cliffs and wide spaces of the quarry under a mournful mist, Mark proceeded to the aperture at the·farther end. Then he left the rill which ran out from this exit and soon stood

by the bungalow. It was now the dinner hour.
Half a dozen masons and carpenters were eating
their meal in a wooden shed near the building and
with them sat two constables and their superior
officer.

Inspector Halfyard rose as Brendon appeared,
came forward, and shook hands.

"Lucky you was on the spot, my dear," he said
in his homely Devon way. "Not that it begins to
look as if there was anything here deep enough to
ask for your cleverness."

Inspector Halfyard stood six feet high
and had curiously broad, square shoulders; but
his imposing torso was ill supported. His legs
were very thin and long, and they turned out a
trifle. With his prominent nose, small head, and
bright little slate-grey eyes, he looked rather like a
stork. He was rheumatic, too, and walked stiffly.

"This here hole is no place for my legs," he
confessed. "But from the facts, so far as we've
got 'em, Foggintor quarry don't come into the
story, though it looks as if it ought to. But the
murder was done here—inside this bungalow—and
the chap that's done it hadn't any use for such a
likely sort of hiding-place."

"Have you searched the quarries?"

"Not yet. 'Tis no good turning fifty men into
this jakes of a hole till we know whether it will be
needful; but all points to somewhere else. A
terrible strange job—so strange, in fact, that we
shall probably find a criminal lunatic at the
bottom of it. Everything looks pretty clear, but
it don't look sane."

"You haven't found the body?"

"No; but you can often prove murder mighty well without it—as now. Come out to the bungalow and I'll tell you what there is to tell. There's been a murder all right, but we're more likely to find the murderer than his victim."

They went out together and soon stood in the building.

"Now let's have the story from where you come in," said Brendon, and Inspector Halfyard told his tale.

"Somewhere about a quarter after midnight I was knocked up. Down I came and Constable Ford, on duty at the time, told me that Mrs. Pendean was wishful to see me. I knew her and her husband very well, for they'd been the life and soul of the Moss Supply Depôt, run at Princetown during the war.

"Her husband and her uncle, Captain Redmayne, had gone to the bungalow, as they often did after working hours, to carry on a bit; but at midnight they hadn't come home, and she was put about for 'em. Hearing of the motor bike, I thought there might have been a breakdown, if not an accident, so I told Ford to knock up another chap and go down along the road. Which they did do—and Ford came back at half after three with ugly news that they'd seen nobody, but they'd found a great pool of blood inside the bungalow—as if somebody had been sticking a pig there. 'Twas daylight by then and I motored out instanter. The mess is in the room that will

be the kitchen, and there's blood on the lintel of
the back door which opens into the kitchen.

"I looked round very carefully for anything in
the nature of a clue, but I couldn't see so much
as a button. What makes any work here wasted,
so far as I can see, is the evidence of the people at
the cottages in the by-road to Foggintor, where
we came in. A few qarrymen and their families
live there, and also Tom Ringrose, the water bailiff down on Walkham River. The quarrymen
don't work here because this place hasn't been
open for more than a hundred years; but they go
to Duke's quarry down at Merivale, and most of
'em have push bikes to take 'em to and from their
job.

"At these cottages, on my way back to breakfast, I got some information of a very definite
kind. Two men told the same tale and they hadn't
met before they told it. One was Jim Bassett,
under foreman at Duke's quarry, and one was
Ringrose, the water bailiff who lives in the end
cottage. Bassett has been at the bungalow once
or twice, as granite for it comes from the quarry
at Merivale. He knew Mr. Pendean and Captain
Redmayne by sight and, last night, somewhere
about ten o'clock by summer time, while it was
still light, he saw the captain leave and pass
the cottages. Bassett was smoking at his door at
the time and Robert Redmayne came alone, pushing his motor bicycle till he reached the road.
And behind the saddle he had a big sack fastened
to the machine.

"Bassett wished him 'good night' and he returned the compliment; and half a mile down the by-road, Ringrose also passed him. He was now on his machine and riding slowly till he reached the main road. He reached it and then Ringrose heard him open out and get up speed. He proceeded up the hill and the water bailiff supposed that he was going back to Princetown."

Inspector Halfyard stopped.

"And that is all you know?" asked Brendon.

"As to Captain Redmayne's movements—yes," answered the elder. "There will probably be information awaiting us when we return to Princetown, as inquiries are afoot along both roads—to Moreton and Exeter on the one side and by Dartmeet to Ashburton and the coast towns on the other. He must have gone off to the moor by one of those ways, I judge; and if he didn't, then he turned in his tracks and got either to Plymouth, or away to the north. We can't fail to pick up his line pretty quickly. He's a noticeable man."

"Did Ringrose also report the sack behind the motor bicycle?"

"He did."

"Before you mentioned it?"

"Yes, he volunteered that item, just as Bassett had done."

"Let me see what's to be seen here, then," said Brendon, and they entered the kitchen of the bungalow together.

CHAPTER III

THE MYSTERY

BRENDON followed Halfyard into the apartment destined to be the kitchen of Michael Pendean's bungalow, and the inspector lifted some tarpaulins that had been thrown upon a corner of the room. In the midst stood a carpenter's bench, and the floor, the boards of which had already been laid, was littered with shavings and tools. Under the tarpaulin a great red stain soaked to the walls, where much blood had flowed. It was still wet in places and upon it lay shavings partially ensanguined. At the edge of the central stain were smears and, among them, half the impress of a big, nail-studded boot.

"Have the workmen been in here this morning?" asked Brendon, and Inspector Halfyard answered that they had not.

"Two constables were here last night after one o'clock—the men I sent from Princetown when Mrs. Pendean gave the alarm," he said. "They looked round with an electric torch and found the blood. One came back; the other stopped on the spot all night. I was out here myself before the masons and carpenters came to work, and I forbade them to touch anything till we'd made our examination. Mr. Pendean was in the habit of doing a bit himself after hours."

"Can the men say if anything was done last night—in the way of work on the bungalow?"

"No doubt they'd know."

Brendon sent for a mason and a carpenter; and while the latter alleged that nothing had been added to the last work of himself and his mate, the mason, pointing to a wall which was destined to inclose the garden, declared that some heavy stones had been lifted and mortared into place since he left on the previous evening at five o'clock.

"Pull down all the new work," directed Brendon.

Then he turned to examine the kitchen more closely. A very careful survey produced no results and he could find nothing that the carpenters were not able to account for. There was no evidence of any struggle. A sheep might as easily have been killed in the chamber as a man; but he judged the blood to be human and Halfyard had made one discovery of possible importance. The timbers of the kitchen door were already set up and they had received a preliminary coat of white paint. This was smeared at the height of a man's shoulder with blood.

Brandon then examined the ground immediately outside the kitchen door. It was rough and trampled with many feet of the workmen but gave no special imprints or other indications of the least value. For twenty yards he scrutinized every inch of the ground and presently found indications of a motor bicycle. It had stood here—ten yards from the bungalow—and the marks of the wheels and the rest lowered to support it were clear enough in the peat. He traced the impressions as the machine was wheeled away and observed that at one soft place they had pressed very deeply into the earth. The pattern of the tire was familiar to him, a Dunlop. Half an hour later one of the constables approached, saluted Mark, and made a statement.

"They've pulled down the wall, sir, and found nothing there; but Fulford, the mason, says that a sack is missing. It was a big sack, in the corner of the shed out there, and the cement that it contained is all poured out; but the sack has gone."

The detective visited the spot and turned over the pile of cement, which revealed nothing. Then, having himself searched the workmen's shed without discovering any clue, he strolled in the immediate neighbourhood of the bungalow and examined the adjacent entrance to the quarries. Not the least spark of light rewarded the search. He came back presently out of the rain which had now begun to fall steadily—but not before he had strolled as far as the fishing pools and seen clear marks of naked, adult feet on the sandy brink.

Inspector Halfyard, who had remained in the bungalow, joined him while he examined the other five chambers with close attention. In the apartment destined for a sitting-room, which faced out upon the great view to the southwest, Brendon found a cigar half smoked. It had evidently been flung down alight and had smouldered for some time, scorching the wooden floor before it went out. He found also the end of a broken, brown boot lace with a brass tag. The lace had evidently frayed away and probably had broken when being tied. But he attached not the least importance to either fragment. Nothing that he regarded as of value resulted from inspection of the remaining rooms and Brendon presently decided that he would return to Princetown. He showed Halfyard the footprints by the water and had them protected with a tarpaulin.

"Something tells me that this is a pretty simple business all the same," he said. "We need waste no more time here, inspector—at any rate until we have got back to the telephone and heard the latest."

"What's your idea?"

"I should say we have to do with an unfortunate man who's gone mad," replied the detective; "and a madman doesn't take long to find as a rule. I think it's murder right enough and I believe we shall find that this soldier, who's had shell shock, turned on Pendean and cut his throat, then, fondly hoping to hide the crime, got away with the body. Why I judge him to be mad is because Mrs. Pendean, who has told me the full story of the past, was able to assure me that the men had become exceedingly friendly, and that certain differences, which existed between them at the outbreak of the war, were entirely composed. And even granting that they quarrelled again, the quarrel must have suddenly sprung up. That seems improbable and one can't easily imagine a sudden row so tremendous that it ends in murder.

"Redmayne was a big, powerful man and he

may have struck without intention to kill; but this mess means more than a blow with a fist. I think that he was a homicidal maniac and probably plotted the job beforehand with a madman's limited cunning; and if that is so, there's pretty sure to be news waiting for us at Princetown. Before dark we ought to know where are both the dead and the living man. These footprints mean a bather, or perhaps two. We'll study them later and drag the pond, if necessary.''

The correctness of Brendon's deduction was made manifest within an hour, and the operations of Robert Redmayne defined up to a point. A man was waiting at the police station—George French, ostler at Two Bridges Hotel, on West Dart.

"I knew Captain Redmayne," he said, "because he'd been down once or twice of late to tea at Two Bridges. Last night, at half after ten, I was crossing the road from the garage and suddenly, without warning, a motor bike came over the bridge. I heard the rush of it and only got out of the way by a yard. There was no light showing but the man went through the beam thrown from the open door of the hotel and I saw it was the captain by his great mustache and his red waistcoat.

"He didn't see me, because it was taking him all his time to look after himself, and he'd just let her go, to rush the stiff hill that rises out of Two Bridges. He was gone like a puff of smoke and must have been running terrible fast—fifty mile

an hour I dare say. We heard as there was
trouble at Princetown and master sent me up
over to report what I'd seen."

"Which way did he go after he had passed, Mr.
French?" asked Brendon, who knew the Dartmoor
country well. "The road forks above Two
Bridges. Did he take the right hand for Dartmeet, or the left for Post Bridge and Moreton?"

But George could not say.

" 'Twas like a thunder planet flashing by," he
told Mark, "and I don't know from Adam which
way he went after he'd got up on top."

"Was anybody with him?"

"No, sir. I'd have seen that much; but he
carried a big sack behind the saddle—that I can
swear to."

There had been several telephone calls for Inspector Halfyard during his absence; and now
three separate statements from different districts
awaited him. These were already written out
by a constable, and he took them one by one, read
them, and handed them to Brendon. The
first came from the post office at Post Bridge, and
the post-mistress reported that a man, one Samuel
White, had seen a motor bicycle run at great speed
without lights up the steep hill northward of that
village on the previous night. He gave the time
as between half past ten and eleven o'clock.

"We should have heard of him from Moreton
next," said Halfyard; "but, no. He must have
branched under Hameldown and gone south, for
the next news is from Ashburton."

The second message told how a garage keeper

was knocked up at Ashburton, just after midnight, in order that petrol might be obtained for a motor bicycle. The description of the purchaser corresponded to Redmayne and the message added that the bicycle had a large sack tied behind it. The rider was in no hurry; he smoked a cigarette, swore because he could not get a drink, lighted his lamps, and then proceeded by the Totnes road which wound through the valley of the Dart southward.

The third communication came from the police station at Brixham and was somewhat lengthy. It ran thus:

"At ten minutes after two o'clock last night P. C. Widgery, on night duty at Brixham, saw a man on a motor bicycle with a large parcel behind him run through the town square. He proceeded down the main street and was gone for the best part of an hour; but, before three o'clock, Widgery saw him return without his parcel. He went fast up the hill out of Brixham, the way he came. Inquiries to-day show that he passed the Brixham coast-guard station about a quarter after two o'clock, and he must have lifted his machine over the barrier at the end of the coast-guard road, because he was seen by a boy, from Berry Head lighthouse, pushing it up the steep path that runs to the downs. The boy was going for a doctor, because his father, one of the lighthouse watchers, had been taken ill. The boy says the motor bicyclist was a big man and he was blowing, because the machine was heavy and the road just there very steep and rough. He saw no more of him on returning from the doctor. We are searching the Head and cliffs round about."

Inspector Halfyard waited until Brendon had read the messages and put them down.

"About as easy as shelling peas—eh?" he asked.

"I expected an arrest," answered the detective. "It can't be long delayed."

As though to confirm him the telephone bell rang and Halfyard rose and entered the box to receive the latest information.

"Paignton speaking," said the message. "We have just called at address of Captain Redmayne —No. 7 Marine Terrace. He was expected last night—had wired yesterday to say he'd be home. They left supper for him, as usual when he is expected, and went to bed. Didn't hear him return, but found on going down house next morning that he had come—supper eaten, motor bike in tool house in back yard, where he keeps it. They called him at ten o'clock—no answer. They went in his room. Not there and bed not slept in and his clothes not changed. He's not been seen since."

"Hold on. Mark Brendon's here and has the case. He'll speak."

Inspector Halfyard reported the statement and Brendon picked up the mouthpiece.

"Detective Brendon speaking. Who is it?"

"Inspector Reece, Paignton."

"Let me hear at five o'clock if arrest has been made. Failing arrest I will motor down to you after that hour."

"Very good, sir. I expect to hear he's taken any minute."

"Nothing from Berry Head?"

"We've got a lot of men there and all round under the cliffs, but nothing yet."

"All right, inspector. I'll come down if I don't hear to the contrary by five."

He hung up the receiver.

"All over bar shouting, I reckon," said Half-yard.

"It looks like it. He's mad, poor devil."

"It's the dead man I'm sorry for."

Brendon considered, having first looked at his watch. Personal thoughts would thrust them-selves upon him, though he felt both surprise and shame that they could do so. Certain realities were clear enough to his mind, however future de-tails might develop. And the overmastering fact was that Jenny Pendean had lost her husband. If she were, indeed, a widow——

He shook his head impatiently and turned to Halfyard.

"Should Robert Redmayne not be taken to-day, one or two things must be done," he said. "You'd better have some of that blood collected and the fact proved that it is human. And keep the cigar and boot lace here for the minute, though I attach no importance to either. Now I'll go and get some food and see Mrs. Pendean. Then I'll come back. I'll take the police car for Paignton at half past five if we hear nothing to alter my plans."

"You will. This isn't going to spoil your holi-day, after all."

"What is it going to do, I wonder?" thought Brendon. But he said no more and prepared to go on his way. It was now three o'clock. Suddenly he turned and asked Halfyard a question.

"What do you think of Mrs. Pendean, inspector?"

"I think two things about her," answered the elder. "I think she's such a lovely piece that it's hard to believe she's just flesh and blood, like other women; and I think I never saw such worship for a man as she had for her husband. This will knock her right bang out."

These opinions made the detective melancholy; but he had not yet begun to reflect on how the passing of a dearly loved husband would change the life of Mrs. Pendean. He suddenly felt himself thrust out of the situation forever, yet resented his own conviction as irrational.

"What sort of a man was he?"

"A friendly fashion of chap—Cornish—a pacifist at heart I reckon; but we never talked war politics."

"What was his age?"

"Couldn't tell you—doubtful—might have been anything between twenty-five and thirty-five. A man with weak eyes and a brown beard. He wore double eye-glasses for close work, but his long sight he said was good."

After a meal Brendon went again to Mrs. Pendean; but many rumours had reached her through the morning and she already knew most of what he had to tell. A change had come over her; she was very silent and very pale. Mark knew that she had grasped the truth and knew that her husband must probably be dead.

She was, however, anxious to learn if Brendon could explain what had happened.

"Have you ever met with any such thing before?" she asked.

"No case is quite like another. They all have their differences. I think that Captain Redmayne, who has suffered from shell shock, must have been overtaken by loss of reason. Shell shock often produces dementia of varying degrees—some lasting, some fleeting. I'm afraid your uncle went out of his mind and, in a moment of madness, may have done a dreadful thing. Then he set out, while he was still insane, to cover up his action. So far as we can judge, he took away his victim and meant apparently to throw him into the sea. I feel only too sure that your husband has lost his life, Mrs. Pendean. You must be prepared to accept that unspeakable misfortune."

"It is hard to accept," she answered, "because they were good friends again."

"Something of which you do not know may have cropped up between them to upset Redmayne. When he comes to his senses, he will probably think the whole thing an evil dream. Have you a portrait of your husband?"

She left the room and returned in a few moments with a photograph. It presented a man of meditative countenance, wide forehead, and steadfast eyes. He wore a beard, mustache and whiskers, and his hair was rather long.

"Is that like him?"

"Yes; but it does not show his expression. It

is not quite natural—he was more animated than that."

"How old was he?"

"Not thirty, Mr. Brendon, but he looked considerably older."

Brendon studied the photograph.

"You can take it with you if you wish to do so. I have another copy," said Mrs. Pendean.

"I shall remember very accurately," answered Brendon. "I am tolerably certain that poor Mr. Pendean's body was thrown into the sea and may already be recovered. That appears to have been Captain Redmayne's purpose. Can you tell me anything about the lady to ·whom your uncle is engaged?"

"I can give you her name and address. But I have never seen her."

"Had your husband seen her?"

"Not to my knowledge. Indeed I can say certainly that he never had. She is a Miss Flora Reed and she is stopping with her mother and father at the Singer Hotel, Paignton. Her brother, my uncle's friend in France, is also there I believe."

"Thank you very much. If I hear nothing further, I go to Paignton this evening."

"Why?"

"To pursue my inquiry and see all those who know your uncle. It has puzzled me a little that he has not already been found, because a man suffering from such an upset of mind could make no successful attempt to evade a professional search for long. Nor, so far as we know, has he apparently attempted to escape. After going to Berry Head early this morning, he returned to his lodgings, ate a meal, left his motor bicycle. and then went out again—still in his tweed suit with the red waistcoat."

"You'll see Flora Reed?"

"If necessary; but I shall not go if Robert Redmayne has been found."

"You think it is all very simple and straightforward, then?"

"So it appears. The best that one can hope is that the unfortunate man may come back to his senses and give a clear account of everything. And may I ask what you design to do and if it is in my power to serve you personally in any way?"

Jenny Pendean showed surprise at this question. She lifted her face to Brendon's and a slight warmth touched its pallor.

"That is kind of you," she said. "I will not forget. But when we know more, I shall probably leave here. If my husband has indeed lost his life, the bungalow will not be finished by me. I shall go, of course."

"May I hope that you have friends who are coming forward?"

She shook her head.

"As a matter of fact I am much alone in the world. My husband was everything—everything. And I was everything to him also. You know my story—I told you all there was to tell this morning. There remain to me only my father's two brothers—Uncle Bendigo in England, and

Uncle Albert in Italy. I wrote them both to-day.''

Mark rose.

''You shall hear from me to-morrow,'' he said, ''and if I do not go to Paignton, I will see you again to-night.''

''Thank you—you are very kind.''

''Let me ask you to consider yourself and your own health under this great strain. People can endure anything, but often they find afterwards that they have put too heavy a call on nature, when it comes to pay the bill. Would you care to see a medical man?''

''No, Mr. Brendon—that is not necessary. If my husband should be—as we think, then my own life has no further interest for me. I may end it.''

''For God's sake don't allow yourself to speak in that way,'' said Brendon. ''Look forward. If we can no longer be happy in the world, that is not to deny us the power and privilege of being useful in it. Think what your husband would have wished you to do and how he would have expected you to face any great tragedy, or grief.''

''You are a good man,'' said Mrs. Pendean quietly. ''I appreciate what you have said. You will see me again.''

She took his hand and pressed it. Then he left her, bewildered by the subtle atmosphere that seemed to surround her. He did not fear her threat. There was a vitality and self-command about Mrs. Pendean that seemed to shut out any likelihood of self-destruction. She was young and time could be trusted to do its inevitable work. But he perceived the quality of her love for the man who was too certainly destroyed. She might face life, proceed with her own existence, and bring happiness into other lives; but it did not follow that she would ever forget her husband or consent to wed another.

He returned to the police station and was astonished to find that Robert Redmayne continued at large. No news concerning him had been reported; but there came a minor item of information from the searchers at Berry Head. The cement sack had been found in the mouth of a rabbit hole to the west of the Head above a precipice. The sack was bloodstained and contained some small tufts of hair and the dust of cement.

An hour later Mark Brendon had packed a bag and started in a police motor car for Paignton; but there was no more to be learned when he arrived. Inspector Reece shared Brendon's surprise that Redmayne had not been arrested. He explained that fishermen and coast guards were dragging the sea, as far as it was possible to do so, beneath the cliff on which the sack had been found; but the tide ran strongly here and local men suspected the current might well have carried a body out to sea. They judged that the corpse would be found floating within a mile or two of the Head in a week's time, if no means had been taken to anchor it at the bottom.

Brendon called at Robert Redmayne's lodgings after he had eaten some supper at the

Singer Hotel. There he had taken a room, that
he might see and hear something of the vanished
man's future wife and her family. At No. 7
Marine Terrace the landlady, a Mrs. Medway,
could say little. Captain Redmayne was a genial,
kind-hearted, but hot-headed gentleman, she told
Mark. He was irregular in his hours and they
never expected him until they saw him. He
often thus returned from excursions after the
household was gone to bed. She did not know at
what hour he had come back on the previous
night, or at what hour he had gone out again;
but he had not changed his clothes or apparently
taken anything away with him.

Brendon examined the motor bicycle with meticulous care. There was a rest behind the saddle
made of light iron bars, and here he detected
stains of blood. A fragment of tough string tied
to the rest was also stained. It had been cut—no
doubt when Redmayne cast his burden loose on
reaching the cliffs. Nothing offered any difficulty in the chain of circumstantial evidence,
nor did another morning furnish further problems save the supreme and sustained mystery of
Robert Redmayne's continued disappearance.

Brendon visited Berry Head before breakfast
on the following day and examined the cliff. It
fell in broad scales of limestone, whereon grew
thistles and the white rock-rose, sea pinks and
furze. Rabbits dwelt here and the bloodstained
sack had been discovered by a dog. It was
thrust into a hole, but the terrier had easily
reached it and dragged it into light.

Immediately beneath the spot, the cliffs fell starkly into the sea—a drop of three hundred feet. Beneath was deep water and only an occasional cleft or cranny broke the face of the shining precipice, where green things made shift to live and the gulls built their rough nests with scurvy grass. No sign marked the cliff edge, but beneath, on the green sea, were boats from which fishermen still dredged for the dead. This work, long continued, had yielded no results whatever.

Later in the day Brendon returned to his hotel and introduced himself to Miss Reed and her family to find that her brother, Robert Redmayne's friend, had returned to London. She and her parents were sitting together in the lounge when he joined them. All three appeared to be much shocked and painfully mystified. None could throw any light. Mr. and Mrs. Reed were quiet, elderly people who kept a draper shop in London; their daughter revealed more character. She was a head taller than her father and cast in a generous mould. She exhibited a good deal of manner and less actual sorrow than might have been expected; but Brendon discovered that she had only known Robert Redmayne for half a year and their actual engagement was not of much more than a month's duration. Miss Reed was dark, animated, and commonplace of mind. Her ambition had been to go upon the stage and she had acted on tour in the country; but she declared that theatrical life wearied her and she had promised her future husband to abandon the art.

"Did you ever hear Captain Redmayne speak

of his niece and her husband?'' Brendon inquired, and Flora Reed answered:

"He did; and he always said that Michael Pendean was a 'shirker' and a coward. He also assured me that he had done with his niece and should never forgive her for marrying her husband. But that was before Bob went to Princetown, six days ago. From there he wrote quite a different story. He had met them by chance and he found that Mr. Pendean had not shirked but done good work in the war and got the O. B. E. After that discovery, Bob changed and he was certainly on the best of terms with the Pendeans before this awful thing happened. He had already made them promise to come here for the regattas.''

"You have neither seen nor heard of the captain since?''

"Indeed, no. My last letter, which you can see, came three days ago. In it he merely said he would be back yesterday and meet me to bathe as usual. I went to bathe and looked out for him, but of course he didn't come.''

"Tell me a little about him, Miss Reed,'' said Mark. "It is good of you to give me this interview, for we are up against a curious problem and the situation, as it appears at present, may be illusive and quite unlike the real facts. Captain Redmayne, I hear, had suffered from shell shock and a breath of poison gas also. Did you ever notice any signs that these troubles had left any mark upon him?''

"Yes,'' she answered. "We all did. My

mother was the first to point out that Bob often repeated himself. He was a man of great good temper, but the war had made him rough and cynical in some respects. He was impatient, yet, after he quarrelled or had a difference with anybody, he would be quickly sorry; and he was never ashamed to apologize.''

"Did he quarrel often?"

"He was very opinionated and, of course, he had seen a good deal of actual war. It had made him a little callous and he would sometimes say things that shocked civilians. Then they would protest and make him angry."

"You cared much for him? Forgive the question."

"I admired him and I had a good influence over him. There were fine things in him—great bravery and honesty. Yes, I loved him and was proud of him. I think he would have become calmer and less excitable and impatient in time. Doctors had told him that he would outgrow all effects of his shock."

"Was he a man you can conceive of as capable of striking or killing a fellow creature?"

The lady hesitated.

"I only want to help him," she answered. "Therefore I say that, given sufficient provocation, I can imagine Bob's temper flaring out, and I can see that it would have been possible to him, in a moment of passion, to strike down a man. He had seen much death and was himself absolutely indifferent to danger. Yes, I can imagine him doing an enemy, or fancied enemy, a hurt; but what I cannot imagine him doing is what he is supposed to have done afterwards—evade the consequence of a mistaken act.''

''And yet we have the strongest testimony that he has tried to conceal a murder—whether committed by himself, or somebody else, we cannot yet say.''

''I only hope and pray, for all our sakes, that you will find him,'' she replied, ''but if, indeed, he has been betrayed into such an awful crime, I do not think you will find him.''

''Why not, Miss Reed? But I think I know. What is in your mind has already passed through my own. The thought of suicide.''

She nodded and put her handkerchief to her eyes.

''Yes; if poor Bob lost himself and then found himself and discovered that he had killed an innocent man in a moment of passion, he would, if I know him, do one of two things—either give himself up instantly and explain all that had happened, or else destroy himself as quickly as he could.''

''Motive is not always adequate,'' Brendon told them. ''A swift, passing storm of temper has often destroyed a life with no more evil intent than a flash of lightning. In this case, only such a storm seems to be the explanation. But how a man of the Pendean type could have provoked such a storm I have yet to learn. So far the testimony of Mrs. Pendean and the assurances of Inspector Halfyard at Princetown indicate an amiable and quiet person, slow to anger. Inspector Halfyard knew him quite well at the Moss Depôt, where he worked through two years of the war. He was apparently not a man to have infuriated Captain Redmayne or anybody else.''

Mark then related his own brief personal experience of Redmayne on the occasion of their meeting by the quarry pools. For some reason this personal anecdote touched Flora Reed and the detective observed that she was genuinely moved by it.

Indeed she began to weep and presently rose and left them. Her parents were able to speak more freely upon her departure.

Mr. Reed indeed, from being somewhat silent and indifferent, grew voluble.

''I think it right to tell you,'' he said, ''that my wife and I never cared much for this engagement. Redmayne meant well and had a good heart I believe. He was free-handed and exceedingly enamoured of Flora. He made violent love from the first and his affection was returned. But I never could see him a steady, married man. He was a rover and the war had made him—not exactly inhuman, but apparently unconscious of his own obligations to society and his own duty, as a reasonable being, to help build up the broken organization of social life. He only lived for pleasure and sport or spending money; and though I do not suggest he would have been a bad husband, I did not see the makings of a stable home in his ideas of the future. He had inherited some forty thousand pounds, but he was very ignorant of the value of money and he showed no particular good sense on the subject of his coming responsibilities."

Mark Brendon thanked them for their information and repeated his growing conviction that the subject of their speech had probably committed suicide.

"Every hour which fails to account for him increases my fear," he said. "Indeed it may be a good thing to happen; for the alternative can at best be Broadmoor; and it is a hateful thought that a man who has fought for his country, and fought well, should end his days in a criminal lunatic asylum."

For two days the detective remained at Paignton and devoted all his energy, invention, and experience to the task of discovering the vanished men. But, neither alive nor dead, did either appear, and not a particle of information came from Princetown or elsewhere. Portraits of Robert Redmayne were printed and soon hung on the notice board of every police station in the west and south; but one or two mistaken arrests alone resulted from this publicity. A tramp with a big red mustache was detained in North Devon and a recruit arrested at Devonport. This man resembled the photograph and had joined a line regiment twenty-four hours after the disappearance of Redmayne. Both, however, could give a full account of themselves.

Then Brendon prepared to return to Princetown. He wrote his intention to Mrs. Pendean and informed her that he would visit Station Cottages on the following evening. It happened, however, that his letter crossed another and his plans were altered, for Jenny Pendean had already left Princetown and joined Mr. Bendigo Redmayne at his house, "Crow's Nest," beyond Dartmouth. She wrote:

"My uncle has begged me to come and I was thankful to do so. I have to tell you that Uncle Bendigo received a letter yesterday from his brother, Robert. I begged him to let me send it to you instantly, but he declines. Uncle Bendigo is on Captain Redmayne's side I can see. He would not, I am sure, do anything to interfere with the law, but he is convinced that we do not know all there is to be told about this terrible thing. The motor boat from 'Crow's Nest' will be at Kingswear Ferry to meet the train reaching there at two o'clock to-morrow and I hope you may still be at Paignton and able to come here for a few hours."

She added a word of thanks to him and a regret that his holiday was being spoiled by her tragedy.

Whereupon the man's thoughts turned to her entirely and he forgot for a while the significance of her letter. He had expected to see her that night at Princetown. Instead he would find her far nearer, in the house on the cliffs beyond Dartmouth.

He telegraphed presently that he would meet the launch. Then he had leisure to be annoyed that the letter from Robert Redmayne was thus delayed. He speculated on Bendigo Redmayne.

"A brother is a brother," he thought, "and no doubt this old sailor's home would offer a very efficient hiding-place for any vanished man."

CHAPTER IV

A MOTOR boat lay off Kingswear Ferry when Mark Brendon arrived. The famous harbour was new to him and though his mind found itself sufficiently occupied, he still had perception disengaged and could admire the graceful river, the hills towering above the estuary, and the ancient town lying within their infolding and tree-clad slopes. Dominating all stood the Royal Naval College, its great masses of white and red masonry breaking the blue sky.

A perfect little craft awaited him. She was painted white and furnished with teak. Her brasses and machinery glittered; the engines and steering wheel were set forward, while aft of the cabins and saloon an awning was rigged over the stern. The solitary sailor who controlled the launch was in the act of furling this protection against the sun as Mark descended to the water; and while the man did so, Brendon's eyes brightened, for a passenger already occupied the boat: a woman sat there and he saw Jenny Pendean.

She wore black and he found, as he leaped aboard and greeted her, that her mourning attire was an echo to her heart. That had happened

66

which convinced the young wife that all hope
must be abandoned; she knew that she was a
widow, for the letter in her uncle's possession told
her so. She greeted the detective kindly and was
glad that he had responded to her invitation, but
Mark soon found that her attitude of mind had
changed. She now exhibited an extreme listless-
ness and profound melancholy. He told her that
a letter from himself had gone to her at Princetown and he asked her for information respecting the communication received from Captain
Redmayne; but she was not responsive.

"My uncle will tell you what there is to tell,"
she said. "It appears that your original suspicion has proved correct. My husband has lost
his precious life at the hands of a madman."

"Yet it seems incredible, Mrs. Pendean, that
such an afflicted creature, if alive, should still be
evading the general search. Can you tell me
from where this letter came? We ought to have
heard of it instantly."

"So I told my Uncle Bendigo."

"Is he sure that it really does come from his
brother?"

"Yes; there is no doubt about that. The letter
was posted in Plymouth. But please do not ask
me about it, Mr. Brendon. I do not want to think
of it."

"I hope you are keeping well; and I know you
are being brave."

"I am alive," she said, "but my life has none
the less ended."

"You must not think or feel so. Let me say a

thing that comforted me in the mouth of another
when I lost my mother. It was an old clergyman
who said it. 'Think what the dead would wish
and try to please them.' It doesn't sound much;
but if you consider, it is helpful.''

The boat was speedy and she soon slipped out
between the historic castles that stood on either
bank of the entrance to the harbour.

Mrs. Pendean spoke.

''All this loveliness and peace seem to make
my heart more sore. When people suffer, they
should go where nature suffers too—to bleak, sad
regions.''

''You must occupy yourself. You must try to
lose yourself in work—in working your fingers to
the bone if need be. There is nothing like mental
and physical toil at a time of suffering.''

''That is only a drug. You might as well drink,
or take opium. I wouldn't run away from my
grief if I could. I owe it to the dead.''

''You are not a coward. You must live and
make the world happier for your life.''

She smiled for the first time—a flicker, that
lightened her beauty for a moment and quickly
died.

''You are good and kind and wise,'' she answered. Then she changed the subject and
pointed to the man in the bows. He sat upright
with his back to them at the wheel forward. He
had taken off his hat and was singing very gently
to himself, but hardly loud enough to be heard
against the drone of the engines. His song was
from an early opera of Verdi.

"Have you noticed that man?"

Mark shook his head.

"He is an Italian. He comes from Turin but has worked in England for some time. He looks to me more Greek than Italian—not modern Greek but from classical times—the times I used to study as a schoolgirl. He has a head like a statue."

She called to the boatman.

"Stand out a mile or so, Doria," she said. "I want Mr. Brendon to see the coast line."

"Aye, aye, ma'am," he answered and altered their course for the open sea.

He had turned at Jenny Pendean's voice and shown Mark a brown, bright, clean-shorn face of great beauty. It was of classical contour, but lacked the soulless perfection of the Greek ideal. The Italian's black eyes were brilliant and showed intelligence.

"Giuseppe Doria has a wonderful story about himself," continued Mrs. Pendean. "Uncle Ben tells me that he claims descent from a very ancient family and is the last of the Dorias of—I forget—some place near Ventimiglia. My uncle thinks the world of him; but I hope he is as trustworthy and as honest in character as he is handsome in person."

"He certainly might be well born. There is distinction, quality, and breeding about his appearance."

"He is clever, too—an all-round sort of man, like most sailors."

Brendon admired the varied charms of the

Dartmouth coast, the bluffs and green headlands, the rich, red sandstone cliffs, and pearly precipices of limestone that rose above the tranquil waters. The boat turned west presently, passed a panorama of cliffs and little bays with sandy beaches, and anon skirted higher and sterner precipices, which leaped six hundred feet aloft. Perched among them like a bird's nest stood a small house with windows that blinked out over the Channel. It rose to a tower room in the midst, and before the front there stretched a plateau whereon stood a flagstaff and spar, from the point of which fluttered a red ensign. Behind the house opened a narrow coomb and descended a road to the dwelling. Cliffs beetled round about it and the summer waves broke idly below and strung the land with a necklace of pearl. Far beneath the habitation, just above high-tide level, a strip of shingle spread, and above it a sea cave had been turned into a boathouse. Hither came Brendon and his companion.

The motor launch slowed down and presently grounded her bow on the pebbles. Then Doria stopped the engine, flung a gangway stage ashore, and stood by to hand Jenny Pendean and the detective to the beach. The place appeared to have no exit; but, behind a ledge of rock, stairs carved in the stone wound upward, guarded by an iron handrail. Jenny led the way and Mark followed her until two hundred steps were climbed and they stood on the terrace above. It was fifty yards long and covered with sea gravel. Two little brass cannon thrust their muzzles over the parapet to seaward and the central space of grass about the flagpole was neatly surrounded with a decoration of scallop shells.

"Could anybody but an old sailor have created this place?" asked Brendon.

A middle-aged man with a telescope under his arm came along the terrace to greet them. Bendigo Redmayne was square and solid with the cut of the sea about him. His uncovered head blazed with flaming, close-clipped hair and he wore also a short, red beard and whiskers growing grizzled. But his long upper lip was shaved. He had a weather-beaten face—ruddy and deepening to purple about the cheek bones—with eyebrows, rough as bent grass, over deep-set, sulky eyes of reddish brown. His mouth was underhung, giving him a pugnacious and bad-tempered appearance. Nor did his looks appear to libel the old sailor. To Brendon, at any rate, he showed at first no very great consideration.

"You've come I see," he said, shaking hands. "No news?"

"None, Mr. Redmayne."

"Well, well! To think Scotland Yard can't find a poor soul that's gone off his rocker!"

"You might have helped us to do so," said Mark shortly, "if it's true that you've had a letter from your brother."

"I'm doing it, ain't I? It's here for you."

"You've lost two days."

Bendigo Redmayne grunted.

"Come in and see the letter," he said. "I never thought you'd fail. It's all very terrible indeed and I'm damned if I understand anything about it. But one fact is clear: my brother wrote this letter and he wrote it from Plymouth; and since he hasn't been reported from Plymouth, I feel very little doubt the thing he wanted to happen has happened."

Then he turned to his niece.

"We'll have a cup of tea in half an hour, Jenny. Meantime I'll take Mr. Brendon up to the tower room along with me."

Mrs. Pendean disappeared into the house and Mark followed her with the sailor.

They passed through a square hall full of various foreign curiosities collected by the owner. Then they ascended into a large, octagonal chamber, like the lantern of a lighthouse, which surmounted the dwelling.

"My lookout," explained Mr. Redmayne. "In foul weather I spend all my time up here and with yonder strong, three-inch telescope I can pick up what's doing at sea. A bunk in the corner, you see. I often sleep up here, too."

"You might almost as well be afloat," said Brendon, and the remark pleased Bendigo.

"That's how I feel; and I can tell you there's a bit of movement, too, sometimes. I never wish to see bigger water than beat these cliffs during the south-easter last March. We shook to our keel, I can tell you."

He went to a tall cupboard in a corner, unlocked it and brought out a square, wooden desk of old-fashioned pattern. This he opened and produced a letter which he handed to the detective.

Brendon sat down in a chair under the open window and read this communication slowly. The writing was large and sprawling; it sloped slightly upward from left to right across the sheet and left a triangle of white paper at the right-hand bottom corner:

"DEAR BEN: It's all over. I've done in Michael Pendean and put him where only Judgment Day will find him. Something drove me to do it; but all the same I'm sorry now it's done—not for him but myself. I shall clear to-night, with luck, for France. If I can send an address later I will. Look after Jenny—she's well rid of the blighter. When things have blown over I may come back. Tell Albert and tell Flo. Yours,
                                   "R. R."

Brendon examined the letter and the envelope that contained it.

"Have you another communication—something from the past I can compare with this?" he asked.

Bendigo nodded.

"I reckoned you'd want that," he answered and produced a second letter from his desk.

It related to Robert Redmayne's engagement to be married and the writing was identical.

"And what do you think he's done, Mr. Redmayne?" Brendon asked, pocketing the two communications.

"I think he's done what he hoped to do. At this time of year you'll see a dozen Spanish and Brittany onion boats lying down by the Barbican at Plymouth, every day of the week. And if poor Bob got there, no doubt plenty of chaps would

hide him when he offered 'em money enough to
make it worth while. Once aboard one of those
sloops, he'd be about as safe as he would be anywhere. They'd land him at St. Malo, or somewhere down there, and he'd give you the slip."

"And, until it was found out that he was mad,
we might hear no more about him."

"Why should it be found that he was mad?"
asked Bendigo. "He was mad when he killed this
innocent man, no doubt, because none but a lunatic
would have done such an awful thing, or been so
cunning after—with the sort of childish cunning
that gave him away from the start. But once
he'd done what this twist in his brain drove him
to do, then I judge that his madness very likely
left him. If you caught him to-morrow, you'd
possibly find him as sane as yourself—except on
that one subject. He'd worked up his old hatred
of Michael Pendean, as a shirker in the war,
until it festered in his head and poisoned his
mind, so as he couldn't get it under. That's how
I read it. I had a pretty good contempt for the
poor chap myself and was properly savage with
my niece, when she wedded him against our
wishes; but my feeling didn't turn my head, and I
felt glad to hear that Pendean was an honest man,
who did the best he could at the Moss Depôt."

Brendon considered.

"A very sound view," he said, "and likely to
be correct. On the strength of this letter, we may
conclude that when he went home, after disposing
of the body under Berry Head, your brother must
have disguised himself in some way and taken

an early train from Paignton to Newton Abbot and from Newton Abbot to Plymouth. He would already have been there and lying low before the hunt began.''

"That's how I figure it," answered the sailor. "When did you last see him, Mr. Redmayne?"

"Somewhere about a month ago. He came over for the day with Miss Reed—the young woman he was going to marry."

"Was he all right then?"

Bendigo considered and scratched in his red beard.

"Noisy and full of chatter, but much as usual."

"Did he mention Mr. and Mrs. Pendean?"

"Not a word. He was full up with his young woman. They meant to be married in late autumn and go abroad for a run to see my brother Albert.''

"He may correspond with Miss Reed if he gets to France?"

"I can't say what he'll do. Suppose you catch him presently? How would the law stand? A man goes mad and commits a murder. Then you nab him and he's as sane as a judge. You can't hang him for what he did when he was off his head, and you can't shut him up in a lunatic asylum if he's sane."

"A nice problem, no doubt," admitted Brendon, "but be sure the law will take no risks. A homicidal maniac, no matter how sane he is between times, is not going to run loose any more after killing a man."

"Well, that's all there is to it, detective. If I

hear again, I'll let the police know; and if you
take him, of course you'll let me and his brother
know at once. It's a very ugly thing for his family. He did good work in the war and got
honours; and if he's mad, then the war made him
mad.''

''That would be taken very fully into account,
be sure. I'm sorry, both for him and for you,
Mr. Redmayne.''

Bendigo looked sulkily from under his tangled
eyebrows.

''I shouldn't feel no very great call to give him
up to the living death of an asylum, if he hove in
here some night.''

''You'd do your duty—that I will bet,'' replied
Brendon.

They descended to the dining-room, where
Jenny Pendean was waiting to pour out tea. All
were very silent and Mark had leisure to observe
the young widow.

''What shall you do and where may I count
upon finding you if I want you, Mrs. Pendean?''
he asked presently.

She looked at Redmayne, not at Brendon, as
she answered.

''I am in Uncle Bendigo's hands. I know he
will let me stop here for the present.''

''For keeps,'' the old sailor declared. ''This
is your home now, Jenny, and I'm very glad to
have you here. There's only you and your Uncle
Albert and me now, I reckon, for I don't think we
shall ever see poor Bob again.''

An elderly woman came in.

"Doria be wishful to know when you'll want the boat," she said.

"I should like it immediately if possible," begged Brendon. "Much time has been lost."

"Tell them to get aboard, then," directed Brendigo, and in five minutes Mark was taking his leave.

"I'll let you have the earliest intimation of the capture, Mr. Redmayne," he said. "If your poor brother still lives, it seems impossible that he should long be free. His present condition must be one of great torment and anxiety—to him— and for his own sake I hope he will soon surrender or be found—if not in England, then in France."

"Thank you," answered the older man quietly. "What you say is true. I regret the delay myself now. If he is heard of again by me, I'll telegraph to Scotland Yard, or get 'em to do so at Dartmouth. I've slung a telephone wire into the town as you see."

They stood again under the flagstaff on the plateau, and Brendon studied the rugged cliff line and the fields of corn that sloped away inland above it. The district was very lonely and only the rooftree of a solitary farmhouse appeared a mile or more distant to the west.

"If he should come to you—and I have still a fancy that he may do so—take him in and let us know," said Brendon. "Such a necessity will be unspeakably painful, I fear, but I am very sure you will not shrink from it, Mr. Redmayne."

The rough old man had grown more amiable during the detective's visit. It was clear that a natural aversion for Brendon's business no longer extended to the detective himself.

"Duty's duty," he said, "though God keep me from yours. If I can do anything, you may trust me to do it. He's not likely to come here, I think; but he might try and get over to Albert down south. Good-bye to you."

Mr. Redmayne went back to the house, and Jenny, who stood by them, walked as far as the top of the steps with Brendon.

"Don't think I bear any ill will to this poor wretch," she said. "I'm only heartbroken, that's all. I used to declare in my foolishness that I had escaped the war. But no—it is the war that has killed my dear, dear husband—not Uncle Robert. I see that now."

"It is all to the good that you can be so wise," answered Mark quietly. "I admire your splendid patience and courage, Mrs. Pendean, and—and— I would do for you, and will do, everything that wit of man can."

"Thank you, kind friend," she replied. Then she shook his hand and bade him farewell.

"Will you let me know if you leave here?" he asked.

"Yes—since you wish it."

They parted and he ran down the steps, scarcely seeing them. He felt that he already loved this woman with his whole soul. The tremendous emotion swept him, while reason and common sense protested.

Mark leaped aboard the waiting motor boat and they were soon speeding back to Dartmouth, while

Doria spoke eagerly. But the passenger felt little disposed to gratify the Italian's curiosity. Instead he asked him a few questions respecting himself and found that the other delighted to discuss his own affairs. Doria revealed a southern levity and self-satisfaction that furnished Brendon with something to think about before the launch ran to the landing-stage at Dartmouth.

"How comes it you are not back in your own country, now the war is over?" he asked Doria.

"It is because the war is over that I have left my own country, signor," answered Giuseppe. "I fought against Austria on the sea; but now—now Italy is an unhappy place—no home for heroes at present. I am not a common man. I have a great ancestry—the Doria of Dolceaqua in the Alpes Maritimes. You have heard of the Doria?"

"I'm afraid not—history isn't my strong suit."

"On the banks of the River Nervia the Doria had their mighty castle and ruled the land of Dolceaqua. A fighting people. There was a Doria who slew the Prince of Monaco. But great families—they are like nations—their history is a sand hill in the hour-glass of time. They arise and crumble by the process of their own development. Si! Time gives the hour-glass a shake and they are gone—to the last grain. I am the last grain. We sank and sank till only I remain. My father was a cab driver at Bordighera. He died in the war and my mother, too, is dead. I have no brothers, but one sister. She disgraced herself and is, I hope, now dead also. I know her not. So I am left, and the fate of that so mighty family lies with me alone—a family that once reigned as sovereign princes.''

Brendon was sitting beside the boatman in the bows of the launch, and he could not but admire the Italian's amazing good looks. Moreover there were mind and ambition revealed in him, coupled with a frank cynicism which appeared in a moment.

"Families have hung on a thread like that sometimes," said Mark; "the thread of a solitary life. Perhaps you are born to revive the fortunes of your race, Doria?''

"There is no 'perhaps.' I am. I have a good demon who talks to me sometimes. I am born for great deeds. I am very handsome—that was needful; I am very clever—that, too, was needful. There is only one thing that stands between me and the ruined castle of my race at Dolceaqua— only one thing. And that is in the world waiting for me.''

Brendon laughed.

"Then what are you doing in this motor launch?''

"Marking the time. Waiting.''

"For what?''

"A woman—a wife, my friend. The one thing needful is a woman—with much money. My face will win her fortune—you understand. That is why I came to England. Italy has no rich heiresses for the present. But I have made a false step here. I must go among the élite, where there is large money. When gold speaks, all tongues are silent."

"You don't deceive yourself?"

"No—I know what I have to market. Women are very attracted by the beauty of my face, signor."

"Are they?"

"It is the type—classical and ancient—that they adore. Why not? Only a fool pretends that he is less than he is. Such a gifted man as I, with the blood of a proud and a noble race in his veins —everything to be desired—romance—and the gift to love as only an Italian loves—such a man must find a very splendid, rich girl. It is only a question of patience. But such a treasure will not be found with this old sea wolf. He is not of long descent. I did not know. I should have seen him and his little mean hole first before coming to him. I advertise again and get into a higher atmosphere."

Brendon found his thoughts wholly occupied with Jenny Pendean. Was it within the bounds of possibility that she, as time passed to dim her sufferings and sense of loss, might look twice at this extraordinary being? He wondered, but thought it improbable. Moreover the last of the Dorias evidently aimed at greater position and greater wealth than Michael Pendean's widow had to offer. Mark found himself despising the extraordinary creature, who violated so frankly and cheerfully every English standard of reserve and modesty. Yet the other's self-possession and sense of his own value in the market impressed him.

He was glad to give Doria five shillings and leave him at the landing-stage. But none the less Giuseppe haunted his imagination. One might dislike his arrogance, or rejoice in his physical beauty, but to escape his vitality and the electric force of him was impossible.

Brendon soon reached the police station and hastened to communicate with Plymouth, Paignton, and Princetown. To the last place he sent a special direction and told Inspector Halfyard to visit Mrs. Gerry at Station Cottages and make a careful examination of the room which Robert Redmayne had there occupied.

CHAPTER V

A sense of unreality impressed itself upon
Mark Brendon after this stage in his inquiry. A
time was coming when the false atmosphere in
which he moved would be blown away by a
stronger mind and a greater genius than his
own; but already he found himself dimly conscious
that some fundamental error had launched him
along the wrong road—that he was groping in a
blind alley and had missed the only path leading
toward reality.

From Paignton on the following morning he
proceeded to Plymouth and directed a strenuous
and close inquiry. But he knew well enough that
he was probably too late and judged with
certainty that if Robert Redmayne still lived, he
would no longer be in England. Next he returned
to Princetown, that he might go over the ground
again, even while appreciating the futility of so
doing. But the routine had to be observed. The
impressions of naked feet on the sand were carefully protected. They proved too indefinite to be
distinguished, but he satisfied himself that they
represented the footprints of two men, if not three.
He remembered that Robert Redmayne had
spoken of bathing in the pools and he strove to

prove three separate pairs of feet, but could not.

Inspector Halfyard, who had followed the case as closely as it was possible to do so, cast all blame on Bendigo, the brother of the vanished assassin.

"He delayed of set purpose," vowed Halfyard, "and them two days may make just all the difference. Now the murderer's in France, if not Spain."

"Full particulars have been circulated," explained Brendon, but the inspector attached no importance to that fact.

"We know how often foreign police catch a runaway," he said.

"This is no ordinary runaway, however. I still prefer to regard him as insane."

"In that case he'd have been taken before now. And that makes what was simple before more and more of a puzzle in my opinion. I don't believe that the man was mad. I believe he was and is all there; and that being so, you've got to begin over again, Brendon, and find why he did it. Once grant that this was a deliberately planned murder and a mighty sight cleverer than it looked at first sight, then you've got to ferret back into the past and find what motives Redmayne had for doing it."

But Brendon was not convinced.

"I can't agree with you," he answered. "I've already pursued that theory, but it is altogether too fantastic. We know, from impartial testimony, that the men were the best of friends up to the moment they left Princetown together on

Redmayne's motor bicycle the night of the trouble.''

"What impartial testimony? You can't call Mrs. Pendean's evidence impartial.''

"Why not? I feel very certain that it is; but I'm speaking now of what I heard at Paignton from Miss Flora Reed, who was engaged to Robert Redmayne. She said that her betrothed wrote indicating his complete change of opinion; and he also told her that he had asked his niece and her husband to Paignton for the regattas. What is more, both Miss Reed and her parents made it clear that the soldier was of an excitable and uncertain nature. In fact Mr. Reed didn't much approve of the match. He described a man who might very easily slip over the border line between reason and unreason. No, Halfyard, you'll not find any theory to hold water but the theory of a mental breakdown. The letter he wrote to his brother quite confirms it. The very writing shows a lack of restraint and self-control.''

"The writing was really his?''

"I've compared it with another letter in Bendigo Redmayne's possession. It's a peculiar fist. I should say there couldn't be a shadow of doubt.''

"What shall you do next?''

"Get back to Plymouth again and make close inquiries among the onion boats. They go and come and I can trace the craft that left Plymouth during the days that immediately followed the posting of Redmayne's letter. These will probably be back again with another load in a week or two. One ought to be able to check them.''

"A wild-goose chase, Brendon."

"Looks to me as though the whole inquiry had been pretty much so from the first. We've missed the key somewhere. How the man that left Paignton in knickerbockers, and a big check suit and a red waistcoat on the morning after the murder got away with it and never challenged a single eye on rail or road—well, it's such a flat contradiction to reason and experience that I can't easily believe the face value."

"No—there's a breakdown somewhere—that's what I'm telling you; but whether the fault is ours, or a trick has been played to put us fairly out of the running, no doubt you'll find out soon or late. I don't see there's anything more we can do up here whether or no."

"There isn't," admitted Mark. "It's all been routine work and a devil of lot of time wasted in my opinion. Between ourselves, I'm rather ashamed of myself, Halfyard. I've missed something—the thing that most mattered. There's a signpost sticking up somewhere that I never saw."

The inspector nodded.

"It happens so sometimes—cruel vexing—and then people laugh at us and ask how we earn our money. Now and again, as you say, there's a danger signal to a case so clear as the nose on a man's face, and yet, owing to following some other clue, or sticking to a theory that we feel can and must be the only right one, we miss the real, vital point till we go and bark our shins on it. And then, perhaps, it's too late and we look silly."

Brendon admitted the truth of this experience. "There can only be two possible situations," he said; "either this was a motiveless murder—and lack of motive means insanity; or else there was a deep reason for it and Redmayne killed Pendean, after plotting far in advance to do so and get clear himself. In the first case he would have been found, unless he had committed suicide in some such cunning fashion that we can't discover the body. In the second case, he's a very cute bird indeed and the ride to Paignton and disposal of the corpse—that all looked so mad—was supercraft on his part. But, if alive, mad or sane, I'm of opinion he did what he said in his letter to his brother he meant to do, and got off for a French or Spanish port. So that's the next step for me —to try and hunt down the boat that took him."

He pursued this policy, left Princetown for Plymouth on the following day, took a room at a sailors' inn on the Barbican and with the help of the harbour authority followed the voyages of a dozen small vessels which had been berthing at Plymouth during the critical days.

A month of arduous work he devoted to this stage of the inquiry, and his investigation produced nothing whatever. Not a skipper of any vessel involved could furnish the least information and no man resembling Robert Redmayne had been seen by the harbour police, or any independent person at Plymouth, despite sharp watchfulness.

A time came when the detective was recalled to London and heartily chaffed for his failure;

but his own unusual disappointment disarmed the
amusement at his expense. The case had presented such few apparent difficulties that Brendon's complete unsuccess astonished his chief.
He was content, however, to believe Mark's own
conviction: that Robert Redmayne had never left
England but destroyed himself—probably soon
after the dispatch of his letter to Bendigo from
Plymouth.

Much demanded attention and Brendon was
soon devoting himself to a diamond robbery in the
Midlands. Months passed, the body of Michael
Pendean had not been recovered, and the little
world of Scotland Yard pigeon-holed the mystery,
while the larger world forgot all about it.

Meantime, with a sense of secret relief, Mark
Brendon prepared to face what had sprung out of
these incidents, while permitting the events themselves to pass from his present interests. There
remained Jenny Pendean and his mind was deeply
preoccupied with her. Indeed, apart from the
daily toll of work, she filled it to the exclusion of
every other personal consideration. He longed
unspeakably to see her again, for though he had
corresponded during the progress of his inquiries
and kept her closely informed of everything that
he was doing, the excuse for these communications
no longer existed. She had acknowledged every
letter, but her replies were brief and she had
given him no information concerning herself, or
her future intentions, though he had asked her to
do so. One item of information only had she
vouchsafed and he learned that she was finishing

the bungalow to her husband's original plan and then seeking a possible customer to take over her lease. She wrote:

"I cannot see Dartmoor again, for it means my happiest as well as my most unhappy hours. I shall never be so happy again and, I hope, never suffer so unspeakably as I have during the recent past."

He turned over this sentence many times and considered the weight of every word. He concluded from it that Jenny Pendean, while aware that her greatest joys were gone forever, yet looked forward to a time when her present desolation might give place to a truer tranquility and content.

The fact that this should be so, however, astonished Brendon. He judged her words were perhaps ill chosen and that she implied a swifter return to peace than in reality would occur. He had guessed that a year at least, instead of merely these four months, must pass before her terrible sorrow could begin to dim. Indeed he felt sure of it and concluded that he was reading an implication into this pregnant sentence that she had never intended it to carry. He longed to see her and was just planning how to do so, when chance offered an opportunity.

Brendon was called to arrest two Russians, due to arrive at Plymouth from New York upon a day in mid-December; and having identified them and testified to their previous activities in England, he was free for a while. Without sending any warning, he proceeded to Dartmouth, put up there that night, and started, at nine o'clock on the following morning, to walk to "Crow's Nest."

His heart beat hard and two thoughts moved together in it, for not only did he intensely desire to see the widow, but also had a wish to surprise the little community on the cliff for another reason. Still some vague suspicion held his mind that Bendigo Redmayne might be assisting his brother. The idea was shadowy, yet he had never wholly lost it and more than once contemplated such a surprise visit as he was now about to pay.

Suspicion, however, seemed to diminish as he ascended great heights west of the river estuary; and when within the space of two hours he had reached a place from which "Crow's Nest" could be seen, perched between the cliff heights and a grey, wintry sea, nothing but the anticipated vision of the woman held his mind.

He came ignorant of the startling events awaiting him, little guessing how both the story of his secret dream and the chronicle of the quarry crime were destined to be advanced by great incidents before the day was done.

His road ran over the cliffs and about him swept brown and naked fields under the winter sky. Here and there a mewing gull flew overhead and the only sign of other life was a ploughman crawling behind his horses with more sea fowl fluttering in his wake. Brendon came at last to a white gate facing on the highway and found that he had reached his destination. Upon the gate "Crow's

Nest" was written in letters stamped upon a
bronze plate, and above it rose a post with a
receptacle for holding a lamp at night. The road
to the house fell steeply down and, far beneath,
he saw the flagstaff and the tower room rising
above the dwelling. A bleakness and melancholy
seemed to encompass the spot on this sombre day.
The wind sighed and sent a tremor of light
through the dead grass; the horizon was invisible,
for mist concealed it; and from the low and ash-
coloured vapour the sea crept out with its
monotonous, myriad wavelets flecked here and
there by a feather of foam.

As he descended Brendon saw a man at work
in the garden setting up a two-foot barrier of
woven wire. It was evidently intended to keep
the rabbits from the cultivated flower beds which
had been dug from the green slope of the coomb.

He heard a singing voice and perceived that it
was Doria, the motor boatman. Fifty yards
from him Mark stood still, and the gardener abandoned his work and came forward. He was bare-
headed and smoking a thin, black, Tuscan cigar
with the colours of Italy on a band round the
middle of it. Giuseppe recognized him and spoke
first.

"It is Mr. Brendon, the sleuth! He has come
with news for my master?"

"No, Doria—no news, worse luck; but I was
this way—down at Plymouth again—and thought
I'd look up Mrs. Pendean and her uncle. Why
d'you call me sleuth'?"

"I read story-books of crime in which the detectives are 'sleuths.' It is American. Italians say 'sbirro,' England says 'police officer.' "

"How is everybody?"

"Everybody very well. Time passes; tears dry; Providence watches."

"And you are still looking for the rich woman to restore the last of the Dorias to his castle?"

Giuseppe laughed, then he shut his eyes and sucked his evil-smelling cigar.

"We shall see as to that. Man proposes, God disposes. There is a god called Cupid, Mr. Brendon, who overturns our plans as yonder ploughshare overturns the secret homes of beetle and worm."

Mark's pulses quickened. He guessed to what Doria possibly referred and felt concern but no surprise. The other continued.

"Ambition may succumb before beauty. Ancestral castles may crumble before the tide of love, as a child's sand building before the sea. Too true!"

Doria sighed and looked at Brendon closely. The Italian stood in a tight-fitting jersey of brown wool, a very picturesque figure against his dark background. The other had nothing to say and prepared to descend. He guessed what had happened and was concerned rather with Jenny Pendean than the romantic personality before him. But that the stranger could still be here, exiled in this lonely spot, told him quite as much as the man's words. He was not chained to "Crow's Nest" with his great ambitions in abeyance for nothing. Mark, however, pretended to miss the significance of Giuseppe's confession.

"A good master—eh? I expect the old sea wolf is an excellent friend when you know his little ways."

Doria admitted it.

"He is all that I could wish and he likes me, because I understand him and make much of him. Every dog is a lion in his own kennel. Redmayne rules; but what is the good of a home to a man if he does not rule? We are friends. Yet, alas, we may not be for long—when——"

He broke off abruptly, puffed a villainous cloud of smoke, and went back to his wire netting. But he turned a moment and spoke again as Brendon proceeded.

"Madonna is at home," he shouted and Mark understood to whom he referred.

He had reached "Crow's Nest" in five minutes and it was Jenny Pendean who welcomed him.

"Uncle's in his tower," she said. "I'll call him in a minute. But tell me first if there is anything to tell. I am glad to see you—very!"

She was excited and her great, misty blue eyes shone. She seemed more lovely than ever.

"Nothing to report, Mrs. Pendean. At least—no, nothing at all. I've exhausted every possibility. And you—you have nothing, or you would have let me hear it?"

"There is nothing," she said. "Uncle Ben would most certainly have told me if any news had reached him. I am sure that he is dead—Robert Redmayne."

"I think so too. Tell me a little about yourself, if I may venture to ask?"

"You have been so thoughtful for me. And I
appreciated it. I'm all right, Mr. Brendon.
There is still my life to live and I find ways of
being useful here."

"You are contented, then?"

"Yes. Contentment is a poor substitute for
happiness; but I am contented."

He longed to speak intimately, yet had no excuse for doing so.

"How much I wish it was in my power to
brighten your content into happiness again," he
said.

She smiled at him.

"Thank you for such a friendly wish. I am
sure you mean it."

"Indeed I do."

"Perhaps I shall come to London some day, and
then you would befriend me a little."

"How much I hope you will—soon."

"But I am dull and stupid still. I have great
relapses and sometimes cannot even endure my
uncle's voice. Then I shut myself up. I chain
myself like a savage thing, for a time, till I am
patient again."

"You should have distractions."

"There are plenty—even here, though you
might not guess it. Giuseppe Doria sings to me
and I go out in the launch now and then. I
always travel to and fro that way when I have to
visit Dartmouth for Uncle Ben and for the house-

hold provisions. And I am to have chickens to
rear in the spring.''

"The Italian——"

"He is a gentleman, Mr. Brendon—a great
gentleman, you might say. I do not understand
him very well. But I am safe with him. He
would do nothing base or small. He confided in
me when first I came. He then had a dream to
find a rich wife, who would love him and enable
him to restore the castle of the Doria in Italy and
build up the family again. He is full of romance
and has such energy and queer, magnetic power
that I can quite believe he will achieve his hopes
some day.''

"Does he still possess this ambition?''

Jenny was silent for a moment. Her eyes
looked out of the window over the restless sea.

"Why not?'' she asked.

"He is, I should think, a man that women might
fall in love with.''

"Oh, yes—he is amazingly handsome and there
are fine thoughts in him.''

Mark felt disposed to warn her but felt that
any counsel from him would be an impertinence.
She seemed to read his mind, however.

"I shall never marry again,'' she said.

"Nobody would dare to ask you to do so—nobody who knows all that you have been called to
suffer. Not for many a long day yet, I mean,''
he answered awkwardly.

"You understand,'' she replied and took his
hand impulsively. "There is a great gulf I think

fixed between us Anglo-Saxons and the Latins.
Their minds move far more swiftly than ours.
They are more hungry to get everything possible
out of life. Doria is a child in many ways; but a
delightful, poetical child. I think England rather
chills him; yet he vows there are no rich women
in Italy. He longs for Italy all the same. I expect he will go home again presently. He will
leave Uncle Ben in the spring—so he confides to
me; but do not whisper it, for my uncle thinks
highly of him and would hate to lose him. He can
do everything and anticipates our wishes and
whims in the most magical way.''

''Well, I must not keep you any longer.''

''Indeed you are not doing that. I am very,
very glad to see you, Mr. Brendon. You are going
to stop for dinner? We always dine in the middle
of the day.''

''May I?''

''You must. And tea also. Come up to Uncle
Bendigo now. I'll leave you with him for an hour.
Then dinner will be ready. Giuseppe always joins
us. You won't mind?''

''The last of the Doria! I've probably never
shared a meal with such high company!''

She led him up the flight of stairs to the old
sailor's sanctum.

''Mr. Brendon to see us, Uncle Ben,'' she said,
and Mr. Redmayne took his eye from the big
telescope.

''A blow's coming,'' he announced. ''Wind's
shifted a point to southward. Dirty weather already in the Channel.''

He shook hands and Jenny disappeared. Bendigo was pleased to see Brendon, but his interest in his brother had apparently waned. He avoided the subject of Robert Redmayne, though he revealed other matters in his mind which he approached with a directness that rather astonished the detective.

"I'm a rough bird," he said, "but I keep my weather peeper open, and I didn't find it difficult to see. when you were here in the summer, that my fine niece took your fancy. She's the sort, apparently, that makes men lose their balance a bit. For my part I never had any use for a woman since I was weaned, and have always mistrusted the creatures, seeing how many of my messmates ran on the rocks over 'em. But I'm free to grant that Jenny has made my house very comfortable and appears to feel kindly to me."

"Of course she does, Mr. Redmayne."

"Hold on till I've done. At this minute I'm in sight of a very vexatious problem; because my right hand—Giuseppe Doria—has got his eyes on Jenny; and though he's priceless as a single man and she's invaluable as a single woman, if the beggar gets round her and makes her fall in love with him presently, then they'll be married next year and that's good-bye to both of 'em!"

Mark found himself a good deal embarrassed by this confidence.

"In your place," he said, "I should certainly drop Dloria a pretty clear hint. What is good form in Italy he knows better than we do, or ought to, seeing he's a gentleman; but you can

tell him it's damned bad form to court a newly
made widow—especially one who loved her husband as your niece did, and who has been separated from him under such tragic circumstances.''

"That's all right; and if there was only one in
it I might do so; though for that matter I'm afraid
Doria isn't going to stop here much longer in any
case. He doesn't say so, but I can see it's only
Jenny who is keeping him. You've got to consider her too. I'm not going to say she en-
courages the man or anything like that. Of course
she doesn't. But, as I tell you, I'm pretty wide
awake and it's no good denying that she can endure his company without hurting herself. He's a
handsome creature and he's got a way with him,
and she's young.''

"I rather thought he was out for money—
enough money to reëstablish the vanished glories
of his race.''

"So he was and, of course, he knows he can't do
that with Jenny's twenty thousand; but love casts
out a good many things besides fear. It blights
ambition—for the time being anyway—and handicaps a man on every side in the race for life. All
Doria wants now is Jenny Pendean, and he'll get
her if I'm a judge. I wouldn't mind too much
either, if they could stop along with me and go on
as we're going; but of course that wouldn't happen. As it is Doria has come to be a friend. He
does all he's paid to do and a lot more; but he's
more a guest than a servant and I shall miss him
like the devil when he goes.''

"It's hard to see what you can do, Mr. Red-mayne."

"So it is. I don't wish to come between my niece and her happiness, and I can't honestly say that Doria wouldn't be a good husband, though good husbands are rare everywhere and never rarer than in Italy, I believe. He might change his mind after they'd been wed a year and hanker for his ambitions again and money to carry them out. Jenny will have plenty some day, for there's poor Bob's money sooner or late, I sup-pose, and there'll be mine and her Uncle Albert's so far as I know. But, taking it by and large, I'd a good bit sooner it didn't happen. I'll tell you these things because you're a famous man, with plenty of credit for good sense."

"I appreciate the confidence and can return a confidence," answered Brendon after a moment's reflection. "I do admire Mrs. Pendean. She is, of course, amazingly beautiful, and she has a gracious and charming nature. With such dis-tinction of character you may rest assured that nothing will happen yet a while. Your niece will be faithful to her late husband's memory for many a long month, if not forever."

"I believe that," answered Bendigo. "We can mark time, I don't doubt, till the turn of the year or maybe longer. But there it is: they are thrown together every day of their lives and, though Jenny would hide it very carefully from me, and probably from herself also as far as she could, I guess he's going to win out."

Brendon said no more. He was cast down and did not hide the fact.

"Mind you, I'd much prefer an Englishman," admitted the sailor; "but there's nobody to make any running in these parts. Giuseppe's got it all his own way." Then he left the subject. "No news, I suppose, of my poor brother?"

"None, Mr. Redmayne."

"I'd pinned my faith that the whole horrid thing might be capable of explanation along some other lines. But the blood was proved to be human?"

"Yes."

"Another secret for the sea, then, as far as Pendean is concerned. And as for Robert, only doomsday will tell where his bones lie."

"I also feel very little doubt indeed that he is dead."

A few minutes later a gong sounded from beneath and the two men descended to their meal. It was Giuseppe Doria who did the talking while they ate a substantial dinner. He proved a great egotist and delighted to relate his own picturesque ambitions, though he had already confessed that these ambitions were modified.

"We are a race that once lorded it over western Italy," he declared. "Midway inland, between Ventimiglia and Bordighera, is our old fastness beneath the mountains and beside the river. An ancient bridge like a rainbow still spans Nervia, and the houses climb up the hills among the vines and olives, while frowning down upon all things is the mighty ruin of the Doria's castle—a great ghost from the past. In the midst of all the human business and bustle, removed by a century from the concerns of men, it stands, hollow and empty, with life surging round about, like the sea on the precipices below us. The folk throng everywhere—the sort of humble people who of old knelt hatless to my ancestors. The base born wander in our chambers of state, the villagers dry their linen on our marble floors, children play in the closets of great counsellors, bats flutter through the casements where princesses have sat and hoped and feared!

"My people," he continued, "have sunk through many a stage and very swiftly of late. My grandfather was only a woodman, who brought charcoal from the mountains on two mules; my uncle grew lemons at Mentone and saved a few thousand francs for his wife to squander. Now I alone remain—the last of the line—and the home of the Doria has long stood in the open market.

"With the fortress also goes the title—that is our grotesque Italian way. A pork butcher or butter merchant might become Count Doria to-morrow if he would put his hand deep enough in his pocket. But salvation lies this way: that though the property and title are cheap, to restore the ruin and make all magnificent again would demand a millionaire."

He chattered on and after dinner lighted another of his Tuscan cigars, drank a liqueur of some special brandy Mr. Redmayne produced in honour of Brendon, and then left them.

They spoke of him, and Mark was specially interested to learn Jenny's attitude; but she gave no sign and praised Giuseppe only for his voice, his versatility, and good nature.

"He can turn his hand to anything," she said. "He was going fishing this afternoon; but it is too rough, so he will work in the garden again."

She hoped presently that Doria would find a rich wife and reach the summit of his ambitions. It was clear enough that he did not enter into any of Mrs. Pendean's calculations for her own future. But Jenny said one thing to surprise her listener while still speaking of the Italian.

"He doesn't like my sex," she declared. "In fact he makes me cross sometimes with his scornful attitude to us. He's as bad as Uncle Ben, who is a very hard-hearted old bachelor. He says, 'Women, priests, and poultry never have enough.' But I say that men are far greedier than women, and always were."

The sailor laughed and they went out upon the terrace for a time where soon the early dusk began to fall. The storm had not yet developed and there was a fierce and fiery light over the west at sunset while a tremendous wind blew the sky almost clear for a time. When the Start lighthouse opened a white, starry eye over the deepening purple of the sea, and heavy waves beat below them in hollow thunder, they returned to the house and Mr. Redmayne showed Brendon curiosities. They drank tea at five o'clock and an hour later the detective went on his way. A general invitation had been extended to him and the old sailor expressly declared that it would give him pleasure to receive Mark as a guest at any time. It was a suggestion that tempted Brendon not a little.

"You've done a wonderful thing," said Jenny, as she saw him to the outer gate. "You've quite won my uncle, and really that's a feat."

"Would it bore you if I fell in with his proposal and came down for a few days after Christmas?" he asked, and she assured him that it would give her pleasure.

Heartened a little he went his way, but the wave of cheerfulness set flowing by her presence soon ebbed again. He felt full of suspicion and half believed her indifference regarding Doria to be assumed. He guessed that she would be jealous to give no sign until the days of her mourning were numbered, but he felt a melancholy conviction that when another summer was passed, Jenny Pendean would take a second husband.

He debated the wisdom of presently returning to "Crow's Nest" and felt a strong inclination to do so. Little guessing that he would be there again on the morrow, he determined to remind Bendigo Redmayne of his invitation in early spring. By that time much might have happened, for he intended to correspond with Jenny, or at any rate take the first step in a correspondence.

The moon had risen as he pursued his lonely road and it shone clear through a gathering scud that threatened soon to overwhelm the silver light. Clouds flew fast and, above Brendon's head, telegraph wires hummed the song of a gathering storm. The man's thoughts proceeded as irregularly as the fitful and shouting wind. He weighed each word that Jenny had said and strove to understand each look that she had given him.

He tried to convince himself that Bendigo Redmayne's theory must, after all, be false, and he assured himself that by no possibility could the widow of Michael Pendean ever lose her sad heart to this stranger from Italy. The idea was out of the question, for surely a woman of such fine mould, so suddenly and tragically bereaved, would never find in this handsome chatterbox, throbbing with egotism, any solace for sorrow, or promise for future contentment. In theory his view seemed sound. Yet he knew, even while he reflected, that love in its season may shatter all theories and upset even the most consistent of characters.

Still deep in thought Brendon tramped on; and then, where the road fell between a high bank to the windward side and a pine wood on the other, he experienced one of the greatest surprises that life had yet brought him.

At a gate, which hung parallel with the road and opened into the depth of a copse behind, there stood Robert Redmayne.

The five-barred gate alone separated them and the big man lolled over it with his arms crossed on the topmost bar. The moonlight beat full into his face, and overhead the pines uttered a harsh and sullen roar as the wind surged over them; while from far below the shout of an angry

sea upon the cliffs was carried upward. The red
man stood motionless, watchful. He wore the
tweed clothes, cap and red waistcoat that Brendon well remembered at Foggintor; the moonlight flashed on his startled eyes and showed
his great mustache and white teeth visible beneath it. There was dread upon his face and
haggard misery, yet no madness.

It seemed that he kept a tryst there; but it had
not been Mark Brendon that he expected. For a
moment he stared as the detective stopped and
confronted him. He appeared to recognize Mark,
or at any rate regard him as an enemy, for instantly he turned, plunged into the woods behind
him, and disappeared. In a moment he had
vanished and the riot of the storm hid all sounds
of his panic flight.

CHAPTER VI

ROBERT REDMAYNE IS HEARD

FOR some moments Mark stood motionless with his eyes on the moonlit gate and the forest gloom behind it. There rhododendron and laurel made dense evergreen cover beneath the pines and offered inviolable shelter. To follow Robert Redmayne was vain and also dangerous, for in such a spot it might easily happen that the hunter would lie at the mercy of the hunted.

This sudden apparition bewildered Brendon, for it argued much beyond itself. Surely it indicated treachery and falsehood among those he had just left at "Crow's Nest," for it was a coincidence almost inconceivable that on this day of his chance visit, the wanted man should suddenly reappear in the neighbourhood of his brother's house. Yet collusion seemed impossible, for Mark had given no notice to Bendigo Redmayne of his coming.

Brendon asked himself if he had suffered a hallucination, but he knew that his rational mind was not constituted to create ghosts from within. Imagination he had, but therein was a source of strength, not weakness, and no grain of superstition weakened his mental endowment. He knew also that no one had been farther from his

thoughts than Robert Redmayne at the moment
of his sudden appearance. No, he had seen a living man and one who certainly would not willingly
have revealed himself.

He had not the least intention of ignoring his
discovery and was quite prepared to arrest Robert
Redmayne, even under his brother's roof if necessary; but he desired first to hear Jenny Pendean
upon the subject before seeking the assistance of
the Dartmouth police. He felt that she would
not deceive him, or answer a direct appeal with a
lie. And then there flashed upon him the painful
conviction that she must already have lied to him;
for if Redmayne were living concealed at ''Crow's
Nest,'' all the household, including Doria and the
solitary woman servant, would assuredly be in the
secret.

Supposing Jenny begged him to hold his hand
and spare Robert Redmayne, would he then be
justified in keeping his discovery to himself?
Some men might have built up a personal hope
upon this possibility and seen themselves winning
to the summit of their ambition by bending to the
widow's will; but Mark did not confound the
thoughts of duty and love nor did he even dream
that success in one might depend upon neglect
of the other. He had only to raise the question
to answer it, and he swiftly determined that not
Jenny, or her Uncle Bendigo, or anybody on
earth should prevent him from securing Robert
Redmayne on the following day if it came within
his power to do so. Indeed he felt little doubt
that this would happen. For that night there

was no hurry. He slept well after an unusual amount of exercise and emotion; and he rose late. He was dressing at half past eight when there came a chambermaid to the door.

"There's a gentleman must see you this instant moment, please, sir," she said. "He's by the name of Mr. Doria and he comes from Captain Redmayne out over at 'Crow's Nest.'"

Not sorry that his day's work might now be simplified, Mark bade the girl summon his visitor, and in two minutes Giuseppe Doria appeared.

"I was clever to find you," he said, "for we only knew that you were stopping in Dartmouth tonight, but we did not know where. Yet I guessed you would choose the best hotel and I guessed rightly. I will eat my breakfast with you, if you please, and tell you why I am here. The thing was to catch you if we could before you went away. I am glad that I was in time."

"So Robert Redmayne, the murderer of Michael Pendean, has turned up?" asked Brendon, finishing his shaving; and Doria showed astonishment.

"Corpo di Bacco! How did you know that?" he asked.

"I saw him on my way home," replied Mark. "I had already seen him, before the tragedy on Dartmoor, and I remembered him. What is more, I'm not sure that he didn't remember me."

"We are in fear," continued Doria. "He has not been yet to his brother, but he is near."

"How can you tell that he is near, if he has not yet been to his brother?"

"Thus we know it. I go every morning early

to Strete Farm on the hills above us for milk and butter. I go this morning and they have an ugly story. Last night a man entered Strete Farm and took food and drink. The farmer hears him and comes upon him sitting eating in the kitchen —a big man with a red head and a red mustache and a red waistcoat. The man, when he sees Mr. Brook—that is the farmer—he bolts through the back kitchen by which he has come. Mr. Brook knows nothing of the man and he tells me of his adventure, and then I go home to tell padron mio—my master.

"When I describe this man, Mr. Redmayne and Madonna nearly have a fit between them. They recognize him—he is the assassin! They think instantly of you and bid me take my bicycle and ride here at my best speed to catch you, if it may be done before you go. I succeed, but I cannot stay with you; I must return to keep guard. I do not like to feel there is nobody there. My old sea wolf is not frightened of the sea, but I think he is a little frightened of his brother. And Mrs. Jenny—she is very frightened indeed."

"Come to breakfast," said Mark, whose toilet was now completed. "I'll get a motor in a quarter of an hour and run out as quick as may be."

They swallowed a hasty meal and Giuseppe displayed growing excitement. He begged Brendon to bring other policemen with him, but this Mark declined to do.

"Plenty of time for that," he said. "We may catch him easy enough. I shall do nothing until I have seen Mr. Bendigo at 'Crow's Nest' and

heard his views. If Robert Redmayne is breaking into houses for food he must be at the end
of his tether.''

By nine o'clock the Italian had started homeward, and as soon as he was gone, Brendon went
to the police station, borrowed a revolver and a
pair of handcuffs, hinted at his business, and
ordered a police car to be ready as quickly as
possible. A constable drove him and before
setting out he told the local chief of police, one
Inspector Damarell, to await a message over the
telephone in the course of the morning. He en-
joined strictest secrecy for the present.

Mark overtook and passed Doria on his way
home. The storm had nearly blown itself out
and the morning was clear and cold. Beneath
the cliffs a big sea rolled, but it was fast going
down.

Any suspicion that the inhabitants of Bendigo's
home were seeking to create false impressions
left Brendon's mind, when he stood before Jenny
and her uncle. The former was nervous and the
latter beyond measure puzzled. There was now
little doubt that Robert Redmayne must be the
man who broke into Strete Farm for food, since
Mark's experience of the previous night tended
to confirm the fact. He had seen Redmayne some
hours before the fugitive alarmed the household
at Strete. Where was he now and why had he
come hither? All suspected that the unfortunate
man had probably returned from France or Spain,
and now lay hid close at hand, waiting for a safe
opportunity to see the old sailor.

"Your brother has probably got his eye on
the house," said Brendon, "and is considering
how to approach you, Mr. Redmayne, without
risking his own safety."

"There's only one he'll trust, I reckon, and
that's me," declared Bendigo. "If he knew that
Jenny means him no harm, he might trust her,
too, but he may not believe that she's good Christian enough to forgive him. And anyway I guess
he don't know she's with me. I'm talking as
though he was sane, but I doubt it."

Mark, who had studied Mr. Redmayne's large
government survey map of the district, suggested
an immediate search over the most likely regions
in the neighbourhood.

"I think of you and Mrs. Pendean," he explained. "You don't want hue and cry again
and all the past brought up once more. If we
can get to him without calling in the police, then
so much the better. The man must be in extreme
want. His face, as I saw it, was harrowed and
tormented. He has probably reached a mental
condition of tension and torture in which he will
not be sorry to find himself among friendly and
understanding fellow creatures. There are two
districts which especially suggest themselves to
me to search in: the shore, where there are many
caves and crevices above sea level safe from observation; and the dense woods into which he
plunged when I came suddenly upon him last
night. I examined them on my way out this
morning. They appear to be very extensive, but
they are traversed by drives for sportsmen and

you can look up and down these drives for many hundred yards."

Mr. Redmayne summoned Doria who had now reached home again.

"Can the launch go to sea?" he asked. Giuseppe considered that she might. Bendigo then submitted a proposition.

"I'm asking that you'll let this search go on quietly and privately for another twenty-four hours," he said. "Then, if we fail to round him up in a friendly way, so to say, you must, of course, turn the constabulary out and hunt him down. To-day we can go over the places you name and I reckon you've hit the most likely burrows for the poor man. I dare say, if we sat tight and did nothing at all, we might find him creeping here to me after dark pretty soon; but we'll act as you advise and see if the shore or the woods show any sign.

"There's us three who know who he is— Jenny and me and you; and I'd propose that my niece goes down the coast in the motor boat with Giuseppe. They can cruise away to the west, where there's an easy landing here and there at little coves, and they may sight my brother poking about, or hid in some hole down that way. There are caves with tunnels aft that give on the rough lands and coombs behind. It's a pretty lone region and he couldn't hang on long there or find food for his belly. They can try that for a few hours and we'll go up aloft. Or else I'll take you in the boat and they can hunt round Black Woods —whichever you like."

Brendon considered. He inclined to the belief that the hunted man might sooner trust the woods than the coast. Moreover he knew himself an indifferent sailor and perceived that the motor boat could not promise a very even keel in the great swell that followed the storm.

"If Mrs. Pendean doesn't mind the weather and there is no shadow of danger to the launch, then I advise that your niece goes down the coast and has a look into the caves as you propose," he said. "No doubt Doria can be trusted to see sharply after her. Meantime we will quarter the wood. If we could only get into touch with the man, it might be possible to secure him without making any noise."

"There must be a noise if we catch him," declared Doria. "He is a famous criminal and who ever runs him to his earth and pulls him out will make a noise and receive great praise."

He prepared for the coming voyage of discovery and, within half an hour, the motor boat danced out from beneath "Crow's Nest"; then she held a course to the westward, rolling indeed, but not enough to trouble Jenny who sat in the stern and kept a pair of strong Zeiss glasses fixed upon the cliffs and shore. They were soon reduced to a white speck under the misty weather; and after they had gone, Bendigo, in a sailor's pea-jacket and cap, lighted a pipe, took a big black-thorn stick, and set off beside Mark. The police car still stood on the road and, both entering it, they soon reached the gate beside which Robert Redmayne had appeared on the previous night. There they left the motor and entered Black Woods together.

Bendigo still talked of his niece and continued to do so. It was a subject on which the other proved very willing to listen.

"She's at the parting of the ways now," declared Jenny's uncle. "I can see her mind working. I grant she loved her husband dearly enough and he made a pretty deep mark on her character, for she's different from what she was as a girl. But there's very little doubt that Doria's growing awful fond of her—and when that sort loves a woman he generally finds she's not unwilling to meet him halfway. I believe now that my niece can't help caring for the man, but all the time she's secretly ashamed of herself —yes, heartily ashamed—for finding another in her mind only six months after the death of Pendean."

Mark asked a question.

"When you say that her husband altered his wife's character, in what way did he do so?"

"Well—he taught her sense I reckon. You'd never think now, would you, that she was a red Redmayne—one of us—short of temper, peppery, fiery? But she was, as a youngster. Her father had the Redmayne qualities more developed than any of us and he handed 'em down. She was a wilful thing—plucky and fond of mischief. Her school fellows thought the world of her because she laughed at discipline; and from one school she got expelled for some frolics. That was the girl I remembered when Jenny came back to me

a widow. And so I see that Michael Pendean,
what ever else he was, evidently had the trick
character to learn her a bit of sense and
patience.''

"It may be natural development of years and
experience, combined with the sudden, awful
shock of her husband's death. These things
would unite to tone her down and perhaps break
her spirit, if only for a time.''

"True. But she's not a sober-sided woman for
all her calm. She was too full of the joy of life
for Pendean, or any man, to empty it all out of
her in four years. He may have been one of the
Wesleyan sort, like such a lot of the Cornish; he
may have been a kill-joy, too; but whether he was
or not, he hadn't quite converted her in the time,
and what I'm seeing now, I judge, is the young
woman slowly coming back to herself under the
influence of this Latin chap. He's cunning, too.
He knows how to tickle her vanity, for even she
has got a bit of womanly conceit in her, though
less vain of her wonderful face no woman could
be. But Doria has taken good care to hint his
ambition is well lost for love; he's dropped it
very cleverly no doubt and already made her see
which way he's steering. He's put Jenny before
the dollars and the dreams of the castle down
south. In a word, if I'm not a greenhorn, he'll
ask her to marry him as soon as a year is told
and he can touch the subject decently.''

"And you think she will accept him, Mr. Redmayne?''

"At present I'd take long odds about it; but

he's a volatile devil and may change by that
time."

Then Bendigo in his turn asked a question.
"We found no will among my poor brother's
papers, and of course he's had no access to his
money since this bad business. How he's lived
all the time only he himself knows. But suppose
the worst happens presently and he's found to be
a lunatic, what becomes of his stuff?"

"It would ultimately go to you and your
brother."

They tramped the wood and fell in with a
gamekeeper, who greeted the trespassers none
too amiably. But on learning their errand and
receiving a description of the fugitive, he bade
them go where they pleased and himself promised
to keep a sharp watch. He had two mates and
would warn them; and he understood the importance of preserving strict silence concerning the
fugitive until more should be known.

But it was not to Brendon and Robert Redmayne's brother that any information came.
Their hunt produced neither sign nor clue of the
man they sought, and after three hours of steady
tramping, which covered all the ground and exhausted Bendigo, they returned in the motor car
to "Crow's Nest."

News of direct importance awaited them, and
Bendigo proved correct in his suspicion that the
wanted man might have chosen the coast. Jenny
had not only seen Robert Redmayne but had
reached him; and she returned very distressed
and somewhat hysterical, while Doria, having

done great things in the matter, was prepared to brag about them. But he begged Mrs. Pendean, as the heroine of a strange adventure, to tell her story.

She was deeply moved and her voice failed on two or three occasions during the narrative; but the interest of the tale was such that Bendigo lost sight of Jenny in the picture she now painted of his unfortunate brother. They had sighted Robert Redmayne suddenly from the motor boat.

"We saw him," said Jenny, "about two miles down the coast, sitting not fifty yards from the sea, and he, of course, saw us; but he had no glasses and could not recognize me, as we were more than half a mile from shore. Then Giuseppe suggested landing and so approaching him. The thing was to let me reach him, if possible. I felt no fear of him—excepting the fear that, knowing how he had ruined my life, he might shrink from facing me.

"We ran by, as though we had not observed him; then, getting round a little bluff, so that we were hidden, we went ashore, made fast the boat, and regularly stalked him. There was no mistake. I had, of course, recognized Uncle Robert through the glasses; and now Doria went first and crept along, with me behind him, until we had reached to within twenty-five yards. The poor wretch saw us then and leaped up, but it was too late and Giuseppe reached him in a moment and explained that I came as a friend. Doria was prepared to detain him if he endeavoured to escape, but he did not. Robert Redmayne is worn

out. He has been through terrible times. He
shrank at first and nearly collapsed when I came
to him. He went on his knees to me. But I was
patient and made him understand that I had not
come as an enemy."

"Is he sane?" asked Bendigo.

"He appears to be sane," she answered. "He
made no mention of the past and neither spoke of
his crime nor of what he has been doing since;
but he has altered. He seems a ghost of his
former self; his voice has changed from a boom
into a whisper; his eyes are haunted. He is thin
and full of terror. He made me send Doria out
of earshot and then told me that he had only come
here to see you. He has been here some days,
hidden in one of the caves down the coast westward. He wouldn't tell me where, but no doubt
it is near where we found him. He is ragged and
wounded. One of his hands ought to be attended
to."

"And still you say he behaved like a sane man,
Mrs. Pendean?" asked Brendon.

"Yes—except for what seemed an insane fear.
And yet fear was natural enough under the circumstances. He feels, poor creature, that he has
reached the end of his tether; and even if he is insane and will escape the extreme penalty, he
doesn't know that himself. I implored him to
come with me in the boat and see Uncle Bendigo
and trust to the mercy of his fellow men. I
didn't feel a traitor in asking him to do this; for
I imagine, though seemingly sane now, he must
in reality be mad, since only madness could ex-

plain the past, and he will be judged accordingly. But he is very suspicious. He thanked me and grovelled horribly to me; but he would not trust either me or Doria, or think of entering the boat. He is all nerves and soon began to fear we were planning an ambush, or otherwise endangering his freedom.

"I asked him, then, to tell me what he wished and how I could help him. He considered and said that if Uncle Bendigo would see him quite alone and swear, before God, not to hinder his departure in any way after they had met, he would come to 'Crow's Nest' to-night after the household was asleep.

"For the moment he wants food and a lamp to light his hiding-place after dark. But before all else, he begs you, Uncle Ben, to let him come and see you quite alone. Then he told us to be gone if we were honest friends. It is left in this way. If you will see him, he will come any hour you mention after midnight. But first you must give your written oath before God that you will have nobody with you, and that you will neither set a trap for him nor seek to detain him. His hope is that you will give him means and clothes, so that he may leave England safely and get to Uncle Albert in Italy. He made us swear not to say where we had found him, and then he indicated a spot where I was to bring your answer in writing before dark. I am to leave a letter at that spot as soon as I can, and go away at once, and he will come and find your directions."

Mr. Redmayne nodded.

"And at the same time you had better take the poor wretch some food and drink and the lamp. How he has lived for the last six months I cannot understand."

"He has been in France—so he says."

Bendigo did not take long to determine a course of action and Brendon approved his decisions.

"In the first place," declared Robert Redmayne's brother, "the man must be mad, whatever appears to the contrary. This story points to that, and seeing he is still free and has succeeded in existing and avoiding the police in two countries, one can only say that with his madness he has developed amazing cunning too. But, as Jenny reports, he's on his beam ends at last. He knows this house and he knows the way to it. So I'll do this.

"I'll agree to see him to-night—or rather to-morrow morning. I'll bid him come at one o'clock, and he shall find the door open and a light in the hall. He can walk straight in and mount up to me in the tower, and I'll swear the needful oath that he shall see nobody else and be free to go again when he pleases. That will calm him down and give me a chance to study him and try and see where we stand. We might trap him, of course, but I can't lie even to a lunatic."

"There's no reason why you should," said Brendon. "If you feel no personal fear of the man, then you can see him as you suggest. You understand, however, there must be no question of helping him to evade the law, as he wishes?"

Bendigo nodded.

"I suppose not. I can't turn him on to my brother, Albert, anyway. Albert's a weak, nervous sort of man and he'd have a fit if he thought Robert was coming to seek asylum with him."

"The State must provide his asylum," said Mark. "His future is no longer any question for his relations. The best that we can hope is that he may soon be in a position of security, both for himself and other people. You will do well to see him, give him succour, and hear what he has to say. After that, Mr. Redmayne, if I may advise, you will leave the rest to me."

Bendigo lost no time in writing the desired letter inviting Robert Redmayne to meet him in secret at one o'clock during the coming night and promising the fugitive, on oath, that he should be safe and free to depart again when he desired to do so. But, none the less, he expressed an earnest hope that his brother would stop at "Crow's Nest," and be advised as to his future actions. Some provisions were put into the launch and, with the letter in her pocket, Jenny again set out. She was prepared to go alone, for she could handle the boat as cleverly as Doria himself; but this her uncle would not permit.

It was already growing dusk before she left and Giuseppe drove the little vessel to its limit of speed.

Then Brendon was much surprised. He had been standing under the flagstaff with the master of "Crow's Nest," watching the launch, and when she had vanished westward into a grey, still evening, Bendigo challenged the detective with a proposition altogether unexpected.

"See here," he said. "I've got a damned, uneasy feeling about meeting my brother single-handed to-night. I can't tell you what it is. I'm not a coward and never shirked duty yet; but frankly I don't much like facing him for this reason. A madman's a madman, and we can't expect a madman to be any too reasonable if we oppose him, however tactfully. I should be powerless if he got off his head, or resented the advice I should have to give him, or went for me—powerless, I mean, to do anything but stop him with a bullet. But if he's got to be stopped that way, I don't want to be the one to do it.

"I've promised to meet him alone and I shan't be telling the poor man a lie, because, if all's straight and he shows no violence, he needn't know anybody else is there. But if I was put into danger, I might tackle him mercifully with somebody to help, whereas if I was alone and he threatened to do me harm, it would very likely mean something I'd rather not think about."

Brendon saw the force of this observation.

"A very reasonable thing indeed," he answered, "and in a case like this, you couldn't blame yourself even if you didn't keep the letter of your promise."

"In the spirit I shall keep it, however. I've sworn to let him come and go again free, and that oath I must keep if he does nothing that forces me to break it."

"You are wise and I quite agree with you,"

said Mark. "No doubt Doria is a man you can
rely upon in every way and he is powerful too."
But Bendigo shook his head.

"No," he answered. "I've left this question
until Doria and my niece were out of the way, for
a very good reason. I don't want them in this
thing more than they are already; and I don't
want them, or anybody, to know that I've got a
friend hid along with me in the tower when Robert comes. They understand that I am to see
him alone; and I've bade them keep out of the
way and not show themselves for an instant.
What I want up there is you and only you."
Brendon considered.

"I confess the idea occurred to me as soon as
we had your brother's offer; but seeing the terms,
I couldn't press for it," he said. "Now I agree
and, what's more, I think it would be very desirable if nobody—not even the household—knew I
was here."

"That can be done. If you send your car away
and say you'll report to-morrow, then the police
won't trouble us any more till we see what next.
You can go up to the tower and get into the big
case I keep my flags and odds and ends in. There
are holes bored for ventilation at the height of
a man's head from the ground, and if you're
packed in there, you can see and hear everything
and pop out in five seconds if my life is
threatened."

Brendon nodded.

"That's all right," he said. "I'm considering
what follows. Your brother goes free presently;

and no doubt Mrs. Pendean will only wait until he is off to come up to you. I can't stop all night in the cupboard."

"It don't matter a button after he's gone," answered Bendigo. "If you tell your car to go, that's all that signifies for the minute. And all anybody but ourselves will believe is that you've gone back to Dartmouth, and won't be here again until to-morrow morning."

Mark fell in with this plan. He dismissed the car and directed that Inspector Damarell should be told to do nothing more until further information reached him. Then, with the old sailor, he climbed to the tower room, inspected the great cupboard, and found that he could follow the course of events very comfortably from within. Holes of the size of a half-penny piece were bored in each door of this erection and, with a three-inch support under his feet, Brendon found his eyes and ears at the needful level.

"The point is to know how I get clear afterward," considered Brendon, returning to the sequel. "As soon as your brother has left the house, it is certain that Mrs. Pendean, probably Doria also, will hasten to know what has happened and what you have determined."

"Afterward nothing matters," repeated Bendigo. "I'll go down to the door with Robert and you can follow me and slip out as soon as he has got clear. Or else you can appear when he has gone and reveal yourself and tell Jenny that it was your own wish to stop without letting anybody know it but myself. That'll be the best way;

and as soon as she finds you are here, she'll see that you have comfortable quarters for the rest of the night.''

Brendon approved of this plan and when the launch returned, her uncle informed Jenny that the detective had left, to make certain inquiries, but would return early on the following morning. She expressed surprise that he had gone but declared that it would in any case have been necessary for him to do so before the fugitive arrived.

"We left the letter, the lamp, and the food and drink exactly where he indicated," she said, "on a forlorn spot, above that ancient, raised beach, where the great boulders are."

Thus the matter was settled. Mark had already taken up his position in the chamber aloft and Bendigo looked to it that he should not be interfered with. It was Mr. Redmayne's custom to keep the tower room locked when not himself in it, and he did so now until the night should come. He supped with Jenny and the Italian, having already provided Brendon with food in his hiding-place. It was understood that the sailor would ascend to his den about eleven o'clock, by which time Mark undertook to be safely hidden in the cupboard.

At the agreed time Doria and his master came up together, the former carrying a light. Jenny also joined them for a short while, but she stayed only ten minutes and then departed to bed. The weather had turned stormy and wet. A shouting wind from the west shook the lantern of the tower room and flung rain heavily against the glass, while Bendigo moved restlessly about and bent his brows to look out into the blackness of the night.

"The poor devil will be drowned, or break his neck climbing up from the sea in this darkness," he declared.

Giuseppe had brought up a jug of water, a bottle of spirits, a little keg of tobacco, and two or three clay pipes, for the old sea captain never smoked till after supper and then puffed steadily until he went to bed.

He turned now and asked Doria a question.

"You've cast your peepers over the poor chap to-day," he said, "and you're a clever man and know a bit of human nature. What did you make of my brother?"

"I looked closely and listened also," answered the servant; "and this I think—the man is very sick."

"Not likely to break out again and cut another throat?"

"Never again. I say this. When he killed Madonna's husband, he was mad; now he is not mad—not more mad than anybody else. He craves only one thing—peace."

CHAPTER VII

BENDIGO lit his pipe and turned to his only book. It was "Moby Dick." Herman Melville's masterpiece had long ago become for the old sailor the one piece of literature in the world. It comprised all that interested him most in this life, and all that he needed to reconcile him to the approach of death and the thought of a future existence beyond the grave. "Moby Dick" also afforded him that ceaseless companionship with great waters which was essential to content.

"Well," he said to Doria, "get you gone. Look round as usual to see that all's snug aloft and below; then turn in. Leave only the light in the hall and the front door on the latch. Did you mark if he had a watch to know the hour?"

"He had no watch, but Mrs. Pendean thought upon that and lent him hers."

Bendigo nodded and picked up a clay pipe, while Doria spoke again.

"You feel quite steady in your nerves? You would not like me to lie in readiness to come forward if you want me?"

"No, no—turn in and go to sleep. And no spying, as you're a gentleman. I'll talk reason to

127

the poor fellow. I reckon it's going to be all right. We know that he's had shell shock and all the rest of it, so I dare say the law won't be very hard upon him.''

''The dead man's wife was an angel to Robert Redmayne. He thought at first that she had come to give him up. But her eyes showed him that she had come in mercy. May I speak of your niece a moment before I go?''

Bendigo shrugged his round shoulders and pushed his hand through his red hair.

''It's no good speaking of her till you've spoken to her,'' he said. ''I know what you are after very well. But it's up to her, I reckon, not me. She's gone her own way since she was a nipper— got her father's will hid under her woman's shape.''

He reflected uncomfortably that Mark Brendon must hear every word about to pass; but there was no help for that.

''Our Italian way is to approach the parents of the loved one,'' explained Doria. ''To win you is to be far on my way, for you stand to her in the place of parent. Is it not so? She cannot live alone. She was not meant by God to be a single woman, or a widow woman. There is a saying in my tongue, 'She who is born beautiful is born married.' I terribly fear that somebody else will come.''

''But what about your ambitions—to wed an heiress and claim the title and the territory of your vanished forbears?''

Doria swept his hands to right and left with a

great gesture, as though casting away his former hopes.

"It is fate," he said. "I planned my life without love. I had never loved and never wanted to. I guessed that love would appear after I had married money and earned the necessary means and leisure to love. But now all is changed. The arrow has sped. There has come the spirit simpatica instead of the necessary rich woman. Now I do not want the rich woman but only she who wakens my passion, adoration, worship. Life has nothing in it but Madonna—English Jenny. What are castles and titles—pomp and glory—when weighed against her? Dust, padron mio, all dust!"

"And what about her, Giuseppe?"

"Her heart is hidden; but there is that in her eyes that tells me to hope."

"And what about me?"

"Alas! Love is selfish. But you are the last I would seek to hurt or to rob. You have been very good to me and Madonna loves you. It is certain that if the very best happened, she would do nothing to offend one who has been to her as you have been."

"We can stow the subject for six months anyhow," replied Bendigo, lighting his long clay. "I suppose, in your country as well as mine, there's a right and a wrong way to approach a woman; and seeing my girl's a widow—made so under peculiarly sad circumstances—you'll understand that love talk is out of the question for a good bit yet a while."

"Most truly you speak. I hide even the fire in my eyes. I only dare look at her between the lids."

"There's a lot goes to Jenny, and no doubt such a keen blade as you knows that very well. But all's in the air at present. Her husband left no will and that means, since there's nobody else with any claim upon him, she has all his dough— five hundred a year perhaps. But there's much more to her than that in the long run. My brother Albert and I are both old bachelors with nobody so near us as Jenny. In fact you may say that if all goes right, she'll be pretty flush some day. Not enough to waste on ruined castles, but a mighty good income none the less. Then there's poor Bob's money; for however it falls out with him, it don't look as though he'd spend it now."

"All this is wind in the trees and the cackling of hens to me," declared Doria. "I have not thought about it and I do not want to think about it. The criterion of love, such as I feel to Jenny, is that nothing else weighs a mustard seed in the balance against it. If she were a pauper, or if she owned millions, my attitude of heart is not changed. I worship her with the whole of myself —so that there is not a cranny left in my spirit where hunger for money can find foothold, or fear of poverty exist. Happiness never depends upon cash, or the lack of it; but without love no real happiness shall be found in the world."

"That may be bunkum, or it may be God's truth —I don't know. I've never been in love and nobody ever wasted an ounce of affection on me," replied Redmayne. "But you've heard me now. You can sit on the safety valve for six months anyway; and it will probably pay you best to do so; for one thing's certain: Jenny won't love you any better for making love under present circumstances."

"It is too true," answered the other. "Trust me. I will hide my soul and be exquisitely cautious. Her sorrow shall be respected—from no selfish motive only, but because I am a gentleman, as you remind me."

"Youth's youth, and you Italians have a good deal more fire kneaded into you than us northerners."

Suddenly Doria's manner changed and he looked half sternly, half curiously at Bendigo. Then he smiled to himself and ended the conversation.

"Fear nothing," he said. "Trust me. Indeed there is no reason why you should do otherwise. No more of this for half a year. I bid you good night, master."

He was gone and for a moment only the hurtle of the rain on the ground windows of the tower room broke the silence; then Brendon emerged from his hiding-place and stretched his limbs. Bendigo regarded him with an expression half humorous and half grim.

"That's how the land lies," he said. "Now you've got it."

Mark bent his head.

"And you think that she——"

"Yes—I think so. Why not? Did you ever in

your experience hit up against a man more likely
to charm a young woman?''

"Will he keep his word and not try to make the
running for another six months?''

"You're as green about love as I am; but even
I can answer that. Of course he'll make the running. He can't help it. It doesn't need words.''

"The idea of another husband would be abominable to Mrs. Pendean for many years; and no
Englishman worthy of the name would dare to
intrude upon her sacred grief.''

"I don't know anything about that. I only
know that whatever the amount of grief she feels,
she's devilish interested in Giuseppe—and he's
not an Englishman.''

They talked for the best part of an hour and
Mark perceived that the old sailor was something
of a fatalist. He had already concluded that his
niece would presently wed again and with the
Italian. Nor did the prospect do more than annoy
Bendigo from the point of view of his own comfort. Brendon observed that Mr. Redmayne felt
no personal objection or distrust. Jenny's uncle
did not apparently anticipate that she would live
to regret such a second husband; while Mark,
from a standpoint quite independent, honestly
felt that one so volatile and strangely handsome
might sooner or later cloud the young woman's
life with tribulation. He knew the quality of his
own love, but perceived the hopelessness at present
of showing it in any way. For at this juncture
there appeared no possibility of serving her. He
was, however, a patient man and now summoned

hope that in the future it might yet fall within his reach to be of vital use, even though it should never lie in her power to reward his devotion.

He knew himself and he knew that this strange and novel emotion of love was, at least in his case, a deep, omnipotent thing, beyond and above any selfish and purely personal desire for happiness. Even Doria admitted that much probably, though whether, did the test arise, he would put the woman's prosperity before his own passion, Brendon took leave to doubt.

He retreated presently as the hour of one approached, but before doing so, returned to the subject of Robert Redmayne. The elder spoke the last word and left Mark in grave doubt as to what the immediate future might bring.

"If," said Bendigo, "my brother has any just excuse for what he did, or can convince me, for instance, that he took Pendean's life in order to save his own, then I stick by him and don't give him up while I can fight on his side. You'll tell me that I'll be in reach of the law myself if I do any such thing; but that won't frighten me. Blood's thicker than water when you come down to a job like this."

It was a new attitude, but the detective said nothing, and as a clock in the hall below beat the hour of one he returned to the cupboard and drew the door behind him. Bendigo had just lighted another pipe when there came the sound of feet ascending the stair; but it was no doubtful or cautious footfall that they heard. The ascending man neither hesitated nor made any effort to approach without noise. He came swiftly and as the sailor stood up calm and collected, to meet his brother—not Robert Redmayne but Giuseppe Doria appeared.

He was very agitated and his eyes shone. He breathed hard and wiped the hair away from his forehead. He had evidently been out in the rain, for water glistened on his shoulders and face.

"Suffer me to drink," he said. "I have been frightened."

Bendigo pushed the bottle and an empty tumbler across his table and the other sat down and helped himself.

"Be quick; what the devil's the matter? He'll be here in a minute—my brother."

"No, he will not be here. I have seen and spoken with him—he's not coming to you."

Doria helped himself very sparingly to some spirits; then he explained.

"I was going the rounds and just about to turn out the oil lamp over the front gate as usual when I remembered Mr. Redmayne. That is half an hour ago and I thought it would be better to leave the lamp, to guide him, for the night is dark and wild. I came down the ladder therefore; but I had already been seen. He was waiting under the shelter of the rocks on the other side of the road, where there is a pent roof of natural stone; and seeing me he remembered me and came and spoke a little. He was full of new fear and dread. He said that people had been hunting him and that even now men were hidden not far off to take him. I assured him it was not so and swore to him that you were alone and desired only to succour him. I used my best words and prayed him to come in swiftly and let me shut the outer gate and make it fast; but his suspicions grew; the fear of a hunted animal was in his eyes. He misunderstood me. Terror conquered him and what I had said, to make him feel safe, acted in the contrary way. He would not come within the gate but sent a message that you are to come to him instead, if you still will to save him. He is a very sick soul and will not last long. I saw death in his eyes under the lamplight.''

There was a pause while Bendigo slowly took in this change in the situation. Then he lifted his voice and spoke, not to Doria, but to the man in hiding.

"Come right out, Brendon," he said. "The game's up for to-night as you've heard. Doria has seen Bob, and he's frightened the poor beggar off apparently. Anyway he's not coming."

Mark emerged and Giuseppe gazed in astonishment. His mind evidently ran backward and his face flushed with annoyance.

"Corpo di Bacco!" he swore. "Then you heard my confidences. You are a sneak!"

"Stow that," cried Bendigo. "Brendon's here because I wished it for my brother's good. I wanted him to know what passed—and your love affairs are neither here nor there. He'll not use anything he heard that don't concern his proper business. What did Robert say?"

But Doria was angry. He opened his mouth to speak, then shut it again, looked first at Brendon and then at his master and breathed hard.

"Get on," said Bendigo. "Shall I go out to the man, or has he gone?"

"And as for me; don't think twice about it," added Brendon. "I'm here for one reason only, and that you know. You and your private hopes and ambitions have nothing to do with me."

Upon this speech the Italian appeared to regain his composure.

"I am a servant for the moment and my duty is to Mr. Redmayne," he answered. "This is the message that I have been told to bring. The hunted man will not trust himself behind doors or under a roof, until he has seen his brother alone. He is hiding now near the place where Mrs. Pendean and I found him, in a cave beside the sea. It opens upon the water and it can be approached by boat. But there is a way also inside, that enables him to creep down into the cave from the cliffs behind it. He will be in this place until his brother comes, to-morrow night after twelve o'clock. But the way down from the land is hidden very carefully and he will not speak of that. You must go to him from the sea, my master. He thought it out while he spoke to me. He will light his lamp in the cave, and when the light is seen from the launch, you will put in and come to him. That is what he demands shall be done; and if anybody tries to land but only his brother, he will shoot them. So he swears, and he said also that when Bendigo Redmayne knows all, then he will forgive all and be on his side."

"Did he talk like a sane man?" asked Brendon.

"He talked like a sane man; but he is at his last gasp. He must have had mighty strength once, only it is now worn down to nothing."

An uneasy thought passed through the detective's mind. Could it be possible that Doria, while speaking previously to Bendigo about private affairs, had discovered his presence in the great cupboard and then warned Robert Redmayne that he would not meet his brother alone? He dismissed the suspicion, however, for Doria's surprise and anger when he emerged were genuine enough. Moreover there appeared no reason why Giuseppe should side with the fugitive.

Bendigo spoke.

"So be it," he said. "It's a matter of life and death now and I'm sorry we must wait till another night. We'll fetch out in the launch and, when we see the light, go in and hail him."

Then he turned to Brendon.

"I'll ask you to hold off until I've seen the poor chap. As a brother I ask it."

"Trust me. It's quite understood that nothing shall be done now until you have seen him and reported. It may not be regular, but common humanity suggests that."

"You can stop here to-morrow night," continued the sailor. "And if I prevail with the unfortunate man I'll bring him off in the launch. Then we'll talk sense to him. We've got to remember that nobody's ever heard his side."

"If Captain Redmayne had a side he wouldn't have run away, or taken the extraordinary pains that he did take to conceal his victim," answered

Mark. "Don't buoy yourself up to suppose that will be a possible line of defence. We're far more likely to get him off by proving a homicidal act under the influence of shell shock—and the less reason there was for murdering Michael Pendean, the more reason there will be for supposing your brother out of his mind and therefore guiltless when he did it."

"He is a very sane and a very sorry man now," declared Doria. "He will come to your hand like a starved bird, signor."

"So much for that, then; and now we had better turn in," said Bendigo. "I've always got a spare bunk in the spare room and you'll find all you want, barring a razor, in the bathroom. You young men use the newfangled safety razors, so Giuseppe can lend you one no doubt."

Doria promised that a razor should be in the bathroom early on the following morning; then he retired and Bendigo, who found that he was hungry, descended to the dining-room. Brendon and he made a meal before going to bed.

From his couch in a small chamber adjoining the older man's, Mark heard Mr. Redmayne growling to himself in evident sorrow for his brother. Himself he felt moved at a situation so painful, but was glad enough to know that a few more hours would determine it. In his own mind he felt satisfied of the issue and imagined Robert Redmayne as detained for a certain period at the royal pleasure and then, if medical opinion sanctioned the step, once more liberated.

He turned to his own affairs and faced the fact

that his hope of Jenny grew thin. The thought of her was now complicated by her position. He had never considered that in the future she might be rich and possessed of far larger means than he could ever attain. He looked forward and perceived that opportunity would lie with him to enjoy some private conversation on the following day. Yet, when the time came, what was there that he could say to her? The storm had blown itself out and dawn returned before he slept.

With morning Bendigo proved grumpy and desirous to be left alone. He was evidently much perturbed and shut himself into the tower room with his pipe and "Moby Dick." He only cared to see Jenny, who spent some time with him. It was from Brendon that she heard the facts in the morning when, much to her surprise, he appeared at breakfast while she was making tea. Doria joined them a little later, but Mr. Redmayne, usually an early riser, did not appear. Jenny took him his breakfast.

He came down to luncheon and, after that meal, Doria conveyed Brendon in the launch to Dartmouth, where Mark visited the police station and explained the need for further delay. There was now no necessity for the contemplated man hunt and he let Inspector Damarell learn that the fugitive had been found and would probably surrender within four-and-twenty hours. He telephoned to Scotland Yard the same information and presently returned to "Crow's Nest." The day was still and sunless with fine rain falling; but the wind had dropped and the night promised to be calm.

Doria landed Brendon and then put off again, going slowly down the coast. He asked Mark's permission to do so, that he might make a few mental notes of distances for the coming night. The raised beach, on which Robert Redmayne had been first spoken, was about five miles off, and Giuseppe suspected that Redmayne's hiding-place would be found to lie still farther to the west.

He departed therefore at a definite rate of speed and was back again in three quarters of an hour before the dusk had fallen. But he had nothing to report. He had found no cave where he expected one, and now guessed that Robert Redmayne's secret holt must be nearer than they imagined.

The night came at last—very dark overhead but clear and calm. Beneath "Crow's Nest" the waves, sunk to nothing, made a quiet whisper along the feet of the precipices and tinkled on the little beaches that here and there broke the cliff line. The tide was just making and midnight had struck when Bendigo Redmayne, in rough-weather kit, stumped down his long flight of steps and went to sea. Brendon and Jenny stood above under the flagstaff, and soon they heard the launch purr away swiftly under the darkness.

The woman spoke first.

"Thank God we are at the end of this horrible suspense," she said. "It has been a cruel nightmare for me, Mr. Brendon."

"I have felt much for you, Mrs. Pendean, and admired your marvellous patience."

"Who could but be patient with the poor wretch? He has paid the price of what he did. Even I can say that. There are worse things than death, Mr. Brendon, and you will presently see them in Robert Redmayne's eyes. Even Giuseppe was sobered after our first meeting."

That she should use the Italian's Christian name so easily struck unreasoning regret into the heart of Mark. It gave him an excuse for a question.

"Do you believe all Doria tells you? Is he regarded here as a domestic or an equal?"

She smiled.

"As a superior rather than an equal. Yes, I see no reason to doubt his story. He is obviously a great gentleman and a man of natural fine feeling. Breeding and education are different things. He has little education, but a native delicacy of mind belongs to him. You feel it."

"He interests you?"

"He does," she confessed frankly. "Indeed I owe him something, for he has a wonderful art and tact to strike the right note with me."

"He has had rare opportunities," said Brendon grudgingly.

"Yes; but not everybody would have taken them. I came here distracted—half mad. My uncle tried to be kind, but he has no imagination and could rise to nothing higher than reading me passages from 'Moby Dick.' Doria was of my own generation and he has a feminine quality that most men lack."

"I thought women hated feminine qualities in men."

"Perhaps I misuse my words. I mean that he possesses a quick sympathy and a sort of intuition that are oftener found in a woman than a man."

Mark was silent and she asked a question.

"I could not fail to note that you do not like him, or if that is too strong, that you see nothing to admire in him. What is there anti· pathetic in his nature to you, and in yours to him? He doesn't like you either. Yet you both seem to me such gracious, kindly men. Surely you have no bias against other nationalities—a man with a cosmopolitan record like yours?"

At this thrust Brendon perceived how unconsciously he had displayed an aversion for which no real reason existed—no reason, at any rate, that he might fairly declare. And yet he was frank; nor did his response perhaps surprise her, though she appeared to be astonished.

"There's only one answer, Mrs. Pendean: I'm jealous of Signor Doria."

"Jealous! Why, Mr. Brendon—what have you to envy him?"

"You would not be likely to guess," he replied, though in truth Jenny had already done so accurately enough. "I am sure that if Doria is a gentleman I need not be jealous, seeing what is in my thought cannot be spoken to you by any man for many a long day to come. And yet to envy him is natural; and when you ask what I envy, I will be honest and tell you. Fate has given him the privilege of lightening the cruel burden placed upon your shoulders. His sympathy and intuition you admit have succeeded in so doing. You will say that no Englishman could have done that exactly in the way he did—perhaps you are right; but one Englishman regrets from the bottom of his heart that the opportunity was denied him.''

"You have been good and kind, too," she answered. "Do not think I am ungrateful. It was not your fault that you failed to discover Robert Redmayne. And, after all, what would success have amounted to? Only the capture of the unfortunate man a few months sooner. Now, I hope, he will see that there is nothing for it but to give himself up to his brother and trust his fellow creatures to be merciful."

Thus she led conversation away from Doria and herself, and Mark took the hint. He no longer doubted that her regard for the Italian might easily ripen into love. He assured himself that he dreaded this for her, yet suspected all the time that his regret was in reality selfish and inspired by personal disappointment rather than fear for her.

Anon they saw the flash of a ruby and an emerald upon the sea westward and soon heard Redmayne's motor boat returning. Less than half an hour had passed, and Brendon hoped that Robert Redmayne had yielded to his brother's entreaty and was now about to land; but this had not happened. Only Giuseppe Doria ascended the steps and he had little to tell.

"They didn't want me yet, so I ran back," he said. "All goes well; his cavern lies quite near

to us. The lamp flashed out only two miles away
and I ran in; and there was the man standing just
outside a small cave on the little beach before it.
He cried out a strange welcome. He said, 'If any
other lands but you, Ben, I will shoot him!' So
the master shouted that he was to fear nothing,
and he jumped ashore as soon as our nose touched
the sand; then told me to put off instantly. They
went back into the cave together and I am to return within an hour.''

He explained the position of the cave.

"It is above the little beach, revealed at low
tide, where cowries are to be found," he said. "I
took Madonna there on an occasion to gather the
little shells for the fancywork the master makes."

"Uncle Ben fashions all sorts of wonderful
ornaments out of shells," explained Jenny.

Doria smoked some cigarettes and then descended again. In twenty minutes the boat had
gone to sea once more, while Jenny bade Mark
good night and retired. She felt it better not to
meet her uncles on their arrival, and Brendon
agreed with her.

CHAPTER VIII

ALONE, Brendon regarded the future with some melancholy, for he believed that only Chance had robbed him of his great hope. Chance, so often a valued servant, now, in the mightiest matter of his life, turned against him. Not for a moment could he or would he compare himself with the man he now regarded as a successful rival; but accident had given Doria superb opportunities while denying to Brendon any opportunity whatever. He told himself, however, that a cleverer man than he would have made opportunities. What was his love worth if it could not triumph over the handicaps of Chance?

He felt ruled out, and he had not even the excuse to impose himself upon Jenny and still seek to win her by pretending that he was better fitted to make her permanently happy than his rival. Indeed he knew that in the long run such a cheerful and versatile soul as Giuseppe was more likely to satisfy Jenny than he, for Doria would have all his time to devote to her, while marriage and a home must be only a part of Brendon's future existence. There remained his work, and he well knew that, whatever Jenny's position and independence, he would not leave the business that

145

had brought him renown. Only on one ground he
doubted for her, and again and again feared that
such an attractive being as Doria might follow
the tradition of his race and presently weary of
one woman.

Next he considered another aspect of the situation and thought of every word that Jenny had
recently spoken. They pointed to one conclusion
in his judgment and he believed that when a
seemly period had elapsed she would allow herself to love Doria. That was as much as to say
she had already begun to do so, if unconsciously.
This surprised him, for even granting the obvious fascination of the man, he could hardly believe that the image of her first husband had already begun to grow faint in Jenny's memory.
He remembered her grief and protestations at
Princetown; he perceived the deep mourning
which she wore. She was indeed young, but her
character had never appeared to him youthful or
light-hearted. Against that fact, however, he had
certainly only known her after her sorrow and
loss, and he remembered how she had sung on the
moor upon the evening she passed him in
the sunset light. She had probably been cheerful and joyous before her husband's death. But
she surely never possessed a frivolous nature.
His knowledge of character told him that. And
there was strength as well as sweetness in her
face. Serious subjects had interested her in his
small experience of her company; but that might
be because she responded, as a delicate instrument, to her environment; and he himself had

never been anything but serious beside her.
With the Italian, no doubt, there had happened
moments when she could sometimes smile and forget. Doria's own affairs, of which he loved to
chatter, had doubtless often distracted Mrs. Pendean from her own melancholy reflection, and in
any case she could not sigh forever at her age.

The return of the motor boat arrested his reflections. She had been gone about an hour when
Mark perceived her running very swiftly homeward. Guessing that Bendigo Redmayne and his
brother were now aboard, he prepared to retire
until the following day to the room he occupied.
He had arranged to be invisible unless Robert
Redmayne were willing to see him and discuss
the future.

But Doria once more came back to "Crow's
Nest" alone, and what he had to tell soon altered
the detective's plans. For Giuseppe was much
concerned and feared that evil had overtaken his
master.

"After the time was up, I ran in," he said,
"and the rising tide brought me within a few
yards of the mouth of the cave. The light was
burning but I could see neither of them. I hailed
twice and got no answer. All was still as the
grave and I went near enough to the shore to
satisfy myself that there was nobody there. The
cave was empty. Now I am a good deal alarmed
and I come back to you."

"You didn't land?"

"I didn't touch shore, but I was within five
yards of the cave, none the less, for the tide is

now risen. The light shone upon emptiness. I beg you will return with me, for I feel that some evil thing may have happened.''

Much puzzled, Brendon delayed only to get his revolver and an electric torch. He then descended with Doria to the water and they were soon afloat again. The boat ran at full speed for a few minutes; then her course was changed and she turned in under the cliffs. Mark soon saw a solitary gleam of light, like a glowworm, at sea level in the solid darkness of the precipices, and Doria, slowing down, crept in toward it. Presently he shut off his engine and the launch grounded her prow on a little beach before the entrance of Robert Redmayne's hiding-place. The lamp shone brightly, but its illumination, though serving to show the cavern empty, was not sufficient to light its lofty roof, or reveal a second exit, where a tunnel ran up at the rear and could be climbed by steps roughly hewn in the stone.

"It is a place my master showed me long ago," explained Doria. "It was used by smugglers in the old days and they have cut steps that still exist."

Both men landed and Giuseppe made fast the launch. Then immediate evidence of tragedy confronted them. The floor of the cave was of very fine shingle intermixed with sand. The sides were much broken and the strata of the rock had wrinkled and bent in upon itself. The lamp stood on a ledge and flung a radius of light over the floor beneath. Here had been collected the food and drink supplied to Redmayne on the previous day, and it was clear that he had eaten and drunk heartily. But the arresting fact appeared on the beaten and broken surface of the ground. Heavy boots had torn this up and plowed furrows in it. At one spot lay an impression, as though some large object had fallen, and here Brendon saw blood—a dark patch already drying, for the substance of it was soaked away in the sandy shingle on which it had dropped.

It was a blot rather than a pool and under his electric lamp Mark perceived a trail of other drops extending irregularly toward the back of the cavern. From the mark of the fallen body a ridge ploughed through the shingle extending rearward, and he judged that one of the two men had certainly felled the other and then drawn him toward the chimney, or tunnel that opened at the back of the cave. Spots of blood and the dragged impression of some heavy body stretched along the ground to the stone steps and there disappeared.

The detective stopped here and inquired the length of the staircase and whither it led; but for a time his companion appeared too dazed to answer him. Giuseppe showed a good deal of the white feather, combined with sincere emotion at the implicit tragedy.

"This is death—death!" he kept repeating, and between his words his mouth hung open and his eyes rolled fearfully over the shadowy places round about him.

"Pull yourself together and help me if you can," said Brendon. "Every moment may make

all the difference. It looks to me as though somebody had been dragged up here. Is that possible?"

"To a very powerful man it might be. But he
was weak—no good."

"Where does this place lead?"

"There are many shallow steps, then a long
slope and, after that, you have to bend your head
and scramble out through a hole. You are then
on a plateau halfway up the cliff. It is a broad
ledge and from it one only track, rough and steep,
rises up zigzag, like our hairpin roads in Italy,
till you reach the summit of the cliff. But it is
rough and broken—impossible by night."

"We must go that way all the same and make
it possible. Is the boat fast?"

"If you will help me, we will pull her up into
the cave. Then we can hunt and she will not take
harm."

Lamenting the loss of time, Mark lent a hand
and the launch was soon above high-water mark.
Then, with Brendon in front and the light from
his torch upon the steps, they began their ascent.
Save for a drop of blood here and there, the
stone stairway gave no clue; but when they had
reached its summit and the subterranean path
turned to the left, still in a tunnel of the solid
rock, they marked on the ascending slope, slippery
with percolations from the roof, a straight smear
dragged over the muddy surface. Pursued for
fifty yards the tunnel began to narrow and the
roof descend, but still the smooth track of a heavy
object being dragged upward was evident. Save

for an occasional word the men proceeded in silence, but Brendon sometimes heard the Italian speaking to himself. "Padron mio, padron mio —death!" he repeated.

For the last ten yards of the tunnel Mark had to go on his knees and crawl. Then he emerged and found himself in the open air on a shelf hung high between the earth and the sea. All was dark and very silent. He held up his hand to Doria and the two listened intently for some minutes, but only the subdued murmur of the water far beneath reached their ears. No sound broke the stillness round about. Under their feet stretched a ledge of fine turf, browned by winter and covered with the evidence of sea birds. Giuseppe picked up a few grey feathers as the electric torch swept the surface of the plateau.

"For the master's pipe," he explained. "He uses feathers to cleanse it."

Overhead the cliff line stretched black as ink against the sky, making the midnight clouds above it light by contrast. Here Brendon saw evidences that the dead weight dragged from beneath had remained still a while, and he observed an impress near it on the herbage, where doubtless a living man had rested after his exertions. There were clots of blood on the grass near this spot, but no other sign visible in the present condition of darkness. Remembering the death of Michael Pendean, Brendon was already reconstructing, in theory, the events immediately under his notice. That Bendigo Redmayne's brother had slain the elder now appeared too probable;

and he had apparently proceeded as before and removed his victim—in a sack—for the line on the cave floor below and along the path which Mark had just traversed indicated some heavy, rounded object that did not change its shape as it was dragged along.

For two minutes he stood, then spoke.

"Where is the path from here?" he asked, and Doria, proceeding cautiously to the east of the plateau, presently indicated a rocky footpath that ascended from it. The track was rough and evidently seldom used, for brambles and dead vegetation lay across it. They proceeded by this way and Brendon directed the other to disturb nothing, so that careful examination might, if necessary, be made when daylight returned. The path elbowed to right and left sharply, ever ascending, and it was not too steep to prevent steady progress. It ended at last on the summit of the cliffs, where, after a barren space of fifty yards, a low wall ran separating ploughed lands from the precipices. But no sight of any human being awaited them and, on the close sward of the summit, footsteps would have left no record.

"What d'you make of it?" asked Doria. "Your mind is swift and skilled in these deviltries. Is it true that my master and my friend is a dead man—the old sea wolf dead?"

"Yes," said Brendon drearily. "In my mind there is no doubt of it. It is also true that a thing has happened which I should have prevented and a life been lost which might have been saved. From the first I have taken too much on trust in this matter and believed all that I was told too readily."

"That is no blame to you," answered the other. "Why should you have doubted what you heard?"

"Because it was my business to credit nothing and trust nobody. I am not blaming anybody, or suggesting any attempts to deceive me; but I have accepted what sounded obvious and rational, as we all did, instead of examining things for myself. You may not understand this, Doria; but other people will be only too quick to do so."

"You did the best you could; so did everybody. Who was to know that he came here to kill his brother?"

"A madman may do anything. My fault has been to assume his return to sanity."

"What more natural? How could you assume otherwise? Only an insane man would have killed Madonna's husband, and only a very sane one would have escaped the sleuths afterward. So you argued that he was mad and then sane again; yet now he has gone mad once more."

Brendon desired to be at Dartmouth as swiftly as possible, so that a search might be instituted at dawn. Doria considered whether he might make best speed by road or water, and decided that he could bring Mark more quickly to the seaport in the launch than along the highway.

"We must, however, return by the tunnel," he said, "for there is no other route by which we can get back to the boat."

Brendon agreed and they descended the zig-zag path and then, from the plateau, reëntered the tunnel and presently reached the steps again and the cavern beneath. Extinguishing the lamp, which still burned steadily, they were soon afloat, and under a tremor of dawn the little vessel cut her way at her best speed, flinging a sheaf of foam from her bows and leaving a white wake on the still and leaden-coloured sea.

They saw a figure beneath the flagstaff at "Crow's Nest" and both recognized Jenny Pendean. She made no signal, but the sight of her evidently disturbed Giuseppe's mind. He stopped the boat and appealed to Brendon.

"My heart is in my mouth," he said. "A sudden fear has overtaken me. This madman—it may be that he has turned against his own and those who are his best friends. There is a thing lunatics will do. It follows—while we are away —do you not see? There are only two women at 'Crow's Nest' now, and he might come and make a clean sweep—is it not so?"

"You think that?"

"With God and the devil all things are possible," answered the other, his eyes lifted to the house on the cliffs.

"You're right. Run in. There may be a danger for her."

Doria was triumphant.

"Even you do not think of everything," he cried; but the other did not answer. On him lay a load of responsibility and a heavy sense of failure.

He directed Doria how to act, however.

"Tell Mrs. Pendean and the servant to lock up

the house and then join us," he said. "They had better come to Dartmouth, and they can return presently with you, after you have landed me. Beg that they do not delay a moment." Doria obeyed and in ten minutes returned with Jenny, dazed and pale, and the frightened domestic still fumbling at her bodice buttons. They were both in great fear and full of words; but Brendon begged them to be quiet. He warned Jenny that the worst was to be dreaded for her uncle, and their awful news reduced her to silence quickly enough. Thus they sped on their way, leaped between the harbour heads before sunrise, and soon came ashore at the landing stage.

Doria's work was now done and, having directed him to take the women back, Mark bade them all keep the house until more news should reach them.

"Telephone to the police station if you have anything to report," he directed, "but should the man appear and attempt to enter, prevent him from doing so."

He gave them further directions and then they parted.

In half an hour the news had spread, search parties set out by land, and Brendon himself, with Inspector Damarell and two constables, put to sea in the harbour-master's swift steam launch. Some food had been brought aboard and Mark made a meal as he described the incidents of the night. It was eight o'clock before they reached the cavern and began a methodical search over the ground and upward. Mark had arranged with Doria that a signal should fly from "Crow's Nest" for him if there were any news; but nothing had happened, for the flagpole was bare. Then began a laborious hunt in the cave and the tunnel by which it was approached from above. Morning light filled the hollow place and the officers working methodically left no cranny unexplored; but their combined efforts by daylight revealed little more than Brendon had already found for himself in the darkness. There was nothing but the trampled sand, the partially eaten store of food, the lamp on its stone bracket, the black blot of blood, and the shallow trench left by some rounded object that had been dragged to the steps. The tide was down but the little beach only displayed the usual débris at high-water mark. Inspector Damarell returned to the steam launch and bade the skipper go back to Dartmouth.

"We'll ride home by motor from above," he said. "Tell them to bring my runabout car to the top of Hawk Beak Hill; and let 'em fetch along some sandwiches and half a dozen bottles of Bass; I'm thinking we shall want 'em by noon."

The launch was off and once more the chimney with the steps, the inclined plane beyond, and the plateau halfway up the cliff were all examined with patient scrutiny. The police went at a foot's pace, yet nothing appeared save an occasional drop of blood upon a stone and the trail of the object dragged upward on the previous night.

"He must be a Samson," said Mark. "Con-

sider if you or I had to pull a solid, eleven-stone
man in a sack up here.''

"I could not," admitted the inspector. "But
it was done. We're going to have a repetition of
that job at Berry Head in the summer. We shall
hunt the cliffs, like a pack of hounds, and presently find some place hanging over deep water.
Then we shall hit on a sack in a rabbit hole or
badger's earth—and that will be all there is to
it."

On the plateau they rested, while Brendon found
some clear marks of feet—a heavy, iron-shod
boot, which he recognized. They occurred in a
soft place just outside the mouth of the tunnel and
he recollected the toe plates and the triangle-
headed nails that held them.

He called Inspector Damarell.

"When this is compared with the plaster casts
taken at Foggintor, you'll find it's the same
boot," he said. "That's no surprise, of course,
but it proves probably that we are dealing with
the same man."

"And he'll use the same means to vanish into
thin air that he did six months ago," prophesied
the other. "You mark me, Brendon, this is not
one man's work. There's a lot hid under this
job that hasn't seen light—just as there was under
the last. It's very easy to say, because we can't
find a motive, the man's mad. That's the line of
least resistance; but it don't follow by a long
sight that it's the right line. Here's a chap has
lured his brother to death, and very cunning he's
been about it. He's pitched a yarn and then,

after a promise to turn up, he changes his mind and makes a new plan altogether by which old Ben Redmayne is put entirely in his power. Then—"

"But who was to know he meant mischief? We had facts to deal with. Mrs. Pendean herself had seen and spoken to him; so had Doria. In the case of the lady, at any rate, all she said was above suspicion. She hid nothing; she behaved like a Christian woman, wept at the spectacle of his awful misery, and brought his message to his brother. Then sudden, panic fear overtook the man at the last moment—natural enough— and he begged Bendigo Redmayne to see him in his hiding-place alone. It rang true as a bell. For myself I had not a shadow of suspicion."

"That's all right," admitted Damarell, "and I'm not one who pretends to be wise after the event. But, as I told you before, I thought it a mistake to suspend our search and take the matter out of professional hands just when we were safe to nab him. You were in command and we obeyed, but whatever the murderer had to say would as well have been said to us as to his brother—and better; because in any case he might have tempted a brother to break the law for him. Now there's more innocent blood been shed and a damned, dangerous criminal—mad or sane—is still at large. Most likely more than one. However, it is not much use jawing, I grant you. What we've got to do is to catch them—if we can."

Brendon made no reply to this speech. He was

vexed, yet knew that he had heard little more
than the truth.

He examined the plateau and showed again
where some round object had pressed the earth
and where a man had sat beside it. From this
spot it was not possible to dispose of a body in
the sea. Beneath it extended a fall of a hundred
feet to broken ground, which again gave by slop-
ing shelves to the water. Had a corpse been
thrown over here, it must have challenged their
sight beneath; and yet from this standpoint no
sign of the vanished man or his burden appeared.
But the zigzag path to the clifftop revealed neither
any evidence of a weight being dragged upward
nor the impression of the iron-shod foot. Fresh
footprints there were, but they had been made by
Brendon and Doria on the previous night. Now
the police ascended, making careful examination
of every turn in the way, and finally reached the
summit a little after noon. It was a dizzy height,
beetling over the sea beneath; but crags and but-
tresses broke out from the six hundred feet of
precipice and any object thrown over from the
crest of Hawk Beak Hill must have been arrested
many times in its downward progress.

Inspector Damarell stopped to rest and flung
himself panting on the close sward at the crown
of the cliff.

"What do you think?" he asked Brendon; and
the other having made a careful examination of
the ground around them and scanned the peaks
and ledges beneath, answered:

"He never came here—at any rate not until

he had disposed of the body. It's the broken ground under the plateau we must search. There may be a way down that he knew. I guess he threw the body over, then scrambled down himself and covered it deep with stones. It's surely there—for the simple reason that it can't be anywhere else. We should have found out if he'd brought it to the top. And in my judgment, even if he wanted to do so, he would have lacked the physical strength. He must have spent himself getting it to the plateau, however strong he is, and then found that he could do no more. The body, therefore, should be hidden in the rocks below the plateau."

"We can leave it at that then, till we've had something to eat and drink," answered the inspector, and proceeding to the nearest point of the highroad, where a car already waited for them, they made a meal. The constable who drove the car had no news, but Brendon expected that information might await him at Dartmouth. He was convinced that on this occasion the object of their search could not long evade discovery.

They chained up the motor car, and the constable who had driven it joined them when they descended to explore the broken ground beneath the plateau.

"There's nothing more hateful to me than a murder without the body," declared Damarell, on the way down. "You don't even know if you're on firm ground to start with, and every step you take must hang upon a fact that you can't verify except by circumstantial evidence.

Every step may in reality be a false one—and the nearer you appear to be to the truth, the farther you may be going away from it. A pint of blood needn't of necessity mean a murder; but this chap, Robert Redmayne, has a partiality for leaving red traces behind him."

The others listened and then they reached the plateau and went down to the stony space beneath. This was not difficult to reach. A dozen rough-and-ready ways presented themselves to a climber; but neither Brendon nor his companions could find the least indications that any other had recently descended.

Now they quartered out the stone-covered ground and, having first searched every superficial yard for indications of disturbance, proceeded to a methodical and very thorough hunt beneath the surface. The stones were moved and the space critically examined over every square foot, but not a shadow of evidence to show that the spot had been trodden or touched could be discovered. Brendon sought first immediately below the plateau, where the sack and its contents must have fallen, but nothing indicated such an event. The stones were naked and no stain of blood or indication of any intrusion upon the lonely spot rewarded the searchers. For three hours, until dusk began to deepen on the precipices above them, the men worked as skilfully and steadfastly as men might work. Then their fruitless task was done. Brendon's theory, so confidently proclaimed, had broken down and he confessed his failure frankly enough.

They climbed up together once more and reached the summit of the cliffs again. Here, by the main road, they met one or two civilians who had devoted the day to assisting the police; but not one of them reported any sight or rumour of the fugitive.

The entrance of "Crow's Nest" opened upon the highroad which took the police back to Dartmouth, and here Brendon delayed the car and descended alone down the coomb to the house that had so suddenly lost its master. The place seemed mourning and it was very silent. Mark inquired for Jenny and the frightened maid doubted whether she might be seen.

"The poor lady be cruel put about," she explained. "She says she brings evil fortune after her and wishes to God it was her that was dead and not poor master. Mr. Doria tried to comfort her a bit; but he couldn't and she told him to be gone. She's very near cried her eyes out of her head since morning."

"That does not sound much like Mrs. Pendean," he answered. "Where is she, and where is Doria?"

"She's in her room. He is writing letters. He says that he must look after new work pretty quick, because no doubt he won't be wanted here after a month from now."

"Ask Mrs. Pendean if she can see me a moment," he said, and the woman left him to ascertain. But Brendon was disappointed. Jenny sent word that she could not see him to-day and hoped he would take occasion to call on the following morning, when he would find her more composed.

To this he could answer nothing and presently started to rejoin the car. Giuseppe overtook him from the house; but he could only report that the day had passed without event at "Crow's Nest."

"Nobody has come but a clergyman," he told Brendon, "and we have been careful to leave everything just as the old captain left it."

"I will see you to-morrow," promised Mark; then he rejoined the inspector and their car went on its way.

A surprise and a keen disappointment awaited them at Dartmouth. The day's work had produced no result whatever. Not a trace of Robert Redmayne was reported from anywhere and Inspector Damarell offered the former solution of suicide. But Brendon would not hear it now.

"He is no more dead this time than he was six months ago," he answered; "but he has some system of disguise, or concealment, that utterly defeats the ordinary methods of a man hunt. We must try bloodhounds to-morrow, though the scent is spoiled now and we can hardly hope for any useful results."

"Perhaps he'll write from Plymouth again as he did before," suggested the inspector.

Weary and out of spirits, Mark left the police station and went to his hotel. To be baffled was an experience not new to him and thus far he felt no more tribulation than a great cricketer, who occasionally fails and retires for a "duck," knowing that his second innings may still be told in three figures; but what concerned him was the double failure on the same case. He felt puzzled by events and still more puzzled by his own psychology, which seemed incapable of reacting as usual to the stimulus of mystery and the challenge of a problem, apparently ineluctable.

He felt that his wits were playing him false and, instead of cleaving some bold and original way to the heart of a difficulty, as was his wont, he could see no ray of light thrown by the candle of his own inspiration. Inspiration, in fact, he wholly lacked. Once only in the past—after an attack of influenza—had he felt so barren of initiative as now, so feeble and ineffective.

He fell asleep at last, thinking not of the vanished sailor, but Jenny Pendean. That she must suffer at her uncle's sudden death was natural and he had not been surprised to learn of her collapse. For she was sensitive; she had lately been through a terrible personal trial; and to find herself suddenly associated with another tragedy might well induce a nervous breakdown. Who would come to the rescue now? To whom would she look? Whither would she go?

Mark was early astir and with Inspector Damarell he organized an elaborate search system for the day. At nine o'clock a large party had set out, for another morning brought no news by telegram or telephone, and it was clear that Redmayne still continued free.

Brendon proceeded presently to "Crow's Nest," drawn thither solely by thoughts of Jenny, for whatever she might secretly think of Doria and feel toward him, it was certain that he could not be of any great support under present circumstances. Doria was essentially a fair-weather friend. Many were the things that Jenny would be called to do and, so far as Mark knew, there was none to assist her. He found her distressed but calm. She had telegraphed to her uncle in Italy and though she doubted whether he would risk return into an English winter, she hoped that he might do so.

"Everything is chaos," she said, "just as it was at Princetown. Uncle Bendigo told me only a few days before these things happened—when he had made up his mind that his brother Robert must be dead—that the law would not recognize his death for a certain period of years. And now we know that he is not dead but that poor Uncle Bendigo is. Yet the law will not recognize his death, either perhaps, seeing that he has not been found. Uncle Robert's papers and affairs were gone into and he left no will; so his property, when the law sanctions it, would have been divided between his brothers; but now I imagine it all belongs to my uncle in Italy; while, as for poor Uncle Bendigo, I expect that he has made a will, because he was such a methodical man; but what he intended to do with his house and money we cannot tell yet."

Jenny had nothing to say or suggest that could help Brendon and she was very nervous, desiring to leave the lonely habitation on the cliffs as quickly as possible; but she intended to await Albert Redmayne's decision.

"This will greatly upset him, I fear," she said. "He is now the last of 'the red Redmaynes,' as our family was called in Australia."

"Why the adjective?"

"Because we were always red. Every one of my grandfather's children had red hair, and so had he. His wife was also red—and the only living member of the next generation is red, too, as you see."

"You are not red. Your hair is a most wonderful auburn, if I may say so."

She showed no appreciation of the compliment. "It will soon be grey," she answered.

CHAPTER IX

ALBERT REDMAYNE, holding it his duty to come to
England, did so, and Jenny met him at Dartmouth after his long journey.

He was a small, withered man with a big head,
great, luminous eyes, and a bald scalp. Such hair
as yet remained to him was the true Redmayne
scarlet; but the nimbus that still adorned his
naked skull was streaked with silver and his thin,
long beard was also grizzled. He spoke in a gentle, kindly voice, with little Southern gestures.
He was clad in a great Italian cloak and a big,
slouchy hat, which between them, almost served
to extinguish the bookworm.

"Oh, that Peter Ganns were here!" he sighed
again and again, while he thrust himself as near
as possible to a great coal fire, and Jenny told
him every detail of the tragedy.

"They took the bloodhounds to the cave, Uncle
Albert, and Mr. Brendon himself watched them
working, but nothing came of it. The creatures
leaped up the channel from the cave and were
soon upon the plateau where the long tunnel
opens into the air; but there they seemed to lose
their bearings and there was no scent that
attracted them, either up to the summit of the

167

cliffs, or down to the rocky beach underneath. They ran about and bayed and presently returned again down the tunnel to the cave. Mr. Brendon has no belief in the value of bloodhounds for a case like this."

"Nothing further of—of—Robert?"

"Not a trace or sign of him. I'm sure that everything that the wit of man can do has been done; and many clever local people, including the County Commissioner and the highest authorities, have helped Mr. Brendon; but not a glimpse of poor Uncle Robert has been seen and there is nothing to show what happened to him after that terrible night."

"Or to brother Bendigo, either, for that matter," murmured Mr. Redmayne. "It is your poor husband's case over again—blood, alas, but nought else!"

Jenny was haggard and worn. She devoted herself to the old man's comfort and hoped that the journey would not do him any hurt.

Mr. Albert Redmayne slept well, but the morning found him very depressed and melancholy. Things, dreadful enough at a distance, seemed far worse now that he found himself in the theatre of their occurrence. He maintained a long conversation with Mark Brendon and cross-questioned Doria; but their information did not inspire him to a suggestion and, after twenty-four hours, it was clear that the little man could be of no assistance to anybody. He was frightened and awe-stricken. He detested "Crow's Nest" and the melancholy murmur of the sea. He showed the keenest desire to return home at the earliest opportunity and was exceedingly nervous after dark.

"Oh, that Peter Ganns were here!" he exclaimed again and again, as a comment to every incident unfolded by Brendon or Jenny; and then, when she asked him if it might be possible to summon Peter Ganns, Mr. Redmayne explained that he was an American beyond their reach at present.

"Mr. Ganns," he said, "is my best friend in the world—save and excepting one man only. He—my first and most precious intimate—dwells at Bellagio, on the opposite side of Lake Como from myself. Signor Virgilio Poggi is a bibliophile of European eminence and the most brilliant of men—a great genius and my dearest associate for twenty-five years. But Peter Ganns also is a very astounding person—a detective officer by profession—but a man of many parts and full of such genuine understanding of humanity that to know him is to gain priceless insight.

"I myself lack that intimate knowledge of character which is his native gift. Books I know better than men, and it was my peculiar acquaintance with books that brought Ganns and me together in New York. There I served him well in an amazing police case and aided him to prove a crime, the discovery of which turned upon a certain paper manufactured for the Medici. But a greater thing than this criminal incident sprang from it; and that is my friendship with the won-

derful Peter. Not above half a dozen books have
taught me more than that man. He is a Machia-
velli on the side of the angels.''

He expatiated upon Mr. Peter Ganns until his
listeners wearied of the subject. Then Giuseppe
Doria intervened with a personal problem. He
desired to be dismissed and was anxious to learn
from Brendon if the law permitted him to leave
the neighbourhood.

"For my part," he said, "it is an ill wind that
blows good to nobody. I am anxious to go to
London if there is no objection.''

He found himself detained, however, for some
days, until an official examination of the strange
problem was completed. The investigation
achieved nothing and threw no ray of light, either
upon the apparent murder of Bendigo Redmayne,
or the disappearance of his brother. The original mystery at Foggintor Quarry was recalled,
to fill the minds of the morbid and curious; but
no sort of connecting motive between the two
crimes appeared and the problem of Robert Redmayne only grew darker. All purpose was lack-
ing from both tragedies, while even the facts themselves remained in doubt, since neither incident
furnished a dead body to prove murder against the
missing man.

Mr. Albert Redmayne stayed no longer in Devonshire than his duty indicated, for he could
prove of no service to the police. On the night
previous to his departure he went through his
brother's scanty library and found nothing in it
of any interest to a collector. The ancient and

well-thumbed copy of "Moby Dick" he took for sentiment, and he also directed Jenny to pack for him Bendigo's "Log"—a diary in eight or ten volumes. This he proposed to read at his leisure when home again. To the end of his visit he never ceased to lament the absence of Mr. Peter Ganns.

"My friend is actually coming to Europe next year," he explained. "He is, without doubt, the most accomplished of men in the dreadful science of detecting crime and, were he here, he could assuredly read into these abominations a meaning for which we grope in vain. Do not think," he added to Jenny, "that I undervalue the labours of Mr. Brendon and the police, but they have come to naught, for there are strange forces of evil moving here deeper than the plummet of their intelligence can sound."

He departed, assured that his family was the victim of some evil, concealed alike from himself and everybody else; but he promised Jenny that he would presently write to America and lay every incident of the case, so far as it was known and reported, before his friend.

"He will bring a new intelligence to bear upon the tragedy," said Albert. "He will see things that are hidden from us, for his brain has a quality which one can only describe as a mental X-ray, which probes and penetrates in a fashion denied to ordinary thinking apparatus."

Before he returned to the borders of Como and his little villa beneath the mountains, the old scholar took affectionate leave of Jenny and made

her promise to follow him as soon as she was able
to do so.

He had failed to observe the emotional bonds
that united her to Doria; but he had found Giuseppe an attractive personality and welcomed the
Italian's good sense and tact under distressing
circumstances. He made him a present of money
before leaving and promised him testimonials if
he should need them. As for Jenny, she was to
enjoy the bequest under her grandfather's will
when she desired to do so, while for her future,
her uncle trusted that she would make her home
with him.

He soon departed and the Redmayne inquiry,
begun with much zest and determination, gradually faded away and perished of inanition. No
solitary clue or indication of progress rewarded
the investigations. Robert Redmayne had vanished off the face of the earth and his brother
with him. There remained of the family only
Albert and his niece—a fact she imparted, not
without melancholy, to Mark Brendon, when the
day came that he must take his leave of her and
return to other and more profitable fields of work.

He urged her to join her uncle as soon as possible and he begged her to accept his willing service in any way within his power; while she was
gracious and thanked him for all that he had
done.

"I shall never, never forget your patience and
your great goodness," she said. "I am indeed
grateful, Mr. Brendon, and I hope, if only for
your sake, that time will lay bare the truth of

these horrible things. To know that good men, against whom there was no grudge or hate in the world, have been murdered by their fellow men— it is a nightmare. But God will bring the truth to light—I feel positive of that.''

He left her more deeply in love than ever; but there seemed no note of hope or promise in their farewell. And yet he felt a profound conviction that they would meet again. She undertook to acquaint him with her movements and was not sure that she would accept Albert Redmayne's invitation to join him. So Mark left her, believing that Doria was certain to determine her future and guessing that, if she presently proceeded to Como, the lively and indomitable Italian would quickly follow.

For the present, however, Giuseppe seemed to be concerned with his own affairs. He brought Brendon back on his last journey from "Crow's Nest" in the launch and explained that he had already found good work beside the Thames.

"We shall, I hope, meet again," he said, "and you may hear presently of a very wonderful adventure in which Doria shall be l'allegro—the merry man and the hero!"

They talked and Mark became impatient under a growing consciousness that the quicker-witted spirit was pulling his leg. Doria preserved the best possible temper, but his Latin love of a certain sort of fun seemed cynical and almost inhuman under the circumstances.

They spoke of the mystery and, upon that sub-

ject, the motor boatman declared himself as quite
unable to find any explanation; but, with respect
to Brendon's failure, he did not hesitate to make
a sly allusion. Indeed he hinted at things which
Mark was to hear six months later in a more responsible mouth.

"Above all, what has puzzled me most in this
horrid affair is you, Brendon," declared Giuseppe. "You are a great sleuth, we know; yet
you are no better than the rest of us stupid people
before these happenings and horrors. That made
me wonder for a long time; but now I wonder no
longer."

"I'm beat and I own it. I've missed something vital—the keystone of the arch. But why
do you say that you wonder no more? Because
you know me now and find me a very dull dog?"

"Not so, my friend, far from it. You are a
very wily, clever dog. But—well, as we say in
Italy, 'if you put a cat into gloves, she will not
catch mice.' You have been in gloves ever since
you knew Madonna was a widow."

"What do you mean?"

"Very well you know what I mean!"

And that was the end of their conversation, for
Brendon frowned in silence and Giuseppe began
to slack the engines as they reached the landing
stage.

"Something tells me I shall meet you again,
Marco," he said as they shook hands and prepared to part; and Brendon, who shared that
impression strongly enough, nodded.

"It may be so," he answered.

For a period of several months, however, the detective was not to hear more of those who had played their small parts in the unsolved mystery. He was busy enough and in some measure rehabilitated a tarnished reputation by one brilliant achievement in his finest manner. But success did not restore his self-respect; and it diminished in no degree the fever burning at his heart.

Once he received a note from Jenny telling him that she hoped to see him in London before leaving for Italy; and the fact that she had decided to join her uncle gave him some peace; but he heard nothing further and his reply to Mrs. Pendean's communication, which had come from "Crow's Nest," won no response. Weeks passed and whether she remained still in Devonshire, was in London, or had gone to Italy, he could not know, for she did not write again.

He dispatched a long letter in early spring to the care of Albert Redmayne, but this also won no response. And then came an explanation. She had been in London, but kept him ignorant of the fact for sufficient reasons. She had neither thought of him nor wanted him, for her life was full of another.

On a day in late March, Brendon received a little, triangular-shaped box through the post from abroad, and opening it, stared at a wedge of wedding cake. With the gift came a line— one only: "Kind and grateful remembrances from Giuseppe and Jenny Doria."

She sent no direction that might enable him to acknowledge her gift; but there was a postal

stamp upon the covering and Brendon noted that
the box came from Italy—from Ventimiglia,
a town which Doria once mentioned in connection
with the ruined castle and vanished splendours
of his race.

And yet, despite this sudden, though not surprising, event, there persisted with Mark a conviction that this did not mean the end.   Time was to
bring him into close companionship with Jenny
again: he knew it for an integral factor of the
future; but the persistence of this impression
could not serve to lighten his melancholy before
an accomplished fact.   That he might live to be
of infinite service to Jenny a subconscious assurance convinced him; but he must say good-bye
to love forever.   Henceforth hope was dead and
when duty called he knew not what form his duty
might assume.   Through a sleepless night he retraced every moment of his intercourse with
Doria's wife and much tormented himself.

But other recollections awakened by this survey gave him pause and pointed to mysteries
as yet unguessed.   For was it possible that this
tender-natured woman, who had mourned her
husband so bitterly but nine months before,
could now enter with such light-hearted joy into
union with another man?   Was it reasonable
to see Jenny Pendean, as he remembered her in
the agony of her bereavement, already the happy
and contented bride of one a stranger to her until
so recently?

It was indeed possible, because it had happened; but reasons for so untimely an event ex-

isted. They might, if understood, absolve the widow for an apparent levity not consonant with her true and steadfast self. It cast him down, almost as much as his own vanished dream and everlasting loss, that hard-hearted love could work such a miracle and banish the wedded past of this woman's life so completely in favour of a doubtful future with a foreign spouse.

There were things hidden, and he felt a great desire to penetrate them for the credit of the woman he had loved so well.

CHAPTER X

DAWN had broken over Italy and morning, in honeysuckle colours, burned upon the mountain mists. Far beneath a lofty hillside the world still slumbered and the Larian lake, a jewel of gold and turquoise, shone amid her flowery margins. The hour was very silent; the little towns and hamlets scattered beside Como, like clusters of white and rosy shells, dreamed on until thin music broke from their campaniles. Bell answered bell and made a girdle of harmony about the lake, floating along the water and ascending aloft until no louder than the song of birds.

Two women climbed together up the great acclivity of Griante. One was brown and elderly, clad in black with an orange rag wrapped about her brow—a sturdy, muscular creature who carried a great, empty wicker basket upon her shoulders; the other was clad in a rosy jumper of silk: she flashed in the morning fires and brought an added beauty to that beautiful scene.

Jenny ascended the mountain as lightly as a butterfly. She was lovelier than ever in the morning light, yet a misty doubt, a watchful sadness, seemed to hover upon her forehead. Her

178

wonderful eyes looked ahead up the precipitous tract that she and the Italian woman climbed together. She moderated her pace to the slower gait of the elder and presently they both stopped before a little grey chapel perched beside the hill path.

Mr. Albert Redmayne's silkworms, in the great airy shed behind his villa, had nearly all spun their cocoons now, for it was June again and the annual crop of mulberry leaves in the valleys beneath were well-nigh exhausted.

Therefore Assunta Marzelli, the old bibliophile's housekeeper, made holiday with his niece, now upon a visit to him, and together the women climbed, where food might be procured for the last tardy caterpillars to change their state.

They had started in the grey dawn, passed up a dry watercourse, and proceeded where the vine was queen and there fell a scented filigree of dead blossom from flowering olives. They had seen a million clusters of tiny grapes already rounding and had passed through wedges and squares of cultivated earth, where sprang alternate patches of corn yellowing to harvest and the lush green of growing maize. Figs and almonds and rows of red and white mulberries, with naked branches stripped of foliage, broke the lines of the crops. Here hedges sparkled in a harvest of scarlet cherries; and here sheep and goats nibbled over little, bright tracts of sweet grass. Higher yet shone out groves of chestnut trees, all shining with the light of their tassels, very bright by contrast with the gloom of the mountain pines.

And then, where two tall cypresses stood upon either side, Jenny and Assunta found the shrine and stayed a while. Jenny set down the basket which she carried with their midday meal, and her companion dropped the great bin destined to hold mulberry leaves.

The lake below was now reduced to a cup of liquid jade over which shot streamers of light into the mountain shadows at its brink; but there were vessels floating on the waters that held the watchers' eyes.

They looked like twin, toy torpedo boats—mere streaks of red and black upon the water, with Italy's flag at the taffrail. But the little ships were no toys and Assunta hated them, for the strange craft told of the ceaseless battle waged by authority against the mountain smugglers and reminded the widow of her own lawless husband's death ten years before. Cæsar Marzelli had taken his cup to the well once too often and had lost his life in a pitched battle with the officers of the customs.

Long shafts of glory shot between the mountains and drenched the lake; the shoulders of the lesser hills flamed; the waters beneath them flashed; and far away, among the table-lands of the morning mist, against a sapphire sky, there gleamed the last patches of snow.

A cross of rusty iron surmounted the little sanctuary by which they sat, and the roof was of old tiles scorched a mellow tint of brown. To Maris Stella was the shrine dedicated; and within, under the altar, white bones gleamed—skulls and thighs

and ribs of men and women who had perished of
the plague in far-off time.

"*Morti della peste*," read Jenny, on the front
of the altar, and Assunta, in gloomy mood before
the recollection of the past, spoke to her young
mistress and shook her head.

"I envy them sometimes, signora. Their
troubles are ended. Those heads, that have ached
and wept so often, will never ache and weep
again."

She spoke in Italian and Jenny but partially
understood. Yet she joined Assunta on her knees
and together they made their morning prayer to
Mary, Star of the Sea, and asked for what their
souls most desired.

Presently they rose, Assunta the calmer for her
petitions, and together they proceeded upward.
The elder tried to explain what a base and abominable thing it was that her husband, an honest
free trader between Italy and Switzerland, should
have been destroyed by the slaves in the government vessels beneath, and Jenny nodded and
strove to understand. She was making progress
in Italian, though Assunta's swift tongue and
local patois were as yet beyond her comprehen-
sion. But she knew that her dead smuggler husband was the subject on Assunta's lips and nodded her sympathy.

"Sons of dogs!" cried the widow; then a steep
section of their road reduced her to silence.

The great event of that day, which brought
Jenny Doria so violently back into the tragedy of
the past, had yet to happen, and many hours

elapsed before she was confronted with it. The women climbed presently to a little field of meadow grass that sparkled with tiny flowers and spread its alpine sward among thickets of mulberry. Here their work awaited them; but first they ate the eggs and wheaten bread, walnuts and dried figs that they had brought and shared a little flask of red wine. They finished with a handful of cherries and then Assunta began to pluck leaves for her great basket while Jenny loitered a while and smoked a cigarette. It was a new habit acquired since her marriage.

Presently she set to work and assisted her companion until they had gathered a full load of leaves. Then the younger plucked one or two great golden orange lilies that grew in this little glen, and soon the women started upon their homeward way. They had descended about a mile and at a shoulder of Griante sat down to rest in welcome shadow. Beneath, to the northward, lay their home beside the water and, gazing down upon the scattered and clustered habitations of Menaggio, Jenny declared that she saw the red roof of Villa Pianezzo and the brown of the lofty shed behind, where dwelt her uncle's silkworms.

Opposite, on its promontory, stood the little township of Bellagio and behind it flashed the glassy face of Lecco in the cloudless sunshine. And then, suddenly, as if it had been some apparition limned upon the air, there stood in the path the figure of a tall man. His red head was bare and from the face beneath shone a pair of wild and haggard eyes. They saw the stranger's great tawny mustache, his tweed garments and knickerbockers, his red waistcoat, and the cap he carried in his hand.

It was Robert Redmayne. Assunta, who gazed upon him without understanding, suddenly felt Jenny's hand tighten hard upon her arm. Jenny uttered one loud cry of terror and then relaxed and fell unconscious upon the ground. The widow leaped to her aid, cried comfortable words and prayed the young wife to fear nothing; but it was some time before Jenny came to her senses and when she did so her nerve appeared to have deserted her.

"Did you see him?" she gasped, clinging to Assunta and gazing fearfully where her uncle had stood.

"Yes, yes—a big, red man; but he meant us no harm. When you cried out, he was more frightened than we. He leaped down, like a red fox, into the wood and disappeared. He was not an Italian. A German or Englishman, I think. Perhaps a smuggler planning to fetch tea and cigars and coffee and salt from Switzerland. If he leaves enough for the doganieri, they will wink at him. If he does not, they will shoot him— sons of dogs!"

"Remember what you saw!" said Jenny tremulously: "Remember exactly what he looked like, that you may be able to tell Uncle Albert just how it was, Assunta. He is Uncle Albert's brother—Robert Redmayne!"

Assunta Marzelli knew something of the mys-

tery and understood that her master's brother
was being hunted for great crimes.

She crossed herself.

"Merciful God! The evil man. And so red!
Let us fly, signora."

"Which way did he go?"

"Straight down through the wood beneath us."

"Did he recognize me, Assunta? Did he seem
to know me? I dared not look a second time."

Assunta partially followed the question.

"No. He did not look either. He stared out
over the lake and his face was like a lost soul's
face. Then you cried out and still he did not
look but disappeared. He was not angry."

"Why is he here? How has he come and where
from?"

"Who shall say? Perhaps the master will
know."

"I am in great fear for the master, Assunta.
We must go home as quickly as possible."

"Is there danger to the signor from his
brother?"

"I do not know. I think there may be."

Jenny helped Assunta with her great basket,
lifted it on her shoulders and then set off beside
her. But the rate of progress proved too slow
for her patience.

"I have a horrible dread," she said. "Some-
thing tells me that we ought to be going faster.
Would you be frightened if I were to leave you,
Assunta, and make greater haste?"

The other managed to understand and declared
that she felt no fear.

"I have no quarrel with the red man," she said. "Why should he hurt me? Perhaps he was not a man but a spirit, signora."

"I wish he were," declared Jenny. "But it was not a ghost you heard leap into the wood, Assunta. I will run as fast as I can and take the short cuts."

They parted and Jenny hastened, risked her neck sometimes, and sped forward with the energy of youth and on the wings of fear. Assunta saw her stop and turn and listen once or twice; then the crags and hanging thickets hid her from view.

Jenny saw and heard no more of the being who had thus so unexpectedly returned into her life. Her thoughts were wholly with Albert Redmayne and, as she told him when she met him, it remained for him to consider the significance of this event and determine what steps should be taken for his own safety. He was at Bellagio when she reached home, and his manservant, Assunta's brother, Ernesto, explained that Mr. Redmayne had crossed after luncheon to visit his dearest friend, the book lover, Virgilio Poggi.

"A book came by the postman, signora, and the master must needs hire boat and cross at once," explained Ernesto, who spoke good English and was proud of his accomplishment.

Jenny waited impatiently and she was at the landing stage when Albert returned. He smiled to see her and took off his great slouch hat.

"My beloved Virgilio was overjoyed that I should have found the famous book—the veritable

Italian edition of Sir Thomas Browne—his 'Pseu-
dodoxia Epidemica.' A red-letter day for us
both! But—but——" He looked at Jenny's
frightened eyes and felt her hand upon his sleeve.
"Why, what is wrong? You are alarmed. No
ill news of Giuseppe?"

"Come home quickly," she answered, "and I
will explain. A very terrible thing has happened.
I cannot think what we should do. Only this
I know: I am not going to leave you again until
it is cleared up."

At home Albert took off his great hat and cloak.
Then he sat in his study—an amazing chamber,
lined with books to the lofty ceiling and dark in
tone by reason of the prevalent rich but sombre
bindings of five thousand volumes. Jenny told
him that she had seen Robert Redmayne, whereupon her uncle considered for five minutes, then
declared himself both puzzled and alarmed. He
showed no fear, however, and his large, luminous
eyes shone out of his little, withered face un-
shadowed. None the less he was quick to read
danger into this extraordinary incident.

"You are positive?" he asked. "Everything
depends on that. If you have seen my unfortunate, vanished brother again here, so near to
me, it is exceedingly amazing, Jenny. Can you
say positively, without a shadow of doubt, that
the melancholy figure was not a figment of your
imagination, or some stranger who resembled
Robert?"

"I wish to Heaven I could, Uncle Albert. But
I am positive."

"The very fact that he appeared exactly as you saw him last—in the big tweed suit and red waistcoat—would support an argument in favour of hallucination," declared her uncle. "For how on earth can the poor creature, if he be really still alive, have remained in those clothes for a year and travelled half across Europe in them?"

"It is monstrous. And yet there he stood and I saw him as clearly as I see you. He was certainly not in my thoughts. I was thinking of nothing and talking to Assunta about the silkworms, when suddenly he appeared, not twenty yards away."

"What did you do?"

"I made a fool of myself," confessed Jenny. "Assunta says that I cried out very loud and then toppled over and fainted. When I came round there was nothing to be seen."

"The point is then: did Assunta see him also?"

"That was the first thing I found out. I hoped she had not. That would have saved the situation in a way and proved it was only some picture of the mind as you suggest. But she saw him clearly enough—so clearly that she described a red man not Italian, but English or German. She heard him, too. When I cried out he leaped away into the woods."

"Did he see and recognize you?"

"That I do not know. Probably he did."

Mr. Redmayne lighted a cigar which he took from a box on a little table by the open hearth. He drew several deep breaths before he spoke again.

"This is a very disquieting circumstance and I greatly wish it had not happened," he said. "There may be no cause for alarm; but, on the other hand, when we consider the disappearance of my brother Bendigo, I have a right to feel fear. By some miracle, Robert, for the last six months, has continued to evade capture and conceal the fact of his insanity. That means I am now faced with a most formidable danger, Jenny, and it behooves me to exercise the greatest possible care of my person. You, too, for all we can say, may be in peril."

"I may be," she said. "But you matter more. We must do something swiftly, uncle—to-day—this very hour."

"Yes," he admitted. "We are painfully challenged by Providence, my child. Heaven helps those who help themselves, however. I have never before, to my knowledge, been in any physical danger and the sensation is exceedingly unpleasant. We will drink some strong tea and then determine our course of action. I confess that I feel a good deal perturbed."

His words were at variance with his quiet and restrained expression, but Mr. Redmayne had never told a falsehood in his life and Jenny knew that he was indeed alarmed.

"You must not stop here to-night," she said. "You must cross to Bellagio and stay with Signor Poggi until we know more."

"We shall see as to that. Prepare the tea and leave me for half an hour to reflect."

"But—but—Uncle Albert—he—he might come at any moment!"

"Do not think so. He is now, poor soul, a creature of the night. We need not fear that he will intrude in honest sunshine upon the haunts of men. Leave me and tell Ernesto to admit nobody who is not familiar to him. But I repeat, we need fear nothing until after dark."

In half an hour Jenny returned with Mr. Redmayne's tea.

"Assunta has just come back. She has seen nothing more of—of Uncle Robert."

For a time Albert said nothing. He drank, and ate a large macaroon biscuit. Then he told his niece the plans he was prepared to follow.

"Providence is, I think, upon our side, pretty one," he began, "for my amazing friend, Peter Ganns, who designed to visit me in September, has already arrived in England; and when he hears of this ugly sequel to the story I confided in his ears last winter, I am bold to believe that he will hasten to me immediately and not hesitate to modify his plans. He is a methodical creature and hates to change; but circumstances alter cases and I feel justified in telling you that he will come as soon as he conveniently can do so. This I say because he loves me."

"I'm sure he will," declared Jenny.

"Write me two letters," continued Albert. "One to Mr. Mark Brendon, the young detective from Scotland Yard, of whom I entertained a high opinion; and also write to your husband.

Direct Brendon to approach Peter Ganns and beg
them both to come to me as quickly as their affairs
allow. Also bid Giuseppe to return to you immediately. He will serve to protect us, for he is
fearless and resolute."

But Jenny showed no joy at this suggestion.

"I was to have had a peaceful month with you,"
she pouted.

"So indeed I hoped; but it can hardly be peaceful now and I confess that the presence of Doria
would go some way to compose my nerves. He is
powerful, cheerful, and full of resource. He is
also brave. He remembers the past and he knows
poor Robert by sight. If, therefore, my brother
is indeed near at hand and to be expected at any
moment, then I should be glad of some capable
person to stand between us. Should my brother
presently indicate, through you or somebody else,
that he wants to see me alone by night, as in the
case of Bendigo, then I must absolutely decline
any such adventure. We meet in the presence of
armed men, or not at all."

Jenny had left Doria for a time and apparently
felt no desire to see him again until her promised
visit to her uncle should be ended.

"I heard from Giuseppe three days ago," she
said. "He has left Ventimiglia and gone to
Turin, where he used to work and where he has
many friends. He has a project."

"I shall speak with him seriously when next we
meet," declared the old man. "I entertain great
admiration for your attractive spouse, as you

know. He is a delightful person; but it is time we consider the future of your twenty thousand pounds and yourself, Jenny. In the course of nature all that is mine will also be yours, and when the estate of poor Bendigo is wound up, my present income must be nearly doubled. Leave to presume death, however, may be delayed. But the fact remains that you will enjoy the Redmayne money sooner or later, and I want to come to grips with Giuseppe and explain to him that he must understand his responsibilities."

Jenny sighed.

"Nobody will make him understand them, uncle."

"Do not say so. He is intelligent and has, I am sure, a sense of honour as well as a deep and devoted affection for you. But he must not spend your money. I will not allow that. Write to him at Turin and entreat him from me to abandon anything that he may have in hand and join us instantly here. We need not keep him long; but he can look after us for a while until we learn when Ganns and Brendon are to be expected."

Jenny promised, without much enthusiasm, to call her husband to the rescue.

"He will laugh and perhaps refuse to come," she said. "But since you think it wise, I will beg him to hasten and tell him what has happened. Meanwhile what of to-night and to-morrow night?"

"To-night I go across the water to Bellagio and you come with me. It is impossible that

Robert should know we are there. Virgilio Poggi
will take care of us and be very jealous for me
if I hint that I am in any danger."

"I'm sure he will. And should you not warn
the police about Uncle Robert and give them a description of him?"

"I'm not sure as to that. We will consider
to-morrow. I little like the ways of the Italian
police."

"You might have watchers here to-night, ready
to take him if he appears," suggested Jenny.

But Albert finally decided against giving any
information.

"For the moment I shall do nothing. We will
see what another morning may bring forth. To
feel this awful presence suddenly so close is very
distressing and I do not want to think of him any
more until to-morrow. Write the letters and
then we will put a few things together and cross
the lake before it is evening."

"You do not fear for your books, Uncle Albert?"

"No, I have no fear for my books. If there
is a homicidal being here, intent upon my life, he
will not look to the right or the left. Even when
he was sane, poor Robert never knew anything about books or their value. He will not
seek them—nor could he reach them if he did."

"Did he ever visit you here in the past? Does
he know Italy?" she said.

"So far as I am aware he was never here in
his life. Certainly he never visited me. It is,
in fact, so many years since I have seen him that

I might have met him and failed to recognize the unhappy man.''

Jenny wrote the letters and posted them; then she packed for her uncle and herself and presently, having warned Assunta and Ernesto that no stranger must be admitted until his return on the following day, Albert Redmayne prepared to cross the lake. First, however, he locked and barred his library and transferred half a dozen volumes more than commonly precious to a steel safe aloft in his bedroom.

A boatman quickly rowed them to the landing stage of Bellagio and they soon reached the dwelling of Albert's friend, who welcomed them with an equal measure of surprise and delight.

Signor Poggi, a small, fat man with a bald head, broad brow, and twinkling eyes, grasped their hands and listened with wonder to the reason for their arrival. He knew English and always delighted in the practice of that language when opportunity offered.

"But this is beyond belief!" he said. "An enemy for Alberto! Who should be his enemy— he who is the friend of every man? What romance is this, Signora Jenny, that throws danger into the path of your dear uncle?''

"It is the sudden threat and terror of my vanished brother,'' explained Mr. Redmayne. "You are familiar, Virgilio, with the terrible facts concerning Robert's appearance and Bendigo's disappearance. Now, suddenly, when I have long come to believe that my younger brother's lurid career was ended and that he had ceased to be,

he leaps upon the mountains and reappears in his
habit as he lived! Nor can we doubt that he lives
indeed. He is no ghost, my friend, but a solid,
shadow-casting man, who may be seeking my life
by reason of his distempered mind."

"It is romance," declared Virgilio, "but
romance of a very grim and painful description.
You are, however, safe enough with me, for I
would gladly shed my blood to save yours."

"Well I know it, rare Virgilio," declared the
other. "But we shall not long impose ourselves
upon your courage and generosity. We have
written to England for Peter Ganns who, by God's
providence, is now in that country and hoped to
visit me in a few months. We have also called
upon Giuseppe Doria to return at once to us.
When he does so I am content to sleep at home
again; but not sooner."

Signor Poggi hastened to order a meal worthy
of the occasion, while his wife, who was also a devoted admirer of the Englishman, prepared apartments. Nothing but delight filled Poggi's mind
at the opportunity to serve his dearest companion.
An ample meal was planned and Jenny helped
her hostess in its preparation.

Poggi drank to the temporal and eternal welfare of his first friend and Albert returned the
compliment. They enjoyed a pleasant meal and
then sat through the June twilight in Virgilio's
rose garden, smelled the fragrance of oleanders
and myrtles in the evening breeze, saw the fireflies
flash their little lamps over dim olive and dark
cypress, and heard the summer thunder growling

genially over the mountain crowns of Campione and Croce.

Mr. Redmayne's niece retired early and Maria Poggi with her, but Virgilio and Albert talked far into the night and smoked many cigars before they slept.

At nine o'clock next morning Mr. Redmayne and Jenny were rowed home again, only to hear that no intruder had broken upon the nightly peace of Villa Pianezzo. Nor did the day bring any news. Once more they repaired to Bellagio before dark, and for three days lived thus. Then there came a telegram from Turin to say that Doria was returning immediately to Como and might soon be expected via Milan; while on the morning that actually brought him to Menaggio, his wife received a brief letter from Mark Brendon. He had found Mr. Ganns and the two would set forth for Italy within a few days.

"It is impossible that we can receive both here," declared Albert; "but we will engage pleasant apartments with dear Signor Bullo at the Hotel Victoria. They are full, or nearly so; but he will find a corner for any friends of mine."

CHAPTER XI

MR. PETER GANNS

MARK BRENDON received with mingled emotions the long letter from Jenny Doria. It awaited him at New Scotland Yard and, as he took it from the rack, his heart leaped before the well-remembered handwriting. The past very seldom arose to shadow Mark's strenuous present; but now, once more, it seemed that Robert Redmayne was coming between him and his annual holiday. He told himself that he had lived down his greatest disappointment and believed that he could now permit his thoughts to dwell on Jenny without feeling much more than the ache of an old wound. Her letter came a week before the recipient proposed to start upon his vacation. He had intended going to Scotland, having no mind for Dartmoor again at present; but it was not his failure, so complete and bewildering, that had barred a return to familiar haunts. Memory made the thought too painful and poignant, so he designed to break new ground and receive fresh impressions.

Then came this unexpected challenge and he hesitated before accepting it. Yet a second reading of the woman's appeal determined him, for Jenny wrote for herself as well as her uncle.

She reminded Brendon of his goodwill and declared how personally she should welcome him and feel safer and more sanguine for his companionship. She also contrived to let him know that she was not particularly happy. The fact seemed implicitly woven into her long letter, though another, less vitally interested in the writer, might have failed to observe it.

Regretting only that Albert Redmayne's friend must be approached and hoping that Mr. Peter Ganns would at least allow him a few days' start, Brendon sought the famous American and found his direction without difficulty. He had already visited New Scotland Yard, where he numbered several acquaintances, and Mark learned that he was stopping at the Grand Hotel in Trafalgar Square. On sending in his name a messenger boy bade Brendon follow to the smoking-room.

His first glance, however, failed to indicate the great man. The smoking-room was nearly empty on this June morning and Mark observed nobody but a young soldier, writing letters, and a white-haired, somewhat corpulent gentleman sitting with his back to the light reading the *Times*. He was clean shaved, with a heavy face modelled to suggest a rhinoceros. The features were large; the nose swollen and a little veined with purple, the eyes hidden behind owl-like spectacles with tortoise-shell rims, and the brow very broad, but not high. From it abundant white hair was brushed straight back.

Brendon extended his glance elsewhere, but the messenger stopped, turned, and departed, while the stout man rose, revealing a massive frame, wide shoulders, and sturdy legs.

"Glad to meet you, Mr. Brendon," he said in a genial voice; then he shook hands, took off his spectacles, and sat down again.

"This is a pleasure I had meant to give myself before I quitted the city," declared the big man. "I've heard about you and I've taken off my hat to you more than once during the war. You might know me, too."

"Everybody in our business knows you, Mr. Ganns. But I've not come hero-worshipping to waste your time. I'm proud you're pleased to see me and it's a great privilege to meet you; but I've looked in this morning about something that won't wait; and your name is the big noise in a letter I received from Italy to-day."

"Is that so? I'm bound for Italy in the fall."

"The question is whether this letter may change your plans and send you there sooner."

The elder stared, took a golden box out of his waistcoat pocket, opened it, tapped it, and helped himself to a pinch of snuff. The habit explained his somewhat misshapen nose. It was tobacco, not alcohol, that lent its exaggerated lustre and hypertrophied outline to that organ.

"I hate changing my itinerary, once made," replied Mr. Ganns. "I'm the most orderly cuss on earth. So far as I know, there's but one man in all Italy is likely to knock my arrangements on the head; and I'll see him, if all's well, in September next."

Brendon produced Jenny's letter.

"The writer is niece of that man," he said and handed the communication to Mr. Ganns.

Peter put on his spectacles again and read slowly. Indeed Mark had never seen a letter read so slowly before. It might have been in some cryptic tongue which Mr. Ganns could only with difficulty translate. Having finished he handed the communication back to Brendon and indicated a desire for silence. Mark lit a cigarette and sat surveying the other from the corner of his eye.

At last the American spoke.

"What about you? Can you go?"

"Yes; I've appealed to my chief and got permission to pick this up again. My holiday's due and I'll go to Italy instead of Scotland. I was in it from the first, you know."

"I do know—I know all about it, from my old pal, Albert Redmayne. He wrote me the most lucid dispatch that ever I read."

"You can go, Mr. Ganns?"

"I must go, boy. Albert wants me."

"Could you get off in a week?"

"A week! To-night."

"To-night, sir! Do you reckon that Mr. Redmayne is in any danger?"

"Don't you?"

"He's forewarned and you see he's taking great precautions."

"Brendon," said Mr. Ganns, "run round and find when the night boat sails from Dover, or Folkestone. We'll reach Paris to-morrow morning, I guess, catch the *Rapide* for Milan, and be at the Lakes next day. You'll find we can do so. Then telegraph to this dame that we start *a week hence.* You take me?"

"You want to get there before we're expected?"

"Exactly."

"Then you do think Mr. Albert Redmayne is in danger?"

"I don't think about it. I know he is. But as this mystery has only just let loose on him and he's got his weather eye lifting, it will be all right, I hope, for a few hours. Meantime we arrive."

He took another pinch of snuff and picked up the *Times.* "Will you lunch with me here in the grillroom at two o'clock?"

"With pleasure, Mr. Ganns."

"Right. And telegraph, right now, that we hope to get off in a week."

Some hours later they met again and over a steak and green peas Brendon reported that the boat train left Victoria at eleven and that the *Rapide* would start from Paris on the following morning at half past six.

"We reach Bevano some time after noon next day," he said, "and can either go on to Milan and then come back to Como and travel by boat to Menaggio, where Mr. Redmayne lives, or else leave the train at Bevano, take steamer on Maggiore, cross to Lugano, and cross again to Como. That way we land right at Menaggio. There's not much in it for time."

"We'll go that way, then, and I'll see the Lakes."

Peter Ganns spoke little while he partook of a
light meal. He picked a fried sole and drank two
glasses of white wine. Then he ate a dish of
green peas and compared their virtues with
green corn. He enjoyed the spectacle of Brendon's hearty appetite and bewailed his inability
to join him in red meat and a pint of Burton.

"Lucky dog," he said. "When I was young I
did the like. I love food. You need never fear
any rough stuff in business as long as you can eat
beef and drink beer. But nowadays, I don't go
into the rough stuff—too old and fat."

"Of course not, sir. You've done your bit.
Nobody on your side has been at closer quarters
with the big crooks, or heard their guns oftener."

"That's true."

Mr. Ganns held up his left hand, which was de-
formed and had lost the third and little finger.

"The last shot that Billy Benyon ever fired.
A great man—Billy. I'll never see his like
again."

"The Boston murderer? A genius!"

"He was. A marvellous brain. When I sent
him to the chair it was like a Bushman killing an
elephant."

"You're sorry for the under dog sometimes, I
expect?"

"Not always; but now and again I like the bull
to get the toreador, and the savage to eat the
missionary."

They entered the smoking-room presently and
then Brendon, very much to his surprise, heard
an astonishing lecture which left him under the

emotions of a fourth-form schoolboy after an interview with his head master.

Mr. Ganns ordered coffee, took snuff, and bade Mark listen and not interrupt.

"We're going into this thing together and I want you to get a clear hunch on it," he began, "because at present you have not. I don't say we shall see it through; but if we do, the credit's going to be yours, not mine. We'll come to the Redmayne business in a minute. But first let us have a look at Mr. Mark Brendon, if it won't bore you stiff."

The other laughed.

"He's not a very impressive object, so far as this case is concerned, Mr. Ganns."

"He is not," admitted Peter genially. "Quite the reverse, in fact. And his poor showing has puzzled Mr. Brendon a good bit, and some of his superior officers also. So let us examine the situation from that angle before we get up against the problem itself."

He stirred his coffee, poured a thimbleful of cognac into it, sipped it, and then slid into a comfortable position in his armchair, put his big hands into his trousers pockets, and regarded Mark with a steady and unblinking stare. His eyes were pale blue, deeply set and small, but still of a keen brilliancy.

"You're a detective inspector of Scotland Yard," continued Ganns, "and Scotland Yard is still the high-water mark of police organization in the world. The Central Bureau in New York is pretty close up, and I've nothing but admiration for the French and Italian Secret Services; but the fact remains: The Yard is first; and you've won, and fairly won your place there. That's a big thing and you didn't get it without some work and some luck, Brendon. But now— this Redmayne racket. You were right on the spot, hit the trail before it was cold, had everything to help you that heart of man could wish for; yet a guy who had joined the force only a week before could have done no worse. In a word, your conduct of the affair don't square with your reputation. Your dope never cut any ice from the start. And why? Because, without a doubt, you had a theory and got lost in it."

"Don't think that. I never had a theory."

"Is that so? Then failure lies somewhere else. The hopeless way you bitched up this thing interests me quite a lot. Remember that I know the case inside out and I'm not talking through my hat. So now let's see how and why you barked your shins so bad.

"Now, Mark, take a cinema show and consider it. Perhaps it's going to throw some light for you. A cinema film presents two entirely different achievements. It presents ten for that matter; but we'll take just two. It shows you a white sheet with a light thrown on it; it passes the light through a series of stains and shadows and the stains are magnified by lenses before they reach the screen. A most elaborate mechanism, you see, but the spectator never thinks about all that, because the machine produces an appeal to another part of his mind altogether. He forgets sheet, lantern, film, and all they are doing, in the illusion which they create.

"We accept the convention of the moving picture, the light and darkness, the tones and half tones, because these moving stains and shadows take the shape of familiar objects and tell a coherent story, showing life in action. But we know, subconsciously, all the time that it is merely an imitation of reality, as in the case of a picture, a novel, or a stage play. Certain ingenious applications of science and art combined have created the appearance of truth and told a story. Well, in the Redmayne case, certain ingenious operations have combined to tell you a story; and you have found yourself so interested in the yarn that you have quite overlooked the mechanism. But the mechanism should have been the first consideration, and the conjurers, by distracting your attention from it, did just what they were out to do. Let us take a look at the mechanism, my son, and see where the archcrooks behind this thing bluffed you."

Brendon did not hide his emotion, but kept silence while Mr. Ganns helped himself to a pinch of snuff.

"Now the little I've done in the world," he continued, "is thanks not so much to the deductive mind we hear such a lot about, but to the synthetic mind. The linking up of facts has been my strong suit. That's the backbone of success; and where facts can't be linked up, then failure is usually the result. I never waste one moment on a theory until I've got a tough skeleton of facts back of it. It was up to you to hunt facts, Mark; and you didn't hunt facts."

"I had an encyclopedia of facts."

"Granted. But your encyclopedia began at the letter 'B,' instead of the letter 'A.' We'll turn to that in a minute."

"My facts, such as they were, cannot be denied," argued Brendon, a little aggrieved. "They are cast-iron. My eyes and observation are trained to be exact and jealous of facts. No amount of synthesis can prevent two and one from being three, Ganns."

"On the contrary, two and one may be twenty-one, or twelve, or a half. Why jump to any conclusion? You had facts; but you did not have all the available facts—or anything like all. You tried to put on the roof before the walls were up; and, what's more, a great many of your 'cast-iron facts' were no facts at all."

"What were they then?"

"Elaborate and deliberate fictions, Mark."

At this challenge Brendon felt a hot wave of colour mount his cheek; but the other was far too generous and genial a spirit ever to seek any triumph over a younger man. Neither did Brendon feel angry with Mr. Ganns even though his remarks were provocative enough. He was angry with himself. Peter, however, knew his power. He read the detective's mind like a book and well understood that, both by his position and rank, Mark must be far too good a man to chafe at the criticism of a better than himself. He explained.

"Where I've got the pull on you, for the minute, is merely because I've been in the world a few years longer. A time's coming when you'll talk to your juniors as I can talk to you; and they'll listen, with all proper respect and attention, as you are listening. When you are my age, you'll command that perfect confidence which I command. Folks can't trust youth all the way; but you'll win to it; and believe me, in our business, there's no greater asset than the power to command absolute trust. You can't pretend to that power if you haven't got it. Human nature damn soon sees through you, if you're pretending what you don't command. But I'm playing straight across the board, Mark, as my custom is, and I know you are too sane and ambitious a lad to let false pride or self-assurance resent my calling you an ass over this thing."

"Prove it, Ganns, and I'll be the first to climb down. I know I've been an ass for that matter—knew it long ago," confessed Brendon.

"Yes, I'll prove it—that's easy. But what's going to be harder is to find out why you've been an ass. You've no right to be an ass. It's unlike your record and unlike your looks and your general make-up of mind. I mostly read a strange man's brain through his eyes; and your eyes do you justice. So perhaps you'll tell me presently where you went off your rocker. Or perhaps you don't know and I shall have to tell you—when I find the nigger in the woodpile. Now take a look round, and its dollars to doughnuts you'll begin to see the light."

He paused again, applied himself to his gold box, and then proceeded.

"To put it bluntly and drop everybody else but you out of it, for the minute, you went on false assumption from the kick-off, Brendon. To start wrong was not strange. I should have done exactly the same and nobody outside a detective story would have done differently; but to go on wrong—to pile false assumption on false assumption in face of your own reasoning powers and native wits—that strikes me as a very curious catastrophe."

"But you can't get away from facts."

"Nothing easier, surely. You said good-bye to facts when you left Princetown. You don't know the facts any more than I do—or anybody but those responsible for the appearances. You have assumed that the phenomena observed by yourself and reported by other professionals and various members of the public were facts, whereas a little solid thinking must have convinced you that they couldn't be. You didn't give your reason a chance, Mark.

"Now follow me and be honest. You say certain things have happened. I say they didn't, for the very sound reason that they couldn't. I am not going to tell you the truth, because I am a long way from that myself, and I dare say you'll strike it yet before I do; but I am going to prove that a good few things you think are true can't be —that events you take for granted never happened at all. We've got but few senses and they are easily deluded. In fact a man's a darned

clumsy box of tricks at his best and I wouldn't
swap a hill of beans for what my senses can
assure me; but, as a wise man says, 'Art is with
us to save us from too much truth,' so I say
'Reason is with us to save us from too much evidence of our senses—often false.'

"Now see how reason bears on the evidence of
Robert Redmayne and his trick acts since first
he disappeared. A thing occurs and there are
only certain ways—very limited in number—to
explain it. Either Robert Redmayne killed
Michael Pendean, or else he did not. And if he
did, he was sane or insane at the time. That
much can't be denied and is granted. If he was
sane, he committed the murder with a motive;
and pretty careful inquiry proves that no motive
existed. I attach no importance to words, no
matter who may utter them, and the fact that Mrs.
Pendean herself said that her husband and her
uncle were the best of friends don't weigh; but
the fact that Robert Redmayne stopped at
Princetown with the Pendeans for over a week in
friendship and asked them to Paignton, is of
some weight. I'm inclined to believe that Redmayne was perfectly friendly with Michael Pendean up to the time of the latter's disappearance,
and that there was no shadow of motive to explain why Redmayne did in his brother-in-law.
Then, assuming him to be sane, he would not have
committed such a murder. The alternative is
that he was mad at the time and did homicide on
Pendean while out of his mind.

"But what happens to a madman after a crime

of this sort? Does he get off with it and wander over Europe as a free man for a year? Granted the resources of maniacal cunning and all the rest of it, was it ever heard that a lunatic went at large as this man did, and laughed at Scotland Yard's attempt to run him down and capture him? Is it reasonable that he runs away with a corpse, disposes of it safely, returns to his lodgings, makes a meal, and then, in broad daylight, vanishes off the face of the earth for six months, presently to reappear, hoodwink fresh people, and commit another crime? Once more he scorns law and order, vanishes for another six months, and now flaunts his red waistcoat and red mustache in Italy at his remaining brother's door. No, Mark, the man responsible for these impossible things isn't mad. And that brings me back to my preliminary alternative.

"I said just now, 'Either Robert Redmayne killed Michael Pendean, or else he did not.' And we may add that either Robert Redmayne killed Bendigo Redmayne or else he did not. But we'll stick to the first proposition for the moment. And the next question you must ask yourself is this. 'Did Robert Redmayne kill Michael Pendean?' That's where your 'facts,' as you call them, begin to sag a bit, my son. There's only one sure and certain way of knowing that a man is dead; and that is by seeing his body and convincing the law, by the testimony of those who knew the man in life, that the corpse belongs to him and nobody else."

"Good God! You think——"

"I think nothing. I want you to think. This is your funeral—so far; but I want you to come out like the sun from behind a cloud and surprise us yet. Just grasp that matters couldn't have happened as you supposed, and go on from there. Remember, incidentally, that you are quite unable to swear that either Pendean or Bendigo Redmayne is dead at all. They may both be just as much alive as we are. Chew it over. This is a very pretty thing and I believe we're up against some great rascals; but I don't even know that yet for sure. I can see many points that are vital which you are more likely to clear than I. You've been badly handicapped, for reasons I have yet to find out; but if you think over what I told you and look into your brain-pan without prejudice, maybe you'll begin to see them yourself."

"It's sporting of you to suggest that, but I can't offer any such excuse," answered Brendon thoughtfully. "Never did a man go into a case with less handicap. I even had peculiar incentives to make good. I came into it on the top of the tide with everything under my hands. No—what you've said throws rather too bright a light on the truth. Everything looked so straightforward that I never thought the appearances hid an utterly different reality. Now I know they probably did."

"That's what I guess. Somebody palmed a marked card on you, Brendon; and you took it like a lamb. We all have in our time—even the smartest of us. Gaboriau says somewhere,

'Above all, regard with supreme suspicion that which seems probable and begin always by believing what seems incredible.' French exaggeration, of course; but there's truth in it. The obvious always makes me uncomfortable. If a thing is jumping just the way that suits you, distrust it at once. That holds of life as well as business.''

They chatted for half an hour and Mr. Ganns attained his object, which was to fling his companion back to the beginning of the whole problem that had brought them together. He desired that Mark should travel the ground again with an open mind and all preconceptions put behind him.

"To-night, in the train," said Peter, "I shall ask you to give me your version of the case from the moment that Mrs. Pendean invited you to take it up—or from earlier still, if you had to do with any of the people before the catastrophe. I want the whole yarn again from your angle; and after what I've told you, it may be that, as you retrace every incident, light may flash that wasn't there before."

"It is very probable indeed," admitted Mark. Then his generous nature prompted him to praise the elder.

"You're a big man, Peter Ganns, and you've said things to-day that no doubt were elementary to you, but mean a lot to me. You've made me feel mighty small—which I wouldn't own to anybody else; but you know that much without my telling you. I only differ from you on one point and that is the sequel. If this thing is ever cleared, you'll be responsible for clearing it, and I shall see you get the credit."

The other laughed and flung snuff into his purple nostrils.

"Nonsense, nonsense! I'm a back number—almost out of the game now—virtually retired to take my ease and follow my hobbies. This is nothing to do with me. I'm only going to watch you."

"A detective's hobby is generally his old business," said Mark, and Mr. Ganns admitted it. "Literature and crime, nice things to eat and drink, snuff and acrostics—these serve to fill my leisure and represent my vices and virtues," he confessed.

"Each has its appointed place in my life; and now I'm adding travel. I've wanted to see Europe once again before I went into my shell for good; and to enjoy the society of my dear friend, Albert Redmayne, visit his home, and hear his bland and childlike wisdom once more.

"The only shadow thrown by a devoted friendship, Brendon, is the knowledge that it must some day come to an end. And when I say 'good-bye' to the old bookworm I shall know that we are little likely to meet again. Yet who would deny himself the glory of friendship, before the menace that it must sooner or later finish? A close amity and understanding, a discovery of kindred spirits, is among the most precious experiences within the reach of mankind. Love, no doubt, proves a more glorious adventure still; but lightning lurks near the rosy chariot of love, my lad, and we who win the ineffable gift must not whine if the full price has to be paid. For me, cool friendship!''

He chattered amiably and Mark guessed that on the simple and human side Mr. Ganns found himself much at one with his friend, Albert Redmayne. Peter's philosophy seemed to Brendon of a very mild quality, and he wondered how a man who looked at human nature in a spirit so hopeful, if not credulous, should yet own those extraordinary gifts the American possessed. Upon these, surely, and not his genial and elemental faith, was his fame founded.

CHAPTER XII

PETER TAKES THE HELM

As the detectives travelled through night-hidden Kent and presently boarded the packet for Boulogne, Mark Brendon told his story with every detail for the benefit of Mr. Ganns. Before doing so he reread his own notes and was able to set each incident of the case very clearly and copiously before the older man. Peter never once interrupted him, and, at the conclusion of the narrative, complimented Mark on the recital.

"The moving picture is bright but not comprehensive," he said, returning to a former analogy. "In fact I'm beginning to see already that, no matter what we get at the end of the reel, there are still a few preliminary scenes that should come in at the beginning."

"I've begun at the beginning, Mr. Ganns."

But Peter shook his head.

"Half the battle is to know the beginning of a case. I'll almost go so far as to say that, given the real beginning, the end should be assured. You've not begun at the beginning of the Redmayne tangle, Mark. If you had, the clue to this labyrinth might be in your hands to-day. The more I hear and the more I think, the more firmly am I convinced that the truth we are out to find

214

can only be discovered by a deal of hard digging in past times. There is a lot of spade work demanded and you, or I, may have to return to England to do it—unless we can get the information without the labour. But I've no reason to count on any luck of that sort.''

''I should like to know the nature of the ground I failed to cover,'' said Brendon; but Peter was not disposed to enlighten him at present.

''Needn't bother yet,'' he said. ''Now talk about yourself and give the case a rest.''

They chatted until the dawn, by which time their train had reached Paris, and an hour or two later they were on their way to Italy.

Mr. Ganns had determined to cross the Lakes and arrive unexpectedly at Menaggio. He had now turned his mind once more to the problem before him and spoke but little. He sat with his notebook open and made an occasional entry as he pursued his thoughts. Mark read newspapers and presently handed a page to Mr. Ganns.

''What you said about acrostics interested me,'' he began. ''Here's one and I've been trying to guess it for an hour. No doubt it ought to be easy; but I expect there's a catch. Wonder if it will puzzle you.''

Peter smiled and dropped his notebook.

''Acrostics are a habit of mind,'' he said. ''You grow to think acrostically and be up to all the tricks of the trade. You soon get wise to the way that people think who make them; and then you'll find they all think alike and all try to hoodwink you along the same lines. If you tempt me on to acrostics, you'll soon wish you had not."

Mark pointed to the puzzle.

"Try that," he said. "I can't make head or tail of it; yet I dare say you'll thrash it out if you've got the acrostic mind."

Mr. Ganns cast his eye over the puzzle. It ran thus:

> When to the North you go,
> The folk shall greet you so.
>
> .   .   .   .
>
> 1. Upright and light and Source of Light
> 2. And Source of Light, reversed, are plain.
> 3. A term of scorn comes into sight
>   And Source of Light, reversed again.

The American regarded the problem for a minute in silence, then smiled and handed the paper back to Brendon.

"Quite neat, in its little conventional way," he said. "It's on the regular English pattern. Our acrostics are a trifle smarter, but all run into one form. The great acrostic writer isn't born. If acrostics were as big a thing as chess, then we should have masters who would produce masterpieces."

"But this one—d'you see it?"

"Milk for babes, Mark."

Mr. Ganns turned to his notebook, wrote swiftly into it, tore out the page, and handed the solution to his companion.

Brendon read:

G   O   D
Omega   Alph   A
D   O   G

"If you know Knut Hamsun's stories, then you guess it instantly. If not, you might possibly be bothered," he said, while Brendon stared.

"There are two ways with acrostics," continued Peter, full of animation, "the first is to make lights so difficult that they turn your hair grey till you've got them, the second—just traps—perhaps three perfectly sound answers to the same light, but the second just a shade sounder than the first, and the third a shade sounder than either of the others."

"Who makes acrostics like that?"

"Nobody. Life's too short; but if I devoted a year to a perfect acrostic, you bet your life it would take my fellow creatures a year to guess it. The same with cryptography, which we've both run up against, no doubt, in course of business. Cyphers are mostly crude; but I've often thought what a right down beauty it might be possible to make, given a little pains. The detective story writers make very good ones sometimes; but then the smart man, who wipes everybody's eyes, always gets 'em—by pulling down just the right book from the villain's library. My cryptograph won't depend on books."

Peter chattered on; then he suddenly stopped and turned to his notes again.

He looked up presently.

"The hard thing before us is this," he said, "to get into touch with Robert Redmayne, or his ghost. There are two sorts of ghost, Mark; the real thing—in which you don't believe and concerning which I hold a watching brief; and the manufactured article. Now the manufactured article can be quite as useful to the bulls as the crooks."

"You believe in ghosts!"

"I didn't say so. But I keep an open mind. I've heard some funny things from men whose word could be relied upon."

"If this is a ghost, that's a way out, of course; but in that case why are you frightened for Albert Redmayne's life?"

"I don't say he's a ghost and of course I don't think he's a ghost; but——"

He broke off and changed the subject.

"What I'm doing is to compare your verbal statement with Mr. Redmayne's written communication," he said, patting his book. "My old friend goes back a long way farther than you would, because he knows a lot more than you did. It's all here. I've got a regard for my eyes, so I had it typed. You'd better read it, however. You'll find the story of Robert Redmayne from childhood and the story of the girl, his niece, and of her dead father. Mrs. Doria's father was a rough customer—scorpions to Robert's whips apparently—a man a bit out of the common; yet he never came to open clash with the law. You never thought of Robert's dead brother, Henry,

did you? But you'd be surprised how we can get
at character and explain contradictions by study-
ing the different members of a family.''

"I shall like to read the report."

"It's valuable to us, because written without
prejudice. That's where it beats your very lucid
account, Mark. There was something running
through your story, like a thread of silk in
cotton, that you won't find here. It challenged
me from the jump, my boy, and I'm inclined to
think that in that thread of silk I shall just find
the reason of your failure, before I've wound it
up."

"I don't understand you, Ganns."

"You wouldn't—not yet. But we'll change the
metaphor. We'll say there was a red herring
drawn across the trail, and that you took the bait
and, having started right enough, presently for-
sook the right scent for the wrong."

"Puzzle—to find the red herring," said Mark.
Mr. Ganns smiled.

"I think I've found it," he replied. "But on
the other hand, perhaps I haven't. In twenty-
four hours I shall know. I hope I'm right—for
your sake. If I am, then you are discharged
without a stain on your character; if I'm not,
then the case is black against you."

Brendon made no reply. Neither his conscience nor his wit threw any light on the point.
Then Peter, turning to his notes, touched on a
minor incident and showed the other that it admitted of a doubt.

"D'you remember the night you left 'Crow's

Nest' after your first visit? On the way back
to Dartmouth you suddenly saw Robert Redmayne standing by a gate; and when the moonlight revealed you to him, he leaped away and
disappeared into the trees. Why?''

"He knew me."

"How?"

"We had met at Princetown and we had spoken
together for some minutes by the pool in Foggintor Quarry, where I was fishing."

"That's right. But he didn't know who you
were then. Even if he'd remembered meeting
you six months before in the dusk at Foggintor,
why should he think you were a man who was
hunting him?"

Mark reflected.

"That's true," he said. "Probably he'd have
bolted from anybody that night, not wishing to be
seen."

"I only raise the question. Of course it is
easily explained on a general assumption that
Redmayne knew every man's hand was against
him. He would naturally, in his hunted state, fly
the near approach of a man."

"Probably he didn't remember me."

"Probably; but there are possibilities about
the action. He might have been warned against
you."

"There was nobody to warn him. He had not
yet seen his niece, nor spoken with her. Who else
could have warned him—except Bendigo Redmayne himself?"

Peter did not pursue the subject. He shut his

book, yawned, took snuff, and declared himself
ready for a meal. The long day passed and both
men turned in early and slept till daybreak.

Before noon they had left Baveno on a steamer
and were crossing the blue depths of Maggiore.
Brendon had never seen the Italian lakes before
and he fell silent in the presence of such beauty;
nor did Mr. Ganns desire to talk. They sat together and watched the panorama unfold, the
hills and gorges, the glory of the light over earth
and water, the presence of man, his little homes
upon the mountains, his little barques upon the
lake.

At Luino they left the steamer and proceeded
to Tresa. Beside the railroad, on this brief in-
stalment of the journey, there stood lofty pali-
sades of close wire netting hung with bells. Peter,
who had travelled here twenty years earlier, explained that they were erected as a safeguard
against the eternal smuggling between Switzerland and Italy.

" 'Only man is vile' in fact," he concluded and
woke a passing wave of bitterness in his companion's spirit.

"And our life is concerned with his vileness,"
Mark answered. "I hate myself sometimes and
wish I was a grocer or a linen draper or even a
soldier or sailor. It's degrading to let your life's
work depend on the wickedness of your fellow
creatures, Ganns. I hope a time is coming when
our craft will be as obsolete as bows and arrows."

The elder laughed.

"What does Goethe say somewhere?" he asked.

"That if man endures for a million years, he'll never lack obstacles to give him trouble, or the pressure of need to make him conquer them. Then there's Montaigne—you ought to read Montaigne—wisest of men. He'll tell you that human wisdom has never reached the perfection of conduct that itself prescribes; and could it arrive there, it would still dictate to itself others beyond. In a word, the world will never be short of crooks while human nature lasts, nor yet of men trained to lay them by the heels. Crime will continue, in some form or other, as long as men do; and as the criminal gets cleverer, so must we."

"I think better of human nature," answered Mark and his friend applauded him.

"Quite right, my boy—at your age," he said.

They wound over Lugano and came in evening light to its northern shore. Then once more they took train, climbed aloft, and fell at last to Menaggio on Como's brink.

"Now," said Peter, "I guess we'll leave our traps here and beat it to Villa Pianezzo right away. We'll scare the old boy a bit, but can tell him things all fell right and so we found that we could jog along a week before we thought to do so. Not a word that I think him to be in danger."

Within twenty minutes their one-horse vehicle had reached Mr. Redmayne's modest home and they found three persons just about to take an evening meal. Simultaneously there appeared Mr. Redmayne, his niece, and Giuseppe Doria; and while Albert, Italian fashion, embraced Mr. Ganns and planted a kiss upon his cheek, Jenny

greeted Mark Brendon and he looked once more
into her eyes.

There had come new experiences to her and
they did not fail of the man's observation. She
smiled indeed and flushed and proclaimed her
wonder and admiration at the speed which had
brought him across Europe to her uncle's succour; but even in her animation and excitement
the new expression persisted. It set Mark's heart
throbbing vigorously and told him that perchance
he might yet be useful to her. For there hung a
shadow of melancholy on Jenny's face her smiles
could not dispel.

Doria held back a little while his wife welcomed
her uncle's friend; then he came forward, declared his pleasure at meeting Mark again and
his belief that time would soon reveal the truth
and set a period to the sinister story of the
wanderer.

Mr. Redmayne was overjoyed at seeing Ganns
and quite forgot the object of his visit in the
pleasure of receiving him.

"It has been my last and abiding ambition to
introduce you to Virgilio Poggi, dear Peter, so
that you, he and I may sit together, hear each
other's voices and look into each other's eyes.
And now this will happen. Thus the unhappy
spirit who wanders upon the hills has unconsciously accomplished a beautiful thing."

Jenny and Assunta had hastily prepared for
the visitors and now all sat at supper and Brendon learned how rooms were already taken for
him and Mr. Ganns at the Hotel Victoria.

"That's as may be," he declared to Doria's wife. "You will find, I think, that Mr. Ganns is going to stop here. He takes the lead in this affair. Indeed there was no great reason why I should have intruded again, where I have failed so often."

Jenny looked at him softly.

"I am very thankful you have come," she said —in a whisper for his ear alone.

"Then I am very thankful too," he replied.

After a cheerful meal Peter absolutely declined to cross Como and visit Signor Poggi on the instant.

"I've had enough of your lakes for one day, Albert," he announced, "and I want to talk business and get a rough, general idea of what more is known than Mark and I already know. Now what has happened since you wrote, Mrs. Doria?"

"Tell them, Giuseppe," directed Mr. Redmayne.

"Your gift—the gold box—take a pinch," said Peter holding out his snuff to the old bookworm; but the master of Villa Pianezzo refused and lighted a cigar.

"I will have smoke rather than dust, my precious Peter," he said.

"The man has been seen twice since you heard from my wife," began Doria. "Once I met him face to face on the hill, where I walked alone to reflect on my own affairs; and once—the night before last—he came here. Happily Mr. Redmayne's room overlooks the lake and the garden

walls are high, so he could not reach it; but the
bedroom of Mr. Redmayne's man, Ernesto, is upon
the side that stands up to the road.

"Robert Redmayne came at two o'clock, flung
pebbles at the window, wakened Ernesto, and demanded to be let in to see his brother. But the
Italian had been warned exactly what to say and
do if such a thing happened. He speaks English
well and told the unfortunate man that he must
appear by day. Ernesto then mentioned a certain
place, a mile from here in a secluded valley—a
little bridge that spans a stream—and directed
Robert to await his brother at that spot on the
following day at noon. This my Uncle Alberto
had already planned in the event of his brother
reappearing.

"Having heard this, the red man departed without more words and your friend, greatly cour-
ageous, kept the appointment that he had made,
taking only me with him. We were there before
midday and waited until after two o'clock. But
nobody came to us and we saw neither man nor
woman.

"For my own part I feel very certain that
Robert Redmayne was hidden near at hand, and
that he would have come out quickly enough had
his brother been alone; but of course Uncle Alberto would not go alone, and we would not have
allowed him to do so in any case."

Peter listened intently to these words.

"And what of your meeting with him?" he
asked.

"That was clearly an accident on Robert Red-

mayne's part. I happened to be walking, deep in
thought near the spot where my wife first saw him,
and, rounding a corner, I suddenly confronted the
man sitting on a rock by the path. He started at
my footfall, looked up, clearly recognized me,
hesitated, and then leaped into the bushes. I endeavoured to follow but he distanced me. He is
harbouring aloft there and may be in touch with
some charcoal burner above in the mountains.
He was strong and agile and moved swiftly."

"How was he dressed?"

"Exactly as I saw him dressed at 'Crow's
Nest' when Mr. Bendigo Redmayne disappeared."

"I should like to know his tailor," said Mr.
Ganns. "That's a useful suit he wears."

Then he asked a question that seemed to bear
but little on the subject.

"Plenty of smugglers in the mountains I suppose?"

"Plenty," answered Giuseppe, "and my heart
is with them."

"They dodge the customs officers and get across
the frontier by night sometimes I dare say?"

"If I stop here long enough, I shall be better
in a position to know," replied the other cheerfully. "My heart, Signor Ganns, is with these
boys. They are a brave and valiant people and
their lives are very dangerous and thrilling and
interesting. They are heroes and not villains at
all. Our woman, Assunta, is the widow of a free
trader. She has good friends among them."

"Now, Peter, tell us all that is in your mind,"

urged Mr. Redmayne as he poured out five little glasses of golden liqueur. "You hold that I go in some peril from this unhappy man?"

"I do think so, Albert. And as to my mind, it is not by any means made up. You say, 'Catch Robert Redmayne first and decide afterwards.' Yes; but I will tell you an interesting thing. We are not going to catch Robert Redmayne."

"You throw up the sponge, signor?" asked Giuseppe in astonishment.

"Surely you have caught everybody you ever tried to catch, Peter?" asked Albert.

"There is a reason why I shall not catch him," replied Ganns, sipping from his little Venetian glass.

"Can it be that you think him not a man at all but a ghost, Mr. Ganns?" asked Jenny, round-eyed.

"He has already suggested a ghost," said Mark, "but there are different sorts of ghosts, Mrs. Doria. I see that, too. There are ghosts of flesh and blood."

"If he is a ghost, he is a very solid one indeed," declared Doria.

"He is," admitted Peter. "And yet none the less a ghost in my opinion. Now let us generalize. It needn't be a sound maxim to seek the person who benefits by a crime—not always—for often enough the actual legatee of a murdered man may have had nothing whatever to do with his death. Albert, for example, will inherit Mr. Bendigo Redmayne's estate when leave to assume his death is granted by the law; and Mrs. Doria will inherit her late husband's estate in due course. But it isn't suggested that your wife killed her first husband, Signor Doria; and it isn't suggested that my friend here killed his brother.

"None the less, it's a safe question to ask what a suspected man gains by his crime. And, if we put that question, we find that Robert Redmayne gained nothing whatever by killing Michael Pendean—nothing, that is, but the satisfaction of a sudden, ovepowering lust to do so. Pendean's murder made Redmayne a vagabond, deprived him of his income and resources, set every man's hand against him and left him a wanderer haunted by the gallows. Yet, while he evaded the law in a manner that can only be called miraculous, he made no attempt to avert supicion from himself. On the contrary he courted suspicion, took his victim to Berry Head on a motor bicycle and did a thousand things which defiantly proclaim him a lunatic—but for one overmastering fact. A lunatic must have been caught: he was not.

"He vanishes from Paignton, to reappear at 'Crow's Nest'; he takes another life; he apparently commits another senseless murder on the person of his own brother and once more disappears, leaving not a clue. Now, in face of these absurdities, we have a right to brush aside the apparent facts and ask ourselves a very vital question. What is that question, Signor Doria?"

"It is one I have already asked myself," replied Giuseppe. "It is one I have asked my wife. It is a question, however, which I cannot answer, because I do not know enough. There is nobody

in the world who knows enough—unless it be
Robert Redmayne.''

Ganns nodded and took snuff.

"Good," he said.

"But what is the question?" asked Albert Redmayne. "What is the question Giuseppe puts to
himself and, you put to yourself, Peter? We who
are not so clever do not see the question."

"The question, my friend, is this: Did Robert
Redmayne murder Michael Pendean and Bendigo
Redmayne? And you can ask yourself a still
more vital question: Are these two men dead at
all?"

Jenny shivered violently. She put out her
hand instinctively and it clutched Mark Brendon's
arm where he sat next to her. He looked at her
and saw that her eyes were fixed with strange
doubt and horror upon Doria; while the Italian
himself showed a considerable amount of surprise
at Peter's conclusion.

"Corpo di Bacco! Then——" he asked.

"Then we may be said to enlarge the scope of
the inquiry a good deal," answered Mr. Ganns
mildly. He turned to Jenny.

"This is calculated to flutter you, young lady,
when you think of your second marriage," he
said. "But we're not asserting anything; we're
only just having a friendly chat. Facts are what
we want; and if the fact is that Robert Redmayne
didn't kill Michael Pendean, that doesn't mean
for a moment that Mr. Pendean isn't dead. You
must not let theories frighten you now, since you
certainly did not allow them to do so in the past."

"More than ever it is necessary that my unhappy brother should be secured," declared Albert. "It is interesting to remember," he added, "that poor Bendigo first thought he had to do with a ghost when the arrival of his brother was reported to him. He was very superstitious, as sailors often are, and not until Jenny had seen and spoken with her uncle, did Bendigo believe that a living man wanted to see him."

"The fact that it was actually Robert Redmayne and no ghost is proved by that incident, Ganns," added Mark Brendon. "That the man who came to 'Crow's Nest' was in truth Robert Redmayne we can rest assured through Mrs. Doria, who knew her uncle exceedingly well. It only remains to prove with equal certainty that the wanderer here is Redmayne, and one can feel very little question that he is. It is of course marvellous that he escaped discovery and arrest; but it may not be as marvellous as it seems. Stranger things have happened. And who else could it be in any case?"

"That reminds me," replied Ganns. "There has been mention made of Mr. Bendigo's log. He kept a careful diary—so it was reported. I should like to have that book, Albert, for in your statement you tell me that you preserved it."

"I did and it is here," replied his friend. "That and dear Bendigo's 'Bible,' as I call it— a copy of 'Moby Dick'—I brought away. As yet I have not consulted the diary—it was too intimate and distressed me. But I was looking forward to doing so."

"The parcel containing both books is in a drawer in the library. I'll get them," said Jenny. She left the apartment where they sat overlooking the lake and returned immediately with a parcel wrapped in brown paper.

"Why do you need this, Peter?" asked Albert, and while he was satisfied with the reply, Brendon was not.

"It's always interesting to get a thing from every angle," answered Mr. Ganns. "Your brother may have something to tell us."

But whether Bendigo's diary might have proved valuable remained a matter of doubt, for when Jenny opened the parcel, it was not there. A blank book and the famous novel were all the parcel contained.

"But I packed it myself," said Mr. Redmayne. "The diary was bound exactly as this blank volume is bound, yet it is certain that I made no mistake, for I opened my brother's log and read a page or two before completing the parcel."

"He had bought a new diary only the last time he was in Dartmouth," said Doria. "I remember the incident. I asked him what he was going to put into the book, and he said that his log was just running out and he needed a new volume."

"You are sure that you did not mistake the old, full book for the new, empty one, Albert?" asked his friend.

"I cannot be positive, of course, but I feel no shadow of doubt in my own mind."

"Then the one has been substituted for the

other by somebody else. That is a very interesting fact, if true."

"Impossible," declared Jenny. "There was nobody to do such a thing, Mr. Ganns. Who could have felt any interest in poor Uncle Bendigo's diary but ourselves?"

Mr. Ganns considered.

"The answer to that question might save us a very great deal of trouble," he said. "But there may be no answer. Your uncle may be mistaken. On the other hand I have never known him to be mistaken over any question involving a book."

He took up the empty volume and turned its pages; then Brendon declared they must be going.

"I'm afraid we're keeping Mr. Redmayne out of bed, Ganns," he hinted. "Our kits have already been sent to the hotel and as we've got a mile to walk, we'd better be moving. Are you never sleepy?"

He turned to Jenny.

"I don't believe he has closed his eyes since we left England, Mrs. Doria."

But Peter did not laugh: he appeared to be deep in thought. Suddenly he spoke and surprised them.

"I'm afraid you're going to find me the sort of friend that sticketh closer than a brother, Albert. In a word, somebody must go to the hotel and bring back my travelling grip, for I'm not going to lose sight of you again till we've got this thing straightened out."

Mr. Redmayne was delighted.

"How like you, Peter—how typical of your attitude! You shall not leave me, dear friend. You shall sleep in the apartment next my own. It contains many books, but there shall be my great couch moved from my own bedroom and set up there in half an hour. It is as comfortable as a bed."

He turned to his niece.

"Seek Assunta and Ernesto and set the apartment in order for Mr. Ganns, Jenny; and you, Giuseppe, will take Mr. Brendon to the Hotel Victoria and bring back Peter's luggage."

Jenny hastened to do her uncle's bidding, while Brendon made his farewell and promised to return at an early hour on the following morning.

"My plans for to-morrow," said Peter, "subject to Mark's approval, are these. I suggest that Signor Doria should take Brendon to the scene in the hills where Robert Redmayne appeared; while, by her leave, I have a talk with Mrs. Jenny here. I'm going to run her over a bit of the past and she must be brave and give me all her attention."

He started and listened, his ear cocked toward the lake.

"What's that shindy?" he asked. "Sounds like distant cannon."

Doria laughed.

"Only the summer thunder on the mountains, signor," he answered.

CHAPTER XIII

THE SUDDEN RETURN TO ENGLAND

A sucessful detective needs, above all else, the power to see both sides of any problem as it affects those involved in it. Nine times out of ten there is but one side; yet men have often gone to the gallows because their fellow men failed in this particular—followed the line of least resistance and pursued the obvious and patent conclusions to an end only logical upon a false premise.

Peter Ganns did not lack this perspicuity. It was visible in his big face to any student of physiognomy. He smiled with his mouth, but his eyes were grave—never ironical, never satirical, but always set in a stern, not unkindly expression. They were watchful yet tolerant—the eyes of one versed in the weakness as well as the nobility of human nature. He could measure the average, modest intelligence of his fellow creatures as well as estimate the heights of genius to which man's intellect may sometimes attain. His own unusual powers, centred in sound judgment of character and wide experience of the human comedy, had set the seal in his eyes while graving something like a smile upon his full, Egyptian lips.

He sat next day and spoke to Albert Redmayne on a little gallery that extended from the dining-room of the villa and overhung the lake. Here, for half an hour, he talked and listened until Jenny should be ready for him.

The elder expounded his simple philosophy. "I was long out of heart with God, while striv-ing to keep my faith in man, Peter," he declared. "But now I see more clearly and believe that it is only by faith in our Maker that we can under-stand ourselves. 'Better' is ever the enemy of 'good,' and 'best' is a golden word only to be used for martyrs and heroes."

"Men do their best for two things, Albert," re-plied Mr. Ganns. "For love and for hate; and without these tremendous incitements not the least or greatest among us can reach the limit of his powers."

"True, and perhaps that explains the present European attitude. The war has left us inca--pable of any supreme activity. Enthusiasm is dead; consequently the enthusiasm of good-will lacks from our councils and we drift, without any great guiding hand upon the tiller of destiny. Heart and brains are at odds, groping on differ-ent roads instead of advancing together by the one and only road. We see no great men. There are, of course, leaders, great by contrast with those they lead; but history will declare us a gen-eration of dwarfs and show how, for once, man stood at a crisis of his destiny when those mighty enough to face it failed to appear. Now

that is a situation unparalleled in my knowledge
of the past. Until now, the hour has always
brought the man.''

''We drift, as you say,'' answered Ganns, dust-
ing his white waistcoat. ''We are suffering from
a sort of universal shell shock, Albert; and from
my angle of observation I perceive how closely
crime depends upon nerves. Indifference in the
educated takes the shape of lawlessness in the
masses; and the breakdown of our economical
laws provokes to fury and despair. Our equili-
brium is gone in every direction. For example
the balance between work and recreation has been
destroyed. This restless condition will take a dec-
ade of years to control, and the present craving
for that excitement, to which we were painfully
accustomed during the years of war, is leaving a
marked and dangerous brand on the minds of the
rising generation. From this restlessness to
criminal methods of satisfying it is but a step.

''We are sick; our state is pathological. What
we need is a renewal of the discipline that enabled
us to confront and conquer in the past struggle.
We must drill our nerves, Albert, and strive to
restore a balanced and healthy outlook for those
destined to run the world in future. Men are not
by nature lawless. They are rational beings in
the lump; but civilization, depending as it does
on creed and greed, has made no steps as yet,
through education, to arrest our superstition and
selfishness.''

''Once let the light of good-will in upon this
chaos and we should see order beginning to re-

turn," declared Mr. Redmayne. "The problem is how to promote good-will, my dear friend. This should be the great and primal concern of religion; for what, after all, is the basis of all morality? Surely to love our neighbour as ourself."

They set the world right together and their thoughts drifted into a region of benignant aspirations. Then came Jenny and presently the detective followed her into a garden of flowers behind Villa Pianezzo.

"Giuseppe and Mr. Brendon have gone to the hills," she said. "And now I am ready to talk to you, Mr. Ganns. Don't fear to hurt me. I am beyond hurting. I have suffered more in the past year than I should have thought it possible to suffer and keep sane."

He looked at her beautiful face intently. It was certainly sad enough, but to his eye, beneath the lines of sorrow, lay an anxiety that concerned neither the past nor the future, but the immediate present. She was apparently unhappy in her new life.

"Show me the silkworms," he said.

They entered the lofty shed rising above a thicket behind the villa—a shuttered apartment where twilight reigned. The place was fitted with shelves to the ceiling and between the caterpillar trays tall branches of brushwood ascended to the roof. Out of the cool gloom of this silent chamber there glimmered, as it seemed, a thousand little lamps dotted everywhere on the sticks and walls and ceiling. Not a place where a worm could climb or spin was unadorned, for the oval, shining cocoons, scattered like small, ripe fruit upon the twigs, made a delicate light on every side through the sombre dusk. Mr. Redmayne's silkworms were descended, through countless generations, from those historic eggs stolen by Nestorian pilgrims from China, and carried thence secretly in hollow canes to Constantinople some thirteen hundred years before.

The caterpillars had nearly all done their work and completed their silken cases; but a couple of hundred fat, white monsters, each some three inches long, still remained in the trays, and they fastened greedily on fresh mulberry leaves that Jenny brought them. Others were but beginning their shrouds. They had sketched them and appeared to be busily weaving in the preliminary bag made of transparent and glittering filament. A few of the creatures began to turn yellow, though as yet they had not devoured their last meal. Jenny picked them up and held them to the morning light.

"Never mummy was wound so exquisitely as the silkworm's chrysalis," said Peter; and Jenny chatted cheerfully about the silken industry and its varied interests, but found that Mr. Ganns could tell her much more than she was able to tell him.

He listened with attention, however, and only by gradual stages deflected conversation to the affairs that had brought him. Presently he indicated an aspect of her own position arising from his words on the previous night.

"Did it ever strike you that it was a bold thing to marry within little more than nine months of your first husband's disappearance, Mrs. Doria?" he asked.

"It did not; but I shivered when I heard you talking yesterday. And call me 'Jenny,' not 'Mrs. Doria,' Mr. Ganns."

"Love has always been very impatient of law"; he declared, "but the fact is that unless proof of an exceptional character can be submitted, the English law is not prepared to say of any man that he is dead until seven years have passed from the last record of him among the living. Now there is rather a serious difference between seven years and nine months, Jenny."

"Looking back I seem to see nothing but a long nightmare. 'Nine months!' It was a century. Don't think that I didn't love my first husband; I adored him and I adore his memory; but the loneliness and the sudden magic of this man. Besides all that, surely none could question the hideous proofs of what happened? I accepted Michael's death as a fact which need not enter the calculation. My God! Why did not somebody hint to me that I was doing wrong to wed?"

"Did anybody have a chance?"

She looked at him with a face full of unhappiness.

"You are right. I was possessed. I made a terrible mistake; but do not fear that I have escaped the punishment."

He guessed her meaning and led her away from the subject of her husband.

"Tell me, if it won't hurt you too much, a little about Michael Pendean."

But she appeared not to hear him. Her thoughts were concerned entirely with herself and her present situation.

"I can trust you. You are wise and know life. I have not married a man, but a devil!"

Her hands clenched and he saw a flash of her teeth in the gloom of the silent chamber.

He took snuff and listened, while the unfortunate woman raved of her error.

"I hate him. I loathe him," she cried, and heaped hard words on the head of the debonair Giuseppe. She broke off presently panted, and then subsided in tears.

Peter studied her very carefully, yet, for the moment, showed no great sympathy. His answer was tonic rather than sedative.

"You must keep your nerve and be patient," he said. "Even Italy's a free country in some respects; you need not stop with Doria if you don't want to."

"Might my husband be alive? Do you imagine it possible that he could be alive? I think of him as my husband again, now that this midsummer madness is over. I have much to say to you. I want you—I pray you—to help me as well as my uncle. But he must come first, of course."

"We shall possibly find that in helping him we are helping you," answered Peter. "But you ask a question and I always answer a question when it's reasonable to do so. No, Jenny, I cannot think that Michael Pendean is alive. Let us go out into the air; it is stuffy here. But remember I do not say that he is not alive. It was certainly man's blood that an unknown hand shed at Foggintor; it was man's blood in the cave under the cliffs near Mr. Bendigo Redmayne's home; but as yet we know no more, with absolute certainty, who lost it than who spilled it. That is the large problem I am here to solve. And perhaps, if you want to help me, you can do so. This at any rate I promise you: if you help me, you will also help yourself and your Uncle Albert.''

''He is in danger?''

''Consider the situation. In process of time the estate of Albert's two brothers will devolve upon him. That means, I suppose, that sooner or later the bulk of the money must be yours. Albert is frail. I do not think he will be a long-lived man. What follows? Surely that you—the last of the Redmaynes—will inherit everything. And you are married. Here is a proposition, then. And what have you just told me? That your husband is 'a devil,' and that you hate him since you have seen a glimpse of his heart. These facts cannot be entirely separated. They may or may not be closely allied.''

She looked at him steadfastly.

''I have only thought of Giuseppe Doria in connection with myself, never in connection with Uncle Bendigo and Uncle Albert. Uncle Bendigo died—if he is dead—before I consented to marry Doria—before he asked me to do so. But keep my mistake from my uncle. I don't want him to know I'm miserable."

"You must decide where to put your trust, my dear," answered Mr. Ganns. "Otherwise you may find yourself on dangerous ground."

She weighed her answer.

"You are thinking of something," she said.

"Naturally. What you have told me as to your relations with your Italian husband offers considerable food for thought. But consider very carefully. You cannot run with the hare and hunt with the hounds. How many a bad man and, for that matter, how many an innocent man, has come to grief in the attempt. Tell me this. Does Giuseppe know that you no longer love him?"

She shook her head.

"I have hid it. The time has not come to let him know that. He would be revenged, and God knows what form his revenge might take. Till I have escaped from him, he must not dream that I have changed."

"That's your feeling? Well, the questions are two. Do you know enough about him to assist and justify your escape and, if you do, are you prepared to confide your knowledge to me?"

"I do not know enough," she answered. "He is a very clever man under his light-hearted and easy-going manners. He is, I believe, faithful to me, and he takes care never to be unkind in the presence or hearing of a third person. But this I think: that he knows very well what you've just told me—that all the Redmayne money must sooner or later be mine.''

''And yet he behaves to you as though he were a devil? That's not very clever of him.''

''I can't explain. Perhaps I have said too much. His cruelty is very subtle. Italian husbands——''

''I know all about Italian husbands. We'll talk over this again when you have had time to think a little. There's a reason for your hate and distrust of him, no doubt. You would not pretend such emotions. He's faithful, you say, so perhaps that reason is linked with knowledge you do not care to impart to me—or anybody? Perhaps it embraces the mystery man we want to catch—Robert Redmayne? Does Doria know more about him than you or I do? And you have found it out? There may be quite a number of things that make you hate Doria. So think it over and consider if to hear any of them would help me.''

Jenny looked at Peter with profound interest.

''You are a very wonderful man, Mr. Ganns.''

''Not a bit—only practiced in the jig-saw puzzle we call life. Attach no special importance to what I have just said, or the possibilities I have just thrown out. I may be altogether wrong. I have only at present your word that Signor Doria is not a kind husband. I may not agree with you when I know him better. You may not be a judge. Your first husband was perhaps so exceptional that the norm of hus-

bands is unknown to you. My mind is quite
open on the subject, because I have often found
that a wife knows much less about her husband's
character than do other people. Remember that
hate blinds quite as frequently as love; and love
turned to hate is a transformation so complicated
that it takes a cunning psycho-analyst to interpret
it. Therefore to know the importance of your
fears, I must know more about you yourself.

"We'll leave it at that—and all you need think
of me at present is that I want to serve you. But
I am an old bird, while Brendon, on the contrary,
is still young; and youth understands youth.
Remember that in him you have a steadfast and
faithful friend. I shan't be jealous if you can
tell him more than you can tell me."

Jenny's lips moved and were again motionless.
He perceived that she had started to say one
thing, but would now say another. She took his
big hand and pressed it between her own.

"God bless you!" she said. "If I have you
for a friend, I am content. Mr. Brendon has
been very good to me—very, very good. But
you are more likely to serve Uncle Albert than
he."

They parted presently and Jenny returned to
the house, while the detective, finding a comfortable chair under an oleander bush, sniffed the
fragrance of the red blossom above him, regretted
that his vice had largely spoiled his sense of
smell, took snuff and opened his notebook. He
wrote in it steadily for half an hour; then he rose
and joined Albert Redmayne.

The elder was full of an approaching event. "To think that to-day you and Poggi meet!" he exclaimed. "Peter, my dear man, if you do not love Virgilio I shall be broken-hearted." "Albert," answered Mr. Ganns. "I have already loved Poggi for two years. Those you love, I love; and that means that our friendship is on a very high plane indeed; for it oftens happens that nothing puzzles us more infernally than our friends' friends. In our case, however, so entirely do we see alike in everything that matters, that it is beyond possibility you should be devoted to anybody who does not appeal to me. By the same token, how much do you love your niece?"

Mr. Redmayne did not answer instantly.

"I love her," he replied at length, "because I love everything that is lovely; and without prejudice I do honestly believe she is about the loveliest young woman I have ever seen. Her face more nearly resembles that of Botticelli's Venus than any living being in my experience; and it is the sweetest face I know. Therefore I love her outside very much indeed, Peter.

"But when it comes to her inside, I feel not so sure. That is natural, for this reason, that I do not know her at all well yet. I have seldom seen her in childhood, or had any real acquaintance with her until now. When I know her better, it is pretty certain that I shall love her all through; but one must confess I can never know her very well, because the gap in age denies perfect understanding. Nor does she come to me, as it were,

alone. Her life turns to her husband. She is
still a bride and adores him.''

"You have no reason to think her as an unhappy bride?"

"None whatever. Doria is amazingly handsome and attractive—the type a woman generally
worships. I grant that Italo-English marriages
are not remarkable for their success; but—well,
no doubt Jenny's husband is worldly-wise. He
has everything to gain by being good, everything
to lose by behaving badly. Jenny is a proud girl.
She has qualities. There is a distinction about
her. She would stand no nonsense from Doria
and she knows that I would stand no nonsense
from him. I hope to see much of her, though it
appears that their home will be in Turin.''

"He has abandoned his ambitions to recover
the family estates and title and so forth? Brendon told me all about that.''

"Entirely. Besides it seems that one of your
countrymen has secured the castle at Dolceacqua
and bought the title too. Giuseppe was very en-
tertaining on the subject. But I'm afraid he
loves idleness.''

Before luncheon Mark Brendon returned from
the hills with his guide. They had seen nothing
of Robert Redmayne and appeared to be rather
weary of one another's company.

"You must impart your wisdom and gay spirit
to Signor Marco,'' said Giuseppe to Mr. Ganns,
when Brendon was out of earshot with Jenny.
"He is a very dull dog and does not even listen
when I talk. Not simpatico, I suppose. He

will never find out anything. Will you, I wonder? Have you any ideas? A new broom sweeps clean, as you say."

"I must suck your brains before you suck mine, Doria," said Peter genially. "I want to hear what you think of this man in the red waistcoat. We must have a talk."

"Gladly, gladly, Signor Peter. I have seen him now many times—in England three—four times—in Italy once. He is always the same."

"Not a spook?"

"A spirit? No. Very much alive. But how he lives and what he lives for—who can tell?"

"You do not fear on account of Mr. Redmayne?"

"I much fear on account of him," answered Doria. "And when my wife told me that she had seen him, I telegraphed from Turin that they should be careful and run no risk whatever of a meeting. Jenny's uncle is frightened when he thinks about it; but we keep his thoughts away as much as possible. It is bad for him to fear. For the love of Heaven, good signor, get to the bottom of it if you can. My idea is to set a trap for this red man and catch him, like a fox or other wild creature."

"A very cute notion," declared Peter. "We'll rope you in, Giuseppe. Between you and me and the post, our friend Brendon has been barking up the wrong tree, you know. But if you and I and he, together, can't clean this up, then we're not the men I take us for."

Doria laughed.

" 'Deeds are men; words are women,' " he said. "There has been too much chatter about this; but now you are come; we shall see things accomplished."

It was not until after the midday meal that Ganns and Mark were able to get speech together. Then, promising to return in time to meet Virgilio Poggi, who would cross the lake for tea, the two men sauntered beside Como and exchanged experiences. The interview proved painful to the younger, for he found that Peter's doubts were cleared in certain directions. Brendon, indeed, led up to his own chastening very directly.

"It makes me mad," he said, "to see the way that beggar treats his wife—Doria I mean. Pearls before swine. I never hoped much from it; but to think they have only been married three months!"

"How does he treat her?"

"Well, one isn't blind to her appearance. The cause is, of course, concealed; the effect, very visible to my eyes. She's far too plucky to whisper her troubles; but she can't hide her face, where they may be read."

Mr. Ganns said nothing and Mark spoke again.

"Do you begin to see any light?"

"Not much upon the main problem. A minor feature has cleared, however. I know the rock you split upon, my son. You were in love with Jenny Pendean from the moment you knew that she was a widow. And you're in love with Jenny Doria now. And to be in love with one

of the principals in a case, is to handicap yourself
out of the hunt, as far as that case is concerned.''
Brendon stared but made no answer.

"Human nature has its limits, Mark, and love's
a pretty radical passion. No man ever did, or
could, do himself justice in any task whatever—
not while he was blinded with love of a woman.
Love's a jealous party and won't stand com-
petitors. So it follows that if you were in love
anyway you wouldn't be at your best; and how
much more so when the lady in your case was the
lady in *the* case?''

"You wrong me," answered the other rather
hotly. "That is really unreasonable. Emphatically the incident made no sort of difference, for
the very good reason that she was not in the case,
save as an innocent sufferer from the evil actions
of others. She helped me rather than hindered
me. Despite all she was called to endure, she
kept her nerve from the first and fought her own
grief that she might make everything clear to me.
If I did come to love her, that made no sort of
difference to my attitude to my work.''

"But it made a mighty lot of difference to
your attitude to her. However, your word runs
with me, Mark, and I'm very willing to attach all
due importance to your conclusions. But I am
not in the least willing to accept your estimate
of anybody's character without further proofs.
You mustn't feel it personal. Only remember
that I'm not in this case for my health, and, so
far, I have had no reason whatever to eliminate
anybody.''

"We know some things without proof and are proud to take them on trust," answered Brendon. "Have I not seen Mrs. Doria under affliction and in situations unspeakably difficult? She has been marvellously brave. After her own great sorrow, her only thought was her unfortunate relations. She buried her own crushing grief——"

"And in nine months was married to another man."

"She is young and you have seen for yourself what her husband is. Who can tell what measures he took to win her? All I know is that she has made an appalling mistake. Perhaps I feel it rather than know it; but I'm positive."

"Well," said Peter quietly. "It's no good playing about. At a seemly opportunity, after her husband died, I guess you told her you loved her and asked her to marry you. She declined; but it didn't end there. She's got you on the string at this moment."

"That's not true, Ganns. You don't understand me—or her."

"Well, I do not ask much; but since I have picked up this thing for Albert's sake, there's one point on which I insist. If you are going to take Jenny into your confidence and assume that she has no wish or desire other than to see justice done and the mystery cleared, then I can't work with you, Mark."

"You wrong her, but that doesn't matter, I suppose. What does matter is that you wrong me," said Brendon, with fierce eyes fixed upon the elder. "I've never thought or dreamed of confiding in her, or anybody else. I've nothing to confide, for that matter. I did love her, and I do love her, and I'm deeply concerned and troubled to see the mess she's in with this blighter; but I'm a detective first and last and always over this business; and I have some credit in my painful profession.''

"Good. Remember that, whatever happens. And keep your temper with me, too, because nothing is gained by losing it. I'm not saying a word against Mrs. Doria, but inasmuch as she is Mrs. Doria and inasmuch as Doria is as yet very much an unknown quantity to you and me, you must understand that I don't allow appearances to blind my eyes or control my actions. Now if a woman hints, or indicates, that she is unhappily married, then nothing is more natural than that a man like yourself, who entertains the tenderest feelings to the woman, should believe what he sees and regard her melancholy as genuine. It looks all right; but suppose, for their own ends, that Jenny Doria and her spouse want to create this impression? Suppose that their object is to lead you and me to imagine that they are not friends?''

"My God! What would you make of her?''

"It isn't what I'd make of her. It's what she really is. And that I'm going to find out, because a great deal more may depend upon it than you appear to imagine.''

"A moment's reflection will surely convince you that neither she nor Doria——''

"Wait, wait! I'm only saying that we must

not allow character, fancied or real, to dam any channel of investigation. If reflection convinces me that it is impossible for Doria to be in collusion with Robert Redmayne, I shall admit it. As yet that is not so. There are several very interesting points. Have you asked yourself why Bendigo Redmayne's diary is missing?"

"I have—and could not see how it was likely to contain anything dangerous to Robert Redmayne."

Peter did not enlighten him for the moment. Then he spoke and changed the subject.

"I must find out several fundamental facts and I certainly shall not learn them here," he said. "Next week in all probability, unless something unexpected happens to prevent it, I go back to England."

"Can't I go?"

"I shall want you here; but our understanding must be complete before I leave."

"Trust me for that," said Mark.

"I do."

"You want me to look after Mr. Redmayne?"

"No; I look after him. He's my first care. I haven't broke it to him yet; but he's going with me."

Brendon considered and his thought flushed his cheek.

"You can't trust him with me, then?"

"It's not you. Mind, I'm only guessing; but, anyway, the risk is too considerable. I go, because, until I have been, I remain in the dark over some vital matters that must be cleared and can

only be cleared in England. Vital in my opinion,
that is. But in the meantime Albert is not the
sort of a man to be trusted alone, for the reason
that he has no idea whence the danger threatens;
nor can he be trusted with you, either, because you
are equally ignorant.''

''But if the danger lies with Doria, as you seem
to hint, how can you, or anybody else, save Mr.
Redmayne from it? He likes Doria. The
beggar amuses him and is tactful and clever to
please where and when he wants to please. He's
been trying to please me. To-morrow he'll try
to please you.''

''Yes—a very light-hearted, agreeable chap—
and clever as you say. But I don't know yet
whether what you and I see, or even what his
wife sees, is the real Doria.''

''Possibly not.''

Ganns considered and then proceeded.

''I must give you a clear understanding. I'm
so used to playing a lone hand and saying nothing
till I can say everything, that I may be tempted
to treat you in a way you don't deserve. Now
I'll tell you how the cat's jumping. She's jumping in the dark—I'll allow that; but what I seem
to see dimly is this: that Giuseppe Doria knows a
great deal more about the man in the red waistcoat than we do. I hardly think Doria is the man
to murder my old friend; but I'm not so sure that,
if somebody else wanted to take the step, Doria
would prevent him.

''If Albert disappeared, you've got to remember that Doria's wife would be the worldly

gainer. Why anybody should want to kill Albert to put money into Jenny's pocket I cannot say. But it's a feature; and while I'm in England, I'll ask you to keep your eyes skinned and try and find out as much about Giuseppe as you can. Not from his wife, however. I needn't tell you that. You'll be free to poke about and try and surprise 'Red Waistcoat.' Perhaps you'll do the trick; but take care he doesn't surprise you. All I ask is that you don't believe a quarter you hear, or half you see. We must get under the appearances if we're to make good.''

''You think, then, that Doria and Robert Redmayne may be running in double harness? And perhaps you think that Jenny Doria knows this fact and that in this secret knowledge her present misery lies?''

''No need to drag her in; but your own question suggests the possibility.''

''Not against my own knowledge. She could be a willing party to no crime. It is contrary to her inherent character, Ganns.''

''And yet you're a detective 'first and last and always'—eh? One would think that I wanted you to put her through the third degree. Not that I ever put any man or woman through it myself. It is dirty business and quite unworthy of our great service. We'll leave Mrs. Doria, then, and concentrate on her husband. There are a lot of very interesting things to find out about Doria, my boy.''

''You forget that he only came into this business at 'Crow's Nest.' ''

"How can I forget what I don't know? Why do you say he only came into it at 'Crow's Nest'? He may have come into it at Foggintor. Perhaps he and not Robert Redmayne, or any other, cut Michael Pendean's throat?"

"Impossible. Consider. Is not Michael's widow Doria's wife?"

"What, then? I'm not saying she knew he was the murderer."

"Another thing: Doria was the servant of Bendigo Redmayne at the time."

"And how do you know even so much?" Brendon showed impatience.

"My dear Ganns, that's common knowledge."

"Common nothing! You can't swear he was the servant of Bendigo Redmayne on the day that the murder was committed. To prove as much would entail an amount of solid research that might surprise you. Of this crowd, only Doria for certain knows when he joined up at 'Crow's Nest.' His wife may, or may not, know. I'm quite unprepared to take Giuseppe's word for the date."

"That's why you wanted Bendigo Redmayne's log then?"

"One of the reasons certainly. The diary may be here yet. You can use your eyes when we are away and try to find it. If you are allowed to stumble on it, note particularly any pages torn out or erased or faked."

"You still believe that those about Mr. Redmayne are criminals?"

"I believe that it becomes necessary to

prove they are not. Perhaps you'll succeed in doing so before we return. There's a devil of a lot of clearing to be done yet before we begin building. What beats me frankly is the fact that my old friend Albert is still alive. I can see no reason whatever why he should be—and a dozen why he should not.''

"Thanks to your forethought in coming unexpectedly, perhaps."

"With all the will and wit in the world you can't prevent one man from killing another if he wants to do so—that is, assuming the would-be murderer is at liberty and unknown. One more thing, Mark. When I leave with Mr. Redmayne, I disappear altogether, and so does he. It must be understood that nobody here is going to hear anything about us till we come back again. If you want me very urgently, you must telegraph to New Scotland Yard, where my direction will be known, but nowhere else. And look after yourself sharply too. Don't run any needless risks on trust. You may be in danger and certainly will be if you get on the scent."

Two days later the book lover and Peter were taking a steamer for Varenna, whence they would entrain for Milan and so return to England. The meeting of Signor Poggi and Mr. Ganns afforded exquisite satisfaction to Albert, and Peter did not cloud his pleasure with any allusion to the future until the following morning. Then, having expressed his enthusiasm for Virgilio and his hope of better acquaintance on their return, the American broke to Albert their immediate departure.

He anticipated some protest, but Mr. Redmayne was too logical to make any.

"I asked you to solve this enigma," he said, "and I am the last to question your methods of so doing. That you will get to the bottom of these horrid mysteries, Peter, I am quite certain. It is a conviction with me that you are going to explain everything; but I shall support your operations and if you hold it necessary that I go to England, of course, dear friend, I go. You must not, however, count upon me for any practical assistance. It is entirely contrary to my nature to take an active part in this campaign. To put any enterprise or adventure upon me would be to ask for failure."

"Fear nothing at all," answered Ganns. "I don't want you to do anything whatever but lie low and amuse yourself. The danger may follow you, or it may not; but my only wish is to come between you and danger, Albert, and keep you under my own eyes. For the rest we'll hide our tracks. Get Jenny to pack your portmanteau for a ten days' tour. If all's well, you'll be home again at the end of next week."

The morning of departure swiftly arrived and while Mr. Redmayne gave final instructions to his niece, Peter and Mark walked the landing stage as the paddle steamer, *Pliny*, came thudding across from Bellagio to take the travellers on the first stage of their journey. Brendon defined the position.

"It stands thus," he said. "You strongly suspect Doria of being in collusion with another

man, but doubt whether the other man is really
Robert Redmayne. What you want me to do is
to watch Doria and see if I can surprise the great
unknown, or learn the truth about him. Meanwhile you go home, and your work on the case
you prefer to keep to yourself until it is considerably clearer and forwarder than at present.''

''The situation in a nutshell. Keep an open
mind. I ask no more than that.''

''I will,'' answered Brendon. ''Already I suspect the explanation that you have had of Mrs.
Doria's sufferings. It is tolerably clear to me
that she knows more than we do, and has some
secret of her husband's that is causing her unhappiness.''

''A theory capable of proof. You'll see a
good deal of the dame during the coming week
and the time oughtn't to be wasted, if what you
think is true.''

On the steamer stood Virgilio Poggi. He was
come across the water to take leave of Mr. Redmayne and see him as far as Varenna. The three
men departed presently, leaving Mark, Jenny and
her husband together. At Varenna, Virgilio also
took his leave. He was not content with embrac-
ing Albert but clasped Mr. Ganns also in an affectionate farewell.

''We are great men, all three of us,'' said Signor Poggi, ''and greatness cleaves to greatness.
Return as quickly as you can, Albert, and obey
Signor Ganns in everything. May this cloud be
quickly lifted from your life. Meantime you both
have my prayers.''

Albert translated the speech for Peter's benefit; then the train moved forward and Virgilio took the next boat home again. He sneezed all the way, for he had accepted a pinch from Peter's snuffbox ignorant of its effects upon an untrained nose.

CHAPTER XIV

REVOLVER AND PICKAXE

WHILE Brendon entertained no sort of regard for Giuseppe Doria, his balanced mind allowed him to view the man with impartial justice. He discounted the fact of the Italian's victory in love, and, because he knew himself to be an unsuccessful rival, was the more jealous that disappointment should not create any bias. But Doria had failed to make Jenny a happy wife; he understood that well enough, and he could not forget that some future advantage to himself might accrue from this circumstance. The girl's attitude had changed; he was not blind and could not fail to note it. For the present, however, he smothered his own interests and strove with all his strength to advance a solution of the problems before him. He was specially desirous to furnish important information for Peter Ganns on his return.

He did what his judgment indicated but failed to find sufficient reasons for linking Doria with the mystery, or associating him with Robert Redmayne. For despite Peter's luminous analysis, Mark still regarded the unknown as Albert Redmayne's brother; and he could find no reasonable argument for associating Giuseppe with this person, either at present or in the past. Everything rather pointed in a contrary direction. Brendon traversed the incidents cónnected with Bendigo Redmayne's disappearance, yet he could recall nothing suspicious about Giuseppe's conduct at "Crow's Nest"; and if it seemed unreasonable to suppose he had taken a hand in the second tragedy, it appeared still less likely that he could be associated with the first.

It was true that Doria had wedded Pendean's widow; but that he should have slain her husband in order to do so appeared a grotesque assumption. Moreover, as a student of character, Mark could not honestly find in Jenny's husband any characteristics that argued a malevolent attitude to life. He was a pleasure-loving spirit and his outlook and ambitions, while frivolous, were certainly not criminal. He talked of the smugglers a good deal and declared himself in sympathy with them; but it was gasconade; he evinced no particular physical bravery; he was fond of his comforts and seemed little likely to risk his own liberty by association with breakers of law and order.

A startling proof that Mark had not erred in this estimate was afforded by a conversation which he enjoyed with Doria on a day soon after the departure of Albert Redmayne and his friend. Giuseppe and his wife had planned to visit an acquaintance at Colico, to the northward of the lake; and before the steamer started, after noon, the two men took a stroll in the hills a mile above Menaggio. Brendon had asked for some private conversation and the other gladly agreed.

"As you know, I'm going to spend the day in the red man's haunt," explained Mark, "and I'll call at supper time since you wish it; but before you go, I'll ask you to stroll along for an hour. I want to talk to you."

"That will suit me very well," said the other, and in half an hour he returned to Brendon, found him chatting with Jenny in the dark portal of the silkworm house, and drew him away.

"You shall have speech with her to-night after supper," promised Giuseppe. "Now it is my turn. We will ascend to the little shrine on the track above the orchards. There are shrines too many to the Holy Mother, my friend. But this one is not to Madonna of the wind, or the sea, or the stars. I call her 'Madonna del farniente'— the saint for weary people, whose bodies and brains both ache from too much work."

They climbed aloft presently, Doria in a holiday suit of golden-brown cloth with a ruby tie, and Brendon attired in tweeds, his luncheon in his pocket. Then the Italian's manner changed and he dropped his banter. Indeed for a time he grew silent.

Brendon opened the conversation and of course treated the other as though no question existed concerning his honesty.

"What do you think of this business?" he asked. "You have been pretty close to it for a long time now. You must have some theory."

"I have no theory at all," replied Doria. "My own affairs are enough for me and this cursed mystery is thrusting a finger into my life and darkening it. I grow a very anxious and miserable man and I will tell you why, because you are understanding. You must not be angry if I now mention my wife in this affair. A mill and a woman are always in want of something, as our proverb says; but though we may know what a mill requires, who can guess a woman's whims? I am dazed with guessing wrong. I don't intend to be hard or cruel. It is not in me to be cruel to any woman. But how if your own woman is cruel to you?''

They had reached the shrine—a little alcove in a rotting mass of brick and plaster. Beneath it extended a stone seat whereon the wayfarer might kneel or sit; above, in the niche, protected by a wire grating, stood a doll painted with a blue cloak and a golden crown. Offerings of wayside flowers decorated the ledge before the little image.

They sat down and Doria began to smoke his usual Tuscan cigar. His depression increased and with it Brendon's astonishment. The man appeared to be taking exactly that attitude to his wife she had already suggested toward him.

"Il volto sciolto ed i pensieri stretti," declared Giuseppe with gloom. "That is to say 'her countenance may be clear, but her thoughts are dark' —too dark to tell me—her husband.''

"Perhaps she fears you a little. A woman is always helpless before a man who keeps his own secrets hidden.''

"Helpless? Far from it. She is a self-controlled, efficient, hard-headed woman. Her loveliness is a curtain. You have not yet got behind that. You loved her, but she did not love you. She loved me and married me. And it is I who know her character, not you. She is very clever and pretends a great deal more than she feels. If she makes you think she is unhappy and helpless, she does it on purpose. She may be unhappy, because to keep secrets is often to court unhappiness; but she is not helpless at all. Her eyes look helpless; her mouth never. There is power and will between her teeth.''

"Why do you speak of secrets?"

"Because you did. I have no secrets. It is Jenny, my wife, who has secrets. I tell you this. *She knows all about the red man!* She is as deep as hell.''

"You mean that she understands what is happening and will not tell her uncle or you?"

"That is precisely what I mean. She does not care a curse for Alberto. What is born of hen will scrape—remember that. Her father had a temper like a fiend and a cousin of her mother was hanged for murder. These are facts she will not deny. I had them from her uncle. I am frightened of her and I have disappointed her, because I am not what she thought and have ceased to covet my ancestral estates and title.''

Such a monstrous picture of Jenny at first bewildered Brendon and then incensed him. Was it within the bounds of possibility that after six months of wedded life with this woman, any man living would utter such an indictment and believe it?

"She is great in her way—much too great for

me," said Giuseppe frankly. "She should have been a Medici or a Borgia; she should have lived many centuries sooner, before policeman and detective officers were invented. You stare and think I lie. But I do not lie. I see very clearly indeed. I look back at the past and the veil is lifted. I understand much that I did not understand when I was growing blind with love for her. As for this Robert Redmayne—'Robert the Devil,' I call him—once I thought that he was a ghost; but he is not a ghost: he is a live man.

"And presently what will happen if he is not caught and hanged? He will kill Uncle Alberto and perhaps kill me, too. Then he will run away with Jenny. And I tell you this, Brendon: the sooner he does so, if only he leaves me alone, the better pleased I shall be. A hideous speech? Yes, very hideous indeed; but perfectly true, like many hideous things."

"Do you honestly expect that I, who know your wife, am going to believe this grotesque story?"

"I do not mind whether you believe it or no. Feel as savage as you please. For that matter I feel rather savage myself. There is a new ferocity creeping into me. If you keep company with a wolf, you will soon learn to howl—that's why I howl a good deal in secret, I can tell you. Soon I shall howl so that everybody will hear. So now you know how it is with me. I am outside her secrets and feel no wish whatever to learn them, save as they affect me. If she will give me a few thousand pounds and let me

vanish out of her life, I shall be delighted to do
so. I did not marry her for her money; but since
love is dead, I shall like a little of the cash to
start me at Turin. Then she is free as air. It
will pay you quite well to try and arrange the
bargain."

Brendon could hardly believe his ears, but the
Italian appeared very much in earnest. He chattered on for some time. Then he looked at his
watch and declared that he must descend.

"The steamer is coming soon," he said. "Now
I leave you and I hope that I have done good.
Think how to help me and yourself. What she
now feels to you I cannot tell. Your turn may
come. I trust so. I am not at all jealous. But
be warned. This red man—he is no friend to
you or me. You seek him again to-day. So be it.
And if you find him, be careful of your skin. Not
that a man can protect his skin against fate. We
meet at supper."

He swung away, singing a canzonet, and quickly
vanished, while Brendon, overwhelmed by this
extraordinary conversation, sat for an hour motionless and deep in thought. He could hardly
plough his path through what appeared a jungle
of flagrant falsehood. But where another man
had striven to find underlying purpose in this
diatribe and consider Doria's object in choosing
him for a confessor, Brendon, while swift enough
to regard the attack on Jenny as foul and false,
yet did not hesitate to believe that which his own
desire drove him to believe. He sifted the grain
from the chaff, doubtfully guided by his own pas-

sion, and saw the Italian's wife free. But he could not see her false. He scorned the baleful picture that Giuseppe had painted and guessed that his purpose was to cut the ground from under Jenny's feet and accuse her of those identical crimes that he himself had committed. His attitude to Doria was affirmed, and from that hour he believed, with Peter Ganns, that the Italian knew the purposes of the unknown and was assisting him to achieve them. But again his spirit picked and chose. He did not remember how Ganns also, though in more temperate words than Doria's, had warned him for the present to put no trust even in Jenny. He trusted her as he trusted himself; and that also meant distrusting her husband.

He considered now his own course of action and presently proceeded to the region in which Robert Redmayne had been most frequently reported. Certain appearances were chronicled and, before Ganns returned to England, the theory had been accepted that the fugitive hid and dwelt aloft in some fastness with the charcoal burners. Now Brendon felt the need to probe this opinion and determined, if possible, to find the lair of the red man.

Not single-handed did he expect to do so. His purpose henceforth was to watch Doria unseen and so discover whom he served. Thus he would kill two birds with one stone and simplify action for Peter Ganns when he returned.

Brendon climbed steadily upward and presently sat down to rest upon a little, lofty plateau where, in the mountain scrub, grew lilies of the valley and white sun-rose. Idly he sat and smoked, marked the steamers creep, like water-man beetles, upon the shiny surface of the lake stretched far below, watched a brown fox sunning itself on a stone and then plucked a bunch of the fragrant valley lilies to take to Jenny that night when he came to sup at the Villa Pianezzo. But the blossoms never reached the hand of Mrs. Doria.

Suddenly, as he rose from this innocent pastime, Mark became aware that he was watched and found himself face to face with the object of his search. Robert Redmayne stood separated from him by a distance of thirty yards behind the boughs of a breast-high shrub. He stood bare-headed, peering over the thicket, and the sun shone upon his fiery red scalp and tawny mustache. There could be no mistaking the man, and Brendon, rejoicing that daylight would now enable him to come to grips at last, flung down his bouquet and leaped straight for the other.

But it appeared that the watcher desired no closer contact. He turned and ran, heading upward for a wild tract of stone and scrub that spread beneath the last precipices of the mountain. Straight at this cliff, as though familiar with some secret channel of escape, the red man ran and made surprising speed. But Mark found himself gaining. He strove to run the other down as speedily as possible, that he might close, with strength still sufficient to win the inevitable battle that must follow, and effect a capture.

He was disappointed, however, for while still twenty yards behind and forced to make only a moderate progress over the rocky way he saw Robert Redmayne suddenly stop, turn and lift a revolver. The flash of the sun on the barrel and the explosion of the discharge were simultaneous. As the red man fired, the other flung up his arms, plunged forward on his face, gave one convulsive tremor through all his limbs, and moved no more. The discovery, the chase and its termination had occupied but five minutes; and while one big man, panting from his exertions, approached only to see that his fallen victim showed no sign of life, the other, with his face amid the alpine flowers, remained where he had dropped, his arms outstretched, his hands clenched, his body still, blood running from his mouth.

The conqueror took careful note of the spot in which he stood and bringing a knife from his pocket blazed the stem of a young tree that rose not very far from his victim. Then he disappeared and peace reigned above the fallen. So still he lay that another fox, scared from its siesta, poked a black muzzle round a rock and sniffed the air; but it trusted not appearances and having contemplated the recumbent object lifted its head, uttered a dubious bark and trotted away. From on high an eagle also marked the fallen man, but swiftly soared upward to the

crown of the mountain and disappeared. The
spot was lonely enough, yet a track ran within
one hundred yards and it often happened that
charcoal burners and their mules passed that way
to the valleys.

None, however, came now as the sun turned
westward and the cool shadow of the precipice began to creep over the little wilderness at its feet.
Many hours passed and then, after night had
flooded the hollow, there sounded from close at
hand strange noises and the intermittent thud of
some metal weapon striking the earth. The din
ascended from a rock which lifted its grey head
above a thicket of juniper; and here, while the
flat summit of the boulder began to shine whitely
under the rising moon, a lantern flickered and
showed two shadows busy above the excavation of
an oblong hole. They mumbled together and dug
in turn. Then one dark figure came out into the
open, took his bearings, flung lantern light on the
blazed tree trunk, and advanced to a brown,
motionless hump lying hard by.

Infinite silence reigned over that uplifted region. Above, near the summit of the mountain,
flashed the red eye of a charcoal burner's fire;
beneath only the plateau sloped to a ragged edge
easterly, for the lake was hidden under the
shoulder of the hills. No firefly danced upon this
height; but music there was, for a nightingale
bubbled his liquid notes in a great myrtle not ten
yards from where the still shape lay.

The dark, approaching figure saw the object of
his search and came forward. His purpose was

to bury the victim, whom he had lured hither before destroying, and then remove any trace that might linger upon the spot where the body lay. He bent down, put his hands to the jacket of the motionless man, and then, as he exerted his strength, a strange, hideous thing happened. The body under his touch dropped to pieces. Its head rolled away; its trunk became dismembered and he fell backward heaving an amorphous torso into the air. For, exerting the needful pressure to move a heavy weight, he found none and tumbled to the ground, holding up a coat stuffed with grass.

The man was on his feet in an instant, fearing an ambush; but astonishment opened his mouth.

"Corpo di Bacco!" he cried, and the exclamation rang in a note of something like terror against the cliffs and upon the ear of his companion. Yet no swift retribution stayed his steps; no shot rang out to arrest his progress. He leaped away, dodging and bounding like a deer to escape the expected bullet and then disappeared behind the boulder. But neither rascal delayed a moment. Their mingled steps instantly rang out; then the clatter faded swiftly upon the night and silence returned.

For ten minutes nothing happened. Next, out of a lair not fifteen yards from the distorted dummy, rose a figure that shone white as snow under the moon. Mark Brendon approached the snare that he himself had set, shook the grass out of his coat, lifted his hat from the ball of leaves it covered, and presently drew on his knickerboc-

kers, having emptied them of their stuffing. He
was cold and calm. He had learned more than he
expected to learn; for that startled exclamation
left no doubt at all concerning one of the grave-
diggers. It was Giuseppe Doria who had come
to move the body, and there seemed little doubt
that Brendon's would-be murderer was the other.

" 'Corpo di Bacco,' perhaps, but not corpo di
Brendon, my friend," murmured Mark to himself.
Then he turned northward, traversed some harsh
thickets that barred the plateau, and reached a
mule track, a mile beneath, which he had discovered before daylight waned. It led to Menaggio through chestnut woods.

The operations of the detective from the
moment that he fell headlong, apparently to rise
no more, may be briefly chronicled.

When his enemy drew up and fired pointblank
upon him, the bullet passed within an inch of
Brendon's ear and the memory of a similar experience flashed into his mind and led to his subsequent action.

On a previous occasion, having been missed at
close quarters, he pretended to be hit and fell apparently lifeless within fifteen yards of a famous
malefactor. The ruse succeeded; the man crept
back to triumph over an inveterate foe and Brendon shot him dead as he bent to examine a fancied
corpse. With a loaded revolver still in his oppo-
nent's hand, he could take no risk on this second
occasion and fell accordingly. His purpose was
to tempt the red man back and if possible secure
his weapon before he had time to fire again.

But he was disappointed, for the unknown, seeing Mark crash headfirst to the ground, and blood run from his mouth, evidently felt assured that his purpose was accomplished. Brendon had simulated death for a while, but when satisfied of his assailant's departure, presently rose, with no worse hurts than a bruised face, a badly bitten tongue, and a wounded shin.

The situation thus created he weighed in all its bearings and guessed that those who now believed themselves responsible for his death would take occasion to remove the evidence of their crime without much delay. The blazed tree, which he presently noted, confirmed this suspicion. Nobody had ever seen one of Robert Redmayne's victims and the last was little likely to be an exception. Mark guessed that until darkness returned he might expect to be undisturbed. He walked back, therefore, to his starting-place, and found the packet of food which he had brought with him and a flask of red wine left beside it.

After a meal and a pipe he made his plan and presently stood again on the rough ground beneath the cliffs, where he had pretended so realistically to perish. He intended no attempt to arrest; but, having created the effigy of himself and stuffed his knickerbockers and coat to resemble nature and deceive anybody who might return in darkness to his corpse, Brendon found a hiding-place near enough to study what would happen. He expected Redmayne to return and guessed that another would return with him. His

hope was to recognize the accomplice and prove
at least whether Jenny was right in hinting her
husband's secret wickedness, or whether Doria
had justly accused her of collusion with the unknown. It was impossible that both were speaking the truth.

With infinite satisfaction he heard Giuseppe's
voice, and even an element of grim amusement attended the Italian's shock and his subsequent
snipe-like antics as he leaped to safety before an
anticipated revolver barrage.

The adventure told Brendon much and his first
inclination was to arrest Doria on the following
morning; but that desire swiftly passed. A surer
strategy presented itself. From the first ambition—to get Jenny's husband under lock and key
—his mind leaped to a more workmanlike proposition. He suspected, however, that Giuseppe
might take the initiative and deny him any further opportunity of bettering their acquaintance;
and that night as he fell asleep with an aching
shin and cheek, Mark endeavoured to consider
the situation as it must appear from Doria's angle
of vision. Much temporal comfort resulted for
him from this examination.

It seemed clear that Doria and Redmayne were
working to destroy Albert Redmayne for their
common advantage. Let the old book lover disappear and Robert and his niece would be the last
of the Redmaynes to share the fortune of the
vanished brothers. Robert, indeed, could have no
open part in these. advantages, for he was out-
lawed; but it would be possible for him, in process

of time, when Jenny inherited all three estates and Robert, Bendigo and Albert were alike held to be deceased in the eyes of the law, to share the fortune in secret with his niece and her husband. This view explained the prescience of Peter Ganns and his surprise that Albert Redmayne should still be in the land of the living. Ganns, however, was proved mistaken in one vital particular, for there could no longer be any reasonable doubt that Robert Redmayne still lived.

Utterly mistaken as Brendon's theories ultimately proved to be, they bore to his weary brain the stamp of truth and he next proceeded to consider Doria's future attitude before the problem now awaiting him and his companion in crime. Doria could not be sure that he had been recognized or even seen when approaching the supposed corpse of Redmayne's victim; and, in any case, under the darkness, no man might certainly swear that it was Doria who came to dig the grave and dispose of the body. Brendon confessed to himself that only Giuseppe's startled oath had proved his presence, and Jenny's husband might well be expected to offer a sound alibi if arrested. He judged, therefore, that Doria would deny any knowledge of the incident; and time proved that Mark was right enough in that prediction.

CHAPTER XV

A GHOST

THE next morning, while he rubbed his bruises in a hot bath, Brendon determined upon a course of action. He proposed to tell Jenny and her husband exactly what had happened to him, merely concealing the end of the story.

He breakfasted, lighted his pipe and limped over to Villa Pianezzo. He was not in reality very lame, but accentuated the stiffness. Only Assunta appeared, though Brendon's eyes had marked Doria and Jenny together in the neighbourhood of the silkworm house as he entered the garden. He asked for Giuseppe and, having left Brendon in the sitting-room of the villa, Assunta departed. Almost immediately afterward Jenny greeted him with evident pleasure but reproved him.

"We waited an hour for supper," she said, "then Giuseppe would wait no longer. I was beginning to get frightened and I have been frightened all night. I am thankful to see you, for I feared something serious might have happened."

"Something serious did happen. I've got a strange story to tell. Is your husband within

reach? He must hear it, too, I think. He may be
in some danger as well as others.''

She expressed impatience and shook her head.

"Can't you believe me? But of course you
can't. Why should you? Doria in danger!
However, if you want him, you don't want me,
Mark.''

It was the first time that she had thus addressed
him and his heart throbbed; but the temptation to
confide in her lasted not a moment.

"On the contrary I want you both,'' he answered. "I attach very great weight to the hints
you have given me—not only for my sake but for
your own. The end is not yet as far as you're concerned, Jenny, for your welfare is more to me
than anything else in the world—you know it.
Trust me to prove that presently. But other
things come first. I must do what I am here to do,
before I am free to do what I long to do.''

"I trust you—and only you,'' she said. "In
all this bewilderment and misery, you are now
the only steadfast rock to which I can cling.
Don't desert me, that's all that I ask.''

"Never! All that's best in me shall be devoted
to you, thankfully and proudly—now that you
have wished it. Trust me, I say again. Call
your husband. I want to tell you both what
happened to me yesterday.''

Again she hesitated and gazed intently upon
him.

"Are you sure that you are wise? Would Mr.
Ganns like you to tell Doria anything?''

"You will judge better when you have heard me."

Again he longed to confide in her and show her that he understood the truth; but two considerations shut his mouth: the thought of Peter Ganns and the reflection that the more Jenny knew, the greater might be her own peril. This last conviction made him conclude their conference.

"Call him. We must not let him think that we have anything of a private nature to say to each other. It is vital that he should not imagine such a thing."

"You have secrets from me—though I have let you know my own secret," she murmured, preparing to obey him.

"If I keep anything from you, it is for your own good—for your own security," he replied.

She left him then and in a few moments returned with her husband. He was full of curiosity and under his usual assumption of cheerfulness Brendon perceived considerable anxiety.

"An adventure, Signor Marco? I know that without you telling me. Your face is solemn as a raven and you walked stiffly as you came to the door. I saw you from the silkworms. What has happened?"

"I've had a squeak of my life," replied Mark, "and I've made a stupid mistake. You must pay all attention to what I'm going to tell you, Doria, for we can't say who is in danger now and who is not. The shot that very nearly ended my career yesterday might just as easily have been aimed at you, had you been in my place."

"A shot? Not the red man? A smuggler perhaps? You may have stumbled upon some of them, and knowing no Italian——"

"It was Robert Redmayne who fired upon me and missed by a miracle."

Jenny uttered an exclamation of fear. "Thank God!" she said under her breath.

Then Brendon told the story in every detail and explained his own ruse. He related nothing but the truth—up to a certain point; but beyond that he described events that had not taken place.

"Having made the faked figure, I hid just before dusk fairly close to it intending, of course, to keep watch, for I was positive that the murderer, as he would suppose himself to be, must come back after dark to hide his work. But now ensued an awkward contretemps for which I had not provided. I found myself faint—so faint that I began to be alarmed. I had not eaten since the morning and the food and flask which I had brought with me were half a mile and more away. They remained, of course, where I had left them when I started to chase Redmayne. It was a choice between attempting to reach the food while I could do so, or stopping and growing chilled and every moment weaker.

"I am not made of iron and the day had been rather strenuous for me. I was bruised and lame and utterly played out. I decided that I should have time to reach my food and return to my hiding-place before the moon rose. But it was not such an easy or speedy business as I had expected. It took me a long time to get back to the starting-place and when I did, a search was needed before I found my sandwiches and flask of Chianti. Never was a meal more welcome. I soon felt my strength returning and set off in half an hour on the journey back to the plateau.

"Then my troubles began. You'll think the wine got into my head and it may have done so; but at any rate I lost the path most effectually and presently lost myself. I began to despair and had very nearly given up any further attempt to return when, out of the trees, blinked the white face of the precipice under Griante's crown and I recognized the situation. Then I went slowly and silently forward and kept a sharp lookout.

"But I returned too late. Once back again, a glance at the dummy showed me that I had lost my chance. It had been handled. The trunk was in one place, the grass head, with my cap upon it, lay in another. One knew that no fox or other wild creature would have disturbed it thus.

"Dead silence hung over the spot; and now, half fearing an ambush in my turn, I waited an hour before emerging. Not a soul was there. Redmayne had clearly come, discovered my escape and then departed again. Even in that moment I considered what I should have done had he confiscated my clothes! It would then have been necessary to tramp to my hotel in the white shirt and scanty underclothing which was all that remained to me. But now I donned my jacket and knicker-bockers, cap and stockings and then prepared to depart.

"There was a smell of earth in the air—a reek of upturned mould; but what that may have been I cannot say. I soon started downhill and, presently, striking a path to the north, entered the chestnut woods and was at my hotel an hour after midnight. That is my story and I propose to-day to revisit the spot. I shall engage the local police who have orders to assist us—that is, unless you, Doria, can spare time to accompany me yourself. I would rather not ask them; but I do not go there again alone."

Jenny looked at her husband and waited to speak until he had done so. But Giuseppe appeared more interested at what had already happened to Brendon than in what was next to happen. He asked many questions, to which Mark was able to return true replies. Then he declared that he would certainly accompany the detective to the scene of his adventure.

"We will go armed this time," he said.

But Jenny protested.

"Mr. Brendon is not nearly well enough to climb there again to-day," she declared. "He is lame and must be feeling the effects of yesterday. I beg him not to attempt to go again so soon."

Doria said nothing but looked at Mark.

"I shall best lose my stiffness by another climb," he assured them.

"That is very true. We will be in no hurry."

"If you go, I come too," said the woman quietly; and both men protested. But she would take no denial.

"I will carry your meal for you," she said, and though they opposed her again, went off to prepare it. Giuseppe also disappeared, that he might leave an order for the day with Ernesto, and Jenny had joined Brendon again before he returned. He had begged her once more not to accompany them; but she was impatient.

"How dull you are for all your fame, Mark"; she replied. "Can you not think and put two and two together where I am concerned, as you do in everything else? I am safe enough with my husband. It will not pay him to destroy me— yet. But you. Even now I implore you not to go up again alone. He is as wily as a cat. He will make some excuse, disappear and meet the other villain. They won't fail twice—and what can a woman do to help you against two of them?"

"I want no help. I shall be armed."

They started, however, and Jenny's fears were not realized. Doria showed no levity and did nothing suspicious. He kept close to Brendon, offered him an arm at steep places and advanced a dozen theories of the incidents reported. He was deeply interested and reiterated his surprise that the unknown's shot should have missed Brendon.

"It is better to be lucky than wise," he declared. "And yet who shall not call you very wise indeed? That was a great ruse—to fall as though dead when the bullet had missed its billet."

Brendon did not reply and little was said as they proceeded to the scene of his adventures; but presently Doria spoke again.

"One eye of the master sees more than six of his servants. We shall hear how Pietro Ganns understands all this. But I am thinking of the red man. What is in his mind this morning? He is very savage with himself and perhaps frightened. Because he knows that we know. He is a murderer still. He does not repent."

They scoured the scene of Brendon's exploit presently and it was Jenny who found the shallow grave. She was very pale and shivering when they responded to her call.

"That is where you would be now!" she said to Mark.

But he was occupied with the mould piled beside the pit. Here and there were prints of heavy feet and Doria declared that the impression of the nails pointed to such boots as the mountain men habitually wore. Nothing else rewarded the search; but Giuseppe was full of theories and Brendon, occupied with his own thoughts, allowed him to chatter without interruption. For his part he felt doubtful whether any further apparition of Robert Redmayne might be expected. This failure would probably put a period to his activity for a time.

Mark determined to take no action until Mr. Ganns came back to Menaggio. Meanwhile he proposed to occupy himself with the husband and wife and, so far as possible, preserve an attitude of friendship to them both. That relations were secretly strained between them appeared clear enough; and the results of casual but frequent visits to the Villa Pianezzo were summed in the detective's mind before Mr. Redmayne and Peter returned. He believed most firmly that Doria was in collusion with the secret antagonist, and intended ultimate mischief to his wife's uncle for his own ends; and he was equally convinced that Jenny, while conscious enough that her husband could not be trusted and meant evil, as yet hardly guessed the full extent of his infernal purpose.

Had she known that Giuseppe and Robert Redmayne were actually working together to destroy Albert Redmayne, Brendon believed that she would tell him. But he guessed that she knew nothing definite, while suspecting much. She had shown the most acute concern at his own danger, and more than once implored Mark to do nothing but look after his own safety until Peter Ganns was back again. Meantime the rift between her spouse and herself appeared to grow. She was tearful and anxious, yet still chose to be vague, though she did admit that she thought she had glimpsed Robert Redmayne again, one evening. But Brendon did not press her again to confide in him, though Doria showed no sort of jealousy. He often left them together for hours and exhibited to the detective a very amiable attitude. He, too, on more than one occasion confessed that matrimony was a state overvaunted.

"Praise married life by all means, Signor

Marco," he said, "but—keep single. Peace, my friend, is the highest happiness, and the rarest."

The days passed and presently, without any warning, Albert Redmayne and the American suddenly reappeared. They arrived at Menaggio after noon.

Mr. Redmayne was in the highest spirits and delighted to be home again. He knew nothing about Peter's operations and cared less. His visit to England was spent at London, where he had renewed acquaintance with certain book collectors, seen and handled many precious things, and surprised and gratified himself to observe his own physical energies and enterprise.

"I am still wonderfully strong, Jenny," he told his niece. "I have been most active in mind and body and am by no means so far down the hill of old age, that ends by the River of Lethe, as I imagined."

He made a good meal, and then, despite the long night in the train, insisted on sending for a boat and crossing the water to Bellagio.

"I have a present for my Poggi," he said, "and I cannot sleep until I hear his voice and hold his hand."

Ernesto went for a waterman and soon a boat waited at the steps, which descended from Mr. Redmayne's private apartments to the lake. He rowed away and Brendon, who had come to see Doria and found to his surprise that Redmayne and Peter were back again, anticipated some private hours with Mr. Ganns. But the traveller was weary and, after one of Assunta's famous omelettes and three glasses of white wine, he declared that he must retire and sleep as long as nature ordained slumber.

He spoke before the listening Giuseppe, but addressed his remarks to Brendon.

"I'm exceedingly short of rest," he said. "Whether I have done the least good by my inquiries remains to be seen. To be frank, I.doubt it. We'll have a talk to-morrow, Mark; and maybe Doria will remember a thing or two that happened at 'Crow's Nest' and so help me. But until I have slept I am useless."

He withdrew presently, carrying his notebook in his hand, while Brendon, promising to return after breakfast on the following morning, strolled to the silkworm house where the last of the caterpillars had spun its golden shroud. He was not depressed by the weary tones of Peter's voice nor the discouraging nature of his brief statement, for, while speaking, Mr. Ganns had discounted his pessimism by a pregnant wink unseen by Doria. It was clear to Brendon that he had no intention of acquainting Giuseppe with any new facts—if such there might be; and this interested Mark the more because, as yet, Peter was quite ignorant of his own adventure on Griante. He had kept it out of the post, not desiring to obtrude anything between Mr. Ganns and his personal activities.

On the following day it was Mr. Redmayne who found himself weary. Reaction came and he slept all that night and determined to keep his bed for twenty-four hours. It seemed, how-

ever, that he was going to find occupation for
everybody. He directed Doria to visit Milan, on a
mission to secondhand booksellers, and Jenny was
sent to Varenna with a gift for an acquaintance.
Brendon perceived that it was designed to keep
both husband and wife out of the way for a few
hours; but whether Doria suspected the intention
he could not judge. Certainly Jenny did not. She
welcomed the excursion to Varenna, for her uncle's
correspondent was a widow lady and Jenny
already knew her and valued her friendship.

Brendon arrived at Villa Pianezzo just as the
twain were starting on their missions, and he and
Peter walked to the landing stage with them and
saw them departing in different steamers.

Even this arrangement, however, failed to satisfy Ganns. He was mysterious.

"If his steamboat stopped nowhere between
here and Como, we wouldn't need to trouble," he
said; "but as it does, and Doria might hop off
anywhere and come back in an hour, we'll just
drift back to Albert."

"He will be asleep and we can have our yarn out
without fear of interruption," answered Mark.

They soon sat together on a shady seat of the
villa garden from which the entrance was visible, and Peter, bringing out his notebook, took
a great pinch of snuff, set his gold box on a little
table before him, and turned to Brendon.

"You shoot first," he said; "there are three
things I need to know. Have you seen the red
man and what is your present opinion concerning
Doria and his wife? Needn't ask if you found

Bendigo's diary, because I am dead sure you did not."

"I didn't. I directed Jenny to have a hunt and she invited me to help her. For the rest I have seen Robert Redmayne, for we may safely speak of the unknown by that name, and I have come to a very definite conclusion concerning Giuseppe Doria and the unfortunate woman who is at present his wife."

A shadow of a smile passed over the great features of Peter.

He nodded and Mark proceeded to tell his story, beginning with the adventure on the mountain. He omitted no detail and described his talk with Doria, the latter's departure to join Jenny on their expedition to Colico, and his own subsequent surprise and escape from death. He told how he had been fired at and fallen, hoping to tempt the other to him, how his assailant had disappeared, and how, at a late hour, he had planned a dummy and seen Giuseppe Doria arrive to bury him.

He narrated how Giuseppe and Robert Redmayne had departed after their disappointment, how he had decided to give Giuseppe an account of the adventure, in order that he might not guess that his share in it was known; and he told how, on the morrow, the Dorias and himself had returned to the spot and found the empty grave with footmarks of native boots about the margin. He added that Jenny, four days later, had reported a glimpse of a man whom she believed to be her uncle; but it was dark at the time and she could

not be positive, though she felt morally sure of
him. He was standing two hundred yards from
the Villa Pianezzo in a lane from the hills and
had turned and hastened away as she approached.
To this statement Peter listened with the deep-
est attention and he did not disguise his satisfaction when Mark made an end.

"I'm mighty glad for two things," he said.
"First that you're in the land of the living, my
son, and that a certain bullet passed your ear instead of stopping in that fine forehead of yours;
and I'm glad to know what you've told me, because it fits in tolerably well and strengthens an
argument you'll hear later. Your little trap was
quite smart, though I should have worked it a
bit different myself. However, you did a very
clever thing, and to take Doria into your confidence afterward was up to our best traditions.
Your opinion of him needn't detain us now.
There only remains to hear what you may have to
say on the subject of his pretty dame."

"My opinion of a very wonderful and brave
woman remains unchanged," Brendon answered.
"She is the victim of a hateful union and for her
the situation must get worse, I fear, before it can
get better. She is as straight as a line, Ganns;
but of course she knows well enough that her husband's a rascal.

"Needless to say I haven't dropped her a hint
of the truth; but while she is loyal in a sense and
very careful, on her side, to leave her sufferings
or suspicions vague, she doesn't pretend she's
happy and she doesn't pretend that Doria is a

good husband, or a good man. She knows that
I know better. She has been longing for your
return and it is a question with me now whether
we shall not do wisely to take her into our confidence. If she knew even what we know, she
would no doubt see much light herself and afford
much light for us. As to her good faith and
honour, there can be no question whatever.''

"Well—so be it. I've heard you. Now you've
got to hear me. We are up against a very marvellous performance, Mark. This case has some
of the finest features—some unique even in my
experience. Though, as history repeats itself,
I dare say there have been bigger blackguards
than the great unknown—though surely not
many.''

"Robert Redmayne?''

Peter broke off for a brief exposition. He took
snuff, shut his eyes and began.

"Why do you harp on 'Robert Redmayne,'
like a parrot, my son? Just consider all I've
said on that matter and the general subject of
forgeries for a minute. You can forge anything
that man ever made, and a good few things that
God has made. You can forge a picture, a postage stamp, a signature, a finger print; and our
human minds, accustomed to pictures, postage
stamps, finger prints, are easily deceived by
appearances and seldom possess the necessary
expert knowledge to recognize a forgery when
we see it. And now we are dealing with people
who have forged a human being, for that is what
the red man amounts to.

"Didn't you do the same thing last week?
Didn't you forge yourself and leave yourself
dead on the ground? Whether the real Robert
Redmayne is actually a stiff, we can't yet swear,
though for my part I am pretty well prepared to
prove it; but this I do know, that the man who
shot at you and missed you and ran away was
not Robert Redmayne."

Brendon demurred. "Remember, I'm not a
stranger to him, Ganns. I saw and spoke with
him by the pool in Foggintor Quarry before the
murder."

"What of it? You've never spoken with him
since; and, what's more, you've never seen him
since, either. You've seen a forgery. It was a
forgery that looked at you on your way back to
Dartmouth in the moonlight. It was a forgery
that robbed the farm for food and lived in the
cave and cut Bendigo Redmayne's throat. It
was a forgery that tried to shoot you and missed."

Mr. Ganns took snuff again and continued.

But as the course of his inquiries belong
to the terrible culmination of the mystery
and cannot here be told with their just significance, it will suffice to record that Brendon
presently found his brain reeling before a theory
so extravagant that he would instantly have dis-
credited it from any lesser lips than those of the
famous man who propounded them.

"Mind," concluded Peter, who had spoken
without ceasing for nearly two hours, "I'm not
saying that I am right. I'm only saying that,
wild though it sounds, it fits and makes a logical

story even though that story beats all experience. It might have happened; and if it didn't happen, then I'm damned if I know what did, or what is happening at this moment. It is a horrible thing, if true; but it's a beautiful thing from the professional point of view—just as a cancer, or a battle, or an earthquake can be beautiful when put in a category outside humanity.''

Brendon delayed his answer and his face was racked with many poignant emotions.

"I can't believe it," he replied at length, in a voice which indicated the extent of his mental amazement and perturbation; "but I shall nevertheless do exactly as you direct. That is well within my power and obviously my duty.''

"Good boy. And now we'll have something to eat. You've got it clear? The time is all important."

Mark scanned his notebook in which he had made voluminous entries. Then he nodded and shut it.

Suddenly Mr. Ganns laughed. The other's book reminded him of an incident.

"A funny little thing happened yesterday afternoon that I forgot," he said. "I'd turned in, leaving my notebook by my head, when there came a visitor to my room. I was asleep all right, but my heaviest sleep won't hold through the noise of a fly on the windowpane; and lying with my face to the door I heard a tiny sound and lifted one eyelid. The door opened and Signor Doria put his nose in. I'd pulled the

blind, but there was plenty of light and he spotted
my vade-mecum lying on the bed table a couple of
feet from my head. Over he came as quiet as
a spider, and I let him get within a yard. Then
I yawned and shifted. He was gone like a mos-
quito, and half an hour later I heard him again.
But I got up and he didn't do more than listen
outside. He wanted that book bad—you can
guess how bad."

For two days Mr. Ganns declared that he must
rest; and then there came an evening when he
privately invited Doria to take a walk.

"There's a few things I'd like to put to you,"
he said. "You needn't let on to anybody else
about it and we won't start together. You know
my favourite stroll up the hill. Meet me at the
corner—say seven o'clock."

Giuseppe gladly agreed.

"We will go up to the shrine of Madonna del
farniente," he declared; and when the time came,
Peter found him at the spot. They ascended the
hill side by side and the elder invited Doria's aid.

"Between ourselves," he began, "I am not too
well pleased with the way this inquiry is pan-
ning out. Brendon's all right and means as well
as any bull that ever I worked with. He does a
clever thing here and there—as when he shammed
death up on the mountain; but what was the sense
of setting that trap and then missing his man?
I shouldn't have done that. You wouldn't have
done it. In plain words there's some dope coming between Mark and his work, and I should like

to hear what you think of him, you being an independent witness and a pretty shrewd cuss. You've had a chance to study his make-up, so tell me what you think. I'm tired of fooling around this job—and being fooled myself.''

''Marco is in love with my wife,'' answered Giuseppe calmly. ''That is what's the matter with him. And, as I don't trust my wife in this affair and still believe ·that she knows more about the red man than anybody else, I think, as long as she hoodwinks Brendon, he will be no manner of use to you.''

Peter pretended to be much astonished.

''My stars! You take it pretty cool!''

''For the good reason that I am no longer in love with my wife myself. I am not a dog in the manger. I want peace and quietness. I have no use for intrigues and plots. I am a plain man, Signor Pietro. Mystery bores me. Moreover I live in fear of getting into a mess myself. I do not see where I come in at all. My wife and this unknown rascal are after something; and if you want to get to the bottom of this, watch her—not me. The blow you fear may fall at any moment.''

''You'd say trail Jenny?''

''That is what I would say. Sooner or later she'll make an excuse to be off to the mountains alone. Let her start and then follow her up with Brendon. The problem is surely simple enough: to catch this red Redmayne. If you cannot do it, tell the police and the doganieri. There is a force of smuggler hunters always on the spot and ready to your hand. Describe this savage, hu-

man fox and offer a big reward for his brush. He
will be caught quickly enough then.''

Mr. Ganns nodded and stood still.

''I shouldn't wonder if that may not have to be
done; but I'd a deal sooner take him ourselves
if we could. Anyway I must get a move on this
fortnight, for to stop longer in Italy is impossible.
Yet how am I going to beat it and leave my old
friend at the mercy of this threat? While I'm
alongside him, he's safe, I guess; but what may
happen as soon as I turn my back?''

''Can I not help you?''

But Mr. Ganns shook his head.

''Can't work in cahoots with you, son, because
I begin to fear you are right when you say your
wife's against us; and a man isn't to be trusted
to pull down his own wife.''

''If that's all——''

They proceeded slowly and Peter kept the ball
of conversation rolling while he pretended to be
very busy with his plans and projects. He
promised also that, when Jenny went to the hills
alone, he and Brendon would secretly follow her.

Then a very strange thing happened. As the
first firefly streaked the dusk and the ruined
shrine rose beside the way, a tall man suddenly
appeared in front of it. He had not been there
a moment before, yet now he bulked large in the
purple evening light, and it was not yet so dark
but his remarkable features challenged the be-
holders. For there stood Robert Redmayne, his
great, red head and huge mustache thrusting out
of the gloom. He stared quite motionless. His

hands were by his sides; the stripes of his tweed jacket could be seen and the gilt buttons on the familiar red waistcoat.

Doria started violently, then stiffened. For a moment he failed to conceal his surprise and cast one look of evident horror and amazement at the apparition. He clearly knew the tall figure, but there was no friendship or understanding in the bewildered stare he now turned upon the shadow that filled the path. For a moment he brushed his hand over his eyes, as though to remove the object upon which he glared; then he looked again—to find the lane empty and Ganns gazing at him.

"What's wrong?" asked Peter.

"Christ! Did you see him—right in the path —Robert Redmayne?"

But the other only stared at Giuseppe and peered forward.

"I saw nothing," he said; whereupon like light-ning, the Italian's manner changed. His concern vanished and he laughed aloud.

"What a fool—what a fool am I! It was the shadow of the shrine!"

"You've got the red man on your nerves, I guess. I don't blame you. What did you think you saw?"

"No—no, signor; I have no nerves. I saw nothing. It was a shadow."

Ganns instantly dismissed the subject and ap-peared to attach no importance whatever to it; but Doria's mood was altered. He became less expansive and more alert.

"We'll turn now," announced Peter half an hour afterwards. "You're a smart lad and you've given me a bright thought or two. We must lecture Mark. It may be better for you, as her husband, to pretend a bit, even though you don't feel it. Let me know privately when Mrs. Doria is for the hills."

He stopped, kept his eye on Giuseppe and took a pinch of snuff.

"Maybe we'll get a move on to-morrow," he said.

Doria, now self-possessed but fallen taciturn, smiled at him and his white teeth shone through the gloom.

"Of to-morrow nobody is sure," he answered. "The man who knows what is to happen to-morrow would rule the world."

"I'm hopeful of to-morrow all the same."

"A detective must be hopeful," answered Giuseppe. "So often hope is all that he has got."

Chaffing each other amiably they returned together.

CHAPTER XVI

THE LAST OF THE REDMAYNES

FOR the night immediately following Doria's experience at the old shrine, Albert Redmayne and his friend, Virgilio Poggi, had accepted Mark Brendon's invitation to dine at the Hotel Victoria, where he still stayed. Ganns was responsible for the suggestion, and while he knew now that Giuseppe might view the festivity with suspicion, that mattered but little at this crisis.

His purpose in arranging to get Albert Redmayne away from home on this particular night was twofold. It was necessary that Peter himself should see Mark Brendon without interruption; and it was vital that henceforth his friend, the old book lover, should never for an instant lie within the power of any enemy to do him ill. In order, therefore, that he might enjoy private conversation with Brendon and, at the same time, keep a close watch upon Albert, Ganns had proposed the dinner party at the hotel and directed Brendon to issue the invitation as soon as Redmayne returned home.

Wholly unsuspicious, Signor Poggi and Albert appeared in the glory of soft white shirt fronts and rather rusty evening black. A special meal was prepared for their pleasure and the four par-

took of it in a private chamber at the hotel. Then
they adjourned to the smoking-room, and anon,
when Poggi and his companion were deep in their
all-sufficing subject, Peter, a few yards distant
with Mark beside him, related the incident of
Giuseppe's ghost.

"You did the trick to a miracle," he said.
"You're a born actor, my son, and you came and
went and got away with it just as well as mortal
man could wish, and far better than I hoped.
Well, Doria was fine. We stung him all right, and
when he saw and thought he recognized the real
Robert Redmayne, it got him in the solar plexus—
I'm doggone sure of that. For just a moment he
slipped, but how could he help it?

"You see the beauty of his dilemma. If he'd
been straight, he'd have gone for you; but he
wasn't straight. He knew well enough that
his Robert Redmayne—the forgery—wasn't on
the war-path to-night; and when I said I saw
nothing, he pulled himself together and swore he
hadn't either. And the next second he realized
what he had done! But too late. I had my hand
on my shooting iron in my pocket after that, I can
tell you! He was spoiling to hit back—he is now
—he's not wasting to-night. But all that matters
for the moment is that we've put a crimp on him
and he knows it."

"He may be off before you return to the villa."

"Not he. He's going to see this thing through
and finish his job, if we don't prevent it. And
he won't waste any more time either. He's been
playing a game and amusing himself—with us and

Albert yonder—as a cat with a mouse. But he
won't play any more. From to-night he's going
for all three of us bald-headed. He's mad with
himself that he was foolish enough to delay. He's
a wonder for his age, Mark; but a man, after all
—not a superman.''

"What happened exactly, and how does he
stand to what he saw?"

"Can't swear, but I figure it like this. I
watched very close with what I call my third eye
—a sort of receiver in my brain that soaks up
what a man's thinking and draws it out of him.
For the first moment he was nonplussed, lost his
nerve and may even have believed he saw a spirit.
He cried out, 'It's Robert Redmayne!' and instantly asked me if I'd seen him too. I stared
and said I'd seen nothing at all, and then his manner changed and he laughed it off and said it was
only a shadow cast by the shrine. But, on second
thoughts, he knew mighty well it was no shadow,
and presently he fell a bit silent, thinking hard,
while I just chatted about nothing, as I'd done
from the start of our walk. I'd pretended to take
him into my confidence, you see, and I heard from
him just exactly what I thought he was going to
tell me—that you were in love with his wife;
that he had no more use for her; that she knew
all about the red man, and so on.

"Now what passed in his mind? He must
have come to one of two possible conclusions.
Either he suspected that he had been the victim
of hallucination and seen a freak of his own im-

agination, and believed me when I said I had seen nothing; or else he did not. If he had taken it that way, there was nothing more to be said and nothing to worry about as far as I was concerned. But he didn't take it that way and, on second thoughts, he didn't believe me. He knew very well indeed that he was not the sort of person who sees ghosts; he remembered that you'd been away at Milan for a couple of days and he tumbled to it, the moment his wits cleared, that this was a frame-up between me and you to surprise something out of him. And he knew I had got exactly what I wanted, when he swore that he'd seen nothing, after all.

"And that's where he stands now. And he's going to be busy in consequence; but we've got to be busier. What he and his accomplice propose to do is to destroy Albert Redmayne—in such a way that they are not associated with his death; and what they will do, if we let them, is to act as they have already acted in England. Albert would disappear—and we might or might not be invited to look upon his blood; but we shouldn't see him. Como is the grave they probably mean for him."

"You'll go for Doria straight, then?"

"Yes. He's making his plans at this moment, just as we are, and it's up to us to work our wonders so they'll tumble in ahead of his. You see that? There's two of us and two of them, and the next move must be ours, or they'll checkmate our king all right. We've got this great advantage; that Albert is at our beck and call, not theirs; and while he remains safe, our stock's good. Master Giuseppe knows that; but he also suspects that he's no longer safe himself; so he's probably going to take some chances in the next twenty-four hours."

"Everything centres on the present safety of Mr. Redmayne?"

"It does; and we must watch him like a pair of hawks. To me the most interesting aspect of this case is the personal factor that has spoiled it for the master criminal. And the factor is vanity—an overmastering, gigantic, yet boyish vanity, that tempted him to delay his purpose for the simple pleasure of playing, first with you and then with me. It's himself that has given him away; there's mighty little credit to us, Mark. His own pride of intellect has thrown him. If he can win out now I'll forgive the scamp."

"To you all credit—if you are right in what you believe; to me certainly none from first to last," answered Brendon gloomily. "And yet," he added, "you may be mistaken. A man's convictions are not easily uprooted; love is not always blind, and still I feel that, even if I have lost my reputation, I may win something better—after the tale is told."

Ganns patted his arm kindly.

"Hope no such thing, I beg you," he said. "Fight your hope, for it will soon prove to be based on a chimera—on something that doesn't and never did exist. But your reputation is another matter and I pray you won't feel so ready

to let a fine record go down the wind this time to-
morrow.''

"To-morrow?"

"Yes; to-morrow night the bracelets go on
him."

Peter then indicated his purpose.

"He'll not guess we're moving quite so quickly
and, by so doing, we anticipate his stroke. That,
at least, is what I mean to attempt with your
help, if possible. To-night and to-morrow morning I keep beside Albert; then you must do so;
because, after lunch, I have a meeting with the
local police down the lake at Como. The warrant
will be waiting for me and I shall return after
dark in one of the little black boats of the doganieri. We shall come up with lights out and land
at the villa.

"Your part will be to keep Albert in sight and
watch the others. Doria will probably believe
my excuse for going down to Como isn't true, and
he is therefore likely to jump at the opportunity
to get on with it. There's just a chance of poison.
I don't like to get Albert across to Poggi, because
there he would be much easier to tackle than
here.''

"He's awake to the critical situation?"

"Yes, I've made it clear. He's promised not
to eat or drink anything, except what I bring
home with me to-night from here. Our game is
that he'll be indisposed to-morrow and keep his
private rooms. He'll pretend that he's done himself too well with you to-night. I shall be with
him—I don't sleep to-night, but play watch-

dog. To-morrow his breakfast will go away untouched—and mine also. We shall then partake of the secret food.

"After noon it's up to you. I can't say what Doria will do; but you mustn't give him the chance to do anything. If he wants to see Albert, use your authority and tell him he cannot do so until I return. Put the blame on me; and if he's wicked use your iron."

"He may, of course, bolt when he knows the game is up," said Mark. "He may be off already."

"Not he," answered Peter. "It's contrary to reason to suppose he'll guess that I can possibly know what I know. He underrates me far too much to give me credit for that. He won't beat it; he'll bluff it—till too late. I don't fear to lose him; I only fear to lose Albert."

"Trust me that far."

"I'm going to. And I want to plan a little surprise of some sort, so that Albert unconsciously helps us. We can't ask him to do anything cute himself; he's not built that way; but he's the king to be guarded and if the king makes an unexpected move, much may be gained. We've got to be alive to a dozen possibilities. If, for instance, poison is attempted and found to fail——"

"How if we gave it out that it had succeeded and that Mr. Redmayne pretended he was mighty ill an hour after breakfast?"

"I'd thought of that. But the difficulty would be that we shan't be in a position to say if poison is really used. No time for chemistry."

"Try it on the cat."

Peter considered.

"A double cross is often a very pretty thing," he admitted, "but I've seen too many examples among the police of digging a pit and falling in themselves. One difficulty is that we don't want to alarm Albert more than necessary. At present he only knows that I think him in danger; but he has not the most shadowy idea that members of his own household are implicated. He won't know it till I forbid him to touch his breakfast. Yes; we can certainly try a double cross. He shall order bread and milk—we know who will bring it to him. Then his cat, 'Grillo,' shall breakfast upon it." Peter turned to Mark. "That will convince you, my friend."

But the other shook his head.

"It depends upon circumstances. Even granted poison, many an honest man and woman has been the innocent tool of a murderer's will."

"True enough; but we are wasting time upon an improbability. I do not myself think it will be attempted. It is the line of least resistance and the line of least resistance generally means the lines of greatest risk afterward. No—he'll do something smarter than that if he gets half a chance. The grand danger would be that Doria should find himself alone with Albert, even for a moment. That is the situation to circumvent and avoid at any cost. Let nothing induce you to lose sight of one or other; and even should Doria obviously make a run for it before I return, don't be deceived by that, or go after him. He may adopt any ruse to get you guessing when I have gone—that is, if he suspects me of some immediate step. But if I go without leading him to feel any very grave suspicion as to my object in going, we may surprise him before his own stroke is struck. That, in a word, is our objective.''

An hour later the detectives saw Signor Poggi to his boat and then walked home with Mr. Redmayne. Peter had provender concealed about his person and presently he explained to his friend that things were now come to a climax.

''In twenty-four hours I hope we're through with our mysteries and plots, Albert,'' he said; ''but during that time you've got to obey me in every particular and so help me to set you free from this abomination hanging over you. I can trust you; and you must trust me and Mark here till to-morrow night. You'll soon be at peace again with your troubles ended.''

Albert thanked Ganns and expressed his satisfaction that a conclusion was in sight.

''I have seen through the glass darkly,'' he told them. ''Indeed I cannot say that I have seen through the glass at all. I am entirely mystified and shall be glad indeed to know this horror with which I am threatened may be removed. Only my absolute trust in you, dear Peter, has prevented me from becoming distracted.''

At the villa Brendon left them and Jenny welcomed her uncle. The girl begged Mark to come in for a while before returning; but it was late and Mr. Ganns declared that everybody must retire.

"Look us up early, Mark," he directed. "Albert tells me there are some old pictures at Como that have got a lot of kick in them. Maybe we'll all go down the lake for a pleasure party to-morrow, if he thinks it good."

For a moment Brendon and Jenny stood alone before he departed; and she whispered to him.

"Something has happened to Doria to-night. He is struck dumb since his walk with Mr. Ganns."

"Is he at home?"

"Yes; he went to bed many hours ago."

"Avoid him," answered Mark. "Avoid him as far as possible, without rousing his suspicion. Your torments may be at an end sooner than you think for."

He departed without more words. But he presented himself early on the following day. And it was Jenny who first saw him. Then Peter Ganns joined them.

"How is uncle?" asked Mr. Redmayne's niece, and Albert's friend declared the old book lover found himself indisposed.

"He kept it up a bit too late last night at the hotel and drank a little too much white wine," said Peter. "He's all right but feeling a trifle like next morning. He'll stop where he is for a spell and you can take him up a biscuit and a hair of the dog that bit him presently."

Ganns then announced his intention of going later to the town of Como, and he invited Doria and Brendon to accompany him; but Mark, already familiar with the part he had to play, declined, while Giuseppe also declared himself unable to take the trip.

"I must make ready to return to Turin," he said. "The world does not stand still while Signor Pietro is catching his red man. I have business, and there is nothing to keep me here any longer."

He appeared indifferent to the rest of the company and lacked his usual good humour; but the reason Brendon did not learn until a later hour.

After luncheon Mr. Ganns set off—in a white waistcoat and other adornments; Giuseppe also left the villa, promising to return in a few hours; and Brendon joined Albert in his sleeping apartment. For a time they were alone together and then came Jenny with some soup. She stopped to chat for a little while and, finding her uncle apparently somnolent and disinclined to talk, turned to Mark and spoke under her breath. She was still agitated and much preoccupied.

"Later, when we may, I should like to speak to you—indeed I must do so. I am in great danger myself and can only look to you," she whispered. Combined fear and entreaty filled her eyes and she put her hand upon his sleeve. His own caught it and pressed it. He forgot everything before her words. She had come to him at last of her own free will.

"Trust me," he answered, so that only she could hear. "Your welfare and happiness are more to me than anything else on earth."

"Doria will be out again later. Once he has gone—after dusk—we can safely speak," she answered. Then she hastened away.

Albert Redmayne stirred himself as soon as Jenny withdrew. He was dressed and lying on a couch beside the window.

"This subterfuge and simulation of ill health are most painful to me," he declared. "I am exceeding well to-day and all the better for our delightful dinner of last night. For nobody less than dear Peter would I ever sink to pretend anything: it is contrary to my nature and disposition so to do. But since I have his word that to-day light is going to be thrown upon all this doubt and darkness I must possess my soul in patience, Brendon. There are dreadful fears in Peter's mind. I have never known him to be suspicious of good people before. He will not let me eat and drink in my own house to-day! That is as much as to say that I have enemies within my gates. What could be more distressing?"

"A precaution."

"Suspicion is inconceivably painful to me. I will not harbour suspicion. When suspicion dawns in my mind, I instantly throw over the cause of the suspicion. If it is a book, however precious it may be, I drop it once for all. I will not be tormented by doubts or suspicions. In this house are Assunta and Ernesto, my niece and her husband. To suspect any of those excellent and honourable people is abominable and I am quite incapable of doing so."

"Only a few hours. Then, I think, all but one will be exonerated. Indeed I'm sure of it."

"Giuseppe appears to be the storm centre in Peter's mind. It is all beyond my understanding. He has always treated me with courtesy and consideration. He has a sense of humour and perceives that human nature lacks much that we could wish it possessed. He feels rightly toward literature, too, and reads desirable authors. He is a good European and is the only man I know, save Poggi, who understands Nietzsche. All this is in his favor; and yet even Jenny appears to regard Giuseppe as wholly ineffectual. She openly hints that she is disappointed in him. I know what may go to make a man; but am, I confess, quite ignorant of what goes to make a husband. No doubt a good man may be a bad husband, because the female has her own marital standards; yet what she wants, or does not want, I cannot tell."

"You like Doria?"

"I have had no reason to do otherwise. I trust that this unhappy brother of mine—if, indeed, he is what you all think and not an air-drawn vision projected by your subconscious minds—may soon be laid by the heels—for his own sake as much as ours. I will now read in 'The Consolations of Boethius'—last of the Latin authors properly so called—and smoke a cigar. I shall not see Giuseppe. I have promised. It is understood that I am an invalid; but he will certainly be hurt that I deny myself to him. The man has a heart as well as a head."

He rose and went to a little bookshelf of his favourite authors. Then he buried himself in Boethius, and Mark, looking out of the window, saw the life of the lake and the glory of the summer sky reflected. Beyond the shining water Bellagio's towers and cypresses were massed under a little mountain. From time to time there sounded the beat of paddle wheels, as the white steamers came and went.

Doria returned for a while during the afternoon, and Jenny told him that her uncle was better but still thought it wise to keep his room. Her husband appeared to have recovered his good temper. He drank wine, ate fruit and addressed most of his conversation to Brendon, who spoke with him in the dining-room for a while.

"When you and Mr. Ganns are weary of hunting this red shadow, I hope you will come and see me at Turin," he said. "And perhaps you will also be able to convince Jenny that my suggestions are reasonable. What is money for? She has twenty thousand pounds upon her hands and I, her husband, offer such an investment as falls to the chance of few capitalists. You shall come and see what my friends and I are doing at Turin. Then you will make her think better of my sense!"

"A new motor car, you told me?" asked Mark.

"Yes—a car that will be to all other cars as an ocean 'liner' to Noah's Ark. Millions are staring us in the face. Yet we languish for the modest thousands to launch us. The little dogs find the hare; the big dogs hold him."

Jenny said nothing. Then Doria turned to her and bade her pack his clothes.

"I cannot stop here," he said when she had gone. "This is no life for a man. Jenny will probably remain with her uncle. She is fed up, as you say, with me. I am very unfortunate, Marco, for I have not in the least deserved to lose her affection. However, if a new inamorato fills her thoughts, it is idle for me to yelp. Jealousy is a fool's failing. But I must work or I shall be wicked!"

He departed and Brendon joined Albert Redmayne, to find the old man had grown uneasy and fearful.

"I am not happy, Brendon," he said. "There is coming into my mind a cloud—a premonition that very dreadful disasters are going to happen to those I love. When does Ganns return?"

"Soon after dark, Mr. Redmayne. Perhaps about nine o'clock we may expect him. Be patient a little longer."

"It has not happened to me to feel as I do to-day," answered the book lover. "A sense of ill darkens my mind—a suspicion of finality, and Jenny shares it. Something is amiss. She has a presentiment that it is so. It may be, as she suspects, that my second self is not happy either. Virgilio and I are as twins. We have become strangely and psychologically linked together. I am sure that he is uneasy on my account at this moment. I am almost inclined to send Ernesto to see if all be well with him and report that all is well with me."

He rambled on and presently went out upon his balcony and looked across to Bellagio. Then he appeared to forget Signor Poggi for a time and presently ate a little of the store of food brought back in secret by Mr. Ganns on the previous night. "It is a grief to me," he said again, "that Peter fears treachery under this roof. Surely God is all powerful and would not suffer my interesting and harmless life to be snatched away from me by poison? I shall be very thankful when Peter leaves his horrid profession and retires and devotes his noble intellect to purer thoughts."

"What became of the soup, Mr. Redmayne?"

" 'Grillo' drank every drop and, having done so, my beautiful cat purred a grace after meat, according to his custom, then sank into peaceful slumber."

Mark looked at the great blue Persian, who was evidently sleeping in perfect comfort. It woke to his touch, yawned, spread its paws, purred gently and then tucked itself up again.

"He's right enough."

"Of course. Jenny tells me that her husband returns to Turin to-morrow. She, however, will stop here with me for the present. It may be well if they separate for a while."

They talked and smoked, while Mr. Redmayne became reminiscent and amused himself with memories of the past. He forgot his present disquiet amid these recollections and chatted amiably of his earliest days in Australia and his subsequent, successful career as a bookseller and dealer.

Jenny presently joined them and all entered the dining-room together, where tea was served.

"He will be going out soon now," whispered Albert's niece to Brendon; and he knew that she referred to her husband. Mr. Redmayne still declined to eat or drink.

"I did both to excess yesterday," he said, "and must rest my ill-used stomach until to-morrow."

He was chiefly concerned with Doria and had prepared for him various messages to bookmen in Turin. They sat long and the shadows were lengthening before the old man returned to his apartments. Then Giuseppe made a final and humorous appeal to Mark to influence Jenny in favour of the automobiles and presently lit one of his Tuscan cigars, took his hat and left the house.

"At last!" whispered Jenny, her face lighting in relief. "He will be gone for a good two hours now and we can talk."

"Not here, then," Mark answered. "Let us go into the garden. Then I can see when the man comes back."

They proceeded into the gathering dusk and presently sat together on a marble seat under an ilex, so near the entrance that none might arrive without their knowledge.

Presently Ernesto came and turned on an electric bulb that hung over the scrolled iron work of the outer gate. Then they were alone again. and the woman threw off all shadow of reserve and restraint.

"Thank God you can listen at last," she said, then poured out a flood of entreaties. He was swept from every mental hold, drowned in the torrent of her petitions, baffled and bewildered at one moment, filled with joy in the next.

"Save me," she implored, "for only you can do so. I am not worthy of your love and you may well have ceased to care for me or even respect me; but I can still respect myself, because I know well enough now that I was the innocent victim of this accursed man. It was not natural love that made me follow him and wed him; it was a power that he possesses—a magnetic thing—what they call the 'evil eye' in Italy. I have been cruelly and wickedly wronged and I do not deserve all that I have suffered, for it was the magic of hypnotism or some kindred devilry that made me see him falsely and deceived and drove me.

"From the time my uncle died at 'Crow's Nest' Doria has controlled me. I did not know it then, or I would have killed myself rather than sink to be the creature of any man. I thought it was love and so I married him; then the trick became apparent and he cared not how soon my eyes were opened. But I must leave him if I am to remain a sane woman."

For an hour she spoke and detailed all she had been called upon to endure, while he listened with absorbed interest. She often touched Brendon's shoulder, often clasped his hand. Once she kissed it in gratitude, as he promised to dedicate every thought and energy to her salvation. Her breath brushed his cheek, his arm was round her as she sobbed.

"Save me and I will come to you," she prom-

ised. "I am hoodwinked and deceived no longer.
He even owns the trap and laughs horribly at
me by night. He only wants my money, but
thankfully would I give hin every penny, if by so
doing I could be free of him."

And Brendon listened with a rapture that was
almost incredulous; for she loved him at last and
desired nothing better than to come to him and
forget the double tragedy that had ruined her
young life.

She was in his arms now and he sought to
soothe her, sustain her and bring her mind to
regard a future wherein peace, happiness and
content might still be her portion. Another hour
passed, the fireflies danced over their heads;
sweet scents stole through the garden; lights
twinkled from the house; on the lake in the silence
that now fell between them they heard the gentle
thud of a steamer's propeller. Still Doria did
not return and as a church clock struck the hour
Jenny rose. Already she had knelt at his feet
and called him her saviour. Now, still dreaming
of the immense change in his fortunes, already
occupied with the means that must be taken to
free his future wife, Mark was brought back
to the present.

Jenny left him to seek Assunta; and he, hearing
the steamer and guessing that Peter was at hand,
hastened to the house. Silence seemed to fill it,
and, as he lifted his voice and called to Albert
Redmayne, the noise on the water ceased. No
answer reached Mark, and from the library he
proceeded to the adjoining bedroom. It was

empty and he hastened out upon the veranda above the lake. But still the book lover did not appear. A long, black vessel with all lights out had anchored a hundred yards from the Villa Pianezzo, and now a boat put off from the craft of the lake police and paddled to the steps below Brendon.

At the same moment Jenny joined him.

"Where is Uncle Albert?" she asked.

"I do not know. I have called him and got no answer."

"Mark!" she cried with a voice of fear. "Is it possible——" She moved into the house and lifted her voice. Then Brendon heard Assunta answer and in a moment there followed a horrified exclamation from the younger woman.

But Brendon had descended the steps to meet the approaching boat. His mind was still in a whirl of mingled emotions. Above him, as he steadied the boat, stood Jenny and she spoke swiftly.

"He is not in the house! Oh, come quickly if that is Mr. Ganns. My uncle has gone across the water and my husband has not returned."

Peter, with four men, quickly landed and Brendon spoke. He could give no details, however, and Jenny furnished them. While she and Mark sat in the garden, guarding the front door and front gate, behind them to the house there had come a message by boat for Mr. Redmayne from Bellagio. Perhaps there was but one appeal powerful enough to make Albert forget his promises or the danger that he had been as-

sured now threatened him; but it was precisely
this demand which had made the old man hasten
away.

Assunta told them how an Italian had reached
the steps in a skiff from Bellagio; how he had
called her and broken the evil news that Signor
Poggi was fallen dangerously ill; and how he
sent entreaties to his friends to see him without
delay.

"Virgilio Poggi has had a fatal fall and is
dying," said the messenger. "He prays Signor
Redmayne to fly to him before it is too late."

Assunta dared not delay the message. Indeed,
knowing all that this must mean to her master,
she delivered it instantly, and five minutes after
hearing the dreadful news, Albert Redmayne, in
great agony of mind, had embarked, to be rowed
toward the promontory where his friend dwelt.

Assunta declared that her master had been
gone for an hour, if not longer.

"It may be true," said Jenny, but Brendon
knew too well what had happened.

The group formed under Peter's command and
he issued his directions swiftly. He cast one
look at Mark which the detective never forgot;
but none saw it save Brendon himself. Then he
spoke.

"Row this boat back to the steamer, Brendon,"
he said, "and tell them to take you across to
Poggi as quick as may be. If Redmayne is
there, leave him there and return. But he's not
there: he's at the bottom of the lake. Go!"

Mark hastened to the boat and one of the officers

who had come with Ganns wrote a dozen words on a sheet from a notebook. With this Brendon reached the black steamer and in another moment the vessel disappeared at full speed under the darkness in the direction of Bellagio.

Then Peter turned to the rest and bade them all, with Jenny, accompany him to the dwelling room. Supper had been laid here but the apartment was empty.

"What has happened," explained Peter, "is this: Doria has used the only certain means of getting Albert Redmayne out of this house, and his wife has doubtless aided him to the best of her power by arresting the attention of my colleague whom I left in charge. How she did it I can easily guess."

Jenny's horrified eyes flamed at him and her face grew rosy.

"How little you know!" she cried. "This is cruel, infamous! Have I not suffered enough?"

"If I am wrong, I'll be the first to own it, ma'am," he answered. "But I am not wrong. What has happened means that your husband will be back to supper. That's but ten minutes to wait. Assunta, return to the kitchen. Ernesto, hide in the garden and lock the iron gate as soon as Doria has passed through it."

Three big men in plain clothes had these remarks translated to them by the fourth, who was a chief of police. Then Ernesto went into the garden, the officers took their stations, and Mr. Ganns, indicating a chair to Jenny, himself occupied another within reach of her. Once she had tried to leave the room, but Peter forbade it.

"Fear nothing if you're honest," he said, but she ignored him and kept her thoughts to herself. She had grown very pale and her eyes roamed over the strange faces around her. Silence fell and in five minutes came the chink of the iron gate and the footfall of a man without. Doria was singing his canzonet. He came straight into the room, stared about him at the assembled men, then fixed his eyes upon his wife.

"What is this?" he cried in amazement.

"Game's up and you've lost," answered Ganns. "You're a great crook! And your own vanity is all that's beat you!" He turned quickly to the chief of police, who showed a warrant and spoke English.

"Michael Pendean," he said, "you are arrested for the murder of Robert Redmayne and Bendigo Redmayne."

"And add 'Albert Redmayne,'" growled Ganns. He leaped aside with amazing agility as he spoke, for the culprit had seized the weapon nearest his hand and hurled a heavy saltcellar from the table at Peter's head. The mass of glass crashed into an old Italian mirror behind Ganns and at the moment when all eyes instinctively followed the sound, Jenny's husband dashed for the door. Like lightning he turned and was over the threshold before a hand could be lifted to stop him; but one in the room had watched and now he raised his revolver. This young officer—destined for future fame—had never taken his eyes off Doria and now he fired. He was quick but another had been quicker, had seen his purpose and anticipated his action. The bullet meant for Michael Pendean struck down his wife, for Jenny had leaped into the doorway and stopped it.

She fell without a sound, whereupon the fugitive turned instantly, abandoned his flight, ran to her, knelt and lifted her to his breast.

He was harmless now, but he embraced a dead woman and the blood from her mouth, as he kissed her, covered his lips. He made no further fight and, knowing that she was dead, carried her to a couch, laid her gently down, then turned and stretched his arms for the handcuffs.

A moment later Mark Brendon entered from the house.

"Poggi sent no message and Albert Redmayne has not been seen at Bellagio," he said.

CHAPTER XVII

THE METHODS OF PETER GANNS

Two men travelled together in the train de luxe from Milan to Calais. Ganns wore a black band upon the sleeve of his left arm; his companion carried the marks of mourning in his face. It seemed that Brendon had increased in age; his countenance looked haggard; his very voice was older.

Peter tried to distract the younger man, who appeared to listen, though his mind was far away and his thoughts brooding upon a grave.

"The French and Italian police resemble us in the States," said Mr. Ganns. "They are much less reticent in their methods than you English. You, at Scotland Yard, are all for secrecy, and you claim for your system superior results to any other. And figures support you. In New York, in 1917, there were two hundred and thirty-six murders and only sixty-seven convictions. In Chicago, in 1919, there were no less than three hundred and thirty-six murders and forty-four convictions. Pretty steep—eh? In Paris four times as many crimes of violence are committed yearly as in London, though, of course, the population is far smaller. Yet what are the respective achievements of the police? Only half as many crimes are detected by the French as by the British. Your card-index system is to be thanked for that.''

He ran on and then Brendon seemed to come to himself.

"Talk about poor Albert Redmayne," he said.

"There's little to be added to what you know. Since Pendean chooses to keep dumb, at any rate until he's extradited, we can only assume exactly what happened; but I have no doubt of the details. It was Pendean, of course, you saw leave the villa, while his wife held you in conversation, and so ordered her falsehoods that you were swept away from every other consideration save how best to rescue her from her husband.

"She took good care to involve your own future and to say just what was most likely to make you forget your trust. My dear, dear Albert, forgive me if I am blunt; but when you look back, presently, you will see that the great loss is really mine, not yours. Michael Pendean, once out of sight, gets a boat, adopts his disguise —the false beard and mustache found upon him— and presently rows round to Albert's steps. He sees Assunta, who does not recognize him, and says that he has come from Virgilio Poggi, who is at death's door at Bellagio.

"There was no weightier temptation possible than that. Redmayne forgets every other consideration and in five minutes has started for Bellagio. The boat is quickly in mid-lake under the darkness and there Albert meets his death and burial. Pendean undoubtedly murdered him

with a blow—probably just as he murdered
Robert and Bendigo Redmayne; then, no doubt,
he used weights, heavy stones brought for the
purpose, and sank his victim in the tremendous
depths of Como. He was soon back again with
a clean boat and his disguise in his pocket. He
had an alibi also, for we found out that he had
been drinking for more than hour at an *albergo*
before he came back to the villa.''

''Thank you,'' said Brendon humbly. ''There
can be no doubt that it was so. And now I will
ask a final favour, Ganns. What happened has
made my mind a blank in some particulars. I
should be thankful and grateful if you would retrace your steps when you were in England. I
want to go over that ground again. You will not
be at the trial; but I must be; and, praise God,
this is the last time I shall ever appear in a
court of law.''

He referred to a determination that he had already expressed: to leave the police service and
seek other occupation for the remainder of his
life.

''That's as may be,'' answered Peter, bringing
out the gold snuffbox. ''I hope you'll think
better of it. You've had a bitter experience and
learned a great deal that will help you in business as well as in life. Don't be beaten by a bad
woman—only remember that you had the luck to
meet and study one of the rarest female crooks our
mysterious Creator ever turned out. A face like
an angel and a heart like a devil. Let time pass
and presently you'll see that this is merely a

hiatus in a career that is only begun. Much good and valuable work lies before you; and to abandon a profession for which you are specially suited is to fly in the face of Providence anyway.''

After a pause and a long silence, while the train sped through the darkness of the Simplon tunnel, Peter retraced the steps by which he had been enabled to solve the riddle of the Redmaynes.

"I told you that you had not begun at the beginning,'' he said. ''It's really all summed up in that. You occupied an extraordinary position. The criminal himself, in the pride of his craft and by reason of the consuming vanity that finally wrecked him, deliberately brought you in. It was part of his fun—his art if you like—that he should involve a great detective for the added joy of making a fool of him. You were the spice in his bloody cup for Michael Pendean—the salt, the zest. If he had merely stuck to business, not a thousand detectives would ever have queered his pitch. But he was as playful as any other hunting tiger. He rejoiced in adding a thousand details to his original scheme. He was an artist, but too florid, too decadent in his decorations. And so he ruined what might have been the crime of the century. It is just the touch of human fallibility that has brought Nemesis to many a great criminal.

''The machinery he employed focussed attention from the first on the apparent murderer rather than his victim. It appeared impossible to doubt what had happened and Pendean's death was assumed but never proved. Particulars concerning Robert Redmayne were abundant; yet, during the whole course of the official inquiry, none was forthcoming concerning the supposed victim. Of him you had heard from his wife; and her original statement to you at Princetown—when she invited you, doubtless at Pendean's direction, to take up the case—was masterly because so nearly true in every respect.

"But from the time that I met and spoke with Albert's niece I began to reflect upon that statement, and my speedy conviction was this: that a great deal more concerning Jenny's first husband demanded to be known. Do not suppose that I was on the track of the truth at that period. Far from it. I only desired more data and regarded the history of Michael Pendean as being of doubtful value, since his wife alone was responsible for the details. It seemed to me absolutely necessary to learn more than she was prepared to tell. I had questioned her, but found her either ignorant of much concerning him—or else purposely evasive. Of her three uncles, only Robert had ever seen Michael Pendean. Neither Bendigo nor dear Albert had set eyes on him; and that fact, though of no significance at first, of course, became very significant indeed at a later stage of my study.

"I went first to Penzance and devoted several days to learning all possible particulars of the Pendean family. On examining Michael Pendean's ancestry, as a preliminary to finding out everything remembered of Pendean himself, I at once made a highly important discovery. Joseph Pendean, Michael's father, was often in Italy on his pilchard business for the firm, and he married an Italian woman. She lived with her husband at Penzance and bore him one son, and a daughter who died in infancy. The lady seems to have given cause for a certain amount of scandal, for her Latin temperament and lively ways did not commend themselves to the rather austere and religious circle in which her husband and his relations moved.

"She visited Italy sometimes and Joseph Pendean undoubtedly regretted his marriage. He might have divorced her in the opinion of some with whom I spoke; but for the sake of his son he would not take this step. Michael was devoted to his mother and accompanied her frequently to Italy. On one of these occasions, when a boy of seventeen or eighteen, he met with an accident to his head; but I could glean no particulars of its nature. He seems to have been a silent and observant lad and never quarrelled with his father.

"When at last Mrs. Pendean died in Italy, her husband attended the funeral at Naples and returned to England immediately afterward with his son. The boy was subsequently apprenticed to a dentist, having expressed a wish to follow that profession. He promised well, passed his examinations and practised at Penzance for a time. But then he ceased to be interested in the work

and presently joined his father. In connection
with the pilchard trade, he now visited Italy and
often spent a month at a time in that country.

"Few could give me any information as to his
nature, and pictures of him did not apparently
exist; but an elderly relative was able to tell me
that Michael had been a silent, difficult boy. She
also showed me an old photograph of his parents,
taken together with their son when he must have
been a child of three, or thereabout. His father
didn't suggest a man of character; but Mrs.
Pendean appeared to be a very handsome creature indeed, and it was at the moment I studied
her features through a magnifying glass that I
won my first conviction of a familiar likeness.

"It is a rule with me, when any sudden flash
of intuition throws real or false light upon a case,
to submit the inspiration to a most searching and
destructive analysis and bring every known fact
against it. Thus, on seeing a possible glimpse of
Giuseppe Doria's beautiful countenance reflected
upon my eyes from the photograph of the mother
of Michael Pendean, I began to marshal all my
knowledge to confound any deduction from that
accident. But judge of my interest and surprise
when I found nothing that could be pointed to as
absolute refutation of the theory now taking such
swift shape in my mind. Not one sure fact
clashed with the possibility.

"Nothing at present was positively known by
me which made it out of the question that Joseph
Pendean's wife should be the mother of Giuseppe
Doria. But none the less many facts might exist

as yet beyond my knowledge, which would prove such a suspicion vain. I considered how to obtain these facts and naturally my thought turned to Giuseppe himself. To show you by what faltering steps we sometimes climb to safe ground, I may say that at this stage of my inquiry I had not imagined Doria and Michael Pendean were one and the same person. That was to come. For the moment I conceived of the possibility that Madame Pendean, a lady who had caused some fluttering in the Wesleyan dovecots of Penzance, might by chance have been the mother of a second son in her native country. I imagined that Michael and an Italian half brother might know each other, and that the two were working together to destroy the brothers Redmayne, so that Michael's wife should inherit all the family money.

"Having found out what Penzance could tell me, I beat it up to Dartmouth, because I was exceedingly anxious to learn, if possible, the exact date when Giuseppe Doria entered the employment of Bendigo Redmayne as motor boatman. Albert's brother hadn't any friends that I could find; but I traced his doctor and, though he was not in a position to enlighten me, he knew another man—an innkeeper at Tor-cross, some miles away on the coast—who might be familiar with this vital date.

"Mr. Noah Blades proved a very shrewd and capable chap. Bendigo Redmayne had known him well, and it was after spending a week at the Tor-cross Hotel with Blades and going fishing in his motor boat, that the old sailor had decided to start one himself at 'Crow's Nest.' He did so and his first boatman was a failure. Then he advertised for another and received a good many applications. He'd sailed with Italians and liked them on a ship, and he decided for Giuseppe Doria, whose testimonials appeared to be exceptional. The man came along and, two days after his arrival, ran Bendigo down to Tor-cross in his launch to see Blades.

"Redmayne, of course, was full of the murder at Princetown, which had just occurred, and the tragedy proved so interesting that Blades had little time to notice the new motor boatman. But what matters is that we know it was on the day after the murder—on the very day Bendigo heard what his brother, Robert, was supposed to have done at Foggintor Quarry—that his new man, Giuseppe Doria, arrived at 'Crow's Nest' and took on his new duties.

"From that all-important fact I built my case, and you don't need to be told how every step of the way threw light upon the next until I had reached the goal. Robert Redmayne is seen on the night of Michael Pendean's supposed destruction. He is traced home again to Paignton. He leaves his diggings before anybody is up and, from that exit, vanishes off the face of the earth. But during the same day—probably by noon— Giuseppe Doria arrives at 'Crow's Nest'—an Italian whom nobody knows, or has even seen before.

"That meant good-bye to any theory of a half brother for Michael; and it also meant that not Pendean, but his wife's uncle, Robert Redmayne, perished on Dartmoor. And there he lies yet, my son!"

Mr. Ganns took snuff and proceeded.

"Now, having made this tremendous deduction, I looked over all the facts again and they became very much more interesting. Every moment I expected some crushing blow to shake my structure; at every turn I guessed a certainty would come along and bowl my theory over; but no such thing happened. Details, of course, there are— many little pieces of the puzzle now known to only one man alive, and that is Pendean himself; but the main incidents, the true picture, loomed out clear enough for me before I left Dartmouth and came back to Albert in London. The big things were all, not there to be shaken. The picture was fogged at certain points, but I had no doubt as to what it represented, and even the incredible details that seemed to contradict reason were composed and cleaned up when Michael Pendean's own temperament was brought as a solvent to them.

"Here, I think, we may spare a tribute of admiration to Pendean's histrionics. I guess that his original conception and creation of 'Giuseppe Doria' was an exceedingly fine and well thought out piece of acting. He actually lived in the character and day after day exhibited qualities of mind and an attitude to life quite foreign to

his real rather saturnine and reserved nature.
Both he and his wife were heaven-born comedians
as well as hell-born criminals.

"To return; the large particulars, then, were
these: the foreground, the middle distance and
the background made a synthetic whole, logically
consistent, rational even—when you allow for the
artist's make-up. That he will leave a full statement before the end, I venture to prophecy. His
egregious vanity demands it. Nothing that he
writes is likely to be sincere and he'll have his
eye on the spotlight all the time; but you may
expect a pretty complete account of his adventures
before he's hanged; you may even expect something a little new in the suicide line if they give
him a chance; for be sure he's thought of that.

"And now I'll indicate how I brought fact
after fact to bombard my theory, and how the
theory withstood every assault until I was bound
to accept it and act upon it.

"We start with the assumption that Pendean
is living and Robert Redmayne dead. We next
assume that Pendean, having laid out his wife's
uncle at Foggintor, gets into his clothes, puts on
a red mustache and a red wig and starts for Berry
Head on Redmayne's motor bicycle. The sack
supposed to contain the body is found, and that is
all. His purpose is to indicate a hiding-place
for the corpse and lead search in a certain direction; but he is not going to trust the sea; he is
not going to stand the risk of Robert Redmayne's
corpse spoiling his game. No, his victim never

left Foggintor and probably Michael will presently tell us where to find the body.

"Meanwhile a false atmosphere is created under which he proceeds to his engagement at 'Crow's Nest.' And then what happens? The first clue—the forged letter, purporting to come from Robert Redmayne to his brother. Who sent it? Jenny Pendean on her way through Plymouth to her Uncle Bendigo's home. She and her husband are soon together again—working for the next stroke. As I say, they were a pair who ought to have been on the stage, where they would have made darned sight bigger money than the Redmayne capital all told; but crime was in their blood; they must have met like the blades of a scissors and found themselves heart and soul in agreement. Evil was their good; and no doubt, when they understood each other's lawless point of view, both felt they must join forces. A tolerable bad dame, I'm afraid, Mark; but she knew how to love all right; and nobody doubts that bad women can love as well as good ones—often a great deal better.

"They settle down and the supposed death of Michael Pendean blows over. Jenny plays widow but spends as much time as she wants in her husband's arms all the same; and together they plan to put out poor Ben. He'd never seen Pendean, of course, which made the Doria swindle possible. And a great point—that only Michael himself can clear—is the intended order of his murders. That puzzled me a bit, because before Robert Red-

mayne appeared at Princetown and the reconciliation between him and his niece and her husband
was affected, he must already have got the appointment of motor boatman to Bendigo and
known that he was going there presently under
a false name and character. I incline to think
that he meant to begin with the old sailor and
that, when Robert turned up unexpectedly on
Dartmoor, he altered his plans. That accident
opened the way to his first performance if I'm
not wrong; but he'll throw light on that assumption later and show what really did pass through
his mind.

"Now we come to the preliminary steps at
'Crow's Nest' which ended in the death of the
second brother. What plan was to be taken we
cannot be sure, but your second visit to Dartmouth—a surprise visit, remember—quickened
it. You offered just the starting point; and before you left on that rough, moonlight night, Pendean had recreated the forgery of Robert Redmayne and appeared before you in that character.
And not content with this, he kept the part going
for all it was worth. As Robert Redmayne, he
broke into Strete Farm and was seen by Mr.
Brook, the farmer; while as 'Doria,' next morning, he comes to you at Dartmouth to tell you the
murderer of Michael Pendean has reappeared.

"One may easily imagine the joy that he
took in this double impersonation and how easy it
was, with the help of his wife, to fool you to the
top of your bent. He had already derived the
exquisite entertainment of seeing you jealous of

his attentions to Jenny and suspicious that she was yielding to them; while she—well, it is instructive to consider again her treatment of you. Yes, a very great actress; but whether inspired by love for Pendean, or hate for her unfortunate relatives, or just pure creative joy in her own talent, who shall say? Probably all these emotions played their part.

"Now we get to blindman's-buff with the forgery. Follow each step. Bendigo never sees his supposed brother once; you never see him again. Your united search through the woods is futile; but Jenny and her husband in the motor boat bring news of him. She comes back with tears in her eyes. She has seen Robert Redmayne—the murderer of her husband! She and the motor boatman have spoken to him; they describe his miserable condition and intense desire to see his brother. They paint a wonderful and realistic picture. Robert must see Bendigo all alone—and he must have food and a lamp in his secret hiding-place. He has been in France—that was a sop for you, Mark—but can endure suspense no longer.

"Well, it's fixed up and Ben decides to meet his brother after midnight, alone; but the old sailor's pluck wavers—who shall blame him?—and he arranged in secret with you that you should be hidden in his tower room when Robert Redmayne comes to keep the appointment. He writes a letter to his brother, and Jenny and Doria go to sea again and take it, together with stores and a lamp. While they're away, you get planted in the tower room to watch the coming interview; and when the pair in the motor boat return, Jenny's uncle tells her that you've gone back to Dartmouth and will blow in again next morning. You recollect exactly what followed. Night comes and, at the appointed time, footsteps are heard ascending to the observatory and Bendigo prepares to meet his brother. But no Robert Redmayne appears. It is Giuseppe Doria. He has already had a long talk with his master about Jenny Pendean. He has told the old sailor of his love for Jenny and so forth. You, hidden, heard that yarn, and how Bendigo told him to stow the subject and say no more about it for another six months.

"Now the next thing puzzled me for a moment; but I think I know what happened. Only Pendean's final statement, if he ever makes one, will serve to clear the point; but I can guess that at that first interview with Ben he tumbled to the fact that you were hidden in the tower room. He is a man with a power of observation sharp as a razor, and I'm inclined to bet that before he left Bendigo, after their talk over Jenny, he'd got you—knew you were there.

"That being so, his own plans had to be modified pretty extensively. Whether he meant to finish off Ben that night, you can't be sure; but there is very little doubt of it. Everything was planned. The interview with Robert had been arranged and various people, including yourself, knew about it. His wife was ready down below to help him get the body away, and their plans were, no doubt, mature to the last detail. If, therefore, all had gone right with Pendean, if you had really been away that night, next morning you would probably have been greeted with the information that Bendigo had disappeared. You would possibly have found evidences of a struggle in the tower room and a pint of blood judiciously decorating the floor, but nothing else.

"Only on the assumption that Pendean had found you out can I explain why this didn't start under your nose. I imagine that if he had believed his master alone at one o'clock that night, he would have knocked him on the head and proceeded as I suggest. But he does no such thing. He arrives in great excitement to describe another meeting with Robert and to report that the wanderer has changed his mind and will only see his brother in his own secret hiding-place after dark.

"On hearing this, Bendigo bids you come out of your cupboard, and Doria, so to call him, pretends great indignation and surprise.

"Now we get another lifelike report of runaway Robert; and finally Bendigo consents to visit him in his hiding-place. The lamp is going to burn and show the particular cave on that honeycombed coast where Bendigo's brother is supposed to be concealed. Another night comes and Ben goes to his death. Probably he was murdered instantly on landing and disposed of at sea. Again there is going to be no dead man. Pendean returns to you and his wife at 'Crow's Nest.' He reports that the brothers are confer-

ring and reveals the situation of the hiding-place.
He is soon off again and, on his second visit, plays
his tiger tricks, runs a bloody trail up the tunnel
to the plateau, and sets his trap for the police
next morning.

"One needn't go over the futile hunt that followed. Everything worked exactly as Pendean
had planned, and you can very easily picture the
entertainment furnished for that vampire pair by
the course of the subsequent man hunt.

"Two Redmaynes have gone to their account
and there remains but one. Meantime the course
of true love runs smoothly and Doria marries
his wife again. So, at least, they are pleased to
declare, for the satisfaction of Albert Redmayne
and yourself. Needless to say they went south
together as man and wife, reported a ceremony
that did not take place, and after a reasonable
delay turned their attention to my hapless
friend.

"Would you not have thought some ray of
human truth might have touched their hearts in
the company of that childlike and kindly spirit?
Would you not have judged that close acquaintance with one so amiable and large-hearted must
have wakened a spark of compassion in their
souls? No; they came to kill him and the unsus-
pecting victim welcomes his murderers with
friendship. It is interesting to observe that he
prefers Giuseppe to his own niece. He confessed
to me that Jenny puzzled him and it seemed
strange to Albert that she had forgotten her first
husband so easily. His tender sensibilities could

not admire such indifference; and no doubt he also remembered that his niece's early record, in marrying Pendean against her family's wishes, too much reminded him of her father's wilful ways and headstrong passions.

"But they come on their dark business and are welcomed; and then—an insensate act of folly! The weak spot in their remorseless plan! Again Doria rouses Robert Redmayne from the grave; again he challenges you! A thousand simple and safe ways had offered to dispose of Albert Redmayne. The region in which he chose to live and his own trusting and ingenuous character had alike made him the easiest possible prey of any human hunter; but Michael's vanity has grown by what it feeds on. He is an artist, and he desires to complete his masterpiece with all due regard to form. It must be fashioned to endure and take its place forever in the highest categories of crime. His pride rebels against the line of least resistance. All shall end on the same large pattern in which it was originally conceived. He courts danger and creates difficulty that his ultimate achievement may be the more august.

"So the forgery is trotted out once more; and it is not enough that Jenny shall report to her uncle the advent of Robert Redmayne beside Como. An independent witness is demanded and Assunta Marzelli sees the big man with the red mustache, red hair and red waistcoat. She also records the tremendous shock to her mistress that resulted from this sudden apparition. Remember

that Jenny's husband was still supposed by Albert to be in Turin. Then the old game is played;
Doria presently arrives in person; they toy with
their subject; they enrich it with details; awaken
the alarm of their unhappy victim and send for
you, designing to treat you in the same manner
as before.

"Nor does Albert's appeal to me hasten their
operations. Who is Peter Ganns? A famous
American bull. Good! They will have another
victim at their chariot wheels. It shall be an
international triumph. Albert Redmayne must
be murdered before an audience worthy of the
occasion. The combined detective forces of the
States, of Italy, of England, shall seek Robert
Redmayne and succour Albert; but the one shall
evade capture, the other perish under their eyes."
He turned to Brendon. "And they brought it off
—thanks to you, my son."

"And paid for it—thanks to you," answered
Mark.

"We are but men, not machines," answered the
elder. "Love thrust a finger into your brain and
created the inevitable ferment. Of course Pendean was lightning quick to win his account from
that. He may have even calculated upon it when
he made Jenny beg your aid at the outset. He
knew what men thought of her; he had doubtless
taken stock of you at Princetown and probably
learned that you were unmarried. So, when time
has passed and you can look back without a groan,
you will take the large view and, seeing yourself
from the outside, forgive yourself and confess

that your punishment was weightier than your error.''

In gathering dusk the train thundered through the valley of the Rhine while, above, the mountain summits melted upon the night. A steward looked into the carriage.

''Dinner is served, gentlemen,'' he said. ''I will, if you please, make your beds while you are absent.''

They rose and went together to the saloon carriage.

''I'm dry, son, and I've sure earned a drink,'' said Peter.

''You've earned a vast deal more than I or any man can ever pay you, Ganns,'' said Brendon.

''Don't say it, or think it. I've done nothing that you wouldn't have done if you had been free. And always remember this: I shall never blame you, even when I think with dearest affection of my old friend. I shall only blame myself, because the final, fatal mistake was mine—not yours. I was the fool to trust you and had no excuse for doing so. You were not to be trusted for a moment just then, and I ought to have known it. 'Twas our limited capability that made you err, that made me err, that made Michael Pendean err. The best laid plans of mice and men—you know, Mark. The villain mars his villainy; the virtuous smudge their white record; the deep brain suddenly runs dry—all because perfection, in good or evil, is denied to saints and sinners alike.''

CHAPTER XVIII

CONFESSION

DURING the autumn assizes, Michael Pendean was tried at Exeter and condemned to death for the murders of Robert, Bendigo and Albert Redmayne. He offered no defence and he was only impatient to return to his seclusion within the red walls of the county jail, where he occupied the brief balance of his days with just such a statement as Peter Ganns had foretold that he would seek to make.

This extraordinary document was very characteristic of the criminal. It possessed a sort of glamour; but it failed of real distinction and the quality proper to greatness, even as the crimes it recorded and the man responsible for them. Pendean's confession revealed an insensibility, a faulty sense of humour, an affectation and a love for the glittering and the grandiose that robbed it of any supreme claim in the annals or literature of murder. The document ended with an assurance that Michael would never die at the hands of his fellow man. He had repeated this assertion on several occasions and every conceivable precaution was taken to prevent evasion of his sentence—an issue to be recorded in its proper place.

Here is his statement, word for word as he wrote it.

MY APOLOGIA

"Hearken, ye judges! There is another madness besides, and it is before the deed. Ah! Ye have not gone deep enough into this soul! Thus speaketh the red judge: 'Why did this criminal commit murder? He meant to rob.' I tell you, however, that his soul hungered for blood, not booty: he thirsted for the happiness of the knife!"

And again:

"What is this man? A coil of wild serpents at war against themselves—so they are driven apart to seek their prey in the world."

So wrote one whose art and wisdom are nought to this rabbit-brained generation; but it was given to me to find my meat and drink within his pages and to see my own youthful impressions reflected and crystallized with the brilliance of genius in his stupendous mind.

Remember I, who write, am not thirty years old.

As a young man without experience I sometimes asked myself if some spirit from another order of beings than my own had not been slipped into my human carcase. It seemed to me that none with whom I came in contact was built on, or near, my own pattern, for I had only met one person as yet—my mother—who did not suffer from the malady of a bad conscience. My father and his friends wallowed in this complaint. They declared themselves openly to be miserable sinners and apparently held that the one respectable attitude for humanity at large. "Safety" was the only state to seek; "danger" the only condition to avoid. A very cowardice of curs are the Cornish!

I soon found, however, that history abounded in great figures who had thought and acted otherwise; and presently, in the light thrown from the theatre of the past, I recognized myself for what I was.

In what is comprehended under the general and vague term of "crime," everything depends upon the values of the individual performer; and again and again do we find that a criminal has struck before counting the cost to himself, or considering the unsleeping detectives, hidden in his own faulty heart and brain, who will sooner or later discover and denounce him.

The man of conscience, the man capable of remorse, the man who murders at the prompting of a temper uncontrolled—such will swiftly learn that however well the deed is done, a thousand baffling distractions, bred of their own inherent or acquired weakness, must arise to confound them. Remorse, for example, is always a first step to discovery, if not to confession; and any lesser uneasiness similarly tends to trouble of mind and consequent danger of body. Those who hang, in truth deserve to do so; but they who

strike, like myself, for reasons that success cannot shake and from a settled, farsighted resolution
beyond the power of any emotion to assail, should
be safe enough. We rejoice in the sublime mental
gratification that follows success: it is our spiritual support, our sustenance and our reward.

What can offer an experience so tremendous as
murder? What has science, philosophy, religion
to give us comparable with the mysteries, dangers
and triumphs of great crime? All are childish
toys compared to it; and since, in any case, the
next world will surely stultify our knowledge, confound our accepted truths, and reduce the wisdom
of this earth to the prattle of childhood, I
turned from physics and from metaphysics to
action—and happening to taste blood early,
tingled with the joy of it.

At fifteen years of age I killed a man, and
found, in a murder undertaken for very definite
reasons, a thrill beyond expectation. It was as
though I had drunk at a wayside spring and found
an elixir. That incident is unknown; the death
of my father's foreman, Job Trevose, has not been
understood till now. He lived at Paul, a village
upon the heights nigh Penzance, and his walk
to his work took him by the coast-guard track
along lofty cliffs. Among the fish-curing sheds
one day, unseen, I chanced to hear Trevose speak
of my mother to another man and declare that
she did evil and dishonoured my father.

From that moment I doomed Trevose to death
and, some weeks later, after many failures to win
the right conditions, caught him alone in a sea

fog as he returned homeward. There was not a
soul on the cliff path but ourselves; and he was
a small man, I a strong, big boy. I walked beside him for fifty paces, then fell behind, leaped
at his neck and hurled him over the cliff in an
instant. One yell he gave and dropped six hundred feet. Then I fled over meadows inland and
returned home after dark. Neither I nor anybody else was ever associated with the affair, and
the death of Job Trevose has always been as-
cribed to misadventure—the easier to believe
since he was not a temperate man.

From this experience I won, not remorse, but
manhood. I rejoiced in what I had done. But
I did not tell any living soul and only my wife
ever heard the truth. Time passed and I proceeded with my life in normal fashion, learning
myself and increasing my understanding of human nature. I was never under any domination
of passion, but exercised great restraint and
found that only by self-knowledge and self-command comes power. I did not seek forbidden
fruit, but did not shun it. My life proceeded
orderly; I chose the profession of dentist, as being
likely to introduce me to people of a more interesting type than my father's acquaintance; and
I kept an open mind for myself, but a shut mind
for others.

My chief joy at this season was represented by
my occasional visits to Italy with my mother. Already I felt that land to be my home and hated
Cornwall and its bleak inhabitants. Then, at the
psychological moment, a girl woke instincts until

then dormant; I was faced with rarest good fortune and discovered a kindred spirit of the opposite sex. That any woman lived who could see with my eyes, or share my contempt of the trammels set round life, I did not believe until I met with Jenny Redmayne. Women had never interested me, save in the case of my mother, and I had seen none other with her large heart, tolerance, humour and indifference to convention.

Then a chance friend, the brainless Robert Redmayne, brought his niece to spend her school holiday with him and I discovered in the seventeen-year-old schoolgirl a magnificent and pagan simplicity of mind, combined with a Greek loveliness of body that created in me a convulsion. From the day that we met, from the hour that I heard her laugh at her uncle's objection to mixed bathing, I was as one possessed; and my triumphant joy may be judged, though never measured, when I perceived that Jenny recognized in me the complement and precious addition unconsciously sought of her own spirit.

That spirit she had scarcely understood; but now its clean and fierce white light shone in secret for me alone. We loved one another devotedly from the first understanding; and each fresh find in the heart of the other drew us together with increasing worship and passion. We were probably the most exquisite man and woman, the most original, beautiful, fearless and distinguished, that had ever come together in the benighted township of Penzance. People stared at us sometimes as though we were a faun and nymph; but they did not guess that our hearts were formed to match our wondrous bodies. Fire leaped to fire and before the girl finished her education we were dedicated to each other forever.

What she saw in me was my extraordinary masculine beauty, combined with an intellect that set good and evil in their places and soared, by native instinct, above both. What I discovered in her was an attitude of mind so inquiring and so lawless, so utterly devoid of any familar prejudice or mother-taught opinion, that I felt as the finder of a priceless jewel unstained by earth or heaven. Her intellect was pure and not vitiated by any superstition; she revealed a healthy thirst for experience; she adored me and my attitude to life. We made fascinating voyages of discovery into each others' hearts; we experimented from time to time on ordinary people; and we quickly discovered that we both possessed rare histrionic ability.

Indeed she had already entertained ambitions for the stage; but though her dead father would hardly have stood in her way, these ambitions were not encouraged by the three dolts, her uncles, who now supposed themselves to control her future. A glorious actress is lost to the world in my wife.

She had no secrets from me and I soon learned of her expectations; but it was not the prospect of the Redmayne money that shortened her uncles' lives. Jenny and I were never man-eaters; and, while my youthful experience in murder attracted her and increased her admiration for my qualities, it was not at that time in our minds to anticipate events or quarrel with her relations.

Her grandfather still lived, when first I met her, and the extent or disposition of his wealth seldom entered our calculations. For we were then far too much in love to ponder the value of money, and our temperaments proved so distinguished that no sordid calculation ever wasted a moment of our time.

But a year passed; Jenny was ready to wed me and begin life as my twin star; while I longed for her with a great longing. The situation cleared; her grandfather died; she would presently be the possessor of ample means and I already enjoyed an income from the business of Pendean and Trecarrow.

Then came the war and the sentence of death incidently pronounced by that event upon the brothers Redmayne. Their own folly and lack of vision were alone responsible. The facts are familiar, but not the tremendous and shattering emotions I endured on being branded a coward and traitor to my country by these three patriotic idiots. I did not argue with them; it was enough that Jenny swiftly awakened to even a bitterer hatred and a deeper fury of resentment than myself. They had roused the sleeping tempest and our lightning now became only a question of time.

Was I the man to make carrion of myself in national quarrels? Was I the man to sacrifice my glorious life because besotted and third-rate minds, blinded by their own ignorance and fooled by cleverer statesmen than themselves, had suffered England to drift into war with Germany? Was I a sheep to be slaughtered for a government of Nonconformists? Should I consent to be mangled by the Boches because my fatuous country willed to trust the old gang? No!

I had long understood that war was certain; I had already ascended public platforms with that little company who warned the Empire and were derided for their pains by the ruling bats and moles. But to die for the salvation of this diplomatic trash, to suffer untold torments and ultimate extinction for that myopic crew of hypocrites known as the British government—— Never!

I evaded active service with a heart drug, as did some thousands of other intelligent men. I kept a whole skin, stopped at home and received for my share the Order of the British Empire instead of a nameless grave. It was easy enough.

Before Jenny and I were married she knew that my outraged honour had doomed her family to extinction. But they would wait till the war was ended. Germany, indeed, might account for Robert Redmayne; and even the elderly Bendigo, who was appointed to a mine sweeper, might give his life for his country. Meantime we volunteered also and our record of service at Princetown Moss Depôt is not to be assailed.

Already my future intention was colouring my life. I grew a beard, wore glasses and pretended delicacy of constitution; for after the war was done I intended murdering three men, and I proposed to do so in such a manner that society would find it impossible to associate me with the crimes. We devoted many hours to the project, for my wife was, of course, at one with me in my determination. She hated her family, as only relations can hate; and she had her own ground of grievance, in that her legacy of twenty thousand pounds was withheld pending the deliberations of Albert Redmayne. The money interested Jenny more than myself; but she pointed out that her grandfather's fortune, representing considerably over a hundred thousand pounds, was left entirely to her uncles and herself, and that as they were all three bachelors, she might reasonably hope to inherit in fulness of time.

To that end we identified ourselves with war work and expected presently to secure the trust and good-will of the brothers before they were banished off the earth. At Princetown we adopted that strenuous, simple-minded attitude to life most calculated to satisfy those among whom our toil now threw us. We pretended an enthusiasm for the work and an affection for Dartmoor which were alike illusory. As an example of our far-reaching methods I may relate how we returned to the wilderness after the war was done and actually began to build a bungalow upon it, which, needless to say, we never had the least intention of occupying. But the seed was sown and we had created in many minds the impression of a devoted and simple pair—conventional, narrow-minded, ingenuous and therefore attractive to the many.

I now come to my confession and must admit at the outset how circumstance served to modify detail and improve the original plan. My own greatness gradually increases to any intelligent, unprejudiced critic when my adaptability is considered, for that play of blind chance, in which ninety and nine men out of a hundred find themselves entangled throughout their lives, was to me an added inspiration and opportunity. I tamed Chance and put a bit in its jaws, a bridle on its fiery neck. Chance immensely altered my original schemes; but it was powerless to modify my genius; it became the Slave of the Ring, to serve an adamant purpose superior to itself.

The war left the three brothers alive; and I had designed first to destroy Bendigo and Albert Redmayne, who had never seen me, and finally deal with my old friend, Robert; but it was he who came at the critical moment as a lamb to the slaughter and so inspired the superb conception now familiar to the civilized world.

The time was ripe to pluck these men who had insulted and outraged me; and when Bendigo Redmayne advertised for a motor boatman, the challenge was accepted. I left my wife and, from Southampton, offered my services as an Italian marine engineer familiar with this country and now seeking occupation in England. The sea was my playground in youth and I understood very perfectly the mechanism to be under my control.

That Ben would select me seemed improbable and I regarded this tentative opening as unlikely to introduce me to my first objective. I forged certain foreign letters of commendation and left it at that. He approved, however. He liked Italians, from experience of them aboard ship, and he appreciated my letter and my imaginary war record. It was arranged that I should join him on a day in late June; and I returned to Princetown with the interesting intelligence.

My orginal plans need not be related; but any reader of imagination will perceive that Bendigo Redmayne must quickly have been in my power to dispose of as I thought best. Then, within a fortnight of the date fixed for my arrival at "Crow's Nest," all was changed by the advent of Robert Redmayne. Strange to say, upon the day previous to his appearance, my wife had nearly prevailed upon me not to keep my engagement with Bendigo. She had learned that Robert was at Paignton and the danger of a meeting between him and me—the possibility that he might visit his brother and recognize me—was too considerable to risk. I had therefore almost abandoned the impersonation of "Giuseppe Doria" when Robert arrived at Princetown and we were reconciled. But then Jenny, to whom all credit belongs at this stage—my devoted, glorious Jenny!—began to see a glimpse of the dazzling opportunity now presented. Every detail was worked out with meticulous precaution; not a hazard was ignored, not a risk unguarded.

With Robert Redmayne free to visit Bendigo

at any time, "Doria" would obviously be a danger; for, though a man of little perception— a noisy dolt easily enough hoodwinked—there remained strong likelihood that he must recognize me in the Italian "Doria." And the more so that we had now renewed our former friendship. But let Robert Redmayne be reduced to silence, let Robert Redmayne vanish, and I should be safe enough as "Giuseppe Doria" with the old sailor!

From this determination: to obliterate Robert before going to Bendigo, the inevitable means appeared. A week before Robert Redmayne died, every stage of the journey had been planned.

What was the first step? An entreaty from Jenny that I should shave my beard! She begged again and again and appealed to Robert, who supported her. I withstood them until the day of his destruction. Upon that morning I appeared without it and they congratulated me. Other trifling preliminaries there were. On one occasion, when my wife rode down to Plymouth with her uncle on his motor bicycle, she left him to do some shopping and, visiting Burnell's the theatrical costumer, she purchased a red wig for a woman. At home again she transferred it into a red wig for a man. Meantime I had made a pair of large mustaches, helping myself when Mrs. Gerry, our landlady, was out of the way to hair from the brush of one of her stuffed foxes, whose colour exactly resembled the rufous adornments of Robert Redmayne. That was all I wanted. The rest of my disguise would go to the quarry on the person of Robert himself.

But other things went to the quarry also, for I had to look far ahead. When we started on his motor cycle, after tea, to do some work at the bungalow, I took a handbag containing my costume as Giuseppe Doria—a plain, blue serge suit, coat, waistcoat and trousers and yachtsman's cap. I also carried a tool—the little instrument with which I murdered the three Redmaynes. It resembled the head of a butcher's pole-axe, of great weight with the working end sharpened. I made it in a forge at Southampton and it lies to-day under the waters of Como. My bag I had taken on previous occasions to the quarry, with a bottle of whisky and glasses, so Robert thought it not strange that I should do so again.

We started for Foggintor and it was still broad daylight when we got there. I had already studied the quarry and determined on Robert Redmayne's resting-place. You will find him— and the suit of clothes I was wearing that evening—in the moraine, where it opens fanwise from the cliff above and spreads into the bottom beneath. On the right, at its base, water eternally drips from the ledges of the granite and here, two feet beneath the surface, he doubtless still lies. The falling water smooths the slope and the earth descends daily to increase the volume of granite sand and gravel above him. The drip must swiftly have washed away any trace of my handiwork and, even with these directions, it may be hard to find him.

Arrived at the bungalow, Robert's first demand was a bath in the quarry pool. To this I had accustomed him and we stripped and swam for ten minutes. You will perceive the value of this operation. His clothes were ready for me without speck or blemish; and when we returned from the pool into the shelter of the bungalow it was a naked man I smote and dropped with one blow of my formidable weapon. His back was turned and the pole-axe head went through his skull like butter. He was dead before I cut his throat, put on my shoes and hastened, naked, to the moraine with a spade.

I opened the grave under the falling water and dug two feet into the loose stuff, for that was deep enough. Then I carried him and my clothes from the bungalow, interred them, heaped back the soil and left the eternal percolations from above to do the rest. By the following morning it had demanded very keen eyes to discover any disturbance at that spot even had search been instituted at Foggintor. But I did not desire a search and my subsequent measures prevented it. A Ganns might have discovered clues, no doubt; a Brendon was more easily deluded.

I stood now free of the vital object in a murder —the corpse, and it remained for me to create the false appearance of reality with which these operations have always been so successfully enshrouded. I donned Redmayne's clothes. We were men nearly of a size and they fitted closely enough, though too large in detail. I then adjusted my wig and mustaches, drew Robert's cap over my head—it was too large, but that mattered not. I next obtained the sack, touched it in blood

and put into it my handbag and a mass of fern
and litter to fill it out. Then I fastened it behind
the motor bicycle—an unwieldy object designed
to create the necessary suspicion.

There was now nothing of either Redmayne or
myself left at Foggintor. The gloaming had long
thickened to darkness when I went my way and
laid the trail through Two Bridges, Postbridge
and Ashburton to Brixham. Once only was I
bothered—at the gate across the road by Brixham
coast-guard station; but I lifted the motor bicycle
over it and presently ascended to the cliffs of
Berry Head. Fate favoured me in details, for,
despite the hour, there were witnessess to every
step of the route; I even passed a fisher lad, de-
scending from the lighthouse for a doctor, where
no witness might have been hoped for or expected. Thus my course was followed and each
stage of the long journey correctly recorded.

On the cliff I emptied my sack, cast its stuffing
to the winds, fastened my handbag to the bicycle,
thrust the bloodstained sack into a rabbit hole,
where it could not fail to be discovered, and then
returned to Robert Redmayne's lodging at Paignton. There a telegram had already been sent in-
forming the landlady of his return that night.
The place and its details I had gleaned from Redmayne himself; therefore I knew where he kept
his machine and, having put it in its shed, entered
the house about three o'clock with his latchkey
and ate the ample meal left for his consumption.
Only a widow and her servant occupied the dwell·
ing and they slept soundly enough.

I did not venture to seek Bob's bedroom, for I knew not where it might lie; but I changed into the serge suit, cap and brown shoes of Doria and packed Redmayne's clothes, tweeds and showy waistcoat, boots and stockings into my handbag with the wig and mustaches and my weapon. Soon after four o'clock I left—a clean-shorn, brown sailorman: "Guiseppe Doria," of immortal memory.

It was now light, but Paignton slumbered and I did not pass a policeman until half a mile from the watering-place. Having admired the dawn over Torquay, I walked to Newton Abbot and reached that town before six o'clock. At the railway station I breakfasted and presently took a train to Dartmouth. Before noon I reached "Crow's Nest" and made acquaintance with Bendigo Redmayne. He was such a man as Jenny had led me to expect and I found it easy enough to win his friendship and esteem.

But he had little leisure for me at this moment, for there had already come news from his niece of the mysterious fatality on Dartmoor.

Needless to say that my thoughts were now entirely devoted to my wife and I longed for her first communication. Our briefest separation caused me pain, for our souls were as one and we had not been parted, save for my visit to Southampton, since our marriage day.

It was her exquisite thought to involve the man from Scotland Yard. Mark Brendon, then known to be taking holiday at Princetown, had been pointed out to her; she appraised him correctly and her woman's intuition told her what verisimilitude would spring from his active coöperation. Secure in her own genius, she therefore complicated the issues by appealing to Brendon and winning his enthusiastic assistance. Much sprang from this, for the poor fellow was soon a willing victim to Jenny; and while he lent a thousand happy touches to subsequent incidents by his inefficiences and sins of omission, such moderate talent as he possessed was still farther obscured by the emotion of love which sprang up in his heart for my widowed partner. Thus he became exceedingly useful as time passed; yet fortune favours fools and his very stupidity served him well at the end; for when I sought to destroy him on Griante and believed that I had done so, the man displayed an ingenuity for which I did not give him credit and unconsciously laid the foundations of subsequent disaster.

The letter which Bendigo Redmayne received, and supposed had come from his brother at Plymouth, was posted by Jenny on her journey to "Crow's Nest." We had written it together a week earlier and studied her uncle's indifferent penmanship very carefully before doing so. This blind I held valuable, and indeed it proved to be; for it concentrated attention on the port and led to the theory that Robert had escaped to France or Spain.

Thus closed our opening episode. The murder of Michael Pendean became received as a fact capable of everything but proof absolute, while the escape of Robert Redmayne offered an in-

soluble problem to the authorities. Michael Pendean indeed was dead enough, for it had been a
part of my original conception that he should
never reappear. Obviously he could not do so;
and I, who had already created "Doria," now began to live my new part in life with zest and gusto
—a dramatist and actor in one. He did not
spring full-fledged from my brain; but like other
great impersonators, I gradually enlarged and en-
riched the character and finally found myself
actually living and thinking the new being into
which I was translated. Pendean sank to the
shadow of a shade.

My past, by an effort of will, was banished from
my mind. I invented and presently believed in
another past. When my wife returned to my
side, I fell in love with her for the second time;
and so superbly did I enter into the existence and
mental outlook of Giuseppe Doria that I was almost shocked by the familiarity of Jenny when
she kissed me and hugged me at the first con-
venient opportunity after her arrival at "Crow's
Nest"!

And her own echoing genius swiftly accepted
this magnificent apotheosis of her Cornish husband. I became a new man in her eyes also.
With that marvellous power of make-believe, possible only to women of supreme genius, she swiftly
conceived of me as something altogether different
from Michael Pendean—a creature richer and
rarer—and this effort of imagination enabled us
both to create that solid appearance of a new
and quickening understanding that so amply suf-

ficed to deceive Bendigo Redmayne and delude Brendon.

It is impossible to exaggerate the unique entertainment we derived from this phase of our deception. We proposed to let six months pass before the death of Bendigo Redmayne, and we were already contemplating details and considering how best to bring his brother back upon the stage for the purpose of Ben's destruction, when Mark Brendon blundered in upon us once again. He came very pat with calf love in his eyes; and it seemed that he might well assist us once more and apply his limited attainments to the problem of our sea wolf's approaching exit. Because we knew our Marco well, by this time, and perceived how useful he might be in disseminating that atmosphere of reality so desirable in cases such as these.

We were called upon to act quickly—so quickly that the first steps were taken before the last had been fully planned; but the place, the time of long, dark nights and other circumstances—these all lent value and assistance to the acute operations now undertaken. I swiftly brought Robert Redmayne to life; and though, with more leisure for refinements, I should not have clothed him in his old attire, yet that crude detail possessed a value of its own and certainly served to deceive Brendon, who, before the sudden apparition under that night of storm, did not stop to be logical or weigh probability. In the windy moonlight he saw the red head, huge mustache and brass-buttoned waistcoat of Robert Redmayne, and any question of detail escaped him in the whirl of the larger emotions and suspicions awakened by such an unexpected vision.

Doubtless he was thinking of Jenny and speculating with deep unrest how he might approach that lonely and lovely woman. Nor had he missed my attractions and we may feel sure that jealousy shared his heart with passion. Upon these reflections broke Redmayne, the murderer, and Marco's first thought was doubtless unflattering to the residents of "Crow's Nest." What he designed to do next morning I cannot say, but we determined his actions from the other end. Having first appeared before him by Black Wood and lifted the curtain on the second act of my romantic comedy, I remained there a while, then ascended to Strete Farm and presently, in the small hours, awakened the farmer, showed myself stealing food and so hastily departed.

Thus a few hours later, when Giuseppe goes for the milk, he hears of the robbery, returns to "Crow's Nest" and describes a man that Ben has no difficulty in recognizing as his brother, or Jenny as her uncle. Robert Redmayne is on the war-path once more!

Of subsequent events, most are so familiar that there is no need to retrace them. It is to be noted, however, that Robert does not appear again to anybody but Jenny and Doria. In other words, he does not appear again at all. His disguise is doffed—not to be resumed until many months have passed, when once more he leaps out upon the wild ranges of Griante. No. While

alive enough and close enough to impress both
Bendigo and Brendon with his presence as described by Jenny and myself, he has in reality vanished to the void. The "forgery" again goes to
sleep—as soundly as the real man in Foggintor.

Accident, indeed, modified the original scheme
and once more Chance befriended us and enabled
us to improve upon the first intention.

My tears fall when I think of my incomparable
Jenny and her astounding mastery of minutiæ at
"Crow's Nest"—her finesse and exquisite touch,
her kittenlike delicacy, her catlike swiftness and
sureness. The two beings involved were as
children in her hands. Oh, precious phœnix of a
woman, you and I were of the same spirit,
kneaded into our clay! Through your father you
won it—and I had it from my mother—the prime-
val fire that burns through all obstacles to its inveterate purpose!

I say that accident made a radical alteration
of design vital, for I had intended, on the night
when Robert Redmayne would come and see Bendigo, to murder the old sailor in his tower room
and remove him before morning with my wife's
assistance. But the victim postponed his own
destruction, for upon the night when his death
was intended, during my previous conversation
with him touching Jenny, I had perceived, by his
clumsy glances and evidence of anxiety, that somebody else was in the tower room—unseen.

There was but one hiding-place and but one
man likely to occupy it. I did not indicate that
I had discovered the secret and it was not the

detective who gave himself away; but, once alive
to his presence, I swiftly marked a flash of light
at one of the little ventilation holes in the cupboard and perceived that our sleuth stood hid
within it. My plan of campaign was altered accordingly and to great advantage. Indeed, to
have slain Ben in his house, when I should have
appeared instead of the brother he expected, had
been a maladroit achievement, contrasted with
the far more notable feat of the following night.

Having conveyed the old sailor to the cave,
where, on my recent run up the coast after drop-
ping Brendon, I had already looked in and lighted
the lamp, I landed behind him and, as his foot
touched the shore, the pole-axe fell. He was
dead in an instant and five minutes later his blood
ran upon the sand. Next I dug a grave under the
shingle, at a spot destined within half an hour to
be covered by the tide. In less than twenty minutes Bendigo Redmayne reposed beneath three
feet of sand and stone and I was on my way back
again to "Crow's Nest." There I reported to
Brendon that the brothers had met and would expect me again anon. I smoked a cigarette or two,
descended to our little harbour, removed my spade
from the launch to the boathouse, took a sack and
so set out again.

By the time that I had reached the cavern the
waves already flowed over old sea wolf's resting-
place. I landed, half filled my sack with stones
and sand, scattered judicious drops of blood and
climbed the steps and tunnel, laying the trail that
occupied official attention to such poor purpose

during the days that followed. Having reached the plateau, I emptied my sack, casting its contents over the cliff; I then left a good impression or two of Robert Redmayne's shoes, which I had, of course, remembered to put on. They would be recollected by Mark Brendon, for impressions had been found and records taken at Foggintor.

I swiftly descended the tunnel again after these operations, returned to my boathouse, stowed my sack, changed my boots and hastened to Brendon with my story. How we proceeded to the cave, our fruitless inquiries and the subsequent failure to find any solution to the disappearance of Bendigo and the reappearance of Robert are all facts within the memory. I need not tell you that tale again; but may declare how specially attractive it was to picture the puzzled police upon the little beach next day, and know that Bendigo Redmayne lay not a yard beneath their feet.

Once more my amazing wife and I parted for a brief period and then I had the joy of introducing her to Italy, where the remainder of our task awaited us. But we resolved that considerable time should pass before proceeding and we did not appear before her remaining uncle for many months. Meantime we revelled in a second honeymoon, reported our marriage to Albert Redmayne and the egregious Marco, to whom, at Jenny's suggestion we conveyed a piece of wedding cake, that he might the better grasp our achievement. We had not finished yet with the pride of New Scotland Yard.

And now for Italy. It is true that in my early manhood I had suffered a sad accident at Naples, the secret of which was known to my mother and myself alone. I therefore entertained some grudge against her country; but the fact at no time lessened my love for the south; and Jenny and I had always determined that when our task was accomplished the balance of our united life should there be spent in dignity and peace.

CHAPTER XIX

A LEGACY FOR PETER GANNS

IF at any time I entertained one shadow of regret in the execution of those who had traduced me and so earned their destruction, it was after we had dwelt for a season with Albert Redmayne beside Como. The lake itself is so flagrantly sentimental and the environment so serene and suggestive of childlike peace and good-will that I could almost have found it in my heart to lament the innocent book lover's taking off. But Jenny swiftly laughed me out of these emotions.

"Keep your tenderness and sentiment for me," she said. "I will not share them."

We might have killed Albert a thousand times and left no sign—a fact that brings me to that part of my recital I most deplore. But a measure of delay was necessary that we might learn the market value of his books—otherwise Virgilio Poggi would doubtless have robbed us after the old man's death. There was a medieval history of the Borgia family I should myself have greatly treasured under happier circumstances.

Nevertheless, though things difficult and dangerous we had triumphantly achieved, before this task for a child we failed; and the reason for our collapse was not in Jenny but in me. Had

367

I listened to my austere partner I should have
waited only until she had searched for and found
her uncle's will. This she did; and as the instrument proved entirely satisfactory, my duty was
then to proceed about our business and remember that better an egg to-day than a hen to-morrow. Only an artist's fond pride intervened;
nothing but my vanity, my consciousness of
power to excel, upset the rightful climax. We
were, indeed, both artists, but how incomparably
the greater she! How severe and direct, how
scornful of needless elaboration! She belonged,
mind and body, to the finest period of Greek art,
and echoed their stern, soulless simplicity and
perfection. Had she won her way with me, we
should be living now to enjoy the fruits of our
accomplishment.

But though she did not win her way, yet, in de-
feat, her final, glorious deed was to intercept the
death intended for me, that I might still live.
Loyal to the last, she sacrificed herself, forget-
ting, in that supreme moment, how life for me
without her could possess no shadow of compen-
sation. When Jenny shook off the dust of the
world, I was ready and willing to do the same.
As for that future life, in which I most potently
believe, since she and I have merited a like treatment, we shall share eternity together and so be
in heaven, whatever the Great Contriver may desire to the contrary. Yet who shall presume to
dogmatize? "There is nothing either good or
bad, but thinking makes it so." And what the
Almighty Mind may be pleased to think of any hu-

man performance is for the present hidden with Him alone. He did not make the tiger to eat grass or the eagle to feed on honey.

My wife's deeper sanity and clearer vision always inclined her to distrust our American acquaintance, Peter Ganns. From the first moment that Jenny's eyes fell upon that fine figure of a man, she judged him to be built on a very different mental pattern from Brendon. He was no New World edition of our poor, tame Marco; and the preliminary fact that he should have anticipated us and arrived beside Como before he was expected to do so, convinced Jenny that he must prove a factor of extreme gravity in all future calculations. I, too, perceived his force of character, and rejoiced to do so, for here appeared an enemy worthy of my invention and resource.

It seemed clear that Pietro was a skeptical person—doubtless made so by his dreadful trade. "Thomas" rather than "Peter" should have been his name. He had a disconcerting habit of taking nothing for granted; and his "third eye" as he called it—an eye of the mind—saw a great many things concealed from ordinary observers. He would have made a classical criminal.

The artist's pride, that had prevented me from acting so that Ganns should have been invited to discover the murderer of Albert rather than set the task of preserving his friend's life—this false, foolish sense of superiority and security wrecked all. Had Albert slept beneath the waters of Como before Ganns arrived, then not the wit of twenty Peters had ever found him; but while no

man living could have saved the life of Redmayne,
since had I determined to take it, the predestined
sequel to his death was confounded by my own
error. Once more Ganns struck before I expected
him to do so and I was, too late, confronted with
the shattering truth. He had in fact found me
out. He returned to England, worked like a
mole, dug up my history, no doubt, and so came
to the logical conclusion that it appeared more
reasonable Michael Pendean should murder
Robert Redmayne than the opposite. Having
reached this conviction, his reconstruction of each
event threw added light; but even so it must have
been a spark of prodigious inspiration that
identified in Doria the vanished Cornishman.

Ganns is a great man on his own plane. But,
though he is a greedy creature who digs his grave
with his knife and fork, though his habit of
drenching himself with powdered tobacco, instead
of smoking like a gentleman, is disgusting, yet
I have nothing but admiration for him. His
little plot—to treat me to a dose of my own physic
and present a forgery of "Robert Redmayne" in
the evening dusk—was altogether admirable. The
thing came in a manner so sudden and unexpected
that I failed of a perfect riposte. To confess that
I saw the ghost was dangerous; but to pretend
afterwards that I had seen nothing was fatal.
His own immense cleverness, of course, appeared
in assuring me that he saw nothing, thus tempting
me to suspect that I had in reality been a victim
of my own imagination. From that moment the

battle was joined and I stood at grave disadvantage.

How much or how little he had won from my slip I had yet to learn. In any case the time was all too short, for I guessed now that Ganns must at least have associated me with the unknown— he who had worn Redmayne's clothes and had tried to shoot Brendon in his absence. It was Jenny, of course, who had assisted me to dig Marco's grave on Griante and who shared my disappointment when we found that Brendon had escaped my revolver. Even so only the accident of biting his tongue saved him. Had I not seen blood flowing from his lips, I should have fired again.

I was not aware that Peter proposed to arrest me on the night of Albert's death, for upon what ground could he do so? Indeed I judged that after my final operations were completed and Albert destroyed, good Ganns would swiftly prove, to his own satisfaction, that I could not be associated with that crime and so feel his whole theory open to suspicion. Had I known that Peter was at his goal, my first thought might have been to disappear instantly and only appear again under a new impersonation, a year or two later, when the storm was over. In that case I should have indicated how "Guiseppe Doria" had committed suicide and left every tactful and sufficing proof of the fact.

But I never guessed the majestic heights of Peter's genius and, taking the chance of his temporary absence, slew Albert with a simple trick.

There was only Mark Brendon to prevent it; and
Jenny, having reserved her final and irresistible
appeal for some such vital occasion, found no
difficulty in absorbing all Marco's limited intelligence, while awakening for him fond hopes and
visions of a notable future in her arms. It needs
to be pointed out that this worthy person's infatu-
ation served again and again to prosper the situation for us and handicap the efforts of Peter
Ganns; but that Ganns should have trusted him
upon that all-important night to shepherd Albert
from my attention, only shows how Peter never
appreciated the limitations of his assistant. Yes,
even Peter was human, all too human.

While Jenny related her sufferings and made
appeal to her listener's overmastering devotion,
I left the house and Brendon saw me go. To get
a boat, that I might cross to Bellagio, was the
work of ten minutes. I took one without troubling
the owner, loaded a dozen heavy stones and
soon rowed to Villa Pianezzo and ascended the
water steps. A black beard was all the disguise
I used, save that I had left my coat in the boat
and appeared before Redmayne in shirt sleeves.

With trembling accents I related to Assunta,
who of course knew me not, that Poggi was taken
fatally ill and might hardly hope to last an hour.
It was enough. I returned to the boat and in three
minutes Albert joined me and offered me untold
gold to row as I had never rowed before. A hundred and fifty yards from shore I directed him
to pass into the bow of the boat, explaining that
I should so make greater speed. As he passed

me, the little pole-axe fell. He suffered nothing
and in five minutes more, with heavy stones fastened to feet and arms, he sank beneath Como.
The pole-axe followed, its work completed. In
more spacious times the weapon would have become an heirloom. All this happened not two
hundred yards from Villa Pianezzo under the
darkness.

Then I rowed ashore swiftly, returned the boat
to the beach unobserved, hid my disguise in my
pocket and strolled to a familiar inn. I had occupied but twenty-four minutes from the time of
setting out under Brendon's eyes while he sat
in the garden. I stopped at this *albergo* for a
considerable period, that a sufficient alibi might be
established and the moment of my arrival there
prove uncertain, should any future question ever
arise concerning it. Then the crash came. I returned home suspecting nothing—to fall like
Lucifer, to find all lost, to hold my dead wife in
my arms and know that, without her, life was
ended for me.

In seemly, splendid fashion she passed and it
shall not be recorded that the man this glorious
woman loved made an end of his days with less
distinction and propriety. To die on the gallows
is to do what many others have done; I will con-
descend to no such ignominy. Ganns understood
me well enough for that. Did he not warn the
police how I had been a dentist, and advised them
to examine my mouth with care? He alone realized something of my genius, but not all. Only
our peers can judge us; and such men as I

come like lonely comets into the atmosphere of
earth and lonely pass away. Our magnitude
terrifies—and the herd of men thanks God when
we disappear. Indeed I was unusually blessed,
for I had a greater than myself for companion
on my voyage. Like twin stars we cast a blended
light; we shone and vanished together, never to
be named apart henceforth.

Let not my legacy to Peter Ganns be forgotten,
or that I appoint Mark Brendon executor and
residuary legatee. With him I have no quarrel;
he did his best to save the situation for us. You
ask, "How shall a man condemned to death and
watched day and night that he may lay no hand
upon himself—how shall this man make his own
departure?" Before these words are read
throughout the world, you will learn the answer
to that question.

I think there is nothing more to say.

"*Al finir del gioco, si vede chi ha guadagnato.*"
"At the end of the game we may see the winner."
But not always, for sometimes the game is drawn
and honours are easy. I have played a drawn
game with Peter Ganns and he will not pretend a
victory, or withhold the first applause where it
belongs. He knows that, even if we were equal,
the woman was greater than either of us.

Farewell,

GIUSEPPE DORIA.

Ten days after Peter Ganns had read this
narrative and its sequel at his snug home outside
Boston, there awaited him, upon his breakfast

table, a little parcel from England. The packet suggested an addition to Peter's famous collection of snuffboxes. He had left certain commissions behind him in London and doubted not that a new treasure awaited him. But he was disappointed. Something far more amazing than any snuffbox now challenged his astonished eyes· There came a long letter from Mark Brendon also, which repeated information already familiar to Peter through the newspapers; but added other facts for him alone.

NEW SCOTLAND YARD, 20 October 1921.
MY DEAR PETER GANNS: You will have heard of Pendean's confession and message to you; but you may not have read full details as they concern you personally. I inclose his gift; and it is safe to bet that neither you nor any man will henceforth possess anything more remarkable. He made a will in prison and the law decides that I inherit his personal estate; but you will not be surprised to learn that I have handed it over to the police orphanages of my country and yours in equal proportions.

The facts are these. As the day approached for his execution, extraordinary precautions were taken, but Pendean behaved with utmost restraint, gave no trouble and made no threat. Having completed his written statement, he asked to be permitted to copy it on a typewriter, but leave to do so was not granted. He kept the communication on his person and he was promised that no attempt to read it should be made until after his execution. Indeed he received this undertaking before he put pen to paper. He preserved a quiet and orderly manner, ate well, took exercise with his guards and smoked many cigarettes. I may mention that the body of

Robert Redmayne was found where he buried it; but
the tides have deflected the beach gravels of Bendigo's
grave and search there has revealed nothing.

Upon his last night but one, Pendean retired as usual
and apparently slept for some hours with the bedclothes
up to his face. A warder sat on each side of him and a
light was burning. Suddenly he gave a sigh and held
out his hand to the man on his right.

"See that goes to Peter Ganns—it is my legacy," he
said. "And remember that Mark Brendon is my heir."
He then put a small object into the warder's hand. At
the same time he apparently suffered a tremendous physical convulsion, uttered one groan and leaped up into a
sitting position. From this he fell forward unconscious.
One attendant supported him and the other ran for the
prison surgeon. But Pendean was already dead—poisoned with cyanide of potassium.

You will remember two facts which might have thrown
light upon his secret. The first was his accident in Italy
as a youth; the second your constant interest in a
peculiar, inhuman quality of his expression which you
were never able to understand. Both are now explained.
With ordinary eyes the secret would have doubtless been
swiftly discovered by us. But in his case, so dark were
they, that pupil and iris were almost the same colour
and hence our failure to explain the artificial mystery of
his glance. He had, of course, a secret receptacle upon
his person beyond human knowledge or power of discovery, for he says that only his mother knew of his
accident. That accident was the loss of an eye. Behind
an eye of glass that took its place had lain concealed,
until he required it, the capsule of poison found crushed
within his mouth after death.

What the published statement of this knave has done
for me you will guess. I am leaving the detective service

and have found other occupation. One can only seek to live down my awful experience. Next year my work will bring me to America and, when that happens, I shall be very glad to see you again should you permit me to do so—not that we may speak of the past, with all its futility and bitterness for me, but that we may look forward, and that I may see all is well with you in your days of retirement, honour and ease. Until then I subscribe myself, your admirer and faithful friend,

MARK BRENDON.

Peter opened his parcel.

It contained an eye made of glass and very exquisitely fashioned to imitate reality. Its prevailing darkness had prevented the truth from appearing, and yet, perfect though it was in lustre and pigment, the false thing had given to Pendean's expression a quality that never failed to disturb Peter. It was not sinister, yet he remembered no such cast of countenance within his experience.

Mr. Ganns turned over the little object that had so often met his inquiring gaze.

"A rare crook," he said aloud; "but he is right: his wife was greater than either of us. If he'd listened to her and not his own vainglory, both could be alive and flourishing yet."

The dark brown eye seemed to stare up at him with a human twinkle as he brought out his gold snuffbox and took a pinch.

A CATALOGUE OF
SELECTED DOVER BOOKS
IN ALL FIELDS OF INTEREST

A CATALOGUE OF SELECTED DOVER
BOOKS IN ALL FIELDS OF INTEREST

RACKHAM'S COLOR ILLUSTRATIONS FOR WAGNER'S RING. Rackham's finest mature work—all 64 full-color watercolors in a faithful and lush interpretation of the *Ring*. Full-sized plates on coated stock of the paintings used by opera companies for authentic staging of Wagner. Captions aid in following complete Ring cycle. Introduction. 64 illustrations plus vignettes. 72pp. 8⅝ x 11¼.   23779-6 Pa. $6.00

CONTEMPORARY POLISH POSTERS IN FULL COLOR, edited by Joseph Czestochowski. 46 full-color examples of brilliant school of Polish graphic design, selected from world's first museum (near Warsaw) dedicated to poster art. Posters on circuses, films, plays, concerts all show cosmopolitan influences, free imagination. Introduction. 48pp. 9⅜ x 12¼.
                                                23780-X Pa. $6.00

GRAPHIC WORKS OF EDVARD MUNCH, Edvard Munch. 90 haunting, evocative prints by first major Expressionist artist and one of the greatest graphic artists of his time: *The Scream, Anxiety, Death Chamber, The Kiss, Madonna*, etc. Introduction by Alfred Werner. 90pp. 9 x 12.
                                                23765-6 Pa. $5.00

THE GOLDEN AGE OF THE POSTER, Hayward and Blanche Cirker. 70 extraordinary posters in full colors, from Maitres de l'Affiche, Mucha, Lautrec, Bradley, Cheret, Beardsley, many others. Total of 78pp. 9⅜ x 12¼.   22753-7 Pa. $5.95

THE NOTEBOOKS OF LEONARDO DA VINCI, edited by J. P. Richter. Extracts from manuscripts reveal great genius; on painting, sculpture, anatomy, sciences, geography, etc. Both Italian and English. 186 ms. pages reproduced, plus 500 additional drawings, including studies for *Last Supper*, Sforza monument, etc. 860pp. 7⅞ x 10¾. (Available in U.S. only)
                        22572-0, 22573-9 Pa., Two-vol. set $15.90

THE CODEX NUTTALL, as first edited by Zelia Nuttall. Only inexpensive edition, in full color, of a pre-Columbian Mexican (Mixtec) book. 88 color plates show kings, gods, heroes, temples, sacrifices. New explanatory, historical introduction by Arthur G. Miller. 96pp. 11⅜ x 8½. (Available in U.S. only)   23168-2 Pa. $7.95

UNE SEMAINE DE BONTÉ, A SURREALISTIC NOVEL IN COLLAGE, Max Ernst. Masterpiece created out of 19th-century periodical illustrations, explores worlds of terror and surprise. Some consider this Ernst's greatest work. 208pp. 8⅛ x 11.   23252-2 Pa. $5.00

DRAWINGS OF WILLIAM BLAKE, William Blake. 92 plates from Book of Job, *Divine Comedy, Paradise Lost,* visionary heads, mythological figures, Laocoon, etc. Selection, introduction, commentary by Sir Geoffrey Keynes. 178pp. 8⅛ x 11. 22303-5 Pa. $4.00

ENGRAVINGS OF HOGARTH, William Hogarth. 101 of Hogarth's greatest works: *Rake's Progress, Harlot's Progress, Illustrations for Hudibras, Before and After, Beer Street and Gin Lane,* many more. Full commentary. 256pp. 11 x 13¾. 22479-1 Pa. $12.95

DAUMIER: 120 GREAT LITHOGRAPHS, Honore Daumier. Wide-ranging collection of lithographs by the greatest caricaturist of the 19th century. Concentrates on eternally popular series on lawyers, on married life, on liberated women, etc. Selection, introduction, and notes on plates by Charles F. Ramus. Total of 158pp. 9⅜ x 12¼. 23512-2 Pa. $5.50

DRAWINGS OF MUCHA, Alphonse Maria Mucha. Work reveals draftsman of highest caliber: studies for famous posters and paintings, renderings for book illustrations and ads, etc. 70 works, 9 in color; including 6 items not drawings. Introduction. List of illustrations. 72pp. 9⅜ x 12¼. (Available in U.S. only) 23672-2 Pa. $4.00

GIOVANNI BATTISTA PIRANESI: DRAWINGS IN THE PIERPONT MORGAN LIBRARY, Giovanni Battista Piranesi. For first time ever all of Morgan Library's collection, world's largest. 167 illustrations of rare Piranesi drawings—archeological, architectural, decorative and visionary. Essay, detailed list of drawings, chronology, captions. Edited by Felice Stampfle. 144pp. 9⅜ x 12¼. 23714-1 Pa. $7.50

NEW YORK ETCHINGS (1905-1949), John Sloan. All of important American artist's N.Y. life etchings. 67 works include some of his best art; also lively historical record—Greenwich Village, tenement scenes. Edited by Sloan's widow. Introduction and captions. 79pp. 8⅜ x 11¼. 23651-X Pa. $4.00

CHINESE PAINTING AND CALLIGRAPHY: A PICTORIAL SURVEY, Wan-go Weng. 69 fine examples from John M. Crawford's matchless private collection: landscapes, birds, flowers, human figures, etc., plus calligraphy. Every basic form included: hanging scrolls, handscrolls, album leaves, fans, etc. 109 illustrations. Introduction. Captions. 192pp. 8⅞ x 11¾. 23707-9 Pa. $7.95

DRAWINGS OF REMBRANDT, edited by Seymour Slive. Updated Lippmann, Hofstede de Groot edition, with definitive scholarly apparatus. All portraits, biblical sketches, landscapes, nudes, Oriental figures, classical studies, together with selection of work by followers. 550 illustrations. Total of 630pp. 9⅛ x 12¼. 21485-0, 21486-9 Pa., Two-vol. set $15.00

THE DISASTERS OF WAR, Francisco Goya. 83 etchings record horrors of Napoleonic wars in Spain and war in general. Reprint of 1st edition, plus 3 additional plates. Introduction by Philip Hofer. 97pp. 9⅜ x 8¼. 21872-4 Pa. $3.75

THE EARLY WORK OF AUBREY BEARDSLEY, Aubrey Beardsley. 157 plates, 2 in color: *Manon Lescaut, Madame Bovary, Morte Darthur, Salome,* other. Introduction by H. Marillier. 182pp. 8⅛ x 11. 21816-3 Pa. $4.50

THE LATER WORK OF AUBREY BEARDSLEY, Aubrey Beardsley. Exotic masterpieces of full maturity: *Venus and Tannhauser, Lysistrata, Rape of the Lock, Volpone,* Savoy material, etc. 174 plates, 2 in color. 186pp. 8⅛ x 11. 21817-1 Pa. $4.50

THOMAS NAST'S CHRISTMAS DRAWINGS, Thomas Nast. Almost all Christmas drawings by creator of image of Santa Claus as we know it, and one of America's foremost illustrators and political cartoonists. 66 illustrations. 3 illustrations in color on covers. 96pp. 8⅜ x 11¼. 23660-9 Pa. $3.50

THE DORÉ ILLUSTRATIONS FOR DANTE'S DIVINE COMEDY, Gustave Doré. All 135 plates from Inferno, Purgatory, Paradise; fantastic tortures, infernal landscapes, celestial wonders. Each plate with appropriate (translated) verses. 141pp. 9 x 12. 23231-X Pa. $4.50

DORÉ'S ILLUSTRATIONS FOR RABELAIS, Gustave Doré. 252 striking illustrations of *Gargantua and Pantagruel* books by foremost 19th-century illustrator. Including 60 plates, 192 delightful smaller illustrations. 153pp. 9 x 12. 23656-0 Pa. $5.00

LONDON: A PILGRIMAGE, Gustave Doré, Blanchard Jerrold. Squalor, riches, misery, beauty of mid-Victorian metropolis; 55 wonderful plates, 125 other illustrations, full social, cultural text by Jerrold. 191pp. of text. 9⅜ x 12¼. 22306-X Pa. $7.00

THE RIME OF THE ANCIENT MARINER, Gustave Doré, S. T. Coleridge. Dore's finest work, 34 plates capture moods, subtleties of poem. Full text. Introduction by Millicent Rose. 77pp. 9¼ x 12. 22305-1 Pa. $3.50

THE DORE BIBLE ILLUSTRATIONS, Gustave Doré. All wonderful, detailed plates: Adam and Eve, Flood, Babylon, Life of Jesus, etc. Brief King James text with each plate. Introduction by Millicent Rose. 241 plates. 241pp. 9 x 12. 23004-X Pa. $6.00

THE COMPLETE ENGRAVINGS, ETCHINGS AND DRYPOINTS OF ALBRECHT DURER. "Knight, Death and Devil"; "Melencolia," and more—all Dürer's known works in all three media, including 6 works formerly attributed to him. 120 plates. 235pp. 8⅜ x 11¼. 22851-7 Pa. $6.50

MAXIMILIAN'S TRIUMPHAL ARCH, Albrecht Dürer and others. Incredible monument of woodcut art: 8 foot high elaborate arch—heraldic figures, humans, battle scenes, fantastic elements—that you can assemble yourself. Printed on one side, layout for assembly. 143pp. 11 x 16. 21451-6 Pa. $5.00

THE COMPLETE WOODCUTS OF ALBRECHT DURER, edited by Dr. W. Kurth. 346 in all: "Old Testament," "St. Jerome," "Passion," "Life of Virgin," Apocalypse," many others. Introduction by Campbell Dodgson. 285pp. 8½ x 12¼.   21097-9 Pa. $7.50

DRAWINGS OF ALBRECHT DURER, edited by Heinrich Wolfflin. 81 plates show development from youth to full style. Many favorites; many new. Introduction by Alfred Werner. 96pp. 8⅛ x 11.   22352-3 Pa. $5.00

THE HUMAN FIGURE, Albrecht Dürer. Experiments in various techniques—stereometric, progressive proportional, and others. Also life studies that rank among finest ever done. Complete reprinting of *Dresden Sketchbook*. 170 plates. 355pp. 8⅜ x 11¼.   21042-1 Pa. $7.95

OF THE JUST SHAPING OF LETTERS, Albrecht Dürer. Renaissance artist explains design of Roman majuscules by geometry, also Gothic lower and capitals. Grolier Club edition. 43pp. 7⅞ x 10¾   21306-4 Pa. $3.00

TEN BOOKS ON ARCHITECTURE, Vitruvius. The most important book ever written on architecture. Early Roman aesthetics, technology, classical orders, site selection, all other aspects. Stands behind everything since. Morgan translation. 331pp. 5⅜ x 8½.   20645-9 Pa. $4.50

THE FOUR BOOKS OF ARCHITECTURE, Andrea Palladio. 16th-century classic responsible for Palladian movement and style. Covers classical architectural remains, Renaissance revivals, classical orders, etc. 1738 Ware English edition. Introduction by A. Placzek. 216 plates. 110pp. of text. 9½ x 12¾.   21308-0 Pa. $10.00

HORIZONS, Norman Bel Geddes. Great industrialist stage designer, "father of streamlining," on application of aesthetics to transportation, amusement, architecture, etc. 1932 prophetic account; function, theory, specific projects. 222 illustrations. 312pp. 7⅞ x 10¾.   23514-9 Pa. $6.95

FRANK LLOYD WRIGHT'S FALLINGWATER, Donald Hoffmann. Full, illustrated story of conception and building of Wright's masterwork at Bear Run, Pa. 100 photographs of site, construction, and details of completed structure. 112pp. 9¼ x 10.   23671-4 Pa. $5.50

THE ELEMENTS OF DRAWING, John Ruskin. Timeless classic by great Viltorian; starts with basic ideas, works through more difficult. Many practical exercises. 48 illustrations. Introduction by Lawrence Campbell. 228pp. 5⅜ x 8½.   22730-8 Pa. $3.75

GIST OF ART, John Sloan. Greatest modern American teacher, Art Students League, offers innumerable hints, instructions, guided comments to help you in painting. Not a formal course. 46 illustrations. Introduction by Helen Sloan. 200pp. 5⅜ x 8½.   23435-5 Pa. $4.00

THE ANATOMY OF THE HORSE, George Stubbs. Often considered the great masterpiece of animal anatomy. Full reproduction of 1766 edition, plus prospectus; original text and modernized text. 36 plates. Introduction by Eleanor Garvey. 121pp. 11 x 14¾.   23402-9 Pa. $6.00

BRIDGMAN'S LIFE DRAWING, George B. Bridgman. More than 500 illustrative drawings and text teach you to abstract the body into its major masses, use light and shade, proportion; as well as specific areas of anatomy, of which Bridgman is master. 192pp. 6½ x 9¼. (Available in U.S. only)
                                                                    22710-3 Pa. $3.50

ART NOUVEAU DESIGNS IN COLOR, Alphonse Mucha, Maurice Verneuil, Georges Auriol. Full-color reproduction of *Combinaisons ornementales* (c. 1900) by Art Nouveau masters. Floral, animal, geometric, interlacings, swashes—borders, frames, spots—all incredibly beautiful. 60 plates, hundreds of designs. 9⅜ x 8-1/16.   22885-1 Pa. $4.00

FULL-COLOR FLORAL DESIGNS IN THE ART NOUVEAU STYLE, E. A. Seguy. 166 motifs, on 40 plates, from *Les fleurs et leurs applications decoratives* (1902): borders, circular designs, repeats, allovers, "spots." All in authentic Art Nouveau colors. 48pp. 9⅜ x 12¼.
                                                                    23439-8 Pa. $5.00

A DIDEROT PICTORIAL ENCYCLOPEDIA OF TRADES AND IN-DUSTRY, edited by Charles C. Gillispie. 485 most interesting plates from the great French Encyclopedia of the 18th century show hundreds of working figures, artifacts, process, land and cityscapes; glassmaking, paper-making, metal extraction, construction, weaving, making furniture, clothing, wigs, dozens of other activities. Plates fully explained. 920pp. 9 x 12.
                                     22284-5, 22285-3 Clothbd., Two-vol. set $40.00

HANDBOOK OF EARLY ADVERTISING ART, Clarence P. Hornung. Largest collection of copyright-free early and antique advertising art ever compiled. Over 6,000 illustrations, from Franklin's time to the 1890's for special effects, novelty. Valuable source, almost inexhaustible.
Pictorial Volume. Agriculture, the zodiac, animals, autos, birds, Christmas, fire engines, flowers, trees, musical instruments, ships, games and sports, much more. Arranged by subject matter and use. 237 plates. 288pp. 9 x 12.
                                                          20122-8 Clothbd. $14.50

Typographical Volume. Roman and Gothic faces ranging from 10 point to 300 point, "Barnum," German and Old English faces, script, logotypes, scrolls and flourishes, 1115 ornamental initials, 67 complete alphabets, more. 310 plates. 320pp. 9 x 12.   20123-6 Clothbd. $15.00

CALLIGRAPHY (CALLIGRAPHIA LATINA), J. G. Schwandner. High point of 18th-century ornamental calligraphy. Very ornate initials, scrolls, borders, cherubs, birds, lettered examples. 172pp. 9 x 13.
                                                                    20475-8 Pa. $7.00

CATALOGUE OF DOVER BOOKS

ART FORMS IN NATURE, Ernst Haeckel. Multitude of strangely beautiful natural forms: Radiolaria, Foraminifera, jellyfishes, fungi, turtles, bats, etc. All 100 plates of the 19th-century evolutionist's *Kunstformen der Natur* (1904). 100pp. 9⅜ x 12¼. 22987-4 Pa. $5.00

CHILDREN: A PICTORIAL ARCHIVE FROM NINETEENTH-CENTURY SOURCES, edited by Carol Belanger Grafton. 242 rare, copyright-free wood engravings for artists and designers. Widest such selection available. All illustrations in line. 119pp. 8⅜ x 11¼. 23694-3 Pa. $3.50

WOMEN: A PICTORIAL ARCHIVE FROM NINETEENTH-CENTURY SOURCES, edited by Jim Harter. 391 copyright-free wood engravings for artists and designers selected from rare periodicals. Most extensive such collection available. All illustrations in line. 128pp. 9 x 12. 23703-6 Pa. $4.50

ARABIC ART IN COLOR, Prisse d'Avennes. From the greatest ornamentalists of all time—50 plates in color, rarely seen outside the Near East, rich in suggestion and stimulus. Includes 4 plates on covers. 46pp. 9⅜ x 12¼. 23658-7 Pa. $6.00

AUTHENTIC ALGERIAN CARPET DESIGNS AND MOTIFS, edited by June Beveridge. Algerian carpets are world famous. Dozens of geometrical motifs are charted on grids, color-coded, for weavers, needleworkers, craftsmen, designers. 53 illustrations plus 4 in color. 48pp. 8¼ x 11. (Available in U.S. only) 23650-1 Pa. $1.75

DICTIONARY OF AMERICAN PORTRAITS, edited by Hayward and Blanche Cirker. 4000 important Americans, earliest times to 1905, mostly in clear line. Politicians, writers, soldiers, scientists, inventors, industrialists, Indians, Blacks, women, outlaws, etc. Identificatory information. 756pp. 9¼ x 12¾. 21823-6 Clothbd. $40.00

HOW THE OTHER HALF LIVES, Jacob A. Riis. Journalistic record of filth, degradation, upward drive in New York immigrant slums, shops, around 1900. New edition includes 100 original Riis photos, monuments of early photography. 233pp. 10 x 7⅞. 22012-5 Pa. $7.00

NEW YORK IN THE THIRTIES, Berenice Abbott. Noted photographer's fascinating study of city shows new buildings that have become famous and old sights that have disappeared forever. Insightful commentary. 97 photographs. 97pp. 11⅜ x 10. 22967-X Pa. $5.00

MEN AT WORK, Lewis W. Hine. Famous photographic studies of construction workers, railroad men, factory workers and coal miners. New supplement of 18 photos on Empire State building construction. New introduction by Jonathan L. Doherty. Total of 69 photos. 63pp. 8 x 10¾. 23475-4 Pa. $3.00

THE DEPRESSION YEARS AS PHOTOGRAPHED BY ARTHUR ROTH-STEIN, Arthur Rothstein. First collection devoted entirely to the work of outstanding 1930s photographer: famous dust storm photo, ragged children, unemployed, etc. 120 photographs. Captions. 119pp. 9¼ x 10¾.
23590-4 Pa. $5.00

CAMERA WORK: A PICTORIAL GUIDE, Alfred Stieglitz. All 559 illustrations and plates from the most important periodical in the history of art photography, Camera Work (1903-17). Presented four to a page, reduced in size but still clear, in strict chronological order, with complete captions. Three indexes. Glossary. Bibliography. 176pp. 8⅜ x 11¼.
23591-2 Pa. $6.95

ALVIN LANGDON COBURN, PHOTOGRAPHER, Alvin L. Coburn. Revealing autobiography by one of greatest photographers of 20th century gives insider's version of Photo-Secession, plus comments on his own work. 77 photographs by Coburn. Edited by Helmut and Alison Gernsheim. 160pp. 8⅛ x 11.
23685-4 Pa. $6.00

NEW YORK IN THE FORTIES, Andreas Feininger. 162 brilliant photographs by the well-known photographer, formerly with Life magazine, show commuters, shoppers, Times Square at night, Harlem nightclub, Lower East Side, etc. Introduction and full captions by John von Hartz. 181pp. 9¼ x 10¾.
23585-8 Pa. $6.00

GREAT NEWS PHOTOS AND THE STORIES BEHIND THEM, John Faber. Dramatic volume of 140 great news photos, 1855 through 1976, and revealing stories behind them, with both historical and technical information. Hindenburg disaster, shooting of Oswald, nomination of Jimmy Carter, etc. 160pp. 8¼ x 11.
23667-6 Pa. $5.00

THE ART OF THE CINEMATOGRAPHER, Leonard Maltin. Survey of American cinematography history and anecdotal interviews with 5 masters—Arthur Miller, Hal Mohr, Hal Rosson, Lucien Ballard, and Conrad Hall. Very large selection of behind-the-scenes production photos. 105 photographs. Filmographies. Index. Originally Behind the Camera. 144pp. 8¼ x 11.
23686-2 Pa. $5.00

DESIGNS FOR THE THREE-CORNERED HAT (LE TRICORNE), Pablo Picasso. 32 fabulously rare drawings—including 31 color illustrations of costumes and accessories—for 1919 production of famous ballet. Edited by Parmenia Migel, who has written new introduction. 48pp. 9⅜ x 12¼. (Available in U.S. only)
23709-5 Pa. $5.00

NOTES OF A FILM DIRECTOR, Sergei Eisenstein. Greatest Russian filmmaker explains montage, making of Alexander Nevsky, aesthetics; comments on self, associates, great rivals (Chaplin), similar material. 78 illustrations. 240pp. 5⅜ x 8½.
22392-2 Pa. $4.50

HOLLYWOOD GLAMOUR PORTRAITS, edited by John Kobal. 145 photos capture the stars from 1926-49, the high point in portrait photography. Gable, Harlow, Bogart, Bacall, Hedy Lamarr, Marlene Dietrich, Robert Montgomery, Marlon Brando, Veronica Lake; 94 stars in all. Full background on photographers, technical aspects, much more. Total of 160pp. 8⅜ x 11¼. 23352-9 Pa. $6.00

THE NEW YORK STAGE: FAMOUS PRODUCTIONS IN PHOTO-GRAPHS, edited by Stanley Appelbaum. 148 photographs from Museum of City of New York show 142 plays, 1883-1939. *Peter Pan, The Front Page, Dead End, Our Town*, O'Neill, hundreds of actors and actresses, etc. Full indexes. 154pp. 9½ x 10. 23241-7 Pa. $6.00

DIALOGUES CONCERNING TWO NEW SCIENCES, Galileo Galilei. Encompassing 30 years of experiment and thought, these dialogues deal with geometric demonstrations of fracture of solid bodies, cohesion, leverage, speed of light and sound, pendulums, falling bodies, accelerated motion, etc. 300pp. 5⅜ x 8½. 60099-8 Pa. $4.00

THE GREAT OPERA STARS IN HISTORIC PHOTOGRAPHS, edited by James Camner. 343 portraits from the 1850s to the 1940s: Tamburini, Mario, Caliapin, Jeritza, Melchior, Melba, Patti, Pinza, Schipa, Caruso, Farrar, Steber, Gobbi, and many more—270 performers in all. Index. 199pp. 8⅜ x 11¼. 23575-0 Pa. $6.50

J. S. BACH, Albert Schweitzer. Great full-length study of Bach, life, background to music, music, by foremost modern scholar. Ernest Newman translation. 650 musical examples. Total of 928pp. 5⅜ x 8½. (Available in U.S. only) 21631-4, 21632-2 Pa., Two-vol. set $11.00

COMPLETE PIANO SONATAS, Ludwig van Beethoven. All sonatas in the fine Schenker edition, with fingering, analytical material. One of best modern editions. Total of 615pp. 9 x 12. (Available in U.S. only) 23134-8, 23135-6 Pa., Two-vol. set $15.00

KEYBOARD MUSIC, J. S. Bach. Bach-Gesellschaft edition. For harpsichord, piano, other keyboard instruments. English Suites, French Suites, Six Partitas, Goldberg Variations, Two-Part Inventions, Three-Part Sinfonias. 312pp. 8⅛ x 11. (Available in U.S. only) 22360-4 Pa. $6.95

FOUR SYMPHONIES IN FULL SCORE, Franz Schubert. Schubert's four most popular symphonies: No. 4 in C Minor ("Tragic"); No. 5 in B-flat Major; No. 8 in B Minor ("Unfinished"); No. 9 in C Major ("Great"). Breitkopf & Hartel edition. Study score. 261pp. 9⅜ x 12¼. 23681-1 Pa. $6.50

THE AUTHENTIC GILBERT & SULLIVAN SONGBOOK, W. S. Gilbert, A. S. Sullivan. Largest selection available; 92 songs, uncut, original keys, in piano rendering approved by Sullivan. Favorites and lesser-known fine numbers. Edited with plot synopses by James Spero. 3 illustrations. 399pp. 9 x 12. 23482-7 Pa. $9.95

PRINCIPLES OF ORCHESTRATION, Nikolay Rimsky-Korsakov. Great classical orchestrator provides fundamentals of tonal resonance, progression of parts, voice and orchestra, tutti effects, much else in major document. 330pp. of musical excerpts. 489pp. 6½ x 9¼. 21266-1 Pa. $7.50

TRISTAN UND ISOLDE, Richard Wagner. Full orchestral score with complete instrumentation. Do not confuse with piano reduction. Commentary by Felix Mottl, great Wagnerian conductor and scholar. Study score. 655pp. 8⅛ x 11. 22915-7 Pa. $13.95

REQUIEM IN FULL SCORE, Giuseppe Verdi. Immensely popular with choral groups and music lovers. Republication of edition published by C. F. Peters, Leipzig, n. d. German frontmaker in English translation. Glossary. Text in Latin. Study score. 204pp. 9⅜ x 12¼.
23682-X Pa. $6.00

COMPLETE CHAMBER MUSIC FOR STRINGS, Felix Mendelssohn. All of Mendelssohn's chamber music: Octet, 2 Quintets, 6 Quartets, and Four Pieces for String Quartet. (Nothing with piano is included). Complete works edition (1874-7). Study score. 283 pp. 9⅜ x 12¼.
23679-X Pa. $7.50

POPULAR SONGS OF NINETEENTH-CENTURY AMERICA, edited by Richard Jackson. 64 most important songs: "Old Oaken Bucket," "Arkansas Traveler," "Yellow Rose of Texas," etc. Authentic original sheet music, full introduction and commentaries. 290pp. 9 x 12. 23270-0 Pa. $7.95

COLLECTED PIANO WORKS, Scott Joplin. Edited by Vera Brodsky Lawrence. Practically all of Joplin's piano works—rags, two-steps, marches, waltzes, etc., 51 works in all. Extensive introduction by Rudi Blesh. Total of 345pp. 9 x 12. 23106-2 Pa. $14.95

BASIC PRINCIPLES OF CLASSICAL BALLET, Agrippina Vaganova. Great Russian theoretician, teacher explains methods for teaching classical ballet; incorporates best from French, Italian, Russian schools. 118 illustrations. 175pp. 5⅜ x 8½. 22036-2 Pa. $2.50

CHINESE CHARACTERS, L. Wieger. Rich analysis of 2300 characters according to traditional systems into primitives. Historical-semantic analysis to phonetics (Classical Mandarin) and radicals. 820pp. 6⅛ x 9¼.
21321-8 Pa. $10.00

EGYPTIAN LANGUAGE: EASY LESSONS IN EGYPTIAN HIERO-GLYPHICS, E. A. Wallis Budge. Foremost Egyptologist offers Egyptian grammar, explanation of hieroglyphics, many reading texts, dictionary of symbols. 246pp. 5 x 7½. (Available in U.S. only)
21394-3 Clothbd. $7.50

AN ETYMOLOGICAL DICTIONARY OF MODERN ENGLISH, Ernest Weekley. Richest, fullest work, by foremost British lexicographer. Detailed word histories. Inexhaustible. Do not confuse this with *Concise Etymological Dictionary*, which is abridged. Total of 856pp. 6½ x 9¼.
21873-2, 21874-0 Pa., Two-vol. set $12.00

A MAYA GRAMMAR, Alfred M. Tozzer. Practical, useful English-language grammar by the Harvard anthropologist who was one of the three greatest American scholars in the area of Maya culture. Phonetics, grammatical processes, syntax, more. 301pp. 5⅜ x 8½.   23465-7 Pa. $4.00

THE JOURNAL OF HENRY D. THOREAU, edited by Bradford Torrey, F. H. Allen. Complete reprinting of 14 volumes, 1837-61, over two million words; the sourcebooks for *Walden*, etc. Definitive. All original sketches, plus 75 photographs. Introduction by Walter Harding. Total of 1804pp. 8½ x 12¼.   20312-3, 20313-1 Clothbd., Two-vol. set $50.00

CLASSIC GHOST STORIES, Charles Dickens and others. 18 wonderful stories you've wanted to reread: "The Monkey's Paw," "The House and the Brain," "The Upper Berth," "The Signalman," "Dracula's Guest," "The Tapestried Chamber," etc. Dickens, Scott, Mary Shelley, Stoker, etc. 330pp. 5⅜ x 8½.   20735-8 Pa. $4.50

SEVEN SCIENCE FICTION NOVELS, H. G. Wells. Full novels. *First Men in the Moon, Island of Dr. Moreau, War of the Worlds, Food of the Gods, Invisible Man, Time Machine, In the Days of the Comet.* A basic science-fiction library. 1015pp. 5⅜ x 8½. (Available in U.S. only)
                    20264-X Clothbd. $8.95

ARMADALE, Wilkie Collins. Third great mystery novel by the author of *The Woman in White* and *The Moonstone.* Ingeniously plotted narrative shows an exceptional command of character, incident and mood. Original magazine version with 40 illustrations. 597pp. 5⅜ x 8½.
                    23429-0 Pa. $6.00

MASTERS OF MYSTERY, H. Douglas Thomson. The first book in English (1931) devoted to history and aesthetics of detective story. Poe, Doyle, LeFanu, Dickens, many others, up to 1930. New introduction and notes by E. F. Bleiler. 288pp. 5⅜ x 8½. (Available in U.S. only)
                    23606-4 Pa. $4.00

FLATLAND, E. A. Abbott. Science-fiction classic explores life of 2-D being in 3-D world. Read also as introduction to thought about hyperspace. Introduction by Banesh Hoffmann. 16 illustrations. 103pp. 5⅜ x 8½.
                    20001-9 Pa. $2.00

THREE SUPERNATURAL NOVELS OF THE VICTORIAN PERIOD, edited, with an introduction, by E. F. Bleiler. Reprinted complete and unabridged, three great classics of the supernatural: *The Haunted Hotel* by Wilkie Collins, *The Haunted House at Latchford* by Mrs. J. H. Riddell, and *The Lost Stradivarious* by J. Meade Falkner. 325pp. 5⅜ x 8½.
                    22571-2 Pa. $4.00

AYESHA: THE RETURN OF "SHE," H. Rider Haggard. Virtuoso sequel featuring the great mythic creation, Ayesha, in an adventure that is fully as good as the first book, *She.* Original magazine version, with 47 original illustrations by Maurice Greiffenhagen. 189pp. 6½ x 9¼.
                    23649-8 Pa. $3.50

UNCLE SILAS, J. Sheridan LeFanu. Victorian Gothic mystery novel, considered by many best of period, even better than Collins or Dickens. Wonderful psychological terror. Introduction by Frederick Shroyer. 436pp. 5⅜ x 8½. 21715-9 Pa. $6.00

JURGEN, James Branch Cabell. The great erotic fantasy of the 1920's that delighted thousands, shocked thousands more. Full final text, Lane edition with 13 plates by Frank Pape. 346pp. 5⅜ x 8½. 23507-6 Pa. $4.50

THE CLAVERINGS, Anthony Trollope. Major novel, chronicling aspects of British Victorian society, personalities. Reprint of Cornhill serialization, 16 plates by M. Edwards; first reprint of full text. Introduction by Norman Donaldson. 412pp. 5⅜ x 8½. 23464-9 Pa. $5.00

KEPT IN THE DARK, Anthony Trollope. Unusual short novel about Victorian morality and abnormal psychology by the great English author. Probably the first American publication. Frontispiece by Sir John Millais. 92pp. 6½ x 9¼. 23609-9 Pa. $2.50

RALPH THE HEIR, Anthony Trollope. Forgotten tale of illegitimacy, inheritance. Master novel of Trollope's later years. Victorian country estates, clubs, Parliament, fox hunting, world of fully realized characters. Reprint of 1871 edition. 12 illustrations by F. A. Faser. 434pp. of text. 5⅜ x 8½. 23642-0 Pa. $5.00

YEKL and THE IMPORTED BRIDEGROOM AND OTHER STORIES OF THE NEW YORK GHETTO, Abraham Cahan. Film *Hester Street* based on *Yekl* (1896). Novel, other stories among first about Jewish immigrants of N.Y.'s East Side. Highly praised by W. D. Howells—Cahan "a new star of realism." New introduction by Bernard G. Richards. 240pp. 5⅜ x 8½. 22427-9 Pa. $3.50

THE HIGH PLACE, James Branch Cabell. Great fantasy writer's enchanting comedy of disenchantment set in 18th-century France. Considered by some critics to be even better than his famous *Jurgen*. 10 illustrations and numerous vignettes by noted fantasy artist Frank C. Pape. 320pp. 5⅜ x 8½. 23670-6 Pa. $4.00

ALICE'S ADVENTURES UNDER GROUND, Lewis Carroll. Facsimile of ms. Carroll gave Alice Liddell in 1864. Different in many ways from final Alice. Handlettered, illustrated by Carroll. Introduction by Martin Gardner. 128pp. 5⅜ x 8½. 21482-6 Pa. $2.00

FAVORITE ANDREW LANG FAIRY TALE BOOKS IN MANY COLORS, Andrew Lang. The four Lang favorites in a boxed set—the complete *Red*, *Green*, *Yellow* and *Blue* Fairy Books. 164 stories; 439 illustrations by Lancelot Speed, Henry Ford and G. P. Jacomb Hood. Total of about 1500pp. 5⅜ x 8½. 23407-X Boxed set, Pa. $14.95

HOUSEHOLD STORIES BY THE BROTHERS GRIMM. All the great Grimm stories: "Rumpelstiltskin," "Snow White," "Hansel and Gretel," etc., with 114 illustrations by Walter Crane. 269pp. 5⅜ x 8½.
21080-4 Pa. $3.50

SLEEPING BEAUTY, illustrated by Arthur Rackham. Perhaps the fullest, most delightful version ever, told by C. S. Evans. Rackham's best work. 49 illustrations. 110pp. 7⅞ x 10¾.
22756-1 Pa. $2.50

AMERICAN FAIRY TALES, L. Frank Baum. Young cowboy lassoes Father Time; dummy in Mr. Floman's department store window comes to life; and 10 other fairy tales. 41 illustrations by N. P. Hall, Harry Kennedy, Ike Morgan, and Ralph Gardner. 209pp. 5⅜ x 8½.
23643-9 Pa. $3.00

THE WONDERFUL WIZARD OF OZ, L. Frank Baum. Facsimile in full color of America's finest children's classic. Introduction by Martin Gardner. 143 illustrations by W. W. Denslow. 267pp. 5⅜ x 8½.
20691-2 Pa. $3.50

THE TALE OF PETER RABBIT, Beatrix Potter. The inimitable Peter's terrifying adventure in Mr. McGregor's garden, with all 27 wonderful, full-color Potter illustrations. 55pp. 4¼ x 5½. (Available in U.S. only)
22827-4 Pa. $1.25

THE STORY OF KING ARTHUR AND HIS KNIGHTS, Howard Pyle. Finest children's version of life of King Arthur. 48 illustrations by Pyle. 131pp. 6⅛ x 9¼.
21445-1 Pa. $4.95

CARUSO'S CARICATURES, Enrico Caruso. Great tenor's remarkable caricatures of self, fellow musicians, composers, others. Toscanini, Puccini, Farrar, etc. Impish, cutting, insightful. 473 illustrations. Preface by M. Sisca. 217pp. 8⅜ x 11¼.
23528-9 Pa. $6.95

PERSONAL NARRATIVE OF A PILGRIMAGE TO ALMADINAH AND MECCAH, Richard Burton. Great travel classic by remarkably colorful personality. Burton, disguised as a Moroccan, visited sacred shrines of Islam, narrowly escaping death. Wonderful observations of Islamic life, customs, personalities. 47 illustrations. Total of 959pp. 5⅜ x 8½.
21217-3, 21218-1 Pa., Two-vol. set $12.00

INCIDENTS OF TRAVEL IN YUCATAN, John L. Stephens. Classic (1843) exploration of jungles of Yucatan, looking for evidences of Maya civilization. Travel adventures, Mexican and Indian culture, etc. Total of 669pp. 5⅜ x 8½.
20926-1, 20927-X Pa., Two-vol. set $7.90

AMERICAN LITERARY AUTOGRAPHS FROM WASHINGTON IRVING TO HENRY JAMES, Herbert Cahoon, et al. Letters, poems, manuscripts of Hawthorne, Thoreau, Twain, Alcott, Whitman, 67 other prominent American authors. Reproductions, full transcripts and commentary. Plus checklist of all American Literary Autographs in The Pierpont Morgan Library. Printed on exceptionally high-quality paper. 136 illustrations. 212pp. 9⅛ x 12¼.
23548-3 Pa. $12.50

AN AUTOBIOGRAPHY, Margaret Sanger. Exciting personal account of hard-fought battle for woman's right to birth control, against prejudice, church, law. Foremost feminist document. 504pp. 5⅜ x 8½.
20470-7 Pa. $5.50

MY BONDAGE AND MY FREEDOM, Frederick Douglass. Born as a slave, Douglass became outspoken force in antislavery movement. The best of Douglass's autobiographies. Graphic description of slave life. Introduction by P. Foner. 464pp. 5⅜ x 8½. 22457-0 Pa. $5.50

LIVING MY LIFE, Emma Goldman. Candid, no holds barred account by foremost American anarchist: her own life, anarchist movement, famous contemporaries, ideas and their impact. Struggles and confrontations in America, plus deportation to U.S.S.R. Shocking inside account of persecution of anarchists under Lenin. 13 plates. Total of 944pp. 5⅜ x 8½.
22543-7, 22544-5 Pa., Two-vol. set $12.00

LETTERS AND NOTES ON THE MANNERS, CUSTOMS AND CONDITIONS OF THE NORTH AMERICAN INDIANS, George Catlin. Classic account of life among Plains Indians: ceremonies, hunt, warfare, etc. Dover edition reproduces for first time all original paintings. 312 plates. 572pp. of text. 6⅛ x 9¼. 22118-0, 22119-9 Pa.. Two-vol. set $12.00

THE MAYA AND THEIR NEIGHBORS, edited by Clarence L. Hay, others. Synoptic view of Maya civilization in broadest sense, together with Northern, Southern neighbors. Integrates much background, valuable detail not elsewhere. Prepared by greatest scholars: Kroeber, Morley, Thompson, Spinden, Vaillant, many others. Sometimes called Tozzer Memorial Volume. 60 illustrations, linguistic map. 634pp. 5⅜ x 8½.
23510-6 Pa. $7.50

HANDBOOK OF THE INDIANS OF CALIFORNIA, A. L. Kroeber. Foremost American anthropologist offers complete ethnographic study of each group. Monumental classic. 459 illustrations, maps. 995pp. 5⅜ x 8½.
23368-5 Pa. $13.00

SHAKTI AND SHAKTA, Arthur Avalon. First book to give clear, cohesive analysis of Shakta doctrine, Shakta ritual and Kundalini Shakti (yoga). Important work by one of world's foremost students of Shaktic and Tantric thought. 732pp. 5⅜ x 8½. (Available in U.S. only)
23645-5 Pa. $7.95

AN INTRODUCTION TO THE STUDY OF THE MAYA HIEROGLYPHS, Syvanus Griswold Morley. Classic study by one of the truly great figures in hieroglyph research. Still the best introduction for the student for reading Maya hieroglyphs. New introduction by J. Eric S. Thompson. 117 illustrations. 284pp. 5⅜ x 8½. 23108-9 Pa. $4.00

A STUDY OF MAYA ART, Herbert J. Spinden. Landmark classic interprets Maya symbolism, estimates styles, covers ceramics, architecture, murals, stone carvings as artforms. Still a basic book in area. New introduction by J. Eric Thompson. Over 750 illustrations. 341pp. 8⅜ x 11¼.
21235-1 Pa. $6.95

GEOMETRY, RELATIVITY AND THE FOURTH DIMENSION, Rudolf Rucker. Exposition of fourth dimension, means of visualization, concepts of relativity as Flatland characters continue adventures. Popular, easily followed yet accurate, profound. 141 illustrations. 133pp. 5⅜ x 8½.
23400-2 Pa. $2.75

THE ORIGIN OF LIFE, A. I. Oparin. Modern classic in biochemistry, the first rigorous examination of possible evolution of life from nitrocarbon compounds. Non-technical, easily followed. Total of 295pp. 5⅜ x 8½.
60213-3 Pa. $4.00

PLANETS, STARS AND GALAXIES, A. E. Fanning. Comprehensive introductory survey: the sun, solar system, stars, galaxies, universe, cosmology; quasars, radio stars, etc. 24pp. of photographs. 189pp. 5⅜ x 8½. (Available in U.S. only)
21680-2 Pa. $3.75

THE THIRTEEN BOOKS OF EUCLID'S ELEMENTS, translated with introduction and commentary by Sir Thomas L. Heath. Definitive edition. Textual and linguistic notes, mathematical analysis, 2500 years of critical commentary. Do not confuse with abridged school editions. Total of 1414pp. 5⅜ x 8½.   60088-2, 60089-0, 60090-4 Pa., Three-vol. set $18.50